ZANDRU'S FORGE

BOOK TWO OF
The *Clingfire* Trilogy

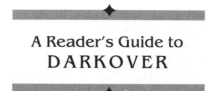

A Reader's Guide to
DARKOVER

THE FOUNDING

A "lost ship" of Terran origin, in the pre-Empire colonizing days, lands on a planet with a dim red star, later to be called Darkover.
DARKOVER LANDFALL

THE AGES OF CHAOS

1,000 years after the original landfall settlement, society has returned to the feudal level. The Darkovans, their Terran technology renounced or forgotten, have turned instead to free-wheeling, out-of-control matrix technology, psi powers and terrible psi weapons. The populace lives under the domination of the Towers and a tyrannical breeding program to staff the Towers with unnaturally powerful, inbred gifts of *laran*.
STORMQUEEN!
HAWKMISTRESS!

THE HUNDRED KINGDOMS

An age of war and strife retaining many of the decimating and disastrous effects of the Ages of Chaos. The lands which are later to become the Seven Domains are divided by continuous border conflicts into a multitude of small, belligerent kingdoms, named for convenience "The Hundred Kingdoms." The close of this era is heralded by the adoption of the Compact, instituted by Varzil the Good. A landmark and turning point in the history of Darkover, the Compact bans all distance weapons, making it a matter of honor that one who seeks to kill must himself face equal risk of death.
TWO TO CONQUER
THE HEIRS OF HAMMERFELL
THE FALL OF NESKAYA
ZANDRU'S FORGE
A FLAME IN HALI*

*Coming in hardcover from DAW Books

THE RENUNCIATES

During the Ages of Chaos and the time of the Hundred Kingdoms, there were two orders of women who set themselves apart from the patriarchal nature of Darkovan feudal society: the priestesses of Avarra, and the warriors of the Sisterhood of the Sword. Eventually these two independent groups merged to form the powerful and legally chartered Order of Renunciates or Free Amazons, a guild of women bound only by oath as a sisterhood of mutual responsibility. Their primary allegiance is to each other rather than to family, clan, caste or any man save a temporary employer. Alone among Darkovan women, they are exempt from the usual legal restrictions and protections. Their reason for existence is to provide the women of Darkover an alternative to their socially restrictive lives.

THE SHATTERED CHAIN
THENDARA HOUSE
CITY OF SORCERY

AGAINST THE TERRANS
—THE FIRST AGE (Recontact)

After the Hastur Wars, the Hundred Kingdoms are consolidated into the Seven Domains, and ruled by a hereditary aristocracy of seven families, called the Comyn, allegedly descended from the legendary Hastur, Lord of Light. It is during this era that the Terran Empire, really a form of confederacy, rediscovers Darkover, which they know as the fourth planet of the Cottman star system. The fact that Darkover is a lost colony of the Empire is not easily or readily acknowledged by Darkovans and their Comyn overlords.

REDISCOVERY *(with Mercedes Lackey)*
THE SPELL SWORD
THE FORBIDDEN TOWER
STAR OF DANGER
WINDS OF DARKOVER

AGAINST THE TERRANS
—THE SECOND AGE (After the Comyn)

With the initial shock of recontact beginning to wear off, and the Terran spaceport a permanent establishment on the outskirts of the city of Thendara, the younger and less traditional elements of Darkovan society begin the first real exchange of knowledge with the Terrans—learning Terran science and technology and teaching Darkovan matrix technology in turn. Eventually Regis Hastur, the young Comyn lord most active in these exchanges, becomes Regent in a provisional government allied to the Terrans. Darkover is once again reunited with its founding Empire.

THE BLOODY SUN
HERITAGE OF HASTUR
THE PLANET SAVERS
SHARRA'S EXILE
WORLD WRECKERS
EXILE'S SONG
THE SHADOW MATRIX
TRAITOR'S SUN

THE DARKOVER ANTHOLOGIES

These volumes of stories, edited by Marion Zimmer Bradley, strive to "fill in the blanks" of Darkovan history and elaborate on the eras, tales and characters which have captured readers' imaginations.

THE KEEPER'S PRICE
SWORD OF CHAOS
FREE AMAZONS OF DARKOVER
THE OTHER SIDE OF THE MIRROR
RED SUN OF DARKOVER
FOUR MOONS OF DARKOVER
DOMAINS OF DARKOVER
RENUNCIATES OF DARKOVER
LERONI OF DARKOVER
TOWERS OF DARKOVER
MARION ZIMMER BRADLEY'S DARKOVER
SNOWS OF DARKOVER

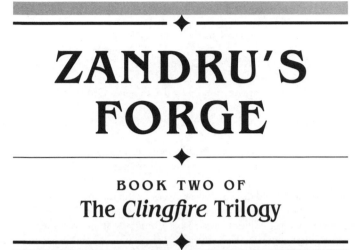

ZANDRU'S FORGE

BOOK TWO OF
The *Clingfire* Trilogy

MARION ZIMMER BRADLEY

AND

DEBORAH J. ROSS

DAW BOOKS, INC.

DONALD A. WOLLHEIM, FOUNDER

375 Hudson Street, New York, NY 10014

ELIZABETH R. WOLLHEIM
SHEILA E. GILBERT
PUBLISHERS

http://www.dawbooks.com

First printing, June 2003

1 2 3 4 5 6 7 8 9 10

DAW TRADEMARK REGISTERED
U.S. PAT. OFF. AND FOREIGN COUNTRIES
—MARCA REGISTRADA
HECHO EN U.S.A.

PRINTED IN THE U.S.A.

For Sarah
Hold fast to your dreams!

ACKNOWLEDGMENTS

My gratitude to those who have graced my life with their compassion, kindness, courage, and hope. You know who you are.

DISCLAIMER

The observant reader may note discrepancies in some details from more contemporary tales. This is undoubtedly due to the fragmentary histories which survive to the present day. Many records were lost during the years following the Ages of Chaos and Hundred Kingdoms and others distorted by oral tradition.

AUTHOR'S NOTE

Immensely generous with "her special world" of Darkover, Marion loved encouraging new writers. We were already friends when she began editing the DARKOVER and SWORD & SORCERESS anthologies. The match between my natural literary "voice" and what she was looking for was extraordinary. She loved to read what I loved to write, and she often cited "The Death of Brendan Ensolare" (FOUR MOONS OF DARKOVER, DAW, 1988) as one of her favorites.

Writing under my married name, Deborah Wheeler, I continued to sell short stories to Marion's anthologies and magazines, and also to ASIMOV'S, FANTASY AND SCIENCE FICTION, STAR WARS: TALES FROM JABBA'S PALACE, and SISTERS OF THE NIGHT. My two science fiction novels, JAYDIUM and NORTHLIGHT, were published by DAW Books.

As Marion's health declined, I was invited to work with her on one or more Darkover novels. We decided that rather than extend the story of "modern" Darkover, we would return to the Ages of Chaos. Marion envisioned a trilogy beginning with the Hastur Rebellion and the fall of Neskaya, the enduring friendship between Varzil the Good and Carolin Hastur, and extending to the fire-bombing of Hali and the signing of the Compact. While I scribbled notes as fast as I could, she would sit back, eyes alight, and begin a story with, "Now, the Hasturs tried to control the worst excesses of *laran* weapons, but there were always others under development . . ." or "Of course, Varzil and Carolin had been brought up on tales of star-crossed lovers who perished in the destruction of Neskaya . . ."

Here is that tale.

Deborah J. Ross

"It is not lily days which shape our souls, but the frozen winter nights, when we find ourselves in the pit of Zandru's Forge and discover who we truly are."

—Felicia Leynier

PROLOGUE

The boy came to bid farewell to his father as the light of dying embers flickered across the fieldstone hearth. He shivered, thinking of the night outside and the horseman who would come to take him away. With a patience beyond his twelve years, he waited for his father to speak the words that would send him away, perhaps forever.

For a long moment, the man swathed in tattered blankets did not move. Only the slow, stuttering rise and fall of his chest and the glitter of his eyes indicated he still lived. The old injury to his lungs, from a time he would never speak of, had brought him to the brink of death before, and each time, he had recovered.

Father, please don't die, the boy thought, and wondered again if this were why he was being sent away. To Arilinn, so far, to live among beasts and wizards.

"Eduin." A whisper, like a fall of ashes. "My son."

Tears stung the boy's eyes, but he fought the longing to throw himself into his father's arms, to bury his face in the wiry gray beard, to feel the iron-thin arms around him.

"I do not know if I shall ever see you again. You are my last hope."

"I won't fail you, Father."

1

The man's shoulders lifted and fell under the layers of blankets. "And what is it you are to do?"

"To go to Arilinn. To become a—" the child stumbled over the unfamiliar word, "—a *laranzu*. The most powerful wizard on all Darkover."

"Like your father before you."

Eduin nodded, brow furrowing. If his father was the mightiest *laranzu* in the world, why did they live so far from everyone? Why did they go hungry and cold in the winter, and wear patched clothing? He knew the Hasturs had something to do with it. His mother, while she still lived, had taught him never to ask. But if he did not, he might never have another chance.

As if sensing his questions, the boy's father gestured him closer and drew him into the shelter of one arm. "You are so young to carry such a burden, yet you are all I have left. Your brothers . . ." His voice trailed off.

They failed.

"Who are you?" his father asked in a different tone.

"Why, Eduin MacEarn, as you named me, Father."

"Listen carefully. Your mother knew nothing of what I am about to tell you. She knew only that I had been wounded in war and that I sought peace and forgetfulness. So I took her name and began a new life here. But the past must be made right."

Eduin shivered on the brink of an enormous mystery.

"Your true name, my son, is Eduin Deslucido and you are the sole heir to what was once a vast kingdom. Your uncle was King Damian Deslucido, a man of surpassing vision, ruler of Ambervale and Linn—" the names rolled off his tongue like incantations, "—and High Kinally and Verdanta and Hawksflight and then Acosta. But it's all gone now, even the memory of that great man. Destroyed by the treacherous Hasturs, may their punishment last a thousand years! In their lust for power, they slaughtered your uncle and your cousin Belisar, who would have been king after him. They rained fire from the heavens and brought two Towers down in ruins. They thought I had perished, too."

"No, Father, not you!"

"But Zandru smiled upon me and I escaped. I came here, took your mother's name, and waited. I thought if I regained my strength, I could go back into the world and bring the Hastur fiends to justice. But," gesturing toward his chest with his free hand, "this body has suffered too much at their hands."

Breath rasped in the old man's lungs. "When your brothers came of age, I began to hope again, that I might send them out in my place. They were good boys, loving sons. They tried their best. I realized then that the Hasturs are too powerful for any ordinary assassin, no matter how just the cause."

Eduin shivered again. He barely remembered his brothers, only that they were tall and strong. How could he possibly succeed where they had failed?

"There is a great sense of justice in all this," the old man said with a wry grin. "That you, the child of Rumail Deslucido, will bring to destruction the children of the accursed witch, Taniquel Hastur-Acosta, and everyone else in that miserable Nest who aided her!"

He broke off into a cascade of racking coughs. The boy scurried to the table across the room and brought back a battered wooden cup of herbal infusion.

"You must never oppose the Hasturs by force of arms," the old man said, "for that way leads only to disaster. Instead, cultivate your talent. Earn your place in the Towers. Watch and learn. Wait. The right time will come. You will meet Hasturs there, of that I am sure. *Laran* talent runs deep in that family, as it does in ours. Make friends with them, gain their trust, obtain entrance into their homes. But never fear their strength. You have a Gift far beyond any of theirs. When the time is right, I will show you how to use it."

The old man paused, but the boy knew there was still more. "Do not betray yourself by striking out at lesser members of that House. Save your efforts for your true targets—the guilty and their descendants. The ghosts of Damian Deslucido, of Prince Belisar, and all those who died in their glorious cause are counting on you. *I am counting on you!*"

Hoofbeats sounded in the yard outside. The boy glanced at the folded cloak laid atop the bundle beside the door. He threw his arms around his father and whispered once more—perhaps for the last time—

"I won't fail you, Father. I won't fail!"

BOOK I

1

The great red sun of Darkover slanted across the courtyard at the entrance to Arilinn Tower on a morning in early autumn. Polished granite interspersed with translucent blue stone formed the floor and two walls. They were shaped and pieced together so artfully that not a blade of grass or tendril of ivy rooted there. Rising sharply, the walls framed a canyon where the chill of the night lingered. At the far end, the graceful sweep of arch enclosed the rainbow-hued Veil through which only those of pure *Comyn* blood, the caste of Darkovan aristocracy Gifted with psychic powers, could pass. In the dawn's oblique light, the Veil resembled a waterfall of coruscating rainbow colors.

When he'd crept into the courtyard in the darkest hour of the night, Varzil Ridenow had not dared to approach the Veil too closely. Even here, in this corner where he'd curled up to doze fitfully until dawn, he felt its power dancing along his nerves.

If there had been any other way . . .

The words echoed in his mind like the refrain of a ballad. He was a Ridenow and he had the gift of *laran*, the true *donas*. He had known this since he first heard the Ya-men singing their laments in the far hills under the four Midsummer moons. He'd been eight, old enough to realize there was something beyond what could be seen or touched, and old enough to know he should keep quiet about it. He'd seen the way his father, *Dom* Felix Ridenow, grew silent and tight-jawed on the subject. Now he was sixteen, older than most when they began their Tower training, and his father would like nothing better than to forget the whole matter and pretend his youngest son was normal.

Varzil had journeyed all the long leagues from his home to Arilinn, along with his father and kinsmen, to be formally presented to the *Comyn* Council. His older brother, Harald, who was heir to Sweetwater, had passed a similar inspection three years ago, but Varzil had been too young to come along then. His present recognition was clearly a political maneuver to bolster the status of the Ridenow. Many of the other great Houses still regarded them as upstarts, barely more civilized than their Dry Towns ancestors. It galled them to accord any Ridenow the respect of a true equal.

The peace that Allart Hastur had forged between his own kingdom and that of Ridenow was neither so long nor so deep to blur the memory of the bloody conflict that had come before. *Dom* Felix was never anything but scrupulously polite to the Hasturs, but Varzil sensed their doubt—their *fear.*

If there had been any other way . . .

He would not have had to creep from the Hidden City at this scandalous hour, to wait half-frozen for someone inside the Tower to let him in. He hoped that would happen soon, before his absence was discovered and a hunt mounted. The Council session was all but over, with little further business to conduct. *Dom* Felix would not tarry, not with catmen sighted in the hills near the sheep pastures.

Varzil drew his cloak more tightly and set his teeth to keep them from chattering. The finely woven garment was meant for courtly show instead of protection against the elements.

Praise Aldones, it had been a clear night.

Through the long hours, Varzil felt the swirl and dance of psychic forces behind the Tower walls. The harsh bright energy of the Veil scoured every nerve raw, leaving him sensitive to the slightest telepathic whisper.

Much of the work of a Tower was done during the hours when ordinary men slept, to minimize the psychic static of so many untrained minds. This close to the city, even the occasional stray thought or burst of emotion, hardly worth calling *laran,* became cumulative, low-grade interference, or so he'd been told. For this reason, Towers like Hali and the now-ruined Tramontana stood apart from other human habitation. In the long quiet hours of darkness, Gifted workers sent messages across hundreds of leagues through the relays, and charged immense *laran* batteries, used for a myriad of purposes, including powering aircars, lighting the palaces of Kings and mining precious minerals, even performing the delicate healing of minds and bodies.

Varzil had drowsed and woken a dozen times that night, each time resonating to a different pattern. Whenever he roused, it seemed that his senses had grown keener. With his mind, he felt colors and music he had never known existed. He heard voices, a word here and there, phrases shimmering with secret meaning that left him hungry for more. The rainbow Veil no longer glinted from a distance, it reverberated through the marrow of his bones.

Movement caught Varzil's attention, a shadow among shadows. Slender, gray-furred, bent over like a little wizened man, a figure slipped through the Veil. It halted, an empty basket clutched in its prehensile fingers, and stared at him.

Varzil sat straighter, pulling his thin cloak more tightly around his shoulders. He recognized the creature as a *kyrri,* although Serrais, seat of the Ridenow, had few of them as servants. They were said to be highly telepathic, but dangerous to approach. His father, in preparing him for the visit to Arilinn, warned him about their protective electrical fields. Nevertheless, he reached out one hand.

"It's all right," he murmured. "I won't hurt you."

Something brushed against the back of Varzil's skull, at once feather-soft and grating, as if sand were being rubbed into his skin. But no, it was *inside* his head. Suddenly, a sensation of curiosity flickered through him and vanished as quickly.

The creature was studying him. Did it want something? He had no food—and then he realized he thought of it as an animal, instead of an intelligent, if nonhuman, being.

Without a sound, the *kyrri* hurried away. Varzil watched as it crossed the outer courtyard and turned aside at the street. He felt as if he had been tested in some mysterious fashion, and he did not know if he had passed.

"Look down there!" a voice cried from above. "Some ne'er-do-well rascal has camped upon our doorstep!"

Varzil craned his neck back to stare up at a balcony running alongside the Tower to either side of the arch of the Veil. Two older boys leaned over, pointing. They looked to be in their late teens, their voices already deepened, waists and hips slender but with the shoulders of young manhood.

"You there! Boy! What are you doing here?"

Something in the voice rankled Varzil's nerves, or perhaps lingering irritability from the encounter with the *kyrri* drove him to snap back, "What business is it of yours? I have come to see the Keeper of Arilinn Tower, and that isn't you!"

"How dare you speak to us in such a manner!" The youth in the Tower leaned over. "You impudent good-for-nothing!"

The second boy pulled his friend back. "Eduin, you gain nothing in taunting him this way. He can do us no harm where he is, and he is clearly no street beggar. These words are unworthy of you." He spoke with the accent of a lowland aristocrat.

Varzil scrambled to his feet, heart pounding. A dozen retorts leaped to his mind. His hands curled into fists. He kept his teeth clamped tightly together, though the breath hissed through them. He had not spent the better part of his years shrugging off far worse insults, only to lose his temper now.

What was he doing, to provoke a confrontation this way? What was wrong with him? Courtesy cost nothing, but insults might well create future enemies. If he succeeded, these boys would become his fellow students. Beside, the only person whose opinion mattered was, after all, the Keeper himself.

Not trusting himself to say anything further, Varzil simply bowed to them. It was the only thing he could think of which would not make matters worse.

The boy named Eduin retreated from the balcony, muttering something about proper respect for the dignity of the Tower. Varzil was concentrating too hard on holding his tongue to catch all the words. But the other youth, the one who had cautioned restraint, remained.

Varzil raised his eyes. The sun caught the brilliant red of the other boy's hair, the luminous gray eyes, the regular features. Both Tower lads wore simple clothing, tunics with wide leather belts, with no clue as to clan or rank.

"Boy," he called down, and this time the word carried no insult. His voice was strong and clear, as if he'd trained as a singer. "What do you want with the Keeper of Arilinn Tower?"

"I've come to—I want to join the Tower." There it was.

For a long moment, the youth continued to study him. With a nod and, "Wait here," he disappeared back into the Tower.

Varzil let out the breath he did not know he had been holding. While he tried to calm himself, the Veil shimmered and parted like an iridescent waterfall. A man in a loose white monitor's robe stepped through. Gray dominated his chestnut-red hair and lines framed his mouth and underscored his eyes. A few paces behind came the youth from the balcony. This close, Varzil was struck by the other boy's commanding sense of presence.

The man in the white robe paused, his gaze flickering over the colors of Varzil's cloak, the gold and green of his clan.

"*Vai dom . . .*" Varzil broke the silence. "I am Varzil Ridenow, younger son of *Dom* Felix of Sweetwater. I have come to seek training here. Will you be so kind as to escort me to the Keeper?"

The taut mouth softened into a glimmer of a smile. "Young sir, I can imagine nothing more appropriate. *I* certainly wouldn't presume to decide what to do with you."

Varzil approached the Veil, as the white-robed man indicated. He'd never been so close to such a powerful matrix device before, only personal starstones or the telepathic damper the Ridenow household *leronis* had used when his mother had one of her fainting spells.

He held up one hand, fingers extended but not daring yet to touch the Veil. Besides a thing of beauty, what was it? Two people—three if he counted the *kyrri*—had passed through it as if it had been a tissue of gauze.

He turned his head to see the monitor watching him intently. Another test, then. He set his jaw and strode ahead.

The Veil looked like a thin rainbow mist, and he had expected it to feel cool and perhaps damp. The instant it touched him, it shifted, engulfing him. He gasped, drawing in breath tainted with the metallic taste of a thunderstorm. The skin of his entire body tingled, each hair erect. The small muscles around his eyes twitched. He could not feel his fingertips.

The next instant, he stood trembling in a windowless cubicle. Although he was no longer directly within a matrix field, he sensed the power in the little room, as if it were itself a *laran* device. Turning to look behind him, he made out shapes, blurred and shadowy. Was this some kind of trap? Another test?

Then the white-robed monitor stepped through the rainbow shimmer. The youth followed him, grinning.

"I told you so," the youth said.

Told him what? Varzil wondered.

The man moved his hands as if manipulating something and Varzil's stomach plummeted to his feet. No, he still stood upon a solid floor, but the *room itself* was rising. It stopped a moment later and they stepped through an arched doorway that appeared in one wall. The lighted room beyond it opened onto a broad terrace.

Surely not even the ballroom of the greatest castle on Darkover could be so grand, Varzil thought. Tapestries covered the walls, glowing with rich colors, depicting scenes of hunting parties, *chieri* dancing in the forest beneath the four moons, eagles soaring over the Hellers. The floor tiles formed an intricate mosaic pattern that was at once lavish and soothing to the eye. At the far end of the room, a fire filled the air with warmth and a touch of incense.

Armchairs and a long bench piled with cushions formed a rough half circle around the fireplace. A woman and two men sat there, talking in low tones. The woman met Varzil's gaze. She was about the age of Varzil's favorite aunt, short and compact without being fat, the wrinkles around her eyes giving her the appearance of being perpetually on the edge of laughter. She got to her feet and dismissed the men with a gesture, something no woman in Varzil's family would ever dare to do.

"Off with you, too, Carlo," she told the red-haired youth.

"But—" he protested.

She folded her arms across her ample, shawl-wrapped chest, silencing him. "What happens now is not your affair."

The youth delivered an impeccably polite bow and left the room through the archway at the far end, but not without a quick wink at Varzil.

Varzil's breath caught in his throat. After the years of longing, the months of planning, the night's escape, and the long hours of waiting, things were happening much too fast.

Once, while climbing the craggy hills near Serrais in search of eagle feathers, Varzil had lost his footing and tumbled down a pebbled slope.

Rock and sky had whirled together as stones pelted his body from a dozen different directions at once. He'd slid to a stop and lain there for a long time, panting and bruised, gazing up at the cloudless sky with amazement that he was still alive.

He felt that way now, although his body was unhurt. Dimly, he heard the woman's voice talking about a hot breakfast. He felt her hands on his shoulders, guiding him to a chair beside the fire.

"Sweet Evanda, you're half frozen!" she exclaimed. "Not to mention—" Varzil could not follow her next words, "—energon channels— just as if you've been working two solid nights without a break!"

The next moment she pressed a cup of steaming *jaco* into his hands. He felt the heat through the heavy ceramic with its intricate incised pattern, the smoothness of the glaze. The *jaco* had been sweetened with honey and laced with some herb he did not recognize. He swallowed it obediently, though it burned his tongue. Only then did he realize how badly he was shivering.

"Here, get this into you," the woman said, handing him a bowl heaped with some kind of nut porridge and topped with cream. "Can you hold the spoon?"

Varzil's fingers curled around the handle. His hand shook, but he managed a mouthful of the stuff. Whatever happened, he was *not* going to be fed like a baby.

The porridge turned out to be a mixture of oats, hazelnuts, and dried apples, seasoned with cinnabark. It tasted wonderful, blending the earthiness of the grain, the crunchiness of the nuts, and the chewiness of the fruit.

Varzil's vision returned to focus and his hands steadied. He thanked the women, adding, "This is very good."

"It should be," she said, again reminding him of his aunt. "Eat it all up. Lord of Light, boy, you look as if you haven't had a decent meal in a tenday!"

Varzil lowered the spoon. "I'm grateful, *vai domna,* but I didn't come here to beg a meal." He handed her back the bowl.

"I won't hear such prideful nonsense," she retorted, shoving it back at him. "I'm house mother to all the novices here and when I say *eat,* they eat. Even the royal ones. Is that clear?"

Varzil had not taken more than another two or three spoonful when the door at the far end swung open and a tall, heavy-shouldered man strode into the room.

Rust and silver mingled in his neatly trimmed beard and hair. His features were too irregular to be conventionally handsome, with his over-large ears and crooked mouth. Eyes blue and dark as lapis regarded Varzil. An aura of steely power hung about the man like a mantle.

Yet he wore ordinary clothing, comfortable and warm, a leather vest trimmed with bright embroidery over a belted *linex* tunic, and loose pants tucked into laced calf-high boots. A chain of dark gray metal hung about his neck, disappearing beneath his shirt.

Two other men entered the room from a door at the opposite end. One was the white-robed man who had taken Varzil into the Tower. The other was robed, too, but in a soft deep green. Yet there was no doubt in Varzil's mind who held the power here.

Varzil got to his feet and bowed deeply to the heavy-shouldered man.

So you are the Ridenow boy who wants to train at Arilinn Tower? The voice rang out like a sword on the anvil. Never had anyone spoken so directly to Varzil's mind, or with such crystalline clarity. Even the household *leronis,* who had given him rudimentary training in the use of his starstone, had sounded muffled, as if in another room, when she used her *laran* to speak with him. Varzil realized that of all the tests he might face, this was the basic and most crucial one of all. He bowed again.

"Vai dom, I am."

"Sit down, then, and let us get to know you a little. Do you know who I am?"

"Sir, you are Auster Syrtis, Keeper of Arilinn Tower."

"One of them, anyway." A smile flickered at the corner of the man's mouth. "What makes you think I am he? How can you be sure?" With one hand, he gestured to his clothing, as if to indicate the absence of the traditional crimson robes.

Does he think I'm such a head-blind fool? Varzil wondered. His indignation evaporated as the man tilted his head back in laughter.

For the next hour, Varzil sat before the fragrant fire, answering questions from the three men. The woman, whose name was Lunilla, alternated between sitting quietly in her own chair and offering the men *jaco* and Varzil food, on some schedule of her own devising. Nobody argued with her.

Varzil showed them the starstone he had been given by the household *leronis,* a light blue crystal the size of his thumbnail. As he had been taught, he kept it wrapped in layers of silk. When he took it out and held it in his bare fingers, the ribbons of twisting brightness in its heart flared to life. The patterns first appeared when he had keyed into the stone. Now, with the prolonged exposure to the psychic energies of Veil and circle, he sensed it as a living thing, responding to his touch. The stone sang to him, danced with him.

Varzil answered questions and performed a few simple *laran* exercises very much like those the Ridenow *leronis* had taught him. Without his starstone, he had very little psychokinesis, although by focusing, he could cause a small feather to quiver. He had no difficulty hearing questions in thought form, rather than spoken aloud. The shifts in mood and emotion appeared to him as clear and distinct as musical phrases played on different instruments.

Even as the examination continued, Varzil sensed an undercurrent beneath the innocent-sounding questions. On one or two occasions, he caught the edge of a quickly-guarded thought, and knew it had nothing to do with the quality of his *laran.*

Again and again, the questions skirted the issue of how he had come, and whether his father knew of this visit and had given his blessing. The Keeper never asked directly, yet suspicion shadowed his words. Perhaps they feared he had come on some purpose other than his own—to penetrate their company, learn their secrets, or somehow weaken them.

But surely they would read the truth in his mind. . . .

Realization dawned slowly. Yes, they were suspicious, but it was because they saw him as sickly and feared he might fall ill under the rigors of training. Since Varzil was a son of Ridenow, there might be serious repercussions if he died. His family might act in retaliation against Hastur or Asturias, destabilizing the balance of power. Political relations continued to be precarious since the last wars. Arilinn itself might be drawn into the conflict. . . .

I will not be a pawn in any lordling's game!

In the middle of a question from the green-robed man, Varzil got to his feet and bowed.

"Vai dom'yn," he said in such a serious tone that the man stopped in midsentence. "I am happy to answer any questions about my background or fitness for Tower work. You have a right to know these things. But—" and here his composure wavered, "—but you must either admit or refuse

me based on my talent. I am here on my own behalf, not anyone else's. Others may use their *laran* to plot and spy, but *I* do not," he said glaring pointedly at Auster.

"Children do not address a Keeper of Arilinn Tower in that manner!" Lunilla gasped. The green-robed man scowled, but Auster bent to look at Varzil even more carefully with those intense blue eyes.

"No, it's all right," said Auster. "He has spoken like a man, so he deserves a man's answer. Young Ridenow, you have undeniable talent, but you have also come here, by your own admission, without your father's permission and against his wishes. We are not prepared to offer you a place here under those circumstances. In these troubled times, it is not a simple matter of accepting anyone with *laran*. We of the Towers must do everything we can to hold ourselves apart from the greater events of the world."

With a sinking heart, Varzil realized that he'd guessed rightly. His admission to Arilinn Tower involved much more than his own desires and abilities. Nothing he could say now would change that fact.

"You seem untroubled by the illnesses which so often accompany the awakening of *laran*," the white-robed monitor said, "so there is no compassionate need for training to save your life or sanity, no emergency which might justify overriding your father's wishes. The training you have already received from your family *leronis* should suffice."

Auster rose, signaling that the interview was over. Stunned, Varzil stood as the *leronyn* left the room, all except the white-robed man. He gestured Varzil to follow him. They retraced their steps, descending in the strange matrix-powered chute as before, guided by ritual hand motions.

In parting, the monitor spoke to Varzil in a kindly tone. "It has been a pleasure to breakfast with you. With the blessing of the gods, you will prosper, sire many sons, and be a credit to your family."

But the waste of talent— Abruptly, the man's mental barriers slammed shut.

Regardless of his private feelings, the *laranzu* would never speak out against his Keeper's verdict.

Varzil thought wildly that in another moment, he would be gone from the Tower. He must find a way back. There was so much he wanted to ask, wanted to know! Words clogged his throat as the seconds slipped by. He found himself standing at the entrance to Arilinn Tower with morning sun filling the streets of the city. When he turned back, the gate had closed.

2

From his turret window, Carolin Hastur, called Carlo after his boyhood nickname, watched the strange boy standing outside the gates of Arilinn. Fists clenched at his sides, back rigid, the boy drew in one heaving breath after another. Carolin himself did not have a vocation in Tower work, but he could recognize it in others. Never before had he seen such passion, such intensity as in that slender form below.

Carolin had only a modest amount of *laran* and no particular interest in closeting himself inside a Tower. He was here for a short time only, for his destiny had been fixed on the day of his birth. He'd been sent to Arilinn last spring, at the age of seventeen, as part of the training suitable for a young man of his caste.

Looking down at the boy below, seeing the bony shoulders rise and fall, the tension in each muscle, Carolin could well believe the boy was born to the Tower, even as he, Carolin, was born to the throne. He remembered how the boy had spoken to the *kyrri,* not only in words, but with a gentle mental touch that even Carolin could sense.

Had he been turned away summarily? Any prospective student applying to the Tower was given hospitality as he was evaluated. Once or twice in Carolin's knowledge, the Keepers sent a likely boy to another Tower. Each circle maintained a balance of different skills and gifts.

17

The Keeper must have a good reason for what he did, he told himself. *And would tell me to keep out of things which are none of my concern.* He slumped in the window seat, wishing it were so simple to banish that slender, ardent figure from his thoughts.

The outer wall of his room was rounded like the turret outside, with a bed built into the single straight wall. Set between the two windows, a rack of hooks held cloaks and ordinary clothing. A small chest of carved blackthorn wood was more than enough room for his few personal possessions. Because he was Hastur, he also had a small heating brazier and a desk. Unlike most of the other novices, he could read and was being tutored in other things a prince must know. He had an aircar at his disposal, a horse stabled below in the town, and many other privileges of his rank.

A copy of Roald McInery's *Military Tactics* lay open on the desk. Carolin strode over and flipped the book closed, impatient with its ponderous style. The material, once he waded through the antiquated language, was interesting enough. McInery wrote sensibly about fortifications, supply lines, and positioning of troops. But he also discussed *laran* weaponry as a natural and inevitable extension of force of arms. Some of the weapons were unknown to Carolin, but others were all too familiar to a royal heir in these chaotic times. Linked telepathically to their trainers, sentry birds could spy out an army's position, *clingfire* could turn man and beast into living torches, relays could send messages faster than horse or aircar, and small circles of *leronyn* could control the very minds of the enemy.

Yet even the powerful Towers of Neskaya and Tramontana could not protect themselves from the strife and chaos of the world outside. Drawn into war a generation ago by the command of their respective liege lords, the two Towers had ended by destroying each other. Most of their highly trained and Gifted workers had been killed or mentally crippled.

No one was sure exactly how it happened, but the ballads suggested that Neskaya had been engaged in the development of a new, fearsome weapon that was accidentally deployed during a crucial confrontation. It was said that deep within the rubble, eerie blue flames still smoldered, feeding on the very substance of the stones.

Once Carolin had met a survivor of that horrendous battle, a distant Hastur cousin who had been *leronis* at Tramontana. Old Lady Bronwyn had escaped the worst of the conflagration, but when he asked her about it, she had turned to him with a look of such desolation that his small boy's heart faltered in his chest. She had not answered; her expression had been enough.

Stories of how the Towers had been drawn into the war between Hastur and a ruthlessly ambitious neighbor, Deslucido of Ambervale, still circulated in the boys' dormitories. It was said that the Keeper of Neskaya, in love with a *leronis* at Tramontana, had sacrificed himself in defiance of his lord's orders in order to save her, but in vain, for both had gone up in flames. He still didn't know if that was true, or any of the other tales whispered around the fireplace during the long winter nights, but he wished they were.

With the defeat of Ambervale and all its conquered provinces, Darkover had achieved only an uneasy peace. A hundred kingdoms still dotted the landscape. Larger ones preyed on the small and then fractured in succession disputes and insurrections. From his earliest boyhood, Carolin had heard the lords of his own family arguing, debating, struggling to restrain the worst abuses of *laran* weaponry. He remembered his uncle Rafael saying, over and over again, "There must be a way."

The ruins of the Towers and the desolation of the Lake of Hali, the result of an ancient disaster known as the Cataclysm, remained as mute witnesses to their failure.

Carolin snapped out of his reverie. He stood before his own door, fingers brushing the wooden latch, as if he'd been caught in a waking dream. When he returned to his window, the Ridenow boy was gone. Carolin knew, with that atavistic certainty, that they would meet again.

◆

Carolin made his way down the stairs and across the central room to the smaller chamber where his afternoon session, practicing the basics of monitoring with the other beginning students, met. He caught a snatch of conversation between the older workers as they sat together before the cold fireplace.

"... Ridenow ..." "... who sent him? ..."

As he crossed the room, the two broke off their conversation. Dark-eyed Marella looked up at Carolin and smiled. Only a few years his senior, she had flirted with him at Midsummer Festival, a tenday after he'd arrived at Arilinn. Despite his efforts to behave properly, she'd figured prominently in his dreams for a while. Carolin knew she was aware of the effect she had on him, for at his grandfather's court, he'd been the target of many feminine wiles. The combination of youth, good looks, and a crown attracted eligible ladies like a honeycomb attracted scorpion-ants. Only with his kinswoman, Maura Elhalyn, and Jandria, the cousin of his foster-brother Orain, did he feel fully at ease, but they were back at Carcosa.

Marella's companion, a slab-faced older man named Richardo, who never seemed to smile at anything, got to his feet. He nodded to Carolin and hurried away. Color rising to her cheeks, Marella followed him, so that Carolin had no chance to ask questions.

It was just as well. He had been at Arilinn long enough to know that telepaths operated under a different set of social proprieties than ordinary people did. Some kinds of privacy were impossible, such as sexual attraction. Casual physical contact could be as offensive as an outright assault when people lived in such intimacy. Yet no code of Tower etiquette could overcome Carolin's inborn curiosity. It was a fault he'd long struggled to overcome.

Although Carolin's family, the Hasturs of Carcosa, worshiped the Lord of Light, as was proper for the *Comyn* caste, he had also studied the teachings of the *cristoforos*. One prayer, in particular, had struck him as appropriate to his own character, *Grant me, O Bearer of the World's Burdens, to know what Thou givest me to know . . .* Sometimes that meant to keep his nose out of affairs which might cause him to lose it, and his entire head as well. At other times, such as this one, the prayer suggested that it was his right and responsibility to find out what was going on, although it did not imply *how* or *when*.

At his uncle's court, there was hardly a moment when some plot or scheme was not simmering. Political undercurrents were as numerous and changing as motes of dust in the air. Carolin had learned patience and the usefulness of a blankly innocent expression. In due time, he would find out.

✦

Carolin focused his thoughts on the task at hand, starstone practice with the other beginners. The class took place in a small, airy room that had been pleasant when he arrived at Arilinn in the summer, but now felt drafty. In another month or so, they would all be bundled in outdoor clothing against the chill.

He took his place around the worktable with the other students,

three boys he didn't know well. Their teacher was Cerriana, an older girl
with fiery red hair who had little interest in socializing with boys the age
of her baby brother. She worked as a monitor while she continued her
own training.

Valentina, youngest of the novices, was absent, probably because she
was ill again. Like many of her family, the Aillards, she was in frail health
and had been sent to Arilinn in the hope that, with skilled help, she might
survive the turmoil of threshold sickness. Carolin had developed a light
case of it himself, a few months of queasiness and quick temper. He'd
been told that it was often severe, even life-threatening, in those with
exceptional talent. The combination of the awakening of *laran* and adolescent sexual energy, which were carried by the same energon channels
in the body, could create fatal overloads. Fidelis, the senior monitor, had
mentioned that rarely, perhaps once or twice in a generation, *laran* of
extraordinary power arose earlier, in childhood, so smoothly and completely there was never any difficulty.

With her usual methodical care, Cerriana directed the students
through the morning's routine. Together, they took out their starstones
and began as usual by simply gazing into them, watching the patterns of
blue light.

Like all the members of his family, Carolin had been given a stone
of superior quality, medium-sized but beautifully cut, clear and faintly
luminescent. Now as he cupped it in his bare hand, the stone warmed
against his skin. His starstone had grown noticeably brighter since his
arrival at Arilinn, the flashes of brilliance more intense. Sometimes he
sensed the crystalline structure that would focus and amplify his own
natural psychic abilities. Cerriana had said that the more he worked with
the stone, the more it would become attuned to him.

After the preliminary exercises, Cerriana brought out a collection of
objects—feathers, thin silver coins, small cubes and dowels of wood—
and distributed them to the students. Using their starstones, the students
were to focus their minds upon the object with the goal of either lifting
or sliding it across the table.

Carolin, as a beginner, was still working with feathers. The task,
which had seemed all but impossible when he first attempted it, now
began to make sense, although he had not as yet had any luck in producing so much as a quiver in the feather. He'd made the mistake of looking
directly at it, as if by sheer force of will he could cause it to rise. Now he

gazed at it only long enough to fix its features in his mind, its size and color, the curve of the quill, the curl of the down. Then he looked deep into his starstone, building a mental picture of the feather. He tried to imagine the air beneath it rising like the waves of heat above a summer field.

The feather quivered, tilted. He sensed tiny currents of air pressing against its weight. This time, he decided to keep his attention on the air as it swirled upward.

Let the feather go where it wills, he told himself.

The air felt hot, exciting. He thought of storm clouds, mountains of gray-white, billowing to fill the sky. A taste and flash like lightning flickered across his senses.

"Carolin!"

He jumped, his vision leaping into focus. The feather sat on the table just as before. Then it burst into flame.

Lord of Light!

Without thinking, Carolin grabbed the feather. The fire went out immediately, but not before it had singed his fingers. He yelped and clutched his hand. His starstone went rolling across the table. Cerriana caught it just before it tumbled off the edge.

Fire erupted inside Carolin's skull. He could no longer feel his burned hand. For an awful moment, his lungs locked, unable to draw in air. He heard confused voices in the distance.

The next instant, something small and cool was pressed into his hand. He could breathe again. His vision seeped back and he looked into Cerriana's eyes. They were dark with concern. Her hand overlaid his, curling his fingers around his starstone.

"What—" *What happened to me?*

"I touched your starstone. I must now monitor you to make sure you have taken no harm from it."

Carolin's eyes stung and he felt shaken to his bones. He was grateful when Cerriana dismissed the class. All he wanted was to be left alone. He clenched the starstone, pressing it to his heart. His fingers throbbed where he'd touched the burning feather. The muscles of his belly quivered. But he was Hastur, heir to the throne, and it was not proper that he behave like a whimpering child.

Only a moment had passed. Cerriana still waited for the answer to her request. As an Arilinn-trained monitor, she scrupulously observed the formalities of permission. This was not an emergency; she would not enter the energy fields of his body against his will. Finally, he lifted his head and gestured to Cerriana that he was ready.

As she worked, relief and a sense of well-being spread throughout his body. Frayed nerves relaxed and the burns on his fingers cooled. His heartbeat steadied and his breathing came more freely.

A short time later, she announced with a smile that he had not been damaged by either the fire or the accidental contact with his starstone.

"I don't understand," Carolin said. Although he felt physically well enough, except for the fading heat on his palms, he couldn't think straight. His skull seemed to be packed with feathers. "Other people have handled my stone before—Hanna at home, you and Fidelis and Auster here. I've never had a reaction like this."

"It's usually safe enough at this stage," Cerriana answered. "Few of the novices have keyed into their stones strongly enough to carry any risk in a trained monitor handling them. You certainly hadn't, not at the beginning of our session. Whatever you were doing must have accelerated the process." She looked thoughtful. "Sometimes there's a plateau in *laran* development and then a cascading effect. Contact with a catalyst telepath will do it, too."

She sat back, still studying him with renewed composure. "Listen, Carolin. This is very important. Now that you have attuned with your matrix, you must never let anyone touch it except a Keeper, and then it should be only your own Keeper. I cannot emphasize this strongly enough. Even though I am trained to oversee the physical and psychic well-being of those entrusted to my care, I am only a monitor. With all the best intentions, I could have seriously injured you. The only reason I did not is that I held your stone for only a moment. Do you understand?"

"Oh," he said with a wry smile, "I have no intention of repeating *that* experience." With hands that still trembled a little, he folded the starstone back into its pouch of insulating silk.

She nodded gravely. "I don't think you have the aptitude for psychokinesis. The question remains whether you have a separate talent for creating fire or whether this—" she gestured at the few bits of charred feather on the table, "—was due simply to the energies generated by keying into your starstone."

"Well," Carolin said with his usual levity, "at least it'll be better than staring at those damned feathers."

◆

The next morning, Carolin and Eduin passed beneath the archways of the Tower on their way into Arilinn City, headed for the morning marketplace accompanied by one of the *kyrri*. Since only nonhumans and *Comyn* could pass the Veil, everyone took turns with daily household tasks, even the youngest novices. The autumn day was crisp. Last night's rain had washed any hint of dust from the air and the city sparkled. Beyond it loomed the Twin Peaks, their pinnacles shimmering.

Carolin paused at the place where the Ridenow boy had stood. Although no visible trace remained, no stain or mark on the age-smoothed stone, Carolin felt a sense of lingering presence so strong he could have sworn there was indeed someone there. Images flashed through his mind, half memory, half something else. He pictured the boy, not as young as he'd first supposed, only thin and undersized, his face pale and very serious.

As Carolin watched, Varzil's features shifted into those of an older boy, then to a mature man. He was still slender, but held himself with a quiet confidence Carolin had seen in expert swordsmen. Silver glinted in his hair and lines bracketed his eyes and mouth. An expression of compassion touched with sadness lay upon his face. He wore a dark, loosely belted robe, but Carolin could not make out the color, red or brown, as the vision began to fade. Varzil raised one hand in greeting and a gem-set ring flashed white.

The sense of prescience lifted, and Carolin stood with his market basket in hand.

"Let's get on with it, Carlo," Eduin said. He used the familiar nickname, although they didn't know each other well. Carolin had only been at Arilinn a few months, whereas Eduin had begun his training there four years ago. That had been long enough for Eduin to know his own worth. He had a life in the Towers and would certainly make a skillful matrix mechanic or technician, perhaps even a Keeper if he could accept the discipline.

Carolin hung back. He had no doubt of what he'd seen. He was no *laranzu,* but he was of the true *Comyn* blood. The powers of the mind were every bit as real as what he could lift and handle. And he himself could not go on with the mundane tasks of the morning, as if nothing had happened.

"Go on," he said absently. "I'll be along shortly."

"But, Carlo, we're already late—the best sweet-gourds will be gone—"

"Not if we get them first!"

Eduin sauntered off, the *kyrri* scurrying in his wake. A few minutes later, Carolin strode down the corridor to the Keeper's chambers. Two of the senior technicians were just about to enter. One was Gavin Elhalyn, second only to Auster in position in the Tower. He was also Carolin's distant kinsman.

"I must speak with Auster," Carolin said. "It's important."

Gavin frowned, clearly torn between his responsibility and his blood relationship to Carolin. He was *Comyn* and *laranzu,* but Carolin would someday be King.

Lerrys moved into the breach. "Whatever it is can wait, lad. Auster himself summoned us."

Carolin held back a retort, realizing too late how useless that was. This was, after all, a Tower, where people spoke with their minds as freely as they did with their mouths. He was coming to understand why he had been sent here to Arilinn. It was not just to cultivate his modest *laran,* but to groom him for the exacting demands of kingship. At home, he had learned to speak with care; here in the Tower, he would learn to guard his very thoughts.

"It's all right." Auster swung the door open. His face looked drained, but not the light in his eyes. "Carlo will only pester us until he has his say. It's a family trait. The Hasturs have never backed down easily. Come in, all of you, and in a moment I'll hear the boy out."

Auster returned to his usual place, a padded armchair. The two other men took up positions inside the door, as if awaiting orders.

As long as he'd thought of Auster as the second cousin of his aunt Ramona Castamir, Carolin had no doubts of success. But now, Auster's formal crimson robes glowed in the reflected firelight, the remains of a small blaze laid in against the autumn night chill. Carolin remembered this was one of the most powerful men on Darkover, and within these walls, his word was absolute.

There is more than one kind of power, Carolin told himself, *just as there is more than one kind of truth.*

A fourth man waited inside the chambers, shifting uneasily from one foot to the other. Carolin did not recognize him, only the subtle richness of his garb, a padded velvet jacket edged with fur, thick woolen breeches above boots of buttery-soft leather, the fine lace at his cuffs and throat, the chain of gold-and-copper links about his neck. Carolin instantly recognized his air of authority.

In a blink, the man's gaze took him in. Something whispered through Carolin's mind, wordless. The man's expression did not change, yet Carolin felt the shift in him, could almost catch his thought, *So this is Hastur's cub.*

Carolin, stung by the undercurrent of animosity, took a moment to study the older man's face. Was this man an enemy? His tutors had always made it a great point to remember both names and appearances. But no, he could not detect even a hint of familiarity.

In that instant, he picked up a surge of tightly controlled anger.

How dare they? How dare they question me?

Neither Auster nor Gavin gave any sign they'd read the man's thoughts, though the room vibrated with tension.

"It is just as I told you," the older man said. "My son came on his own accord, without my knowledge or approval." *And only Aldones knows what trouble will come from this!* "Nothing you can say will alter my decision."

"You—you are the father of the boy who came to seek admission to the Tower this morning," Carolin said.

The man inclined his head and answered politely, "I am Felix Ridenow."

"We thank you for the courtesy of your visit," Auster said. "And we will, of course, consider all the factors involved in this case."

"There is nothing to consider, *vai tenerézu.* My son's ill-considered adventure is over. He returns home with me as planned. I bid you good day."

Gavin and Lerrys escorted *Dom* Felix from the room with impeccable courtesy and equally unmistakable suspicion.

What was going on here? With a shiver, Carolin knew.

No matter how talented this Varzil might be, he is suspect simply because he is a Ridenow! And his own father will not agree to his staying for exactly the same reason. This feud should have been settled long ago!

Carolin had been brought up on court intrigue, but had always believed the Towers above those petty maneuverings. The unfairness rankled like poison beneath his skin.

Varzil had been so filled with passion. Even from his perch on the balcony, Carolin had felt it. Varzil had passed the Veil, thus proving his pure *Comyn* blood, and the *kyrri* had answered him. They didn't often do that. And now, for Auster to dismiss his potential, his dedication, to question this dignified man who was his father, all from political motives! It was not just. More than that, it was not honorable.

Auster shifted, gesturing for Carolin to sit. "You are concerned about the Ridenow boy."

Sitting, Carolin nodded. "I know it's not my place to question your decisions, but it's—it's wrong to send him away."

"Wrong?" One eyebrow arched upward, but not in anger.

Carolin, knowing Auster would pick up the emotion behind his thought, if not the exact meaning, lifted his eyes in a direct gaze. "What I mean is—it isn't fair to not even give him a chance because of his family."

"You, a Hastur, say this?"

Anger sparked in Carolin. *Am I never to forget who I am? Am I to choose my friends by their parentage instead of their character?* "I speak of what is right, not necessarily of what is expedient. Is it not better to take a longer perspective on this matter? After all, it is said the only way to truly eliminate an enemy is to turn him into a friend."

Auster leaned back in his chair, the slightest transfer of weight. "It is also said that it is better to leave a sleeping banshee alone. In this case, the boy's own father has forbidden his son to come here, and we dare not take any contrary action."

"What about Varzil's own desires—what about his destiny? Are you, the Keeper of Arilinn Tower, intimidated by a minor Ridenow lord?"

"Carlo, now it is I who remind you to take the longer view. Going against the father's expressed wishes could cause incalculable harm to every faction involved. Leave it. Let the hot feelings die down. Practice the discipline of the work. In a few years, the boy will have made his peace with his father's decision, and no harm will have been done."

"A great deal of harm will have been done!" Carolin shook his head. How could Auster and the others not see it? If Varzil were an ordinary lad, he might well forget his childhood dream, but he was not ordinary. Carolin had sensed the strength of his *laran* and the passion that could be so easily turned for good or for ill.

He is important—to me, to all of Darkover.

The shift in Auster's eyes told Carolin he had picked up the thought.

Some Hasturs have the gift of prescience. Auster spoke mind to mind. *It is said that Allart Hastur, who forged the peace between your clan and the Ridenow, could see into the future. There is more at stake here than one undersized boy.*

Yes! Carolin shot back at him. *Yes, there is!* He took a breath. *And I will use all the power of my rank to make sure he gets his chance.*

Auster shook his head again. "I advise you to stay out of it. It is best for everyone to let these things run their natural course."

"And allow the grudges of generations long past to dictate everything we do now?" Carolin shot back.

"You are not a private person, to think only of yourself," Auster reminded him. "In some things, not even the King of the Hasturs can have his way. The world will go as it wills, and not as you or I—or even this Ridenow boy—will have it."

"I understand your meaning plain enough, Auster. I know very well what is at stake here and I have no wish to set the whole countryside aflame in war. But there must be another way!" *And I will find it!*

"Consider the consequences. For if you take any action, Carolin Hastur, you will be responsible for whatever comes of it, for good or for ill."

"Then that is my choice and my burden." Carolin lifted his chin. "Is there nothing I can say to convince you?"

"Oh," Auster said, a ghost of a smile flitting across his mouth. "You have already done that. If this lad returns to us with his father's blessing, we will of course welcome him, whether he be Ridenow or not. Rest content with that."

Carolin knew when he was dismissed. At least, Auster had given him a germ of hope. If he could not directly change the minds of Auster and *Dom* Felix, then at least he could seize upon whatever opening chance presented him with. He felt certain there would be one.

3

In the Ridenow quarters of Arilinn's Hidden City, Varzil waited for his father's return. Each major house had access to private apartments, clean and warm but austere. Despite the banners of green and gold, these were only slightly more luxurious than trail shelters, and maintained under the same conditions of truce.

Not two hours ago, *Dom* Felix had been summoned, with a great show of politeness but absolute command, to the Keeper of Arilinn Tower. Then he would learn that Varzil had slipped away from the evening gathering of the *Comyn* Council, where his presence would have served his family, and stayed out all night without permission or letting anyone know where he was. *Dom* Felix would never have approved of his plan, so in essence he had done what would surely have been forbidden. Now Varzil had been found out, his act of disobedience made public. If only Arilinn had taken him in—but it had not, and now he would pay doubly, for trying and for failing. The result would not be pleasant.

Varzil awaited his father's return with equanimity, for he had always borne the punishments meted out for childhood mischief with patience. No action, whether grand or trivial, was without consequence. At Sweetwater, the family estate, he saw this on a daily basis. A seed planted with care became a vine laden with sweet-gourds in the fall. A hand raised in temper against a half-broken colt gave rise to a sullen, unreliable mount. A cat whose tail was pulled would turn and scratch. A kind word and smile to the cook resulted in a treat at bedtime. A dreamy summer afternoon in the orchards, playing the flute and watching the patterns of clouds, was followed by extra hours with wooden practice swords.

As he sensed his father's approach, Varzil prepared himself for the usual litany. He could recite it himself: "When will you get your head out of the clouds and pay attention? I bring you all the way to Arilinn for a most solemn occasion and you go running off on some irresponsible lark! You know how important the *Comyn* Council is—its influence, its politics. We Ridenow need powerful alliances, whether by treaty or marriage, and it is here they will be forged! You've made us a laughingstock with your reckless prank!"

Dom Felix threw open the door to the central sitting room. Varzil scrambled to his feet and braced himself. With a rapid glance, he took in his father's flushed complexion, the dark brows drawn together and bracketed by incised lines. His father's agitation swept over Varzil in a turbulence of sound and color.

Dom Felix unclasped his cloak and draped it over the nearest chairs. No servant came forward to put the garment away, for like the Tower itself, only those of pure *Comyn* blood could enter the Hidden City.

"You know I don't approve of what you did, running off to the Tower like that," *Dom* Felix began without preamble. Pacing, he pounded one fist into the open palm of his other hand. "But those—nine-fathered sandal-wearers had the effrontery to question me—*me!*—as if I were a landless nobody! I refused to give them any satisfaction, of course. They can take their suspicions and shove them up Zandru's icy arse!"

Dom Felix came to the end of the room and his breath at the same time. He paused, visibly collecting himself, and turned to his son.

"Ah well, all that no longer matters. We're well done with them. Come now, we have preparations to make. I mean to be on the road home before first light tomorrow." Slinging his cloak over one shoulder, he started toward the sleeping chambers.

Varzil remained where he was. His heart hammered against the cage of his bony chest. Sweat sprang up on his brow. His knees quivered. If he gave in now, he might never have another chance. Even the slim hope he might be able to persuade the Keeper through sheer persistence and endurance was better than nothing.

"No, Father."

Dom Felix paused at the inner doorway. It took him an instant to understand. Dark brows furrowed. "What do you mean, *no?*"

"I mean—" Varzil rushed on, afraid that if he once faltered in his resolve, his courage would utterly desert him. "—I'm not going home with you. I must stay until they let me in."

"*Arilinn?*" His father paused. "That is a hopeless cause. Even if I *had* given you my permission, you could not associate with anyone who holds the honor of our family in such contempt. The way they treated me speaks for itself."

Varzil took a step backward. "Truly, they should have offered you proper respect, but that is their offense against you alone. For myself, I belong there. If they will not admit me today, then I will sit at their gates until they do."

"You'll have a long wait."

Varzil lifted his chin. "Waiting will not change my mind."

"There is nothing to change. You are coming home tomorrow."

"No, I am not."

"I don't believe what I'm hearing. Whatever were you thinking of, to have any dealings whatsoever with those—those *Hali'imyn?* Have they poisoned your mind with their sorcery? I would not have thought it possible in so short a time."

"They did nothing to me," Varzil replied with a touch of temper. He suppressed it and continued, as calmly and reasonably as he could. "Asking for admission there was my own idea. I'm sorry I didn't discuss it with you first. I know it was wrong to sneak away in the middle of the night and I apologize for the worry I caused you. If I'd seen any other way, I would have much preferred to do this openly, with your blessing. I was afraid you'd disapprove without even listening to me, and that's exactly what has happened."

"Where did you *get* such ideas? Neither your brother nor your sisters can be a tenth as stubborn as you!" *Dom* Felix raised his hands in mock exasperation. "Was it a fever of the brain that left you willful as well as puny? Was it something I ate on the night I fathered you? Did the forge-folk leave you in place of a human baby when your nurse wasn't looking?"

Varzil almost laughed aloud. "Whatever it was, Father, I am as the gods made me."

"And what you are is a *laranzu* of Arilinn, is that what you mean to say? What a ridiculous notion! Wipe it from your mind. The matter is settled. There is nothing more to say."

"You are right," Varzil replied, though his belly trembled. "There is nothing more to discuss. I do not expect you to agree with me, only to accept this is what I must do."

"Why *must?*" *Dom* Felix's voice roughened. "Who holds a sword to your throat and forces you do this thing? And since when have you earned the right to tell your father what you will and will not do? I assure you, being sealed to the *Comyn* Council has granted you no such privilege."

Fighting the sting of tears, Varzil said, "Father, please. I've always tried to be a good son, but I can't—I can't follow your wishes in this. I beg you—try to understand." He lifted one hand to his heart. "It *is* in me. I—"

"This foolish notion will result in nothing but embarrassment for your entire family. If you cannot behave with proper dignity, then at least think of the rest of us. Nothing good will come of this."

"I tried—Father, I tried—"

Varzil's voice broke as he remembered the nights he'd lain awake, watching the pattern of colored light from Darkover's four moons slowly shift across the stone walls of his room. He had struggled not to feel, not to hear, not to respond to the surges of inexpressible energy that left him quivering like the strings of a lute. Some mornings he would awaken with blood on his lips where he had bitten them, his hands aching from clenching into fists. Finally, he understood. It was no use. There was nothing he could do to give back his Gift. He could no more escape his *laran* than he could tear out his own tongue or put out his eyes.

For a year now, he'd hoped that the training he received from the Ridenow household *leronis* would be enough. He tried his best to be the son his father wanted, or a close enough counterfeit. It had quickly become obvious this would never work.

Varzil had lived in two worlds—the ordinary one of daily work as unofficial assistant *coridom* and unsworn paxman to his older brother, Harald—and the one which became stronger and more vivid every day. He felt as if he were a single droplet in a vast living river, so that each time the Ya-men howled their secret laments, or the scullery maid stirred awake with a nightmare, or a stallion sensed the rising heat in a nearby mare, the hot, raw sensations ripped though him.

In his bones, he knew that to go on like this would only drive him mad. He sensed, too, that without his conscious control, his Gift might prove to be far deadlier to those he loved than to himself. The only solution was to master it, to swim as a fish in that surging tide. But how?

The *leronis* who had taught him as a child had clearly reached the limit of her ability. He must go to a Tower. And what better Tower than fabled Arilinn?

If only he could find some way to make father understand!

"You and your hopeless dreams!" *Dom* Felix brushed aside Varzil's explanations. "You always were one for mooning around when there was work to be done, or ranting about *chieri* singing."

"They weren't *chieri*. No man has seen or heard of them since the Ages of Chaos. They were Ya-men. And I really heard them."

"Ya-men, fairies, demons from Zandru's seventh hell! It's all the same. Your whole life has been devoted to one romantic notion after another. This is just the latest one. I've indulged you in the past, perhaps more than was good for you. Now I must correct that. It's one thing to bring shame upon yourself by behaving in such an undignified manner, begging for admission where you're not wanted. I will not allow you to besmirch the honor of your house, not after the way they treated me. And all for what? Do you really believe you're worth training? Even if you weren't a Ridenow, they'd never waste their time on you. Of course you have some degree of *laran*—the Council placed its seal on you in attestation to that fact. But a *laranzu?* You've been inhaling ghostweed to think such a thing. You never had threshold sickness worth noticing, and everyone knows that's what indicates strong *laran*."

Varzil hung his head. He didn't know what to say. His father had calmed down, but he knew that tone of voice. It would be easier to move the Kadarin River from its banks than to get his father to change his mind when he was in one of these moods.

"There, I've done all I can to reason with you and that's an end to it. No more discussion. You will do as I say."

Chest heaving, head still bowed, Varzil said, "I will not give it up. I cannot."

"*Cannot?* You are never to say that!" Felix thundered as he jabbed a blunt index finger in Varzil's direction. "I gave you life, I can take it away again, and you will be and do what *I* say! Now get on with your packing!"

Varzil had flinched reflexively at his father's first shouted words, but he held his ground. "I will do no such thing. I am staying here until Arilinn admits me."

"You will return home on a horse or strapped across it with your rump so sore you can't sit on it. That would be a fine fate for someone just accepted by the Council as a true *Comyn!*"

"I don't mean to defy you, Father. It's just—just—"

In a single stride, *Dom* Felix crossed the space between them and struck his son with a roundhouse punch. The blow caught Varzil on the cheek and spun his head around. He reeled, so stunned that for a long moment, he could not even breathe.

The impact ran deeper than knuckles on flesh. It resonated along every nerve and fiber of Varzil's body. Beneath his skin, fire raced along the network of energy channels, which carried his *laran.*

Varzil staggered and caught himself on the back of the wooden chair. His vision whirled. Unable to speak, he shook his head.

"No?" Felix raised his fist again. "*NO?*"

Father, please! I would do anything else you asked, but do not—do not—

Varzil's eyes swam with tears. His knees buckled and he fell to the floor. One hand clenched the side of the chair, but he was too disoriented to pull himself upright.

The old man's face loomed over him. White ringed *Dom* Felix's eyes. His lips drew back from his teeth. Veins stood out along his temples.

Father, no!

For a terrifying moment, Varzil thought his father had been taken away and one of Zandru's demons left in his place. There would be no mercy, no respite until the fury had run its course. Varzil knew his father's explosive temper. Even the family dogs knew when to hide when their master's voice rose. If Varzil passed out, he would not feel anything after that. It would be far from pleasant to wake up afterward, but he could endure that. He threw up one hand over his face and braced himself for the next blow.

It never came. A heartbeat passed and then another. Varzil lowered his arm. His father stared at the palms of his hands with an expression of confusion and yes, horror.

What have I done?

Tears bleared the old man's eyes. The loose skin along his jaw quivered, revealing the shape of the mortal skull beneath. Yet the old man's pride pressed his lips together, holding in his words.

If he must cling to his pride, Varzil thought, *then I must be humble. If he will not be the first to speak, then I will.*

Varzil scrambled to a kneeling position. He reached up to take his father's hands. Their positions resembled those of vassal and lord when exchanging oaths of fealty, but with a subtle difference. Varzil took his father's hands between his own. "Please forgive me. I was rude and disrespectful. I would never wish to bring dishonor upon my family."

When it came to speaking the words that would surrender his dream, however, his throat closed up.

Dom Felix pulled Varzil to his feet and clasped him in a rough embrace. "I'll hear no more of that. You're a good son, or as good as you can be. Nothing I can say will get you to see sense on it, even a blind man can see that. The thing will just have to run its course. Things will be better once we're out of this thrice-cursed city and back at Sweetwater."

Too heartsick to protest further, Varzil nodded. He had made peace with his father, but at what price?

4

Despite *Dom* Felix's intentions of an early departure, the Ridenow party did not pass the outskirts of Arilinn City until the great red sun was well into the sky. The grass along the road had lost its coating of dew hours before. The promise of the autumn day's fleeting warmth rose from the land. The men were anxious to return, wearied of celebratory evenings that were more political sparring than entertainment. Varzil rode silently in the position in which his father had placed him, second in the procession. He did not speak, even when a casual comment was thrown his way. His inner senses strained backward, toward Arilinn and his fading dreams.

The road before him wavered in his sight. Colors blurred together—the red-brown rump of the horse in front of him, the gold of the sun-parched grasses, the gray of the stones, the layered haze of the sky. He let the reins fall loose on the neck of his mount and pressed both hands over the pain in his chest. An invisible rope tethered the very core of him to the Tower which had by now disappeared from sight. He thought he must be bleeding, though his heart beat steadily, and then he realized it was not a physical pain.

"Varzil, lad?" A voice reached him from a distance. It was Gwilliam, the stout young horse handler who had stayed with the animals in the stables on the outskirts of Arilinn.

"Let him be." That was his father's voice. "Once we're home, he'll be all right."

I am not all right. I have never been all right.

Is this how a laranzu *of Arilinn thinks? Wallowing in self-pity like a spoiled child?* The words resounded through his skull.

He knew that mental voice, so clear and powerful. Who else could reach him this far, or speak to him this clearly?

Auster!

The same. You could not have stayed with us against your father's opposition. But do not doubt your Gift. Never doubt that. If it is the will of the gods, we will meet again. Do not lose heart.

Before Varzil could phrase a response, the telepathic contact vanished. In front of him, beyond the nodding head of his horse, the road stretched away through the Plains of Arilinn. To either side, heavy-headed grasses bent under their own ripe weight. Every line of stalk and sun-bronzed leaf shone with crystalline clarity. The pain in his body subsided to an ache.

Varzil straightened in the saddle and lifted the reins. The horse, sensing new energy in its rider, picked up the pace.

When *Dom* Felix said, "What did I tell you?" Varzil only nodded.

They rode on through what was left of the morning. To either side, harvesters and haywains traced measured patterns through the fields.

As they rested in the heat of noon, a breeze sprang up, laden with the musty, honeyed scent of grain. Insects whined and clicked. The horses pulled at their bits to snatch stalks close to the edge of the road.

The heat softened the remaining tension in Varzil's muscles and he found himself nodding in the saddle. His father no longer sat quite so straight, but there would be no stopping for a nap. So he settled himself, loosened his feet in the stirrups, and let his thoughts wander.

Thin clouds spread across the sky, turning it almost white. Light beat down upon them. A few copses and hedgerows near the road provided dappled shade, nearly as hot as the road. The horses had long ago dropped from a brisk walk to an amble and then to a plod. Sweat streaked their necks and flanks.

Dom Felix called a halt in midafternoon at a little stream that meandered near the road. The horses thrust their muzzles beneath the rippling surface. The men dismounted, drank their fill upstream, and washed their hands and faces. *Dom* Felix sat stoically on his horse, although he accepted a cup. His face had paled to the color of chalk and the muscles of his jaw bulged from clenching his teeth.

Varzil walked to where his father's kinsman, Black Eiric, was helping Gwilliam check the saddle blankets for burrs or wrinkles. Eiric Ridenow was not he of the same name who had just been made Lord of Serrais, but of a far lesser branch and called so because he was born with a full head of dark hair. The hair had since turned to a deep russet, but the childhood name stuck. Now he was a sturdy man well into middle age, solidly competent, often acting in the capacity as paxman to *Dom* Felix.

"My father does not look well," Varzil said in a low voice. "He will not listen to me, but I think he should rest."

"Aye, that's truth," Eiric replied in his easy country way. "I'll see to it. If he will not bide here for his own health, then he will for the sake of the horses. I can't remember an autumn day this hot."

Varzil nodded his thanks and watched while the other man ambled over to *Dom* Felix's horse. As if probing an old wound, he reached out for Arilinn in his thoughts, but felt nothing beyond the faint scintillation—half music, half light—of the Veil. He wondered if it would always be with him in memory.

How long he stood there, listening with that inner sense, he could not have said, before he became aware of a faint thrumming underfoot. At first, he felt it with his mind, like a basso counterpoint to the Veil. After a few moments, though, he realized it was a physical vibration. It grew stronger and louder.

Hoofbeats—

Varzil spotted a line of billowing dust, rapidly approaching. He spied a galloping horse, though he could not make out the rider. A sense of urgency rang in the back of his mind like a bell, an almost-familiar touch—

Carlo. The flame-haired youth from Arilinn.

They waited while the rider drew up. Yellow foam dotted the horse's neck and flanks and lined the breast-strap, but it moved as strong and fresh as if it had just left the stables. Varzil knew horses. This one must have exceptional stamina. Surely it must be one of the fabled black steeds bred at the Alton estates at Armida.

"Aldones be praised! I've found you!" Carlo brought the beast to a halt in front of *Dom* Felix. The black horse pulled at the bit, sides heaving like bellows. Everyone else crowded around. He wore a light summer-weight shirt open to the neck, and no cloak, but the saddle blankets were blue, stitched with the Hastur emblem of the silver fir tree. Carlo must come from an influential family indeed to be able to borrow such a mount.

Carlo kicked his feet free from the stirrups and jumped lightly to the ground. From his expression, *Dom* Felix was not pleased to see him.

"Come, sir, let us talk privately," Carlo said with a brief but impeccably polite bow. "I bring news from Arilinn."

What could those Hali-imyn have to say of any possible interest to me? was Dom Felix's surly thought.

"Sir, it is your place and not mine to decide what you will tell your people," Carlo said. If he'd caught *Dom* Varzil's angry thought, he gave no sign. His expression continued as respectful as before, his gray eyes steady.

The old man frowned, but he dismounted stiffly and gestured that Carlo should follow him. "And you, too," he said to Varzil, "for this undoubtedly concerns some trouble you have stirred up."

Carlo handed the reins of the black horse to Gwilliam, bidding him walk the animal before letting him drink. They went a little way off, upriver. Here, willows arched over the water to trail leafy fingers in the eddies. A cool, sweet scent arose from the banks, mixed with the smell of churned mud and the tang of river-wet stones.

Carlo moved closer to *Dom* Felix, lowering his voice. Varzil felt as well as heard his perfectly enunciated words. "Word came to Arilinn Tower from the *leronis* at Serrais after you had already departed."

"Serrais?" *Dom* Felix repeated the name of the seat of the Ridenow. "There is trouble at Serrais?"

No, not at Serrais. Varzil knew without asking.

Carlo shook his head. "From your own home—Sweetwater, it is called? Three days ago, catmen raided the sheep pastures. Some were killed and others carried off. A group of men captained by your oldest son were near enough to come to the aid of the shepherds. There was a fight. The terrain was very bad—"

An image flashed through Varzil's mind, though he could not have named its source. He saw the jagged hillside, the stones dotting the wind-swept heather as clearly as if he stood there.

Two men in the sheepskin vests and woolen breeches of shepherds crouched near the top of the hill, one holding his upper arm. Wetness seeped through his fingers.

The red light of the lowering sun flashed on drawn swords—straight blades of men even now scrambling for room to use their weapons—curved shorter blades in the hands of the agile furred creatures. The catmen fought to cover their retreat as they herded a double handful of terrified sheep along the crevasse.

A man with a black beard stumbled when the rock beneath his feet gave way. A catman leaped for him, curved sword blurring in motion. The man twisted away an instant before the blade would have slit open his belly.

Even as the catman recovered its own balance, a second man scrambled to the side of the first. His approach took him within reach of the catman's sword. Reversing its blade with inhuman speed, the feline slashed again. The farthest edge caught the man in an upward sweep along his thigh.

Varzil felt the man's scream as a shiver across his own skin. With his next breath, he tasted the coppery reek of blood.

In an instant, the catmen came swarming back. They flowed through the shadows with deadly grace. Perhaps they scented an unexpected victory.

Terror now masked the images. Varzil could no longer see the hillside clearly, yet he sensed each slice, each thrust, each gasping breath. The musky reek of the catmen washed over him. Adrenaline hung bitter in the cooling night air.

Varzil gave a shudder, returning to himself. Only an instant had passed, barely a phrase or two of the conversation. Yet the images burned inside him, as vivid as if he stood on that hillside beneath the setting sun. As Carlo finished his tale, gazing at Varzil with a curious, penetrating expression.

"And the other two men?" *Dom* Felix asked in a hoarse voice. Varzil had never heard such fear in his father.

"After the battle was over and the catmen fled, a pair of shepherds brought the bodies of the slain men back to Sweetwater. Your son and the other man were not among them."

"The catmen carried them away?" Felix asked, incredulous.

"Either that, or they fled and may yet still live, wounded and in hiding," Carlo said. "Your household *leronis* could not reach the mind of your son, nor could the folk at Serrais."

"I must return at once!" Felix cried, taking a step back toward the watering horses. Then he paused, as the enormity of the distance impressed itself upon him. No horse alive, not even the magnificent black which Carlo had ridden so hard, could cover the leagues in less than a tenday. By then, Harald could be dead or, at very best, the trail too cold to follow.

Varzil caught a flicker of emotion from Carlo. The red-haired youth bowed again to *Dom* Felix.

"If you would care to return to Arilinn with me," Carlo said, "an aircar will be placed at your disposal. With luck and a clear sky, you can arrive at Sweetwater this very evening."

Varzil drew in his breath at the generosity of the offer. *Laran*-powered aircars were fabulously expensive to own and operate, a luxury restricted to kings and the very wealthy. Aircars depended upon technology developed in the Ages of Chaos, much of it now lost. Even now, few were used outside of warfare and the most urgent diplomatic missions. The Lord of Serrais had one which he never entrusted to anyone else, lest it be damaged. Had Auster used his influence as Keeper to secure one—and why would he go to such lengths to help someone he hardly knew?

"Who arranged this?" *Dom* Felix said, scowling. "And what will it cost me?"

"The owner wishes to remain unknown, for reasons you must surely comprehend," Carlo said. "And there is no price. Only a word of advice. There is room for three passengers. You could do no better than to take your younger son."

"Varzil?" *He is no tracker, nor has he any great skill with a sword. And if a trained* leronis *cannot reach Harald with her mind, what could this pup do?*

Dom Felix made a rumbling sound in his throat. He clearly didn't want to refuse so magnanimous a gift or to make a powerful enemy by an ungracious reply. Varzil almost heard the thoughts in his father's mind. The important thing was that he reach Sweetwater as soon as possible, assess the situation, and take swift action. If it meant dragging along his useless younger son, that was a small price to pay.

◆

They returned to Arilinn at a somewhat quicker pace. Even Carlo's black horse picked up its feet as it headed toward the stables it knew. *Dom* Felix rode ahead with Black Eiric, giving orders for the return of the rest of the party.

Carlo nudged his horse even with Varzil's. They rode near the rear of the Ridenow party, far enough from Varzil's father so they could not be easily overheard.

"When I was telling your father the news from the relays," Carlo said, pausing faintly over the next words, "what did you . . . *see?*"

Varzil startled, quickly masking the lapse by adjusting the reins. Then he remembered that Carlo had Tower training, so he must sense *something*. He did not believe Carlo was his enemy.

"I—it was as if I were there, watching the battle. I saw two men fall, the catmen with their curved swords. I saw the hill, the rocks . . ." *The blood.*

Carlo's gray eyes widened. "I am not so strong a telepath for you to have taken that from my mind."

Varzil looked down at his hands, the reins worn soft and dark by much usage. The horses moved on, shod hooves clicking against small stones on the road. Stirrup leathers creaked.

"*I* am not so strong a telepath . . ." Carlo's words hung in the silence.

"Your father *must* allow you to return to Arilinn," Carlo said with same tone of command he had used to suggest that *Dom* Felix take Varzil in the aircar.

Varzil shrugged. "I see little chance of that. Even without the political aspects, my father believes I have so little talent, Arilinn would not have me, whether he granted his blessing or not. I will go to Sweetwater in your aircar if that is his wish, and I will do whatever I can to find my brother, but I do not hope for anything further coming of it."

"How can you give up so easily?" Carlo responded with heat. "Was camping out all night at the gates of Arilinn some sort of prank? If so, you possess an astonishing ability to dissemble. You have truly mastered the art of double tongues, for you managed to convince me—us—that you truly desired admittance. *Desire* would have struck me as too mild a word."

Stung, Varzil replied, "I pretended nothing. I—" *I still want it more than I've ever wanted anything, but what is the use of tormenting myself?* He went on in a tightly controlled voice, "I cannot defy my father, especially with my older brother gone missing. To lose us both would kill him. Nor do I believe Arilinn would have such a man who would so easily forsake his duty and his honor."

A frown darkened Carlo's handsome features, like a cloud passing across the sun. He said nothing more of the matter.

They rode no farther than the field on the city outskirts, where an aircar sat ready. Varzil had never seen one so close before. It was shaped like an elongated teardrop, crafted of a glassy material which was clear in some areas and cloudy or completely opaque in others. A hinged door stood open to reveal a narrow compartment. Banks of instruments of the same substance, some fashioned with strips of polished metal, lined the nose of the craft. There was one seat facing the controls, another by its side and two more in the broader belly. Behind the seats lay a compartment for storage.

A man in livery of blue and silver stood beside the aircar. With the air of one who is sure of his competence, he indicated where the baggage was to be placed and then set about securing it with straps. Then he assisted *Dom* Felix into the forward passenger seat.

Carlo took Varzil aside. "Whatever happens, you must convince your father to let you come back." Then, before Varzil could frame an objection, he was being helped into the aircar, to sit beside Black Eiric. Within a few short minutes, they were aloft.

5

Varzil had never traveled by aircar before, and he found the experience unsettling. Lord Serrais had one, and Varzil had caught a glimpse of another as it landed on the airfield at Arilinn before the Council meeting. He'd admired its silent grace, the skill and cunning of its fashioning.

He sat behind the pilot, watching the man's fingers on the controls or making cryptic gestures. From the belly of the car, *laran* batteries sent a stream of harnessed energy to the propulsion and guidance mechanisms.

Varzil's contact with the Tower telepaths had opened him up to new, disturbing sensations. He felt the stored power like a caged predator, rumbling and lurking. Even through the exhilaration of soaring, he sensed how easily so much power could be turned to other, deadlier purposes. Like so many other things, *laran* could cure or kill, serve or destroy.

The pilot glanced over his shoulder at Varzil. "There's nothing to fear. It's not magic, but a technique which anyone with skill and training can master."

"Anyone with the riches to afford something like this," *Dom* Felix grunted.

"Yes, they are costly, but that is because there are so few with the Gift and the discipline to operate them," the pilot replied. He spoke politely enough, but without the deference ordinarily due from a servant to a lord, however minor.

He is no servant, Varzil thought. *He is a laranzu in his own right.*

"What is your name, pilot?" he asked.

"Jeronimo Lanart," came the response without any added "m'lord" or *"vai dom."*

Varzil caught the edge of the man's thought. *Lord Carolin must have thought it important to speed these two home, or he would never have commanded his own aircar to bring them.*

Lord Carolin? The heir to the Hastur throne? Was he at Arilinn for the Council session?

A sudden gust swerved them off course, and the pilot bent over his instrument panel again. Varzil hunched forward in his seat, straining for a better view. Once they were set right, he asked about the controls.

"Some have mechanical linkages." Jeronimo explained the simpler levers. "Others require shaping thought. The guidance systems are tuned to specific *laran* patterns. We use standard gestures for uniformity. Here—" He held up one hand and moved his fingers from one position slowly to another and then a third. "You try it."

The gestures were easy enough to copy. "Now, follow my movements like this—"

An image appeared in Varzil's mind, a hawk extending its wings in the air. Varzil echoed the thought along with the finger pattern. The movement shaped the energy of his mind to slide along the matrix guides within the aircar. An answering surge of power lifted the stubby wings of the craft.

"You see," the pilot said, "it's not so mysterious. You could learn to do it."

"We'll have no such talk," *Dom* Felix said, shifting uneasily, "or any more idle diversions. Your instructions were to take us to Sweetwater as quickly as may be, and we have no time for dalliance."

"As you wish, though we are already making the best possible speed, so there is nothing lost in a simple demonstration," Jeronimo answered. "In my experience, nothing learned is ever a waste of time." However, he refrained from further comment.

In the silence of the remaining flight, Varzil tried to imagine what might have befallen his brother Harald. They were not especially close, for they were separated in age by the twins, Ann'dra and Silvie, who had both perished in adolescence from threshold sickness, and by Joenna. A third sister, Dyannis, was still a child. Varzil had been eight when the twins died, about the time he first heard the Ya-men singing in the hills. Joenna was now betrothed to the son of a wealthy Alardyn lord, and much more interested in her upcoming wedding than anything having to do with *laran.*

Of all his siblings, Varzil felt the deepest kinship with Dyannis. Her own Gift had not yet shown itself, but he never doubted she had one, for she always seemed to know what he was thinking before he spoke.

Harald was fair, bespeaking the Dry Towns ancestry of the Ridenow. Like many of his family, he had a talent for working with livestock. In his memory, Varzil saw his brother, golden hair tied back with a rawhide thong, sitting on the back of a green-broken colt, stroking the trembling animal, calming its fears with mind as well as words. A big man he was, strong in the shoulders, with gentle hands, a weather-reddened face, an easy laugh. . . .

Darkness. A line of fire along his ribs, stiff with crusted blood. Pain throbbing deep within his shoulder. Thirst. Adrenaline like coppery ashes in his mouth. A sword hilt hard and sure in his hand. Light seeping through the crevice above. The musty spoor of cat. A voice, hoarse with urgency—"Did they see us, m'lord?"

With a jerk, the aircar touched ground. Varzil blinked, staring through the transparent panel. His stomach lurched. The darkness of his vision receded to reveal familiar surroundings. They were a little distance from the main house at Sweetwater, in the field by the paddocks. A handful of men ran to meet them. *Dom* Felix clambered down from the aircar, shouting for saddled horses and torches.

Black Eiric jumped to the ground. "*Vai dom,* you cannot mean to ride tonight! The sun is already near set! Not even the best tracker can follow a trail in those hills in the dark. The catmen could as easily ambush you, too."

"My son, my Harald, is out there! I must go!"

Varzil heard the brittle desperation in his father's voice. The old man had been pale with exhaustion even before they'd started back to Arilinn. He had rested a little in the aircar, but only because he had no choice, confined as he was within its narrow space.

"Father, you will make yourself ill if you keep on like this." Varzil touched his father's arm.

Before his father could protest, Varzil rushed on. "What can you accomplish that Eiric and his men cannot? Can you see in the dark? Can you track better than they? What will become of Sweetwater if there is a fight and you are wounded?"

"You young pup—" *You think to give me orders?*

Though his father pulled against his grasp, Varzil held him firm. Through the layers of his father's clothing, he felt a faint, bone-deep trembling.

"You are lord and master here!" Varzil said. "This entire estate depends upon you, from ordering the day's work to speaking for us at *Comyn* Council. You are not an ordinary man, who can risk himself at his pleasure!"

"I will risk myself as I please!" *Dom* Felix cried, "How can I sit by my own fireplace like a useless old woman? My son is lost in those hills, perhaps dying!"

You have another son, Varzil thought, *who stands before you now.* But he could not bring himself to say it.

They glared at one another, barely able to see each other's features in the gloom. "A Ridenow of his own blood should go after him," *Dom* Felix said in a thick voice.

Varzil leaped into the opening. "Then let me go!" When his father hesitated, he pushed on. "You are always urging me to take my place here, to be responsible—so let me! Give me the command of these men and let me lead the rescue. I swear that whether Harald still lives or not, I will bring him back to you!"

He felt the slight sagging of the old man's body in his grasp, the burst of quickly suppressed relief.

If only Varzil could become such a son to me, a credit to his house! But he is a green boy, weak, and given to moony dreams. These men are used to hardened leaders. I have ruled them with an iron hand. They will not follow a weakling.

There was only one way to find out. Varzil released his father, calling to Eiric. "Take my father back to the house and see him properly cared for, then return. You others, bring the horses and torches. We will ride for the hills!"

"You men," Felix said, his voice roughened by emotion and fatigue, "you heard the words of my son. Obey him as you would me."

Varzil mounted up and in short order selected the men who were to come with him. One of the shepherds had been summoned to lead them into the hills. His hardy little *chervine* was almost as shaggy as its master. The beast trotted along the thread of a path, as surefooted as if it had been a wide road at midday.

After they were well beyond the outer buildings, Eiric spoke to Varzil as they rode side by side. Eiric held his torch high, to cast a flickering light over the next few feet of trail and the bobbing form of the shepherd's white fleece jacket.

"Master Varzil," Eiric said, "this is madness, and cruel besides to get the old man's hopes up. Yon shepherd can take us to the place, right enough. It's said that they can see in the dark as well as their beasts. But what then? We cannot summon a track out of nothing. For all we know, this quest is for naught and the young master is already perished."

Darkness. Harsh breathing. The dull sick throbbing of a wound turning bad.

"He is still alive," Varzil said with a sureness that surprised him. He could not see in the dark any better now than before, yet other, newer senses awoke in him, ignited by the intense contact with the folk at Arilinn. He had no words for his knowledge, only the absolute certainty of its truth.

"We must find him soon," Varzil said, half to himself. "He is hurt, and the catmen are still on his trail. For the moment, though, he is safe."

"Now, how could you be knowing that?" Eiric's voice raised in pitch. Then he fell silent and Varzil touched his thoughts. *From the time he were a laddie, he had the Gift. The old lord tried to hush it up, but you cannot ignore such a thing forever. And he's been to Arilinn, that nest of sorcery. Something happened to him there, it's plain to see. Don't know if it were good or bad. Time alone will tell. But if he can find our young lord and spare the old man's heart, it's worth the chance.*

They rode on, more slowly now as the land rose and turned rocky. The last rust-tinged light left the sky. With the luck of Aldones, three of the four moons were shining in the cloudless night sky.

The land sloped sharply away. Granite boulders shimmered in the multihued light. Iridescent flecks gleamed in the rock. Some were as large as cart horses, others fist-sized. Between them the shadows lay dark and darker.

Years ago, Varzil had explored the area when he was supposed to be rounding up lost sheep or riding the borders. The hills were riddled with caves, wonderful places to seek blessed coolness during the few hot days of summer.

"This is the place?" one of the men behind Varzil asked.

The shepherd mumbled something. His *chervine* tossed its antlers to the jangling of bells.

"Go home," Varzil told him. "You have done a great service this night."

With another muttered comment and a tug at his forelock, the man wheeled his mount and disappeared.

Varzil nudged his horse forward, letting the animal pick its way through the jumbled rocks. Eiric rode a pace behind with the torch held overhead. Its light flickered over muted grasses. The clotted shadows below resolved into shapes, the bodies of two men, one fallen across the other. Nearby, sprawled three or four dead catmen.

Varzil swing down from his horse and approached the two fallen men. Kneeling beside them, he shivered in the sensation of emptiness, the utter absence of life spark. It was not the motionlessness of their limbs or the silence of their heartbeats that touched him. All around, he felt energy—the slow patient grass, the bright motes of insects, the twitter of rabbit-horns in their burrows, the far-off glide of an owl. He had seen death before, in both beasts and men. He had been present when his grand-father took his final shuddering breath. The awe and terror of that myste-rious moment still haunted his dreams.

But this, this was something different. He sensed an incompleteness, like a still-bleeding wound. There was none of the peace of his grand-father's passing. As he reached out with his newly-enhanced *laran,* he could almost taste the final moments of these men's lives. Something of them still lingered, the door between life and death held ajar by the shock of their parting.

Yes, now that he focused on it, he saw that emptiness was an un-healed rift. Gray lapped his vision. With an effort, he turned from the seductive urge to follow where these men had gone.

He spotted no weapons, neither the men's straight swords nor the curved blades of their feline attackers. Metal was too precious to be casu-ally abandoned. He only hoped that he would not find one of his father's own swords turned against him.

Eiric dismounted and traced a widening circle, scanning the ground. "Ah, it's all either too hardscrabble for aught to show or else amuck with tracks every which way. Catmen don't leave much trace with those soft paws. It would take Aldones' own miracle to find a chance sign of their passing."

"Or Zandru's accursed luck," one of the other men muttered.

"Aye, that," Eiric nodded. He pointed north, where the hillside met another in a narrow defile. "It's my guess the catmen are laired up yonder. There are caves all through here."

Stumbling over stones and fallen furred bodies, racing downhill, stopping to slash and parry. The image of thin lips drawn over fangs, a hissing cry of pain. Running, more running. The caves our only hope . . .

Varzil gestured to the north. "Harald is there."

Eiric nodded. The movement threw spectral shadows across his cragged features. "Aye, if he had the chance to get to safety, that's where he'd go. He'd come up here of a Midsummer. Once young master Ann'-dra followed them, d'you remember?"

Varzil remembered hearing the story told, though at the time he was too young to join the escapades of his older brothers. He stood still and tried to focus his thoughts. If he could somehow let Harald know he was here and help was on the way . . .

Moments passed, but there was no response, not even another fleeting contact. Eiric spoke to him again, breaking his reverie, and they headed downslope. From time to time, Varzil halted to search with his mind. No impressions came to him. Having once touched his brother's mind, he felt sure he would know if Harald were no longer living. There could be other explanations for the absence of contact. Perhaps Harald was unconscious or so lost in the delirium of infection to be beyond coherent thought. Either way, time was running out.

The horses stumbled on the increasingly rocky ground. Eiric's mount tripped on loose stone and fell to its knees. When it scrambled up, the beast was bloodied but not lame. One of the other men gave Eiric his own mount.

After that, they went on foot, leading their horses. They moved more slowly, keeping together. This far into the cave-pocked hills, with catmen lurking anywhere, their greatest protection was their numbers.

Time wore on as the moons swung through the sky. Idriel set. The night became darker and then lighter, a milky tinge along the eastern horizon. Torches burned lower. When they guttered out, Eiric did not order new ones lit.

Varzil shivered as if ice pierced the very marrow of his bones. He rubbed his arms with his hands, chafing the skin. Exhaling, he expected to see his breath as frosty mist.

Cold . . . shivering . . . A voice he should know, hands on his shoulders, sword hilt shaking between his hands . . . "Quiet, m'lord, or they'll hear us!"

The ice lay not inside him, then, but in his brother's fevered body.

Varzil had to reach him—but how? He had never been taught to use his starstone to enhance a telepathic contact, but he knew it could be done. He drew out his the blue gem from where it hung, wrapped in triple-layered silk, from a cord around his neck, and focused on it. The blue fire, which had flared to brilliance at Arilinn Tower, filled his sight. He drew it in through his eyes, through his breath.

Harald! Can you hear me?

A stirring. *No, it cannot be! It is the fever putting words in my mind. I am hearing the voices of those I love, nothing more.*

"Master Varzil?" Eiric asked.

Varzil waved him to silence. Dimly, he knew the men were staring at him. They would see his face blank and set, his posture of intense listening.

What does he hear, that none of us can? Their thoughts, like stinging insects, buzzed in his ears.

Impatiently, he handed the reins of his horse to Eiric and, gesturing for the others to follow him, went on in front. They had been traveling on a thread of a trail, barely wide enough for a horse to find footing. He strode along it like a hound on the scent.

Harald! Harald!

Ah, it is a dream. Who calls to me in the darkness, where I cannot hear? Armand is gone. I pray the catmen have not found him.

It's me, Varzil—where are you?

No, Varzil is at Arilinn. How could he reach me here? Get away, you spirits! I am not yet ready to give myself over to you! The darkness is spinning. I see lights—are they catmen or more of those accursed will-o-wisps? Has Aldones, Lord of Light, come to take me from this place?

Harald!

Not yet, O Lord, not yet the gray land of the dead! I cannot leave my father like this—a little more time, I beg of you, just a little more time—

Harald! Where are you?

Why, you know where I am. You know everything. I am where you have

placed me, in darkness . . . And now you send the dancing lights. Ah, how
beautiful they are, like flickering gems. Am I already dead, to see them? But
I am cold, so cold. I must be in Zandru's coldest hell.

Varzil tried several more times, but could not penetrate his brother's
ravings. He feared the infection from Harald's wound had spread to his
brain.

"I can sense his thoughts," Varzil said to Eiric, "but he thinks I am—
He cannot tell me where he is."

"What are we to do then? You say he is still alive, but beset by a fever
dream. If that is so, he cannot help himself."

Lord of Light, what do I do now? He must go on and pray that something more would come to him. Perhaps his senses would sharpen once
he was inside the caves themselves, where the darkness would be akin to
that which surrounded Harald.

He did not know if any one cave in particular was Harald's favorite,
but there was one where he himself had always felt safe. Facing westward,
it had a broad outer ledge, perfect for sunset picnics. A narrow tunnel led
into the cliff face, forcing pursuers to enter one at a time. Harald would
choose such a defensible place, if he had any choice.

In the muted dawn light, the cave entrance eluded him. After several
tries, however, he managed to locate it. They had to leave the horses at
the bottom and climb to the ledge on foot. As a boy, he'd scrambled up
with ease. A man burdened with a sword, or wounded perhaps, would
have more difficulty.

Eiric stopped to light one of the torches, despite the risk of making
them visible to any catmen lurking within. He insisted on going first, for
if there was any trouble, he told Varzil, it was his sword that would defend
the young master. Slowly, they made their way single file through the
narrow tunnel. The walls smelled dank and the wan light glittered on
runnels of condensation. In the close space, the breathing of the men
turned whispery. They trudged on, their footfalls muffled. Once or twice,
Varzil thought he saw the scuff marks of a boot.

After a short distance, the tunnel opened out into the heart of the
mountainside. Darkness pressed in on Varzil, swallowing the sound of his
heart.

6

They had gone only a short way into the mountainside when Black Eiric spotted signs of a struggle—spatters of dried blood, boot marks in the dust, rocks recently overturned. The tunnel branched into one path which continued in roughly the same direction, and two side passages. One was little more than a crevice, barely able to admit a slender youth moving sideways. Pebbles covered the floor of the main artery, showing no footprints or other signs of disturbance.

The hairs along the back of Varzil's neck prickled. When Eiric gestured that they should proceed along the broadest way, his feet froze to the spot. He shook his head as his inner reluctance mounted.

Varzil could not understand his own reaction. It made sense to take the wider passageway with this many men, where they might have a hope of using their weapons. He could think of no reason why Harald, wounded and perhaps sorely pressed, would have chosen the slower, more tortuous route.

He said none of this aloud. Eiric asked if his *laran* told him anything new, but he had nothing to offer. "Then we will go on," Eiric said. "Eyes sharp now, and be ready for anything."

They crept on, with Varzil in the rear. Eiric's torch cast wavering shadows. The slither of boot over coarse sand and the occasional brush of leather against rock wall rasped along Varzil's nerves. He strained his ears for a feline hiss, the moan of a wounded man; what more, he did not know.

When he tried reaching out with his mind, he caught only a jittery tension, a coiling of invisible forces he had no words for. No more images came, whether from Harald or anywhere else.

Varzil's heart beat an uneven tattoo against his ribs. His throat turned dry and his palms moist. His stomach knotted sickeningly. They passed a subsidiary branch, a pit of darkness, and then another. The air smelled thick and dank.

"Careful now," Eiric's half-whisper came ghosting back. "We're near to a bend."

They went on, even more slowly. The tunnel fell away to the right and disappeared. Varzil caught a musky reek like that of a mountain cat. The torch, which Eiric had lifted high above his head, suddenly plummeted to the floor. An inhuman yowl fractured into a pandemonium of echoes. The tunnel exploded with frenzied action, dimly glimpsed in the light of the fallen, guttering torch. One moment, there had been a column of men, moving single file, the next, there were twice as many bodies, some of them furred in gray or ocher, all of them struggling, dodging, leaping.

A sword, short and curved, glinted. A man screamed. Adrenaline and battle heat drenched the air.

Varzil, standing behind the other men, could not get a clear view of the fight, beyond confusion. The torch, kicked to one side, would last only a few moments. He didn't know how well the catmen could see in perfect darkness, but he couldn't.

The fighting surged farther along the tunnel. Standing pressed against the wall, Varzil spied the torch on the ground. Without thinking, he dashed for it. His fingers curled around the base, the strips of resinous wood bound together.

In the flare of brightness, the face of a catman leaped into focus. Eyes met his, green-gold with slitted pupils flared wide but now constricting. Great curved ears tufted with black lifted, then flattened against the short neck.

Varzil sensed a tumble of emotions—hunger . . . desperation . . . hatred, deep and wordless.

The catman whirled away in a blur—gray fur crossed by leather straps, claws, short curved sword, blood welling along hard-muscled thigh. Another cry shocked through the air.

Along the tunnel walls, shadows milled and broke. One of the men was hurt, hand clutching ribs low on his side. Blood so dark it looked black flowed over the man's fingers. His back was to one wall, feet braced and sword in free hand. Even as Varzil watched, the man's knees buckled and he began to sink.

"After them!" Eiric screamed. The wounded man heaved himself to his feet.

They rushed down the tunnel. Varzil thrust the torch aloft, running as fast as he could, and tried to keep his footing. The floor sloped away and turned rough. A few moments later, the wavering light of the torch touched a furred back. Eyes gleamed red as the nonhuman glanced back.

Someone behind Varzil shouted, "Got them!"

In an instant, Eiric had the catman within sword's reach. He slashed, and the catman rolled, shrieking.

Varzil, carried by the press of men behind him, raced past the fallen catman. The white of its belly fur glimmered in the light. It was weaponless, the leather sheath hanging from its cross-shoulder straps empty. The reek of fresh blood stained the air. He had no idea how badly hurt the creature was, or whether it could find its way back to its own kind if it lived.

They went on, scrambling over strange rock formations, stumbling, leaping up again. The tunnel veered sharply left and then began to rise. Varzil struggled to keep up with the mad careening pursuit. He could not get the smell of the catman's blood out of his lungs.

Harald . . .

In an instant, he sensed his brother's mind, very close now. He could see the crossroads ahead, a branching so narrow and cramped that it could hardly be called a cave. Here was where the two paths converged once more. Dark droplets trickled across the coarse sand of the floor.

Eiric rushed to the opening, his sword in ready position. His body blocked what lay beyond, but Varzil caught his surge of dismay. He barked out an order that made the other men scramble back. Varzil raised the torch. Its light filled the little space.

Harald . . . and a wounded catman with claws knotted in his hair, his head back at a joint-straining angle, a curved blade at his throat.

Huddled beyond them, a trio of catmen clung to each other. Their mouths opened to reveal needle-thin fangs. Varzil could not read their expressions. No human could.

Terror . . . terror and despair, pulsed wordlessly through his mind.

Eiric inched forward, his sword still poised. The catman reacted instantly, jerking Harald's head even farther back. The curved blade bit into his skin, sending a rivulet of blood along his exposed neck. A flush darkened his face. He tried to speak. The catman silenced him with a warning hiss and a dig of the blade.

Strange notions surged beneath the catman's emotions, a dimly-glimpsed code of honor Varzil could not understand.

One thing was clear. The catmen were trapped here, their escape blocked. They would make their last stand . . . over Harald's lifeless body.

Varzil laid on hand on Eiric's shoulder, gently so as not to startle him into a rash move. "Lower your sword."

"Are ye daft, boy? What's to stop them—"

"Eiric, lower your sword." Varzil spoke with a calm, instinctive certainty. The older man's eyes flashed white as he let the tip of the blade fall.

Varzil slid past Eiric, scraping along the rough surface of the rock. Behind him, the other men murmured, half in protest, half in awe.

. . . know what he's doing? . . .

. . . taking a terrible risk . . . get Lord Harald and half of us killed . . .

. . . none of us get out of here alive . . .

And the single word that echoed in each man's mind, *Laranzu!*

From the catman came a pulse of *fear-hatred-hunger* and the contorted dance of thought forms. They tasted like a maze of iron, though Varzil could not guess how the catmen knew of that precious mineral. Darkover was poor in metals, and the sword that the catman still held to Harald's throat had come from trading with the Dry Towners of Shainsa or Ardcarran.

Perhaps whatever is in the creature's mind is as precious to him as iron.

Varzil approached slowly, hands held low and away from his body. He deliberately halted at such a distance that the catman could, with its superior speed, release its prisoner and slash his own throat if it chose.

In the dim orange light, slitted pupils dilated a fraction more, though the catman gave no other sign of recognition. Varzil had placed himself at risk, and therefore within the catman's power. He wished he could read some expression in the lean muscled body, the eyes so like a cat's.

He suppressed an impulse to reach out for physical contact, as if by sinking his fingers into the gray fur, he could also link to the creature's mind. His overture might seem a preemptive attack to the catman. He dared not risk it.

The image of reaching out filled his thoughts. In an instant, he saw the catman's mind as a gleaming metallic cage set with jewels and sigils of incomprehensible design. There was beauty and meaning in the pattern, although so far from his human experience, he could not even guess what it was.

Hunger and fear . . . Those he knew.

He built a scene in his thoughts, focusing on each element until it was as clear as a painting. The hillside—green grass, rocks, a few clumps of brush, tendrilled windweed. Sheep—two, no, four—gray-white fleece hanging in tangles, narrow feet finding traction on the rocks, muzzles nipping at the new growth, bobbed tails wagging. The mingled smells of sheep manure and dew-damp wool.

A stirring . . . *arousal-interest-memory . . .*

Varzil pictured a shepherd, not any shepherd but the one called Donny. The shepherd perched just above the sheep, crooked staff resting on his shoulder, in his fleece jacket, with his weather-worn face and alert eyes.

Fear-hatred-hunger. Although not as strong as before, the response was unmistakable. *Sheep good, man bad.*

Varzil imagined the shepherd rising to his feet, walking slowly uphill, away from the flock. He tried to make the mental picture as vivid as before—the shadow falling across the stone, the heavier breathing as the shepherd reached the top and stood silhouetted against the bright sky . . . the sheep grazing on, undisturbed . . . the shepherd's distant form disappearing over the crest of the hill.

Now Varzil visualized a catman crouched where the shepherd had been sitting. Its dark-tufted ears lifted in an attitude he hoped was friendly, relaxed. The sheep grazed on, unguarded.

In the cave, the real catman froze its position. Varzil could not even make out its breathing. The last jolt of *fear-hatred-hunger* fell away like dust settling from the air, to be replaced by a sense of *alertness-waiting.*

The catman in Varzil's vision got to its feet. It moved stiffly, since he'd had little opportunity to observe how they moved when at ease. But there was no flare of hostility or disbelief from the real catman, only that *alertness-waiting.* Closer and closer, the imaginary catman drew to the sheep until it halted a few paces from the flock. One sheep, a fat ewe, looked up and, with total absence of concern, ambled toward the catman until the feline nonhuman could easily touch her.

Alertness-waiting flared into *hunger-arousal!*

The imaginary catman stretched out one clawed hand to the sheep. The sheep placidly approached and allowed herself to be picked up and slung over the catman's shoulders, much as Varzil had seen shepherds do with injured animals or lambs too young to scamper over pastures still half-frozen in spring.

Hunger-arousal! Disbelief . . . Hunger! Hope-hope-hope!

Varzil lifted one hand, palm facing away and fingers spread wide to show he carried no weapon. The catman in the cave riveted its attention on the gesture. Its three fellows also came to rough attention. They seemed to be waiting for some signal, although none made any gesture toward their weapons.

Varzil heard the sharp exhalations of the men behind him, the rustle of cloth over leather. The answering surge of tension from the catmen struck him like a physical blow. He prayed Eiric had enough control of his men to keep them in check. If he shifted his own focus, the fragmentary rapport would shatter.

Praying to whatever god would listen, Varzil closed his eyes and concentrated on the image of the cave, just as he'd seen it a moment ago. In his mind, the catman still held its curved sword against Harald's neck, dark blood trickled down his brother's neck, the other nonhumans poised for action in the flickering torchlight. Now Varzil showed the catman lowering its weapon.

With as much authority as he could summon, Varzil switched to the mental picture of the catman carrying away the sheep. The figure of the nonhuman dwindled in size as it progressed up the valley. Varzil showed it following the same route these very catmen had fled along. He made it clear that this time, the valley was empty. There would be no pursuit.

Again, he projected the image of the catman dropping its sword and Harald going free, followed immediately with a vision of the catman with the sheep.

Let my brother go, and you may keep the sheep you have taken. We will not hinder you. Though he doubted the catman could understand his human words, Varzil drew a measure of assurance from hearing them in his own mind.

The last picture he formed was of the cave and Harald rushing forward, free. As the moments trickled by, the sharp lines of the image blurred, like a reflection in a pool stirred by a stick. In the ripples, he caught a flash of distorted shapes, a background of fire-lapped darkness. Catmen—slinking, crouching, flowing as swiftly through the shadows as a hawk piercing the air. They carried sheep, gray and lumpy, slung over their shoulders.

The next moment, the image vanished. The real Harald slumped over, the sword no longer pressed against his throat.

"Laddie," Eiric called to Harald, "get yourself over here."

Varzil held himself steady as Harald lurched past him and into the arms of his people. Varzil's eyes never left those of the catman. In the back of his mind, he tasted iron once again. The catmen were watching to see if he kept his promise.

Eiric's men retreated down the tunnel, supporting Harald. They'd taken the torch; only an unsteady glimmer lit the little cave. The eyes of the catman flashed red and then vanished. Even as Varzil turned to follow the men, he knew that he was alone in the cave.

He caught up with them in a few turnings, for Eiric had called a halt to wait for him. Harald was still on his feet, but wavering. Despite the fever from his wound, his dark eyes were clear.

"What—what happened?" Harald asked.

"A sorcerer, your brother is," one of the men said.

"Varzil?"

Varzil took one of Harald's arms and Eiric took the other. "Let's get out of here. That bunch is no longer our concern."

"Now we know where they've laired, or nearabouts, we can come after them as it suits us," Eiric said.

"No." Varzil spoke the word quietly, but he sensed its effect upon the men. "That you must not do. I made a bargain with them. The sheep and immunity in exchange for Harald."

"Bargain?" Eiric said, but his voice betrayed him. He was ready to believe anything, for there was no other explanation for what he himself had witnessed. "I . . . I saw no bargain."

"I have given the word of the Ridenow, as close as these creatures can understand. You will not dishonor that oath."

They spoke no more until they had come out on the ledge and gazed down upon the hillside in the full morning sun. Once they'd reached the horses, with food and water in the saddlebags, they halted to wash and dress Harald's wounds.

Varzil knelt at Harald's side and took the fevered hands within his own. With a tug, Harald indicated he should bend down for private speech.

"At first, I thought you were just another dream," Harald said in a half-whisper. "A raving born from my poisoned wound. But you were calling to me, weren't you? And you somehow touched the mind of that cat-monster, near enough to get it to back off."

"I offered it the sheep, free and clear, if it would let you go."

"They would as like have had the sheep anyway." Harald coughed, shifted. "We'll have to get moving soon. Father will be half beside himself."

"Oh, he's already that," Varzil replied.

"How—how did you know to do that? We've had the same lessons and I know I could never have communicated with that creature. Yet . . . you've never been to a Tower."

"No, but I want to."

Something happened to me at Arilinn—an awakening, an opening—or I would not have been able to do what I did here.

No, Arilinn was behind him, no matter what Auster said. He had made his choice—to be his father's son.

Varzil's fingers clenched around his brother's, loosening only at the reflexive wince. "Father thinks—" the words came tumbling out with all the pent-up intensity of the last few hours, "he thinks I have not enough *laran* to be worth training." He broke off. He would not beg, not from his father, not from anyone in the Ridenow clan.

Harald's brow furrowed, his eyes darkening. "Not enough *laran*—only enough to do what no one has ever done before, forge a bargain with a catman!" His gaze flickered to Varzil's. "I would not be alive without this *laran* of yours. Such a Gift must not be lost. Arilinn it shall be, if I have to storm their walls myself. I will speak with Father. You will have your chance."

✦

By the time the rescue party stumbled into the yard at Sweetwater, Harald's fever had broken. He swayed in the saddle, his face pasty with weakness, but he refused a makeshift litter. In that, Varzil thought he was very like their father. As soon as they were spotted, a group of men came galloping to meet them. *Dom* Felix rode at their head.

Varzil watched his father take his oldest son and heir into his arms, the old eyes reddening with tears. For an instant, he wished his father could embrace him with the same unabashed love. He knew, with a strange new certainty that had grown upon him since his visit to Arilinn, that his father *did* love him, and that love underlay his resistance in sending a frail and undersized child into such a den of wizardry. Like the Keeper at Arilinn, he worried what might happen to Varzil's health.

Unlike Varzil, who wanted peculiar and unheard-of things, Harald was an uncomplicated son, his desires as clear and straightforward to *Dom* Felix as his own. They were of a mind; they understood one another. *Dom* Felix could never comprehend a temperament like Varzil's, and no amount of paternal love could overcome such an absence of sympathy.

Once they'd come up to the main house at Sweetwater, Varzil went to help put the horses away. He fully expected that Harald's fever would sweep away his promise, and he held out small hope of his brother being able to persuade Lord Felix.

So Varzil was a little surprised when, the next morning, his father summoned him to a private conversation. The old man stood before him, cheeks dusky, shifting minutely from one foot to the other.

"Harald has told me of the circumstances of his rescue. He said that you *negotiated* with the catmen for his release. How were you able to do that? They have no language a man can speak."

Either he will believe me or he will not, but I will speak the truth. "I was able to reach their leader with my thoughts."

"By *laran?*"

Varzil nodded. *By that very* laran *you say is not worth training.* Without meaning to, he projected the thought.

Dom Felix drew in a breath and his eyes, rheumy with the intense emotions of the last few days, brightened.

"I—I may have been mistaken. You were a dreamstruck, idle youngster, but you have always been truthful. If you say you communicated with the catman by *laran,* then that is what happened. Such a Gift cannot be ignored or discarded. You must have proper training—if not at Arilinn, then somewhere else."

Varzil lifted his chin, unable to speak.

"If you wish it, my son, to Arilinn you shall go this very morning, with not only my blessing but my humble request for your admittance." At Varzil's astonished expression, he hastened to add, "I have done you wrong in thinking you less than you are, and I would make things right."

Your brother lives because of your Gift; it would be as ill-done to keep you here as to chain a dragon to roast my meat.

Varzil could not speak, only move into the circle of his father's arms. When he could finally draw away and gather up the few possessions he cared to take, the aircar was waiting to take him back to Arilinn.

7

Varzil paused beneath the arches leading to the central chamber of Arilinn Tower. It was hard to believe he was really here to stay. Even as the aircar returned him to the city of Arilinn, he'd braced himself for some last-minute disappointment. Perhaps the Keeper would stand by his first refusal or his father would summon him back home on some pretext. But nothing he feared had come to pass. The Keeper offered no explanation for his change of heart, only conveyed his willingness to give Varzil a place as a probationary novice. Bewildered by the rapidity of recent events and their unexpected reversals, Varzil asked no questions. It was enough to be here, to belong here.

Tapestries and floor mosaics glowed in gemstone hues. A fire danced in the hearth, casting a friendly orange light on the faces of the people seated in a rough semicircle on the chairs and cushioned benches. He had not realized how many lived and worked at Arilinn.

To one side, a young woman with hair so intensely red it rivaled the flames plucked a small harp known as a *rryl*. Varzil didn't know her, although he'd been introduced to the man accompanying her on lap drum—Fidelis, who had taken him inside the Tower on that very first morning and would teach him monitoring. The middle-aged woman warbling her way through ballad verses in an obscure dialect of *cahuenga* was

Lunilla, house mother and matrix mechanic. He'd met her and several of the others during his first visit here and could still remember how she'd bossed him about like his aunt Ysabet.

In that instant, he knew she was aware of him, though she went right on with the next verse. She, and everyone else in the room. The sense of being stranded in a foreign country intensified. More than firelight bound these people to one another. Something in the air . . . a humming along his nerves.

Varzil? Fidelis turned to look directly at him, a smile crinkling the corners of his eyes. He was the same age as *Dom* Felix, with only a trace of chestnut left in his white hair.

Varzil wondered uneasily whether he should reply aloud.

It's quite all right. I just wanted to see if you heard me. We don't read each other's minds casually or without permission. But even Durraman's donkey, blind as the hills and twice as deaf, could tell how awkward you feel, standing there alone. Come over and join us.

Varzil lifted his chin and walked into the room. He was too shy to join in, for his singing voice, never very good, would probably come out like the croak of the frog hidden in Fra' Domenic's infamous pockets. He hesitated to join the older people's conversations, not before he'd sorted out the lines of influence, who had opposed his admission and who had taken his part. Then he spotted Carlo and the other youth from the balcony, sitting over a board game. Carlo's height and fiery hair were unmistakable.

Carlo gestured him closer. "Do you play castles? We need a fresh challenger."

Varzil dipped his head. "Yes, I used to play with my grandfather. But I don't want to interrupt your game."

"Oh, this one's dead anyway." Carlo indicated the pieces spread across the board. "We've worn the play to exhaustion, just like a bad war. Now there's nothing left but to thwack away at each other until the bitter end. What's the fun in that?"

"That's the point of the entire game," said the other boy, "to persevere until victory."

Now that he saw the other boy close up, Varzil was struck by how serious, almost grim, he looked. Unlike most of the others, his hair was brown rather than red, his arched brows dark against pale, unblemished skin. His features were thin, the deep blue eyes stark, the mouth small above a pointed chin. Yet there was no delicacy about him, rather a steely strength.

"I rather thought," Carlo said dryly, "that the point was to exercise one's mind. Not to mention an amusing way of passing the hours on long winter nights. Stubborn endurance has nothing to do with it."

Endurance—the very word which had sprung to Varzil's mind as he'd steeled himself for the long wait outside Arilinn Tower on that first frosty morning.

"I think endurance has everything to do with it," he said, clearly startling the others. "Sometimes the board is very tidy and full of possibilities. But sometimes," he copied Carlo's gesture, encompassing the board with its assortment of lackluster pieces, "it's like this, and you just have to keep trying. That's the real challenge, isn't it? To create something of meaning when all seems lost."

Eduin gave him a surprised look, but Carlo laughed. "You remind me of my riding master, who said the true test of a horseman was not what he could do on a spirited horse, for any ham-handed dolt could look good on a beast that's prancing and eager to go. To take a worn-out stable drudge with a mouth like saddle leather and bring it to life—*that* requires real skill."

"He's mocking us, Carlo," Eduin said, glaring at Varzil.

"You have little grounds to object," Carlo replied with good humor. "After all, he's taking *your* part."

Varzil did not know what he had done to provoke Eduin, but clearly the dark-haired boy disliked him. In another circumstance, he would have apologized, but he sensed that nothing he said would appease Eduin. So he pulled the third stool back a little from the table and sat down, murmuring, "Please go on."

Eduin turned away, but before Carlo could comment, an older man in formal green robes rose. There was a general bustle as most of the others put away books or musical instruments. One woman tucked away her sewing in a basket and got to her feet.

"Well, that settles it," Eduin said with an obvious attempt at better humor. "You two can *thwack away* at each other all night." *Some of us have work to do.*

Carlo shrugged and turned back to the board. In a few minutes, only the red-haired girl and another younger one, with a mass of strawberry-blonde ringlets pulled back with a ribbon, and the two boys were left in the room.

The red-haired girl began singing a ballad in a low, sweet voice. Varzil could not make out all the words, but he recognized the melody. The song told the story of the fall of Neskaya and Tramontana, how the folk in one Tower had been forced to rain psychic lightnings upon their kin-folk in the other. Torn between love and duty, sworn brothers had chosen to immolate themselves rather than commit such an atrocity. It was a stirring melody, one which sent blood pounding and toes tapping.

Carlo hummed along, his body swaying unself-consciously. Finally, the last refrain came to an end and the girls headed off toward their chambers.

After they had gone, Varzil could not have said what part of the song moved him. He had heard it many times in different versions over the years. Nor was the girl's performance, while pleasant enough, especially compelling. He only knew that the boy beside him had felt the same stirring of emotion. Perhaps, he told himself, it was being here in Arilinn, a place very much like the Towers of the song, among people very like those same heroes, and knowing himself to be one of them. Would he come to value them as ardently? Auster and Fidelis, even Lunilla, already had his respect and admiration. In time, Carlo would, too—but Eduin?

Varzil took a breath and let it out in a sigh. "I'm afraid I've already made an enemy," he said. "And I don't know why."

"You mean Eduin? I'm glad you don't consider *me* one." Carlo said with an engaging grin. "Don't worry about him. He's a good enough sort once you get to know him. He is a bit serious, I suppose. He's been here four years and is already training at the higher levels. He has a right to feel a bit superior to those of us who don't have work in the circles."

"You don't?"

"Oh, sometimes, when the work's not too technically demanding. I do whatever I'm allowed to, but everyone knows I'm not here to stay. I suppose you could say I'm on sojourn, training for the throne and not the Tower."

"The—? Who—who *are* you, Carlo?"

Carlo dipped his head, showing the first hint of diffidence. "I thought you knew." Eyes filled with gray light met Varzil's. "I'm Carolin Hastur."

Carolin Hastur. Hastur of Hastur, nephew and heir to King Felix.

The death of Rafael II made Carolin the next ruler of the most powerful branch of the Hastur Kingdom.

It had been over two centuries since the Peace of Allart Hastur, which had brought an end to the long, bloody conflict between Ridenow and Hastur. Yet war still smoldered in the Hundred Kingdoms, breaking out in a dozen smaller conflicts. Hastur and Ridenow had not found themselves on opposing sides . . . yet.

On impulse, Varzil reached out and placed his fingers between Carolin's loosely folded hands. It was not quite a gesture of fealty, and it would not have been fitting in any case.

Whatever happens, we two will be as brothers.

We must, came Carolin's thought. Then, aloud, "I do not know why, but you belong here in this Tower, just as I belong in the world, and that for the sake of our world, we must build a bridge between the two."

Like the bredini *of the song.* Embarrassed by his own romantic sentiment, Varzil pulled away. Without the physical contact, they dropped out of rapport. Something remained, as if they had indeed sworn themselves in that brief moment.

✦

Everyone at Arilinn worked, not only at study and the discipline of *laran,* but the physical labor of maintaining the Tower. Lunilla was a masterful organizer, so within a week of Varzil's arrival, he was taking his turns at pot scrubbing, floor sweeping, onion peeling, bundling linens into the town for laundry, and other errands.

"The *kyrri* are useful in their fashion," she said, forestalling objections she'd heard a hundred times, "but they don't think the way humans do. We've learned never to let them near a dirty plate or a basket of apples."

One frosty morning about a month after he'd arrived at Arilinn, Varzil went out with Carolin, Eduin, Cerriana, and young Valentina, the girl with the ringlets, to pick apples. A small orchard of tart green fruit, perfect for pies and sauces, had been donated to the Tower by a grateful merchant whose wife and son had been saved in childbirth by the Tower monitors.

They made a festive caravan with Carolin mounted on his fine horse, Eduin on a mule, and the rest trotting along on pannier-laden stag ponies. Varzil had to cross his legs over the beast's withers because of the huge wicker baskets. He jounced along the road, his rump getting ever more bruised.

By the time the young people arrived at the orchard, the sun had already melted the frost, although white still laced the shadows. The orchard lay on the lowest slopes of the western Twin Peak. Many of the trees were old, misshapen by decades of neglect. Someone with more enthusiasm than skill had taken a pruning saw to them, Varzil saw. Heavily knotted branches stretched out in unbalanced array, giving the trees the appearance of dancers in a tipsy Midsummer revel. The branches bowed under the glossy emerald-toned fruit.

They hobbled the horse and mule, leaving the *chervines* to graze. Eduin and Cerriana, who had worked in this orchard in seasons past, drew out the wooden ladders and aprons from the little shed. In her enormous canvas apron, Valentina looked like a doll dressed by a seaman.

Cerriana had no head for heights, so she and Valentina took the lowest branches, those which could be reached on foot. Eduin and Carolin started on the biggest tree, at the end of the row. Within a few minutes, they'd left the ladder behind to perch on the twisted branches.

Varzil placed his ladder in his usual careful way, studying the branches. Applewood wasn't supple like willow. Those limbs, as heavily laden as they were, could snap in a rough wind. As he climbed, the tree creaked under his weight.

He began picking, dropping the apples into his pocketed apron. The aroma of the fruit filled his head, sweet with lazy summer afternoons. He bit into one. The skin was tough, the flesh crisp, the juice a burst of honeyed tartness.

Valentina, the youngest, began a song in her sweet child's voice, and Cerriana joined in. Eduin sang in a surprisingly good tenor, as did Carolin. Varzil, with no singing voice of his own, was content to simply listen. He kept his eyes on the apples and his mind on judging how much weight each branch could take.

Crack! Crash! came from across the orchard.

Thud!

Varzil grabbed the nearest branch as the ladder went tumbling out from under him. He wrapped his legs around the branch, even as the tree swayed under his weight.

"Carlo!" Cerriana shrieked.

Varzil, clinging to his perch, couldn't see exactly what had happened. Cerriana and Valentina rushed to the other tree.

Varzil shimmied down until he could get a foothold on the lowest branch and from there, drop to the ground. By some miracle, he managed to land on both feet.

Now he got a good look at the tree where Eduin and Carolin had been picking. Eduin still stood atop his own ladder. His thin features were set and ashen, his blue eyes lit with an unreadable expression. A massive branch had snapped off and crashed to the ground.

Carolin lay unmoving under the thickest part of the bough.

8

Cerriana threw herself down beside Carolin's half-hidden form. With one hand, she touched his bare, outstretched hand.

"He's alive."

She was a monitor, Varzil told himself, and would know from a touch. Still, his heart stuttered as he rushed over.

He wrapped his hands around the thick, splintered branch and pulled. It was surprisingly heavy. He staggered under its weight. Valentina tugged uselessly at one of the smaller offshoots. Cerriana made no attempt to help, but reached underneath, toward Carolin's head.

With her other hand, Cerriana took out her starstone, a chip of faceted, blue-tinged fire set in a filigree of copper on a long chain between her breasts. It glimmered into life at her touch. Varzil could almost see a halo of *laran* sparks surrounding her hands as she worked.

Valentina sniffled, but sat quietly. Her round eyes took on the serious, inward-focused look that Varzil already associated with matrix work. She was following Cerriana's mind.

Varzil felt Cerriana's concentration, the surge of her *laran* as she examined Carolin. But Eduin—Eduin's mind was a blank. Varzil glanced up to see the older boy climbing down, rung by slow, studied rung.

Varzil inhaled deeply, filling his chest, just as he'd seen men on his father's estate do when faced with some feat of strength. Letting the breath out in a rush, he tightened his grasp on the branch and heaved with all his strength. Not straight up, against the weight of the dense-grained wood, but sideways, pivoting the branch. To his surprise, it moved.

"Let's get him out!" Cerriana sprang to life. "There's nothing broken—it's safe to move him." She grabbed one of Carolin's arms and Valentina, the other. Together, they managed to pull him clear away. Varzil lowered the branch.

Carolin lay motionless, head lolling, eyes closed. Thick lashes curled over pale cheeks. One arm stretched at an awkward angle and the shoulder bulged unnaturally.

Varzil sensed a faint presence. *Carlo? Can you hear me?*

Silence answered him.

As Varzil knelt by his friend's side, he felt Eduin's approach as a prickle of the hairs at the back of his neck.

"He—he fell," Eduin said. "There was nothing I could do." He swallowed hard.

Through Eduin's barriers, Varzil caught a tinge of intense emotion, fear and concern and an odd desperation, all blurred together.

Cerriana, once more in rapport with the unconscious youth, did not respond, but Valentina blinked.

"Don't—" Varzil began, meaning to say, *Don't distract her.*

"Don't tell me what to do!" Eduin snarled. He circled the branch to crouch beside Cerriana.

No, shuddered through Varzil. He bit back an exclamation. What was wrong with him? Eduin was Carolin's friend, and he had four years of Tower training.

Just as Eduin stretched out his hand, Carolin's eyelids fluttered. He took a deep, heaving breath. Moaning, he raised one hand to his forehead. "What happened—?"

"Hush," Cerriana said. "Lie still while I monitor you."

"No, I'm all right." Carolin lifted his head and struggled to sit up. The brief tint of color immediately drained from his face. He fell back.

Varzil took Carolin's hand between his. "Let Cerriana finish her work. It will take only a few minutes. If you sit up too soon, you'll faint and get Valentina upset."

Valentina had been sitting, watching quietly without the slightest evidence of any distress.

Carolin's mouth quirked upward at one corner, but he made no further attempts to rise. Cerriana continued her scan of his body. Eduin mirrored her from the other side.

Watching Eduin's serious expression and the care with which he examined Carolin's shoulder, Varzil felt ashamed of his suspicions. Had he held a stupid grudge against Eduin for having greeted him so rudely on that first morning?

"You managed to hit your head pretty hard, Carlo," Cerriana said, sitting back. "There's no bleeding inside that thick skull of yours and your neck is intact. Your shoulder's dislocated, but that seems to be the worst of it. I've done what I can, short of compressing two weeks' rest into five minutes. There'll be no more apple picking for you today, I fear." She laughed. "A rather extreme method of getting out of work, I must say."

Cerriana helped Carolin to sit up. He gasped in pain and grabbed his injured shoulder. His arm hung at an odd angle.

"Ah!" Carolin winced.

"Alas, I have not the skill to set it back," Cerriana said. "Fidelis tried to teach me, but I'm not strong enough and I kept getting the angle wrong. I doubt you'd appreciate me putting my foot in your armpit and pulling as hard as I can. No, we'd best put the arm in a sling and get you back."

"By then, the joint will have swollen. Putting it back will be much more difficult," Varzil said.

"How would you know?" Eduin demanded.

Cerriana looked at Varzil, assessing him. *He's so small, he must have grown up in a monastery. What could he know of such injuries?*

Varzil shrugged. "The oldest son of my father's paxman had his shoulder torn half out of its socket by a colt that had gotten into ghost-weed."

Memories rushed over him. He'd been watching from the pole corral, along with Harald and a few of the men. The horse had been one of a herd brought in from winter pasture for the yearlings to be branded, trained to halter, and then turned out for another season before being broken for riding. Kevan, Black Eiric's teenaged son, had roped and haltered the colt.

The three-year-old, driven into a frenzy by the toxic weed, had thrown himself over backward to escape an imagined terror. Kevan's hand had caught in the halter rope, spinning his body around and jerking his arm behind him before he could release himself.

Varzil had jumped into the enclosure a moment after Harald did. Harald had waved his arms to shoo the horse away. Squealing, the beast had shied and bolted for the other side of the pen, where it had stood, trembling and dripping foam from its nostrils. The other horses had whirled and bunched together at the far end.

Varzil had bent over Kevan, who clutched his shoulder even as Carolin did now. Kevan had cursed under his breath and the skin around his mouth had turned white with pain. The oldest of the stable men, Raul, had evaluated the damage with a few deft touches, the same care as he would use for a frightened foal. Raul himself was a wizened nut of a man, a head shorter than the others, his back bowed and knotted with years of battling bad weather and rough livestock.

"Slid your shoulder out of its socket, you have, young Kevan," he had said in a kindly voice. "But we'll soon put it to rights. Now you watch this, Master Varzil. The usual way's to stick your boot in the poor man's armpit and haul away like crazy. It works but tears the muscles something fierce. Sometimes the cure's worst than the illness. But see here, you can do it smart instead of strong."

Raul had placed Kevan on his back and, continuing to speak in a soothing tone, had bent his arm, pulling gently at the elbow. "Ah now, I'm waiting for the moment when the muscles relax. Easy is best, with men as well as horses. Can you feel it start to give? There, now."

He had slowly brought Kevan's elbow to his side and rotated the entire arm so that the hand lay on the opposite shoulder. Varzil heard a soft *pop!* An expression of incredulous relief spread over Kevan's face.

"Once it's been out, a shoulder likes to wander," Raul had said as Kevan got to his feet. "Like some fillies I've known, and more than a few husbands. With a shoulder, the trick is to get it back in before the muscles bind up." He gave a wink to indicate there was no known treatment for either of the other offenders.

"I know about shoulders," Kevan had admitted with a sheepish grin. "'Tis the third time for me, but the puttin' back's always worse than the puttin' out. Never had it so easy as this." He had thanked the stable man and went off toward the main house to have his shoulder bound.

The puttin' back's always worse than the puttin' out. The phrase stayed with Varzil, along with the memory.

"Let me try," he said, gently pushing Carolin down.

"You?" Eduin demanded. "What can you do? Cerriana, this is a terrible idea—he has no monitor training—he could make the damage worse—"

"No," Carolin said. "I trust Varzil. Let him try."

Ignoring Eduin's taunt, Varzil positioned his hands around Carolin's forearm, exerting a steady, gentle traction on the shoulder. At first, he felt resistance, as if he were pulling on a tightly knotted rope. The muscles had already gone stiff with pain. Carolin's face tensed.

Do not fight it, bredu, he spoke mentally to Carolin. *I know it hurts, but can you place your arm into my hands?*

Carolin, who had been holding his breath, let it out. Varzil felt the muscles soften and lengthen. Now was the moment.

Praying his memory was correct, Varzil drew Carolin's elbow to his side, hand rotated backward. He felt something high in the arm begin to slide. With the next slow movement, Varzil moved Carolin's hand toward the opposite shoulder, continuing to hold his elbow at his side.

"Ah!" Carolin cried.

Varzil sensed rather than heard the arm bone slide back into its socket. Warmth spread through the surrounding tissues. Varzil sat back on his heels, aware that he was sweating.

"Now, where is that sling?" he said.

Cerriana, eyes wide, went to get cloth from the picnic basket. Deftly, she knotted it around Carolin's arm.

After Carolin declared he felt well enough to travel, Cerriana announced that she and Valentina would return with him to Arilinn.

"There's no sense all of us leaving," Eduin said. "Varzil and I can keep picking."

With Carolin safely astride his fine black horse and Valentina on the mule, Cerriana bustled her little party back to the Tower. Varzil turned back to the tree where he'd been picking. He lifted the ladder from the ground.

"If you expect to be treated like some kind of hero, you're going to be disappointed." Eduin came up behind him.

Varzil suppressed his startlement. He didn't like the glint in Eduin's eyes, nor did the older boy's words bode him any good will. His former unease returned.

"I just did what needed to be done," he said quietly. "I don't expect any reward."

Eduin's tone slipped toward an outright sneer. "If you know what's good for you, you'll stay away from Carlo from now on."

"What concern is it of yours?" The words burst from Varzil's mouth before he could consider them. Anger pulsed through his belly.

Perhaps, he realized, he disliked Eduin because he sensed how much Eduin disliked *him*.

Why? He was no threat to Eduin's position in the Tower, nor was he aware of any feud between their families. Zandru's scorpions, he didn't even know who Eduin's father was! What difference could that make?

Eduin took a step closer. He was a head taller than Varzil, so that now he glowered down at him. His lips drew back from his teeth. He poked one finger into Varzil's chest. It would have been an offensive gesture under any circumstances, but for telepaths accustomed to respectful physical restraint, it was an outright insult.

Varzil might be new to the Tower, but not so new that he did not catch the implication. He was acutely aware that they were alone together, that Eduin was not only older and taller, but heavier. He'd never been a fighter; if Eduin decided to enforce his point with fists instead of words, his only option would be to run. That would only delay the inevitable.

"Mind your own business," Eduin said, biting off each word. "Nobody wanted you here to begin with, but since we have to put up with you, you'd better stick to your own place. Which is away from me and Carolin Hastur."

Varzil's thoughts skidded to a halt. Eduin was telling him that Carolin was his private preserve and that no outside friendships would be tolerated. They weren't lovers; Varzil would have known if they were, and Tower folk weren't prudish. He'd realized that from his first night when Cerriana and Richardo had gone off together.

He's nothing but a bully.

Varzil squared his shoulders and met the older boy's gaze steadily. "I will associate with anyone I please. It is for Carlo to say who his friends are, not you."

As for his own place, that was at Arilinn Tower. Something held him back from throwing the words in Eduin's face. Perhaps it was the old habit of keeping his thoughts to himself, or he sensed that even a bully might have influence beyond his words.

Eduin was clearly a favorite, advancing rapidly through the ranks of Tower workers. If he fulfilled his promise, he would make a dangerous enemy.

What was really important here? Facing down a bully or following his own dreams, to be here at last at Arilinn Tower?

Or was this a grudge which would grow and fester until it escaped all bounds of reason? He had heard tales of such feuds, running for generations.

Instinctively, Varzil reached out to Eduin's mind. If he could establish a primitive communication with a catman, who wasn't even human, he might also be able to bridge whatever separated him from this young man.

Varzil met a wall, as smooth and blank as a polished shield. He drew back, astonished at the completeness of the barrier. Eduin's thoughts seemed only to reflect, not to penetrate.

Polished . . . as if from years of needing to draw apart, to keep secret. This was not just against him for this moment, Varzil realized, but simply the way Eduin habitually shielded his thoughts. Yet in the Tower, where men spoke mind to mind, what could be kept hidden? Why this desperate need for privacy?

And how terribly lonely he must feel. What could have happened to him, to produce so complete a rift?

Compassion washed through Varzil. He himself had felt compelled to keep secrets for most of his young life. A few early mistakes, like speaking of the Ya-men wailing beneath the moons, had convinced him of the danger of openness. Here in the Tower, he hoped he could finally be himself, among people who understood. How infinitely sad that Eduin, who had been here for four years, still could not trust anyone with the hidden recesses of his mind.

Ah well, that was truly none of his business. And if Eduin felt drawn to Carolin in fellowship and trust, it was better for him to have a single friend than to be so terribly alone.

Silently, Varzil went back to picking apples. His hands and feet moved of their own accord, climbing the wooden rungs, reaching for one green sphere after another. But as he worked, the lingering poison of

Eduin's attack continued to eat away at him. He no longer smelled the honey-tart aroma of the apples. The colors of the day dimmed, as if a mist had passed over the cloudless sky. He emptied the pockets of his apron over and over into the panniers until four of them were full. Leaving the last stag pony for Eduin, he took the lead lines of the other two and trudged back to Arilinn.

9

Snow covered the turrets and courtyards of Arilinn when Varzil took his place as a member of a working circle for the first time. Ordinarily, this would have required years of training, but Varzil had shown aptitude and there was such need that his progress had been accelerated. This night, he was to join Fidelis and Cerriana as part of a *laran* healing.

A handful of families, left homeless and desperate after the last skirmishes between Alton and Esperanza, had tried to farm the Drycreek area. These broken borderlands, adjacent to the Hastur kingdoms, had been contaminated with bonewater dust a generation ago and deserted ever since. The farmers thought enough time had passed for the land to be safe, but after some months, their children sickened. As Midwinter neared, they came to Arilinn, half-starved and suffering from frostbite as well as bonewater poisoning. The Tower's monitors separated out the less afflicted, but it would take the combined efforts of the two strongest healers, along with a full circle, to save the worst. Fidelis recommended that Varzil be included, young though he was.

Varzil arrived early at the designated chamber to compose himself and to calm his rising excitement at this new responsibility. Auster had placed great faith in him and he wanted to prove himself worthy.

Most monitors were healers, skilled in using the body's own energy system to repair and rebuild. Some of the best were women, although no one had offered Varzil an explanation why. Everyone at Arilinn had basic monitor training, and all novices studied the energy patterns of the human body.

Varzil paused to catch his breath just inside the door. A row of cots had been set up around the charcoal brazier, bathed in its gentle warmth. One of the patients, a child wrapped in a thick white blanket, coughed fitfully. He blinked, not sure if he had seen a fine green haze in the air, or only felt the sickness of the children. Something—a smell, a taste like rotted meat—slithered up the back of his throat. The fine hairs along the back of his neck rose.

Fidelis came into the room, touching his fingertips to the back of Varzil's hand in passing and then proceeding to the first cot. As usual, he wore the loosely belted white robe of a monitor. Deep lines bracketed his mouth and eyes.

The monitor bent over the little girl who lay there, her hair spilling over the pillow. "Come here, Varzil. Look at this."

Swallowing, Varzil bent over the child, taking in the milk-pale cheeks, the tracery of blue veins beneath the skin, the hollows around the eyes, the frost-chapped lips. The girl stirred and opened her eyes. She looked to be about four years old. Something in the shape of her eyes reminded him of Dyannis, his youngest sister.

On impulse, he knelt beside the cot and took her hand. Fingers, as slender as a fairy's, tightened around his. With his mind, he followed the energon channels of her body, by layers going deeper into the tissues, the congested red passages, the ruptured cells. He had not the training to completely understand what he saw, the pattern of damage and reaction as her body struggled to defend itself.

This way . . . As gentle and firm as a guiding hand, Fidelis directed his awareness to the core of the girl's bones, where germ cells lined the cavities, dying. Here and there, however, a tiny mote pulsed with unnatural energy. Varzil felt each pinpoint as a dot of lurid phosphorescence, green like the miasma in the room. The girl might survive for a time, but the deep changes in her marrow would eventually kill her. Even now, he could taste her death. Looking up at Fidelis, he sought to put what he saw into words.

Fidelis nodded in agreement. *It is ever so with bonewater dust. Some die within days of exposure, their nerves burned out. Others survive, only to perish a tenday later from vomiting and purging. But these, especially the very young . . . they seem to heal, they lighten our hearts with hope, but theirs is the longer, more tragic death.*

"What must we do? How can we save her?" Varzil forced the words through a throat gone suddenly dry.

Fidelis tilted his head to one side, as if considering. *If we are not too late, I believe it is possible, even though no one today has much experience with such early treatment. The techniques from the Ages of Chaos are lost. Those affected are usually considered beyond help, even if they can still walk. I have heard that some men who survived the seeding of Drycreek seemed unharmed, but they all died a decade later from wasting illnesses or tumors. By the time any of them sought healing at a Tower, there was nothing we could do. Perhaps if we had known earlier . . .*

If we had considered it our responsibility to find out, said Auster.

"Who knew?" Auster spoke aloud as he entered the room. His eyes reflected the light of the globes set about the walls as if it were flame. His physical appearance commanded attention, with his heavy shoulders, rust-streaked beard, and intense eyes, but it was his mantle of energy which filled the room.

Auster went to the girl's cot. "Bonewater dust is a weapon of war. If people have not the wit to avoid the proscribed lands, we must nevertheless try to save them from their own folly."

Varzil read no expression in the Keeper's voice. Was Auster saying the use of bonewater was justified and acceptable, that it was the fault of the victims who had deliberately if unknowingly exposed their own families? Varzil had seen the faces of the parents, the tearing guilt behind their eyes. They loved their children no less than his own father loved him. And they were desperate, homeless. . . .

Together, Fidelis and Auster examined each patient. Most of this was done mentally, but occasionally Auster would ask a question about some medical detail. Cerriana joined them, listening quietly. Meanwhile, Lerrys and two others entered and took seats on the benches.

Last of all came Eduin, who went directly to his place without meeting Varzil's glance. They had spoken only a few words since the incident in the apple orchard, for they usually worked and studied separately. Now Varzil caught no hint of animosity from the other youth, only an attitude of serious concentration. Perhaps Eduin had thought better of his outburst, and now realized that Varzil posed no threat to his status in the

Tower or his friendship with Carolin. Varzil resolved to approach the night's task with the same impartiality.

Auster did not entirely leave each patient as he went on to the next. Instead, he seemed to carry each one with him, weaving some part of them into a whole, like a fisherman's net. He did this with such a light, sure touch that Varzil felt his own heartbeat grow steadier, his awareness heighten. Even the lights seemed to glow brighter.

By the time Auster had passed the row of cots and each patient had been discussed, the circle had been assembled. They were already gathered into a unity of mind. Fidelis took his place on his favorite, unpadded stool and Varzil beside him, facing Auster.

Varzil closed his eyes and began the breathing exercises which would attune him to the rhythms of his own body. He began to feel the sensation which, he'd learned, heralded a properly receptive mind.

A melody wove through the back of his mind, a lilting rise and fall like the gentle ripples of a river. Varzil imagined himself lying in a boat, as he had as a child, carried along the stream, watching the leafy branches pass overhead, the hypnotic alternation of shade and eye-searing brightness. Whether it was an hour or a heartbeat later, he became aware of other boats, all gone strangely translucent now, gliding alongside. As skillfully as a master weaver, Auster brought his circle together.

Varzil had never been part of a true circle before. He had touched other minds as part of training exercises, and then only that of his teacher or one or two others. He had never imagined anything like this floating grace. Each mind flowed in the same river, created the same joyous harmony, yet retained its individual uniqueness. There was Cerriana, for all her red hair and fiery temper a jewel of restful green, Fidelis a familiar melody played on a horn so deep and rich it caressed the bones, Lerrys an unfamiliar but heart-stirring beating of wings, gray like a falcon's . . . and the others, each with his own signature.

And finally there was Eduin. Varzil held off turning his attention to him until the end, expecting the opaque barrier he'd glimpsed at the orchard. To his surprise, he did not encounter a blank, mirrored shield. Eduin shone like an intricate net of jewels all strung together by silver wire, the whole twisting and shifting. Despite the beauty and strength flowing through the layered structure, Varzil pulled away after only a moment. He could not see more than a fraction of it at any one time, and something in the movement, the shift of light and power, unsettled him.

Perhaps that was because in his limited experience, he told himself, he had never experienced a mind so dissimilar to his.

Yet Auster had, with ease and skill, woven Eduin's *laran* signature into a seamless unity with the others. Was this what it meant to be a Keeper—to accept each person's Gift exactly as it was, creating harmony and purpose without demanding change?

Varzil had little time to spare for such musings as the work began. Under Auster's steady mental guidance, the group concentrated its energies, giving them freely into his control. Fidelis and Cerriana worked in tandem to identify the areas of greatest pathology in each patient. Varzil marveled at the delicacy of the subcellular manipulations, the surge and ebb of life energies as one or another of the sick children dropped from restless fever into the sleep of true healing.

How long it went on, he could not tell. He lost all sense of time, suspended in the flowing waters of Auster's circle. Sometimes he floated, drinking it all in, suspended in an ocean of silvery gray shot through with colored light. But more and more, he became part of the web itself, willing energy to flow from him, through Auster's skillful psychic guidance, and into the damaged bodies of the patients.

From time to time, he would become aware of others in the web. Even Eduin began to feel familiar. Once someone touched him—a ripple through his mental body, which he realized represented actual physical contact. Cerriana's musical whisper brushed his thoughts.

Breathe more deeply.

In automatic obedience, his chest rose and his lungs filled. Although he could not see it with his material eyes, he sensed Cerriana's answering smile. Her voice faded like droplets of colored water in a still pool. The gray light dimmed, not the darkness of physical distress, but a gradual release of the circle.

"Varzil."

He blinked, surprised to find himself sitting, immobile, on a bench. For a moment, he did not recognize his own name. Fingertips brushed the inside of one wrist.

Fidelis bent over him with a serious expression. Varzil's shoulders trembled. Around him, the other members of the circle were stretching, yawning, rising to their feet, heading for the door. Several others had come in to tend the patients and carry them to the infirmary.

"Go now and eat," Fidelis said.

"I'm not hungry—" Varzil began, as his stomach shifted uneasily at the thought of food. Nausea, he remembered, was a common symptom of the energy depletion that accompanied intense *laran* work. Lunilla had prepared honeyed fruit and nut confections to appeal to uncertain appetites.

"You have surprising strength, and you use it generously," Auster said. They were alone in the chamber, except for Eduin, lingering inside the door. "After you have rested, I want you to begin regular work in a circle, and take private lessons with me. You have talents we have not yet begun to explore."

Varzil wasn't sure how to respond. Not in his wildest imagination had he anticipated such advancement. Some deep part of him craved to return to the circle, to the world he had no words for, to the unity and joy of those hours.

"Good lad," Auster said, as if this happened every day. "Now, food and rest."

Varzil trailed after Auster and Fidelis as they left the room. Eduin joined them, speaking a few low words to the Keeper.

"Yes, you're quite right," Auster murmured, and then began the descent down the stairs. "I'll have someone see to it when there's time."

Eduin paused as Varzil approached, and Varzil had the fleeting impression that this was the real reason he had stayed behind.

"You did well for your first time," Eduin said pleasantly. His expression was friendly, despite the pale skin and hollows around his eyes. Varzil guessed that he himself looked no better. "I—" Eduin paused, clearly gathering his thoughts, "I misjudged you when you first arrived. We get them from time to time, brats from minor houses with no talent who try to wheedle their way in here. It's a waste of everyone's time. But—" slowing now, as if choosing his words with care, "—you've shown your abilities. I . . . ." His voice trailed off, but not before Varzil caught his last thought, *I was wrong about you.*

For an instant, Varzil wanted to say, *And I was wrong about you.* Eduin had been rude, yes, but that was easily forgiven. But he had also threatened Varzil, tried to warn him off being friends with Carolin.

Eduin's overture had been gracious, especially given the awkwardness of the situation. Carolin would have urged that he—or anyone for that matter—be given the benefit of the doubt. So, for Carolin's sake, Varzil would do his best.

Varzil nodded and murmured, "It's all right."

10

A year later, snow was late in falling at Arilinn. Autumn had stretched on, frosty mornings melting into lazy heat. Across the Plains, grasses dried to pale gold. Farmers harvested their crops and then rested, basking in the mild weather. Several weddings, which had been originally planned for the next spring, took place early amid outdoor feasting. Families offered gratitude and prayers for continuing fertility to the goddess Evanda. A few of the gossips down in the city swore that the coming winter would be a bad one, but their warnings met with little credence as Midwinter Festival approached.

On the morning Varzil was to leave for Hali and the Hastur court, the snow shone as if lit from within by its own light. Winter had arrived in earnest only during the last tenday, with falling temperatures and snow-falls overlapping each other. Still, the air of well-being persisted in both city and Tower. Granaries and silos were full, animals fat, tempers sweet.

Varzil stepped through the Veil and made his way along the streets toward the small airstrip. In a little over one short year, he had evolved from awkward newcomer to rising star, the pride of Arilinn. He had made such rapid progress that instead of preparing first as monitor, then rising through the ranks, Auster had decided to take charge of his training directly as under-Keeper. Rumor had it that Auster had long resisted choosing a replacement; now he joked he had only been waiting for the proper student to appear.

Carolin, having completed his time at Arilinn, was returning to the court of his uncle, King Felix, in Hali. As part of the festivities of Midwinter and also to postpone the time of their parting, he had chosen Varzil and Eduin to accompany him.

Varzil never dreamed that his friendship with Carolin might lead him to such august surroundings. Some moments, he didn't know whether he was awake or dreaming—to visit such a fabulous city, as honored guest of its most powerful family, as well as to be chosen as under-Keeper. It had all happened so quickly, Auster's interview followed within days by Carolin's excited invitation. So now he had chosen to walk to the outskirts of Arilinn alone, to where Carolin's aircar waited.

Varzil slung a canvas bag over one shoulder, which contained his best clothing and a few gifts for Carolin's female relatives. His holiday shirt would surely be considered plain by city standards, but it had been made with loving care by his own sister, Dyannis, embroidered in Ridenow gold and green.

Someday, he told himself, *I will wear a Keeper's crimson, and then it will not matter how costly the fabric or how stylish the cut.*

His spirits rose, and not even the thought of a half-day's journey in close confines with Eduin could dampen them. Since the first circle in which they worked together, the bonewater healing over a year ago, relations between the two had been civil, at times almost cordial. Eduin had no family of any distinction, even one as scandalous as the Ridenows; he had few friends other than Carolin who could help him advance in the world. He had strong *laran,* yes, but no hope of political influence. And with his insecurity went a kind of ambition, which Varzil could sense but not understand. Being a *laranzu* of Arilinn, surely the greatest and most prestigious of the modern Towers, must be glory enough. Varzil had the sense to realize that not everyone thought as he did, that one man's dream was another's nightmare.

It was still early when Varzil spotted the very same aircar which had carried him and his father to Sweetwater. The strip itself was little more than a leveled field. The men whose job it was to sweep it had just begun their morning's work. Ice-crusted snow crunched underfoot as Varzil approached the aircar. A man clambered over the arching roof, scraping off snow. Varzil squinted up at the figure silhouetted against the brightness of the eastern sky. Then the man called down to him, greeting him by name, and Varzil recognized the pilot.

"How are you this fine morning?" Varzil cried. "It's Jeronimo, isn't it?"

"The very same, and speak for yourself, laddie. It's not particularly fine to spend one's morning scraping off snow and ice, but I don't trust those rabbit-horn-brains from town with my ship." The pilot dropped lightly to the ground. He held a long horse-bristle brush in one hand and a bone scraper in the other. A towel was tucked through his belt. He grinned broadly. "Ready for another flying lesson? Or is that beneath you now that you're a high and mighty Arilinn *laranzu?*"

"Honest work is beneath no man's dignity." One corner of Varzil's mouth quirked upward. "Unless you're trying to tell me that flying one of these contraptions *isn't* honest work?"

Jeronimo laughed, throwing back his head. "True enough. Some days it's nigh onto stealing, to take m'lord's money for something I'd pay to do!"

He took Varzil's bag, stowed it in the lower compartment, and handed Varzil the brush. "You take the other side and we'll be ready to fly in no time."

They were just finishing up with the aircar and a flurry of jokes when Carolin and Eduin arrived, followed by a cart bearing their baggage. Two of the silent *kyrri* trotted alongside, patting the draft *chervine.*

"Leave it to you, Varzil, to beat us here," Carolin grinned.

Varzil ducked his head, about to protest that he needed the extra time just to keep up. Carolin had teased him more than once about false modesty. After Auster's decision, Varzil could hardly pretend he was only an ordinary student. So he held his tongue while the conversation flowed on.

Jeronimo stowed Carolin's chests, making sure they were well secured. The day was fair enough, but at this season, storms could come sweeping across the Plains with little warning. By now, the takeoff path had been cleared. The pilot gestured for the three passengers to take their places. There was some jostling, and Varzil realized that Eduin intended to sit beside Carolin.

"If you don't mind," Varzil said, "I should like to sit in front, beside the pilot, to study the operation of the aircar."

Carolin looked a bit surprised, but Eduin gave him a look that said how little he regarded such an interest, how inferior to the work of the Towers. Varzil happily took his place beside Jeronimo.

As soon as Jeronimo activated the *laran* apparatus of the aircar and set it into motion, Varzil was struck by the difference between this flight and the one he had taken a year ago. Then the whole process had seemed mysterious. Now, after months of intensive training, his talents heightened by contact with so many Gifted minds, he could follow every movement, every shift in power, as if illuminated by the brightest sun.

Jeronimo paused in the middle of a spoken explanation to gaze at Varzil with an expression of astonishment. Varzil had been in direct contact with his thoughts, following without intrusion as the pilot routed the power stored in the *laran* batteries along the conducting mechanisms. Jeronimo's eyes widened. His hands, forming the complex gestures that supported and guided his thoughts, fell open on his lap.

"Have—have I in some way offended you?" Varzil asked.

"How could you offend me?" *I have not felt such a strong mental touch since I left my own Keeper.* Jeronimo bowed his head. *"Vai dom."* The phrase meant "worthy lord" and betokened the respect due to one of greatly superior rank.

"Jero." Varzil reached out to touch the other man lightly on the back of one wrist, Tower-style. "You are a trained *laranzu* in your own right and need never feel less than any other man. Not even a Keeper. For just as each part of the body performs its own function to sustain life, so do we each have our own Gifts. I do not even know what mine is, not entirely. But *yours* is no less because of anything *I* might do. Do you understand?"

Jeronimo's shoulders straightened, though he would not meet Varzil's eyes.

"I thank you for sharing your knowledge with me," Varzil said in the awkward pause that followed.

Hours sped past while below, the snow-blanketed Plains stretched on. Varzil spied a line of purple hills along the horizon. When he asked, Carolin explained they were approaching the southernmost tip of the Kilghard Hills. Northward, toward the land of the Altons, the hills grew wilder until they blended into the savage Hellers. But here, on the brink of the lowlands, they seemed tame and pleasant.

For a time, the hills seemed no closer. Then they disappeared from sight. Varzil, looking up from the afternoon meal of cold roast lamb and bread smeared with ripened *chervine* cheese, thought Jeronimo had turned the aircar to face the wrong direction. The sky itself turned hazy, all color bled away.

Varzil shivered. "Must we go through that to reach Hali?"

"It's nothing, *vai*— Lord Varzil," Jeronimo said, following his gaze. "Low-lying clouds, most likely."

From the back seat, Carolin said, "The winter winds often blow fog banks up against the hills. They look worse than they are. Jero has flown through them dozens of times."

No, these are no ordinary clouds.

Varzil reached out with his mind, tasting the air ahead, cold and moist, tinged with the metallic hint of ozone. He did not have strongly-developed weather sense, as some others at Arilinn did. A trained circle could shift a rain-laden cloud from one course to the other by manipulating the winds. It was said that those with Aldaran lineage could not only redirect natural weather patterns, but create new ones, sucking up water vapor from rivers and lakes, building gauzy clouds into massive thunderheads, moving storms wherever they wished.

In Varzil's mind, the clouds billowed, piling one on the other and darkening with urgency. He seemed to be soaring above them, diving into them. He gasped, struck by the dense wet anger of their weight, the quicksilver lacing of electricity. The clouds formed a body, giant and misshapen, with nerves of jagged brilliance. Varzil felt himself a mote battered in its turbulence, hurled into a maelstrom of white and gray. Powerless to resist, he tumbled through ever-darkening, narrowing circles, drawing closer, ever closer to the black heart of the storm. In an instant, the surging darkness cleared and he glimpsed a Tower below. It stood, pure and white against the shadow, as if caught in a single ray of sunlight.

Energy, stark and acrid, condensed into light. A cascade of lightning poured forth, raging toward the Tower.

NO!

The word tore through him. In its reverberation, his vision cleared and he looked down once more on the snow-crusted Plains of Arilinn, rising now into gentle hills. Fog, soft and translucent, gathered in the crevices at their feet. The aircar rocked like a cradle.

"It is as I said," Jeronimo said. "A little wind, nothing more. Some men have weak bellies for such things, but that's hardly a source of shame. Is it so with you?"

Varzil shook his head, wishing it were as simple a matter as an uneasy stomach. He'd seen a storm, a terrible storm, with lightnings hurling at a Tower. Perhaps it had only been his imagination, fed by stories of the destruction of Neskaya. Even as he hoped so, he knew it was not. He had seen a real storm, in another place, another time.

But where? And when?

✦

Hali, as seen from the air, rose like a glittering mountain of turrets. A Tower rose, solitary, from the far outskirts of the city. Shrouded in the distance, invisible in the gathering gloom, lay the fabled Lake.

The aircar began its descent and the Tower was lost to view. The late afternoon sun flashed crimson off the many-paned windows of the city and bathed the buildings in a dusky glow. As they drew nearer, Varzil noticed pennants hanging like multihued streamers, giving the appearance of ongoing holiday. He stared at the houses of stone and wood, sprawled across the city's length. People on foot, riders and vehicles of every description filled the streets, from rude haywains to elegant carriages and litters. He longed to walk those streets, to see and touch and taste for himself.

Jeronimo guided the aircar into the very heart of the city and set it down in a spacious courtyard of what must surely be the largest, grandest castle of them all. When they came to a halt, Varzil sat immobile, overwhelmed.

"Wake up, blockhead!" Carolin reached forward and tapped him on the shoulder. "This is home."

By the time the door swung open and they descended to the pavement, a small crowd surrounded them.

"Carlo!" A young woman with red-gold hair, wearing a gown of soft gray-green and bundled in a shawl of the same hue, cried out. She had been standing a little apart from the others, holding herself with poise beyond her years, but when she saw Carolin, she rushed forward. "We've missed you so! I can hardly believe you're here!"

Carolin grasped her outstretched hands. "I've missed you, too, Maura, more than I can say—and you," turning to the tall angular man at her side, "Orain. Are your wife and son here with you? Alderic must be a fine boy now."

"He is well enough, thank you."

"Jandria," Carolin continued, "how good it is to see you all again! Here—these are my friends, Eduin and Varzil."

Orain gave a polite bow, his face with its lean hatchet jaw betraying little feeling. Jandria curtsied, grinning broadly, but Maura gave a dignified nod. Her manner was not unfriendly, simply reserved. Varzil had seen that remoteness before, in his fellow Tower workers. His mind brushed against hers. Her eyes lit in recognition.

"It is Varzil of Arilinn!" Although she did not offer her hands in greeting, her whole form lightened in joy. "And Eduin! Of course! Forgive me—I did not recognize you!"

"Nor we, you," Eduin said warmly, "although we have talked many times through the relays."

"We all assumed Carlo was bringing a couple of his drinking companions from the town." Jandria's grin turned mischievous. "Not such fine company! I hope you are not too exalted to enjoy dancing, or we shall all pass the Festival as gloomy as *cristoforos!*"

Maura turned to Varzil, lowering her gaze shyly. "We are also distant kin, did you know? My mother was a Ridenow. When she married my father, half of Elhalyn went up in scandal as hot as any forest fire and then hushed up the whole business. She felt it better to say little about her family after that." She tossed her head, expressing her opinion of the situation. "Our cousin, Ranald, was with us here a season ago, but you will not meet him this time."

"I knew nothing of this," Varzil said slowly. "I thought—" *I thought there was such ancient suspicion between Ridenow and Hastur that such a thing was impossible.*

"Where is my cousin Rakhal?" Carolin broke in, his eyes searching the knot of servants who were even now unloading the luggage and carrying it to the castle. "Is he ill, that he is not come to greet us? And Lyondri?"

"Oh!" Jandria made a face, slipping one hand through Carolin's arm. "They're inside, dancing attendance on your uncle. As if the King could not settle on the proper dinner menu without their help!"

"Dinner!" Carolin clapped one hand to his stomach in a dramatic gesture. "I'm starving!"

They proceeded toward the castle. Maura walked at Varzil's side. "You may not have heard. Your sister, Dyannis, has just come to us at Hali to begin her training."

Varzil brightened. His own struggles for his father's permission had borne unexpected fruit, then. Otherwise, *Dom* Felix would surely have kept Dyannis at home until he could find a suitably noble husband to enhance the family's prestige. He caught an image of doors opening in every direction, Hastur and Ridenow as allies, men settling their differences at the Council tables instead of the bloodied fields.

"Dyannis has great talent," Maura went on, with that directness so characteristic of a skilled Tower worker. "And she is sorely needed. We cannot afford to turn away any with the Gift. Is it not so at Arilinn?"

"Varzil has just been chosen to train as under-Keeper," Carolin said, climbing the wide steps leading to the castle gates.

"Indeed?" Maura turned to Varzil, her gray eyes wide. "That is wonderful news. And you, Eduin, we have heard of what a powerful *laranzu* you have become."

But not a Keeper. Not yet. Varzil felt the bitterness in Eduin's unguarded thought.

Maura continued, unconcerned. "Carlo, what do you think? Shall I ask the Keepers if Dyannis may join us? Then all the family will be together for the holiday."

"It is just like you, Maura, to be so thoughtful."

"To be so bossy," Jandria teased, "arranging everything her own way! It's a lucky thing that women can't be Keepers, or she'd have us all dancing in a circle!"

"Janni!" Orain exclaimed, with the easy familiarity of a kinsman. "It is not seemly to say such things."

"Oh, I don't mind," Maura said with good humor. "These are modern times, after all, and just because there never *have* been women Keepers doesn't mean there never *will* be. As for myself, my dear foster-sister, I am content with the Gifts of the Sight."

That explained Maura's innocent self-assurance. She was not only a *leronis,* but one of a select few women, highly trained and pledged to virginity for their clairvoyant talents.

They passed through the massive gates and into an entry hall. Within moments, Varzil and the others were separated and led to their private quarters. Varzil's chamber at Arilinn was spacious yet simply furnished, a place of quiet retreat rather than an entertainment in itself. Now he stood in the middle of an antechamber leading to an entire suite of rooms, easily as spacious as the entire Ridenow apartment in the Hidden City.

Tapestries covered every wall, many of them depicting scenes from the "Ballad of Hastur and Cassilda" in tribute to the august ancestry of the house. Every piece of furniture seemed to be carved, gilded, or inlaid with mother-of-pearl. The bed in the inner chamber stood upon a platform, covered in wine-colored brocade, which could easily have accommodated a Dry Towner and any number of wives and concubines. Beside it stood an armoire huge enough to walk into and a heavy, sumptuously carved dresser topped with a slab of marble so highly polished Varzil could see his reflection in it. The basin and ewer of rose-scented water were costly porcelain, painted in fanciful designs.

Varzil's single bag lay in a misshapen heap at the foot of the platform. He picked it up and carried it to the armoire, carefully placing his few articles of clothing on the shelves. The wood of the interior smelled pleasantly of cedar and lavender, but clashed with the fragrance of the bathing water. If he had to sleep shut up with so many incompatible scents, he would awaken with Zandru's own headache.

He started at a knock on the door. A man in a fine jacket and breeches of Hastur blue and silver entered. Varzil stared. The fellow couldn't have been more than a year or two his elder, but his natural features were masked behind a thick coating of powder, his cheeks and lips painted crimson. Surely hair did not grow that brassy color or have such a lacquered gloss. The courtier reeked of yet another perfume, this one a mixture of incense resin and something musky.

With a respectful half bow, the courtier said that if the young lord would prepare himself, His Majesty would receive him shortly before dinner. The man's eyes flickered to the opened armoire. He added that attire suitable for court could be made available for guests.

Indignation flared. Varzil fought to keep his composure. His own awe at finding himself in the midst of such ostentatious wealth vanished in an instant. He knew what the courtier saw—a poor boy, undernourished and badly brought up, a nobody from nowhere, here only by Carolin's graciousness in sharing a holiday with the less fortunate.

I am a laranzu *of Arilinn, and I am a Ridenow, of a noble house. I will hide neither, and certainly not behind borrowed finery!*

He said, in as mild a voice as he could summon, "I thank you for your courtesy. I am quite content as I am."

The man's eyes widened in disbelief. Varzil almost laughed aloud at his discomfiture as he bowed again and retreated.

Varzil donned his best holiday shirt and a vest with the Ridenow colors when a page, young and sweet-faced, came to escort him to the throne room. Varzil heard the throng before he fully descended the stairs. Court had clearly been in session and petitioners as well as courtiers, spectators, castle servants and guards in Hastur colors filled the enormous room.

So many people in one place! Not for the first time, Varzil silently blessed the training that protected him from the psychic onslaught. Every person possessed some small degree of *laran,* which in ordinary people manifested as intuition or sympathy, sometimes as an aptitude for animal husbandry or languages. At a gathering such as this one, with so many Hastur kin and minor clansmen, the small amount of *laran* of each, taken together, was enough to batter a susceptible mind.

It would be unthinkably rude to read the thoughts that swirled around him, but more than that, Varzil knew all too well that to open himself to the chatter and surge of emotions would quickly make him frantic. He took a deep breath, touched the silk pouch containing his starstone to help him focus, and thought of stone walls. It was a technique Auster had drilled into him, for the more vivid and detailed the visualization, the more solid the buffer. Varzil's image included the seams between the gray stones, their surfaces worn by season upon season of rain, the flecks of black and reflective mica, the streak of pink granite running through the central block. . . .

The mental turmoil receded to a hum. Varzil breathed more easily, the muscles of his shoulders relaxing. He descended the last two stairs and crossed the wide hallway into the throne room. Before he could be swept up in the throng of courtiers, he spotted Carolin near the front of the room.

Tall and handsome, his flame-red hair impeccably cut, Carolin would have stood out, even in this elegant gathering. He wore a suite of dove-gray suede trimmed with blue bands embroidered with the silver fir tree emblem of the Hasturs. It seemed to glow faintly, creating a subtle aura of power, or perhaps the effect was due to his carriage, graceful and proud, and the contrast with the garish costumes around him.

At some distance, Orain stood beside a short woman in extravagantly layered gilt lace. She looked considerably older than he and would have been pretty, but for the lines etched around her eyes and mouth. She held the hand of a bright-faced lad who kept glancing at Orain. Although the boy could not have been more than nine or ten, the promise of his *laran* surrounded him like an invisible corona.

A herald called out Varzil's name, along with Eduin's. He hurried forward. The crowd parted in front of him, as if an invisible shield had pushed them out of the way.

Eduin had been standing near the front of the audience, prepared to take his turn, splendid in a jacket and breeches of shimmering ivory brocade, his shirt of fine Dry Towns *linex* trimmed with lace at throat and wrist. Even his boots, of buttery leather, were those of a noble courtier. From this close, Varzil could see the pins tucking in the jacket and the way the tops of the boots pinched the flesh of Eduin's calves.

Standing at the foot of the dais, Carolin smiled, his gray eyes warm, and beckoned the two of them forward.

Varzil took a deep breath and prepared to meet King Felix Hastur, the most powerful man on Darkover.

11

An immense, age-darkened throne dominated the dais, looming over the assembled crowd. Strands of silver wire glinted along the armrests and high back, highlighting the carved fir tree of the Hasturs and contrasting with the thick blue cushions.

The throne dwarfed the figure perched there like a child's forgotten doll. For a moment, Varzil could hardly believe this old man was truly Felix Hastur, ruler of the most powerful Kingdom on Darkover. He had expected someone more heroic in appearance, but then, what did he know of kings? Like everyone else, he had heard stories that Felix Hastur was *emmasca,* neither male nor female. Such folk were often very long lived and Gifted, but sterile. Hence, Felix's heir must be the oldest son of his next younger brother, since he had no progeny of his own. His two marriages had failed to produce even a single pregnancy. If he'd ever sired a *nedestro* son, no one had ever heard of it.

It was hard to believe that Carolin's father had been this ancient King's brother, though Carolin had explained there were nearly two decades between their births. Their own father, he who ruled in Carcosa before Felix, had buried several wives and sired his two surviving sons when his contemporaries were long in their graves.

King Felix may have once been an imposing presence, but now his skin hung over his bones like an oversized garment, powdered and draped to dry. Behind him, their postures respectful, stood an array of attendants. Most were gray-haired and somber in their robes of fur and jewel-toned velvet. They must be counselors, Varzil thought, or kinsmen, especially the two young men with the red hair of the *Comyn* who stood the closest, within easy hearing. Somehow, they reminded Varzil of a pack of dogs circling an old wolf, uncertain of the beast's strength, unwilling to risk a charge, waiting. Waiting . . .

The king straightened on his throne. One hand, skin flecked with age spots, lifted; one bony finger pointed at Eduin and Varzil. The room hushed.

"Where is Gerrel, my brother?" King Felix demanded querulously. "Why is he not here to attend me?"

One of the youths beside the throne bent closer. His elaborately cut velvets could not entirely disguise his stocky build or the flush over his cheeks, the puffiness beneath his restless eyes. Though he spoke in a low, soothing voice, his words meant only for the king, Varzil made out their meaning.

"Your Majesty will recall that Prince Gerrel is dead these past twelve years. These are Prince Carolin's friends, come with him from Arilinn to celebrate Midwinter Festival with us."

"Oh?" Something flared in the rheumy eyes, and Varzil sensed the keen alertness, the confidence of a century and more of undisputed rule. "Yes, of course, we must extend the hospitality of the Hasturs and bid them a proper welcome. Carolin, my boy, come here. You have been away too long."

Carolin paused before the dais to perform an impeccably respectful bow, then stepped up and kissed the old king on the cheek. His natural affection and ease smoothed away the moment of awkwardness.

"I'm home now, Uncle. I've finished my time at Arilinn and have learned all they could teach me, all that befits a Prince of Hastur. It was for this you sent me there. I've brought my new friends to present to you." Carolin gestured for Varzil and Eduin to approach the throne.

The old man's face had brightened at Carolin's first words. But now he glared at the newcomers. His eyes reflected a pellucid, colorless light, suggesting the fabled *chieri* blood coursed through his veins.

He has been king for a long time, Varzil thought. *Who am I to judge, if the weight of so many years lies heavy upon him?*

Old and tired though he might be, for the sake of Hastur and hence for all of Darkover, this frail old man must somehow muster the strength to continue until his nephew was properly trained to rule. Younger men than Carolin had been thrust into positions of power, even less well prepared than he, and fallen prey to the machinations of those with ambition far exceeding their station.

Carlo trusts too much, Varzil thought. *And this court is no place for such a generous heart. He will need loyal friends.* But who among this painted, perfumed crowd could truly be counted as a friend?

King Felix spoke again, drawing Varzil's attention. It took a few moments for the crowd to become quiet enough to hear his words.

". . . royal pleasure to announce that the wedding of Prince Carolin and Lady Alianora Ysabet Ardais has been set for Midsummer festival . . ."

Varzil strained for a look at his friend. An elderly courtier turned to his neighbor and said, "What a relief to have that settled at last. It's a brilliant match, of course. She's to inherit all the borderlands along the Scaravel River."

"Aye, that will stabilize the whole region," his companion nodded.

At that point, a round of cheering erupted spontaneously. Carolin turned to the crowd and bowed his head in acknowledgment. Varzil could read nothing of his friend's thoughts, or see anything behind the graciousness of his smile.

Carolin, like any young man of his caste, would have been betrothed as soon as it was certain he would survive infancy. His foster-brother, Orain, was not only married, but had a son. The only reason Varzil himself had not already been promised in marriage was his sickly boyhood constitution. Had the catmen rescue not intervened, his father would probably have set about finding a suitable alliance for him shortly after his presentation at the *Comyn* Council. It was the way of the world.

Carolin had never spoken of his betrothal, which suggested he hardly knew the girl. This, too, was the usual custom. Varzil's own parents had never set eyes upon each other before their wedding day and they had lived amicably enough together, producing six children, four of them living. A man couldn't ask for more in these uncertain times. An ordinary man, that is.

But Carolin was *not* ordinary. He had *laran* enough to be trained in a Tower and his very nature—passionate, romantic, loving honor and learning—set him apart. Although Varzil had yet to take a lover at Arilinn, he knew the impossibility of a telepath attempting physical intimacy where there was no sympathy of mind, no direct communion of the heart. It would amount to coupling with a dumb beast. He knew himself incapable of such a thing.

Varzil, watching Carolin receive the congratulations of his royal cousins, felt a pang of loss and of disappointment. Already, his friend had moved beyond the world they'd shared to a place he could not—and had no wish to—follow.

◆

After the formal reception concluded, the king withdrew to his own quarters, where he would dine with his family and their guests later that evening. Those courtiers and holiday guests staying at the castle would be provided for in the old style, at trestle tables to be set up in this central hall. As soon as King Felix departed, servants began rushing this way and that in preparation. Maura, Jandria, and Orain disappeared in the crush.

Courtiers gathered in swirls and knots, and Varzil noticed how they maneuvered for advantage among themselves. There were subtle distinctions here, of who greeted whom, who was the first to withdraw. He caught snatches of conversation. Two ladies, elegantly dressed in the tartans of Hastur of Carcosa, speculated in shrill voices on the problems of genetic recessive traits in the Scaravel Ardais.

"At least, inbreeding won't be an issue," one sniffed.

"Oh, I had thought it a sure thing for Prince Rakhal and Lady Maura, for all she's an Elhalyn and therefore, kin."

"Not that close," the first lady said, tapping her friend's arm with her folded fan. "Nothing can move forward on that match until she's released from her Tower and, if you ask me, that's not likely any time soon. It's no wonder his attention strays."

"Dear me! I was sure they were meant for each other, being fostered together since they were children."

"Mark my words, if she delays long enough, the King will find him another match. I wouldn't be surprised if we see a whole flurry of weddings. I'll have to order a dozen new gowns at least. The King's positively enraptured with the idea—"

The lady's gaze passed over Varzil as she moved by. She lifted her chin and turned, making her way through the assembly.

The stocky youth who had reminded King Felix of the death of Carolin's father now pushed his way through the throng to greet Carolin. They embraced as kinsmen.

"These are my friends from Arilinn. My cousin, Rakhal." Carolin bent toward Rakhal so that he could be heard without shouting. "My uncle—how long he been like this?"

"He'll be better now that you're here," Rakhal answered in the same private tone. "I must attend him in his quarters now. Today's excitement has clearly been too much. He's not strong, you know. He sat for hours all last tenday, hearing cases that should have gone to the *cortes*. But a little care will see him right." Rakhal bowed and headed back toward the dais.

The second youth lingered behind. Varzil regarded him curiously, for the initial resemblance to both Carolin and the departed Rakhal was strong, going far beyond their striking red hair. He'd been mistaken, though. These three might be blood kin, but they were nothing alike. Whereas Carolin held himself with an unconscious grace and Rakhal seemed stolid, a man who might run to fat without the habits of exercise and self-restraint, this youth was thin and nervy, unsettled in himself. He would have benefited, Varzil thought, with a season or two of Tower training.

Jandria emerged from the crowd, walking arm and arm with Maura like sisters. Her eyes flickered to the empty dais. "We'll see little of Rakhal tonight, as he's taken over all the personal duties of the King's paxman," she commented to no one in particular.

"You say that as if it is not a good and noble thing," the second youth said.

"Don't be so sensitive, Lyondri!" Jandria replied.

"We are all aware of how dutiful Rakhal is," Maura said at the same time.

"And if one of us should happen to forget," Jandria went on without drawing breath, "*you* will surely remind us. Ay, me! They will be at least an hour setting up here and in the King's quarters. Let's find Orain and sneak off."

"I'm here," Orain spoke from a pace behind Carolin. He moved so silently and stood so still, Varzil had not noticed him approach. Courtiers edged by them, muttering excuses. "Rakhal sends his compliments and bids us go on without him."

"Then let's get out of here before we're trampled." Maura flinched visibly as a courtier brushed against her. "We're directly in the path of the kitchen traffic." She turned to Lyondri. "You'll join us?"

Lyondri nodded and held out his arm for her. Jandria followed by herself and Orain beside Carolin, leaving Varzil and Eduin to follow.

A young servant girl, flushed with exertion, jumped sideways to avoid a lady's beribboned skirts and stumbled under the weight of her burden, a huge pottery jar. She collided with Eduin and the jar splashed wine in every direction before sliding, miraculously unbroken, to the floor. Dropping to her knees, she tipped it upright, but not before a pool of garnet liquid had escaped. Then she looked up to see the dark splatters across Eduin's fine *linex* shirt and jacket.

"Oh, sir!" she cried, her face reddening even more. "I'm so sorry, sir!"

Eduin brushed at his jacket, but it was no use. The droplets had already sunk into the fabric.

"Oh, sir!" The girl was almost in tears, growing more incoherent by the instant. With her bare hands, she tried to scoop up the spreading puddle. She reached up as if to wipe Eduin's clothing, but he jumped back.

"You stupid—" Eduin cried. "Don't you touch me! Haven't you done enough?"

The girl cringed, bracing herself for a blow.

She has been struck before. No servant at Sweetwater was ever beaten, no matter what the shortcoming. Dismissed, yes, or judged and punished. *Dom* Felix had once ordered a man hanged for poisoning a well that led to the deaths of two children. But that had been an act of deliberate malice. A beating would scarcely improve bad luck.

"Eduin, you're flustering the poor child—" Varzil began.

"Look at these stains! How can I dine with the King looking like this?"

Varzil had never seen Eduin so distressed, and over such a trivial matter. Then he remembered how Eduin had strutted his borrowed finery earlier in the evening. Varzil's own family might live simply, but they had lands and servants, warm clothing, decent food, fine horses to ride. No necessity of life was ever lacking. He had been presented to the *Comyn* Council in attire as fine as theirs, had been accepted among them as an equal. He had never—and now he looked at Eduin with new insight—been poor.

Other details came back to him, Eduin's obscure origins, the rumors of his birth being the unwelcome result of a liaison between a well-born lady and a stable hand, even his hair, muddy brown instead of the shades of red so common in those with *laran*. No wonder Eduin had always seemed so serious, often grim, about his status at Arilinn. No wonder he had reacted with jealousy to any intrusion into his friendship with Carolin, his resentment of Varzil's more rapid advancement. Varzil could only imagine what scars he hid behind those polished barriers, what fears that the little he had in life might be so easily taken from him.

Varzil crouched beside the girl, focusing his *laran* through his starstone. It was a simple enough matter to increase the surface tension of the wine. Instead of a sheet of liquid, quickly spreading on the tile floor, it assumed a rounded shape. By further tightening the outer layer, Varzil was able to gather it up like a bag of jelly and ease it back into the jar. The girl, who had been watching with fists pressed over her mouth in astonishment, gave a little cry.

Varzil helped her lift the jar and balance it in her arms. With a look of naked adoration, she hurried away.

"Watch where you're going!" Eduin called after her. "Varzil, I am not the Keeper of your conscience, but you need not have wasted your *laran* trying to help. The chit was clumsy and should have had to clean up after herself. That's the only way people like her will ever learn."

Varzil doubted that being publicly humiliated and beaten would teach the girl anything except that nobles were to be avoided. Remembering Lunilla's kitchen wisdom, he said, "Those wine stains should lift out easily, especially if we do it before they set." He lowered his *laran* barriers in an overture to work together.

"I don't want your sympathy!" Eduin snapped. "And I certainly don't need your help!"

Varzil drew back in surprise. Eduin had been courteous, if not overtly friendly, since they'd worked together in the circle this last year. He had no idea what he had done to deserve such a response—maybe nothing. Perhaps he was merely a convenient target.

Ah, Varzil thought, not all the smiths in Zandru's forge could mend a broken egg or a man's stubborn nature, or so his father was fond of saying.

"Shall I tell the others you will join us shortly, then?" Varzil said. Under other circumstances, he would have remained behind, so that Eduin would not be left alone in such a bewildering place. Clearly, his own presence was as much an irritant as the splatters on the ivory brocade.

◆

Varzil wandered down the corridor to Carolin's chambers, past standing guards and closed doors. Maura stuck her head out of the largest door and beckoned to him. "Sean," she called to the guard at his post outside, "watch out for Eduin."

Carolin's sitting room was almost as large as the family gathering hall at Sweetwater. If all the suites were this big, it was no wonder the castle sprawled over so much territory. Varzil glanced around at the richly patterned Ardcarran carpets, the panels of pale blue translucent stone, so smooth and perfectly matched that they could only have been set by matrix work, the deeply cushioned chairs and divan, the low table of blackwood set in a mosaic of ash and mother-of-pearl. Warmth swept across his bare face from the fireplace with its marble mantle carved in a life-sized relief of Aldones, Lord of Light, and his son, the very first Hastur, the one who had become mortal for love of the Blessed Cassilda and thereby founded the clan of his name.

Carolin and Orain had already made themselves comfortable on the divan facing the fireplace, with Jandria in an armchair. Lyondri shifted from one foot to the other as if unable to make up his mind whether to stay.

Maura drew up one of the two remaining chairs at a comfortable distance from the fireplace and gestured for Varzil to do the same. The chair was wooden, although of graceful design and excellent crafting, softened only by a needlepoint cushion. She settled herself, back straight, feet primly tucked beneath her skirts and hands folded in her lap.

Varzil took his own seat. "There isn't another chair for Eduin."

"We can send Sean for one," Carolin said.

"That rather defeats the purpose of posting a guard, if you insist on ordering him about on menial errands," Lyondri said. "Maybe things are different at Arilinn."

"I think the three of us can manage to defend the honor of the ladies, if that's what you're worried about," Orain said laconically.

Lyondri scowled and was about to respond when Jandria broke into laughter and said, "Orain, we can take care of our own honor!"

Maura added, lightly, that with two and a half Tower-trained *leronyn,* the half being Carolin, or three and a half when Eduin showed up—they had nothing to fear. "I rather suspect it is *we* would end up defending poor Sean and not the other way around."

But no one made any comment about there being nothing to fear, here in the family seat of the Hasturs. The powerful Kingdom of Hastur might be at peace for the moment, but that did not guarantee personal safety for the King or his heir.

Arilinn, with its Veil which admitted only those Gifted with *laran,* was an isolated fortress. In a circle, in the training rooms, even in the evening gatherings, people shared an intimacy of mind. Surely no outsider could penetrate that community.

"What is it?" Maura bent toward him.

Varzil shook his head. A little shiver, half premonition, crossed his shoulders. "I was thinking about Arilinn, which is so—so self-contained."

Lyondri asked where he had come from before Arilinn. Though the question was posed politely enough, it had an edge, like a blade slipping noiselessly from its scabbard.

Varzil took no offense, though he knew one was intended. There were currents within currents here, like a river with hidden rocks and shoals, deepness and unexpected eddies, rapids to slam a boat onto hungry rocks. The sunny moss-laced banks, like the sumptuous furnishings, were a lure and soporific for the unwary. He did not yet know where his allies lay, or which practiced smile masked self-interest and malicious intent.

He replied, pretending the question was nothing more than a courteous inquiry, but before he had said more than a few words, Eduin arrived at the same time as a bevy of servants bearing trays of hot spiced ale, bread, and winter-crisp apples and bowls heaped with honey-glazed nuts and round cookies redolent with spicebark. Varzil recognized them as a special Midwinter treat, with their dusting of sparkling honey crystals. He noticed, too, that Eduin's jacket had once more been restored to its pristine appearance. Varzil felt the faint residue of the mental power Eduin had used to remove the wine stains.

"Ah, Eduin! You have saved us from starvation!" Carolin cried. Taking the bowl of nuts, he offered them to the others. Maura took a few, as did Orain and Lyondri, but Jandria said she'd wait for a proper dinner.

At the smell of the food, Varzil felt a thrill of nausea. He instantly identified it as a combination of the natural fatigue of a long journey and the expenditure of his *laran* in gathering up the wine. He bit into a sweet bun and refused the hot wine, knowing how potent it would be, as hungry as he was. He needed to keep all his wits about him.

Eduin, too, helped himself to the energy-replenishing sweets, although he accepted a steaming goblet. For a long, awkward moment after the servants had left, the new friends sat or stood, feigning concentration on their food.

Carolin broke the silence, directing his words at his cousin, Lyondri. "Rakhal is slow in joining us tonight. Has he forsworn our company?"

"He is much in the King's attendance since you went to Arilinn," Orain said with an odd hesitation.

"You say that as if it were not the proper role for a kinsman," Maura replied tartly. "Yet who else should tend His Majesty in his time of need?"

Carolin paused, setting the nut bowl beside the other vessels. His brow furrowed and a tightness crept into his voice. "I was not informed the King was ill. Why was word not sent to me at Arilinn?"

"He hasn't been ill, not exactly, nothing more than the natural infirmities of age," Maura said. "For some ailments, there is no cure."

"There was no reason to disturb you," Lyondri added. "Prince Rakhal has personally supervised every aspect of the King's care."

"*Prince* Rakhal?" Carolin said, his head coming up. "Have we become so formal with one another?"

"He is the son of the King's younger brother," Lyondri said, bowing to Carolin, "even as you are of the older, Your Highness. "Your return to Hali has brought you one step closer to the day when you take the throne. You must therefore assume the dignity of your rank."

Carolin glanced from Maura to Orain and his cousin, Jandria, to see if any of them took this statement seriously.

"We are no longer playfellows together, with no greater thought than tomorrow's amusement," Maura said gravely. "Lyondri has the right of it."

"Maura, I never wish to be anything but your true friend," Carolin said.

"You will someday be my King," she insisted, "and that is a fate neither of us can escape."

Carolin reseated himself beside Orain and stretched his legs out toward the fire. "Please do not trouble yourself on the matter of titles. There are enough forces in the world to drive even brothers apart, without the need for artificial distinctions. Here, in this room, we are cousins and friends together. Surely we all remember the hours we played together as children in these very halls. Come now, sit here at my side, Lyondri. Be at ease. Let us enjoy this festival time, renewing our ties with old friends and greeting new ones. There will be time enough later to discuss affairs of state."

A strange look passed over Lyondri's features as he lowered himself to the chair. The significance of being seated at Carolin's right hand had clearly not escaped him. The taut lines of jaw and mouth eased, granting him a more open, generous expression.

And so they sat, talking of one inconsequential thing or another—the birth of a foal from Orain's favorite mare, the marriage of a lady visibly pregnant with another man's child, the cook's disastrous attempt at a sugar cake in the shape of a dragon in flight—until at last dinner was announced and they went downstairs in amicable relief.

12

In his season at Arilinn, Carolin had gotten into the habit of waking before dawn. With the night's work finished, the circles dispersed and those tasks requiring daylight had not yet commenced. In the summer, when Carolin arrived, this was the most pleasant time, but as the days shortened and ice rimed the balcony outside his room, he continued to rise, bundled in layers of plaid, to look out.

His room had faced the Twin Peaks, earth reaching for sky and man humbled before both. He thought it a fitting reminder for a king-in-waiting. The stillness of the morning settled in his bones and as he watched the great Bloody Sun clear the horizon, staining the heavens with its light, it seemed that all the world stretched before him, silently waiting to see what he would do with it.

He had always known he was no ordinary man, he who would one day be a king. Until he had come to Arilinn and bent his mind to its discipline, he had not realized that an even greater destiny might lie before him.

Wrapped in his fur-lined cloak, Carolin looked out over the courtyards of Hastur Castle and beyond to the roofs of Hali and wondered if he would ever know that same stillness in his heart, in his very soul, again. The castle was never truly quiet. There was always someone up and about, some guard or scullery boy, some counselor bent over his papers, someone in the stable fretting over a lame horse or a whelping bitch.

This is my home, my place, he reminded himself for the hundredth time since he had arrived. Tomorrow would be Midwinter Day and the feasting would continue until the next dawn. A few days after that, Varzil and Eduin would return to their Tower. He would be alone in the midst of a crowd as he had never been, for though he still loved the companions of his childhood, they had not seen what he had seen within his own mind, nor felt what he had felt.

Soon they, too, would go their separate ways. Maura would return to Hali Tower and the difficult, demanding work of the Sight. Orain might remain for a time, for he was Lyondri's sworn man, but eventually must return to his estate and family. It was a pity the marriage, arranged by King Felix, had turned out so badly. It was not in Orain's nature to desire any woman, but the two had despised each other from the start. Orain had a fine son who clearly adored him, but Orain was too consumed with antagonism for the boy's mother to appreciate or even see the love his son had for him.

It was time to leave behind the things of his youth. Soon it would be time to be King. But not quite yet.

Movement caught his eye, a figure slipping out through the kitchen door and into the courtyard, leaving deep footprints in last night's snowfall. From the height, the form inside the bulky clothing was unrecognizable, but Carolin would have known him anywhere. Who else would pause by the well, as if listening to the heart of the earth? Who else needed a moment of private reflection as a fish needed water or a falcon its wings?

"Varzil!" Carolin yelled.

There was no need. His friend had already turned to look up at him and raise one hand in greeting. Carolin hurried down the stairs, brushing past guards and maidservants carrying piles of linens, brooms and buckets, and ewers of steaming, scented water for the royal suites. He rushed through the kitchen, the rooms hot and aromatic with the day's first baking.

Varzil was still standing beside the well when Carolin reached him. The ice-edged air caught in his throat. As he drew near his friend, exhilaration tingled through him.

Let's run away! he wanted to shout. *Let's ride to the end of the Hellers and beyond!*

"What are you doing out here?" he said.

One corner of Varzil's mouth quirked upward in that odd half-smile of his, as if he radiated some secret delight. "What are *you?*"

"Let's go down into the city," Carolin said. "There must be some place we can find *jaco* at this hour."

"An adventure beyond the gates?" Varzil said. "Risking assassination or kidnapping? Lyondri would turn himself inside out if he knew, like the goat in the ballad, although for very different reasons."

"Are you defying your prince?"

"Are you my prince?"

"Impudent Ridenow, have you no respect?" Carolin threw his arm around Varzil's shoulders and started toward the gate. He had been taught at Arilinn to avoid such casual contact, but sensed no recoil from Varzil. The gesture was received as naturally as it was offered.

The guards at the gate looked uncertain whether to let Carolin pass or insist upon accompanying him. Carolin waved them back, saying that only the righteous of heart would be abroad at this hour. Miscreants must surely be in bed, sleeping off their evil deeds. Before the guards could formulate a reply, the two friends swept through the gates and into the city.

Hali, unlike mountain towns like Nevarsin, had been laid out with broad avenues. Snow had been swept from the center of each street and piled alongside the buildings. Here in the lowlands, it was possible to keep the streets clear. Anywhere in the rugged Venza Hills or the Hellers, the drifts would have piled waist-high at this season.

With frost-reddened cheeks, women and a few men went about their business. They called out greetings to one another. Some carried baskets of goods to be delivered, bundles of kindling wood, or yoked buckets of water. One man led a team of pack *chervines,* their harnesses jingling with bells.

Carolin and Varzil headed for the marketplace, where a few hardy souls had already set up booths screened from the wind. Farmers offered winter fare such as apples, cabbages, and redroot, along with barrels of the season's fresh cider. A baker had set out a table in front of his shop with trays of steaming spice buns and braided honey cakes.

"Young lords! Try my fine cakes!" the baker's wife cried, wiping her hands on her apron. Her cheeks glowed in the cold.

"*Jaco!* Hot *jaco!*" someone else called from the far side of the square, echoing the canto and response of the *cristoforo* ceremonies.

"Apples! Who'll buy my apples! Fresh as the day they were picked!"

"Ribbons! Fine ribbons for my lady's hair!"

Carolin ordered two mugs of *jaco* and then realized he'd left the castle without any money. The vendor didn't recognize him, and was clearly suspicious of a richly dressed youth attempting to use his status for a free drink. When Carolin started to direct the man to the castle for payment, Varzil handed the man four or five small silver coins. The man stared at the unfamiliar design stamped on the metal, tested one against his teeth, and pocketed them with a grin.

"And a fine mornin' to ye both, m'lords," he said.

"I guessed the amount, since I don't know your currency," Varzil admitted as they moved away, sipping their hot drinks. "It was probably too much."

"Too much for the *jaco,* yes, but not for the convenience of the hour and the price of the mugs," Carolin said.

After a pause, Varzil said, "He didn't know you."

"No, though some of the richer merchants do, the ones who've been to court. I lived here only a few years before I left for Arilinn. No, I am not a city man, by either birth or choice, though now that must change. I grew up in the country, at my mother's estate of Blue Lake. Very beautiful in the summer. Peaceful, too, although I didn't appreciate it at the time. At Arilinn, I missed it far more than the castle here. Still," he sighed as the pang of homesickness passed, "Hali is a place like no other. There is but one *rhu fead,* where the holy things are kept. There are many lakes, but only one at Hali."

It is the proper abode for a Hastur of my lineage. Blue Lake was my childhood, Arilinn a school holiday. Now my real life begins.

Varzil looked pensive. "I hoped to see the lake. I've heard about it since I was a child, how it contains strange clouds that one can breathe instead of ordinary water, and of the creatures that swim in its depths." He did not add that there would be no convenient time for such an expedition, not with the arrival of more guests and members of the other branches of the Hastur clan, all eager to use the holiday gathering for political stratagems, matchmaking, and gossip.

And then, came the unspoken thought, *Eduin and I leave you to return to Arilinn.*

Carolin had not thought of what it must be like for Varzil, to be here in Hali, a place he'd heard of only in tales and ballads. Even a generation ago, no Ridenow would have dreamed of walking freely in the stronghold of the Hasturs. He himself had been so occupied with his uncle's health, the news of his impending wedding, and catching up with the affairs of the court that he'd had little time to play host. Eduin had happily danced attendance whenever invited. Varzil stayed quietly in the shadows, never drawing attention to himself or asking any favors.

Varzil, as if catching his thought, said quickly. "It doesn't matter. Let us enjoy this brief freedom, until some assistant *coridom* comes to fetch us back."

Carolin, however, was still infected with the wildness of the morning and longing to escape the intrigue and confinement of court. An idea came to him, like many he'd had as a boy. There was a stable where he was known. Money would not be a problem.

He downed the last of his *jaco,* leaving his tongue half-scalded. Grabbing Varzil's mug, he thrust them both at the nearest passerby, a young girl in a threadbare cloak carrying a bolt of cloth. The burden was too big for her, but somehow she managed to keep hold of it and snatch the mugs before they fell. Her eyes shone and Carolin realized that, to her, the crockery represented an unexpected treasure, far better than any her family possessed. There were no beggars in Hali, but not every family was well off.

"Come on!" Grinning, Carolin headed for the stables.

Varzil knew immediately what he intended, for their minds were in light rapport. He did not demur or advance arguments why a prince should not go on such an expedition on the eve of Midwinter Festival. That was one of the things that made Varzil so peaceful to be around. Varzil was always pliant. Carolin had seen his stubborn nature on that morning at the Arilinn gates. Yet Varzil seemed for the most part content to let others run their own lives. . . .

Unlike Lyondri, Carolin thought ruefully, who seemed to know exactly what everyone else's duties were and never hesitated to remind them at every opportunity. Varzil was right. His cousin would create an enormous fuss. This made the prospect of an adventure even more appealing. They must make the most of the morning's freedom.

The man in charge at the stable recognized Carolin and produced
two saddled horses. They were the best of the stock for hire, which meant
they had leather mouths and bone-jarring gaits but no lethal habits like
rearing over backward. Shortly, they took off along the road to the lake.

The horses bobbed their heads in rhythm, blowing vapor from their
nostrils. Ice crunched beneath their shod hooves. As the city fell behind,
banks of untouched snow spread out on either side of the road. Icicles
hung from the split-rail fences and ferny patterns of frost sparkled on the
low stone walls. Hedgerows lined the fields, stark and leafless beneath
their dusting of white.

When they were halfway to their destination, they heard behind them
the sound of galloping hooves. Even as he turned in the saddle, Carolin's
hand went automatically to where his sword should hang beside his knee.
It was not there. He had no need of one within his own quarters and he
had rushed down to the courtyard and then to this morning's adventure
without thought. Even within the fastness of Hastur territory, that was
extreme carelessness.

Black against the fields, a rider urged his horse toward them, still far
enough away to hide his features. He wore no colors, not the blue and
silver of Hastur, nor any other.

We could outrun him—

Varzil's laughter cut the thought off. "We have no need to flee *this*
rider!"

Carolin's horse danced under him, infected by his own agitation.
"How—?"

Stupid to ask. This was *Varzil,* who sometimes knew what he was
thinking before he himself realized it. Varzil who had brought his brother
out alive from the clutches of the catmen, despite the fact they never
bargained or kept prisoners. Varzil who had first touched his mind—and
reset his shoulder—when he'd unaccountably lost his balance in the orchard at Arilinn.

With an odd shiver, the thought came to Carolin that he was safer in
Varzil's presence than anywhere else, even the mightiest fortress.

"Lord Carolin!" the voice ghosted along the road.

"Orain!"

Carolin recognized the horse as one from the very same stables, a
flea-bitten gray with stiff hock joints and a nasty temper. Orain had ridden it hard. Its sides heaved like bellows and dark lines of sweat streaked

its hide. Orain himself looked no better, his angular face set, eyes somber. He was, Carolin noticed, armed.

"What are you doing here?" Carolin asked.

Orain flushed. "What are *you?*"

"Obviously, we're on our way to the lake. Did Lyondri send you to keep an eye on me?"

Varzil flinched at Orain's reaction. "Carlo, Orain couldn't have known where you were going, only that you had left the castle without a proper escort. What else was he to do?"

Carolin felt ashamed at his temper. Love, not the scheming of the court, had sent Orain after him. It was cruel to mock such loyalty.

"I'm sorry," he said to Orain, "it was a lark, just like when we were boys together. I never meant to cause any worry, least of all for you."

"We aren't children any longer," Orain said stiffly.

That's exactly what Maura said.

Carolin's horse shifted uneasily beneath him, catching his wave of emotion. He had only wanted to extend the holiday a little longer before taking on the mantle of the Hasturs, waiting until the time he would be King. At Arilinn, it had been easy to forget, to be simply Carolin.

"Since you've come this far," Carolin said, shaking off the mood, "let's go on together. Your sword and Varzil's thunderbolts will be more than enough protection!" He turned his horse toward the lake and set heels to its sides, not waiting for an answer.

"My *what?*" Varzil cried, kicking his reluctant horse to keep pace.

"Can't you shoot lightning out of your fingertips? I thought all *leronyn* could do that!" Carolin chuckled at Varzil's outraged expression.

It occurred to him later, much later, that was not a thing to joke about.

✦

The lake came into view, just as Carolin remembered it. From a distance, it resembled a ground-fog that never lifted or moved, despite the winds and clearness of the sky. The sun was now full up and glimmered on the misty surface. At the far end, the Tower stretched upward, a slender structure of the pale, translucent stone so treasured by the *Comyn*.

They pulled their horses to a halt near the shore, and heard the soft splashing of the waves that spilled onto the banks. Varzil dismounted to scoop up a handful of the hazy stuff.

"It's neither water nor cloud," Carolin said, repeating what his tutors had said. He swung down from the saddle. "You can walk right through it to the bottom. Orain and I tried that once—what, six years ago?"

Orain nodded. He remained on his horse, his eyes scanning the horizon. That was so like Orain, to keep apart, watchful. In a rush, Carolin resented the reminder of danger.

"Come on." Gesturing to Varzil, Carolin walked into the lake.

Varzil exclaimed as the cloud-water billowed against his boots, more like dew than liquid. He pulled back, trembling. Chest-deep, Carolin turned. "What is it?"

"Can you not feel it?" Varzil asked. "This place—how did you say the lake was formed?"

"We don't know. The event is called the Cataclysm. There may have been records once, but if any still exist, they are lost." And a good thing, too, or someone would surely have resurrected whatever terrible weapon changed an ordinary lake into this ghostly place.

Varzil shook his shoulders and the waters around him quivered with the movement. "It's gone . . ."

"What?"

"For a moment, I thought . . . You know that physical objects can retain *laran* impressions, particularly of strong emotions. Well," with a brightening smile, "we've come this far. Let's go on, so that I can tell the folk back at Arilinn about the bird-fish the minstrels sing of."

They went on. Carolin took a breath and ducked his head beneath the surface. The sun, full up now, filled the waters with its brilliance. Against all his instincts, he opened his mouth and inhaled. It was like breathing thick fog.

The rocks of the shore gave way to sloping, sandy banks. The atmosphere grew denser. Carolin forced himself to breathe regularly and the sensation of suffocation eased.

Below, shimmering green and orange objects flickered in and out of the cloud currents. Carolin touched Varzil's sleeve and pointed.

"Bird-fish." The mist-water muffled his words.

Near the flat bottom, long green grasses waved in an intricate, undulating dance, some longer than the height of a man. Carolin stumbled on a stone beneath the surface of the sand. The light was dimmer here. The brilliantly colored creatures swam or flew in schools, darting and diving in unison. Their hides flashed luminescent whenever a stray beam of sunlight touched them.

Varzil held his hands out to the bird-fish, calling gently to them with his *laran*. The Ridenow were said to have a particular empathy with animals and it must be so, for they clustered around him, the tiny red ones slipping through his outstretched fingers like living ribbons. Varzil's delight rippled through the waters, and, through their faint rapport, Carolin found his own heart lightening.

Carolin would have been content to turn back, but now Varzil took the lead, leading them even deeper. The bird-fish followed them for a distance, darting in and out to nibble at their hair or stare with curious, unblinking eyes. The waters darkened as less light penetrated its depths. Just beyond the limit of vision, pale lights flickered in and out.

More bird-fish? Carolin wondered, *or something even stranger?* The skin along his spine crawled and the sense of freedom faded. Shadows pressed in on him, and the currents created shadowy, inconstant figures among the grasses.

He reached out to Varzil, to draw him back toward the light, but his friend shook his head and went on.

What was he to do, leave him here? Varzil knew nothing of the dangers of the lake at Hali; the need to keep breathing even when the urge was absent, the warning signals of fatigue and confusion.

Just a little more, and then we will leave, if I have to drag him out by force!

Varzil halted, so suddenly that Carolin bumped into him. Varzil pointed, creating swirls of cloud-water with the movement. Ahead, half-seen through the dim currents, lay a huge shape, many times the length of a man. Carolin could not be sure if it really existed or was some trick of the light and turbulent mist.

As they approached, however, he saw solid stone, a single fallen column. Sand and water weeds laced its surface. He could not make out its original color. Even worn by time and the surging cloud-waters, the contours looked smooth, as if they had been worked by matrix technology. There were markings, so obscured he could not decipher them.

Somehow, he did not want to touch it.

Varzil, in his usual fearless way, went right up to the fallen column. It came to the level of his knees. With one arm outstretched for balance, he reached down with the other and laid his palm flat on the stone.

And screamed.

13

A scream resounded through Varzil's mind, drowning out sound and sight. It raced along his nerves, filled the hollow of his bones, shivered through his blood. The dark currents of the cloud-water faded from his vision. All he could see was white haze. Within moments, he lost all awareness of his body and surroundings. He could not even feel his heart beating or remember his name. Like a frozen particle in a vast and nebulous sea, he drifted. The last echoes of the scream died to silence.

As his unblinking eyes cleared, shapes appeared before him. At first they were but silverpoint tracings against the stippled whiteness. Gradually, they took on form and substance. Their outlines remained blurred as if he were peering through a cracked lens.

He looked down upon a Tower as if from a great height, one he had never seen before. The translucent stone shone as if lit from within, but the color was subtly wrong, an uneasy ashen gray.

Then, in the strange way of dreamers, Varzil descended. He passed through the stone walls as if he were no more than a bodiless wraith. Radiance suffused the space in which he found himself. It burned along his ghostly skin.

Laran. The air trembled with it, a type and intensity he had never felt before, not in his work at Arilinn, not even as a child newly-awakened to his powers, listening to the Ya-men wailing out their songs beneath the four moons.

Varzil traced the source of the *laran*. He was inside the Tower now, looking down at a circular room. It appeared subtly wrong, out of focus. The room was a large one, judging by the people gathered there. Seated on their benches, they looked very much like a working circle. A table occupied the center of the room, dominated by a huge artificial matrix.

The matrix was octagonal in shape, easily double the arm span of a man, and so layered as to be half that tall. Pinpoints of blue light sparkled in a frame like a weaving of spiderwebs. The table on which it sat glowed with tiny bits of iridescence, which resonated with the power of the matrix.

Varzil had never seen an artificial matrix of such size and power before. At Arilinn, circles worked up to sixth or seventh level. A sixth-level matrix required six trained workers plus a Keeper in order to operate it safely, and the conservative Arilinn circles rarely exceeded that number. Theoretically, it was possible to construct matrices of any order—nine, ten, even more—but the higher the level, the greater the potential for disaster. A single weak link in the circle, a faltering heart or lapse in concentration, could unleash the power of the matrix in some uncontrollable direction. Neither Auster nor any other ethical Keeper would countenance the risk.

By the energies which surged through it, this must be a twelfth-level matrix, or possibly higher. Varzil counted fifteen people in the room, most of them robed in muddied gray, plus a single man in the crimson that had been reserved, from time immemorial, for Keepers.

Where on the face of Darkover could such a thing be? How had it remained hidden?

And what did this nameless circle intend to do with it?

Power crackled through the lattice, threads of brightness that lingered in his vision like phosphorescent vapors. It made him uneasy to look at them. Visceral-level revulsion to the thing built inside him.

Varzil could not understand his reaction, unless it was some effect of the strange condition in which he found himself. He had encountered *laran* power before—in the matrices at Arilinn, in the circles there, within himself. He respected it but did not fear it.

Suddenly, he realized why this matrix was different. All of the other devices and natural uses of *laran* he had known had been, in their very essence, human. Starstones worked by concentrating and focusing natural mental talent. They did not generate it of their own, nor did they draw power from any other source. *Laran* energy, created by individual *leronyn* or by circles working together, could be stored in batteries and other apparatus constructed of smaller, individual starstones.

But this one—somehow, against all his experience and everything he had been taught, it tapped into another source. The origin of the power was not human, of that he was certain. He was not sure it was even alive. It both terrified and fascinated him.

Although it was the last thing he wanted to do, he forced himself to open to the enormous matrix. Sensory impressions flooded his mind, too intense and brief to identify. He caught the ozone reek of lightning, of water, of ashes, and yet none of these was right.

"Va'acqualle—spies! 'imyn! . . ."

". . . kiarren . . . put an end to it . . ."

From the circle of workers below came voices, muffled and oddly cadenced. The fleeting contact with the matrix had brought Varzil more firmly into this world. They had become aware of him. One woman, her hair now visible as a wash of pale red against the misty gray, glanced up in his direction. Varzil drew back, suddenly reluctant to make himself known before he understood what was going on here. The woman's gaze continued across the room without stopping. Her mental query slipped past him as if he was not there. The feeling of dislocation, of seeing and hearing echoes, sharpened. This *leronis* was both alert and skillful, yet she could not see him.

What was going on?

Was he looking into the past, into events imprinted into the very substance of the stone pillar?

Yes, that must be it. Those words he had been able to distinguish were strangely accented and archaic in pattern. But if he were glimpsing some ancient circle at work, did that mean a Tower once stood here, in the middle of the lake? Why was there no record of it, not even in the archives of Arilinn?

Where was he? *When* was he?

Below, the woman who had glanced up now returned to her work. Varzil felt the Keeper reach out for his circle and begin forming them into a single unit. The Keeper's *laran* felt dim and distant. With a technique completely unfamiliar to Varzil, he joined the individual members. If Varzil was not very much mistaken, this Keeper wove their human minds into the pattern of the matrix itself. Not only that, he was doing this with an offhanded ease that suggested he had done it many times before, nor was there any hint of resistance from the circle. They, too, accepted this melding of their human minds with the inorganic, mechanical structure of the matrix lattice as normal.

What Varzil was witnessing should not have been possible—starstones, even joined and tuned at a very high level, could only *amplify* the natural mental energies that passed through them. It was the stones that served the humans, not the other way around.

Lord of Light! What unholy thing was taking place? And what did they intend to do next?

It took all his Arilinn discipline to hold himself immobile, not to take some precipitous action and by doing so, reveal himself. He must not risk an emotional but ineffective outburst.

As the circle members dropped, one by one, into unity with the matrix, their individual personalities dissipated. The stones of the lattice pulsated, at first slowly, then gaining speed and brightness as more minds were added. The outlines of the men and women blurred and the room darkened, but perhaps that was only in contrast to the increasing brilliance of the matrix. Each new burst of radiance cast a wash of blue-gray on the faces of the workers.

The room itself seemed to slip and distort. Outside, mountains like jagged fangs rose treeless and dim under a single moon. Varzil knew only one place on Darkover where such bleak, lifeless peaks reached their lonely heads to the empty sky.

This cannot be Hali, Varzil realized. *It must be somewhere deep in the Hellers.* But since the destruction of Tramontana Tower a generation ago, there was no working circle in all that mountain range.

No wonder his senses kept unsettling, no wonder the odd echo of sight and sound. He was not only looking into the past, but across the distance of half a continent. A thought crept through the back reaches of his mind, one he did not like at all.

Aldaran.

The thought brought a sickening realization. For the circle below him was now complete, in obscene union with the gigantic matrix. The impression of lightning and ashes escalated until it permeated every fiber of his presence. Yet the focus of the energies was not skyward, toward cloud or rain, but down. The circle reached toward the core of the planet, seeking the lines of its magnetic fields.

To gather those vast inhuman forces—and do what? Send them where?

Hali. The Tower at Hali?

The thought rang out in his mind like the clanging of bells.

Hali! Hali! Hali!

A surge of alertness answered him, a break in the concentration of the circle below. They had heard him.

"*Hali-daemon! Spy!*" Like sickly green fire, *laran* burst from the circle toward him. Reflexively, he threw himself back.

No! I come as a friend!

"*Hold thair imyn!*"

The next lash of power, following a heartbeat after the first attack, spread out like a burning net. In horror, Varzil watched it speed toward him. The room twisted around him.

The first of the tendrils touched him. It lanced through his astral form, as caustic as acid. Agony shocked through him. Breath burst from his lungs. His vision went white, then gray. He could not see the circle below him, not even the once-brilliant pulsations of the matrix nor his own ghostly form. He shriveled to a mote of pain, a mote that was moving, slowly and inexorably, downward. A maw of darkness gaped wide to swallow him.

No!

His mental cry sounded feeble and tinny, but at least he had a voice. He threw all his determination into the next outburst.

"*NO!*"

The echoes beat back the grayness. Dimly, he made out the circle, the dots of overshadowed light, the pallid walls. Power gathered below him, murky and swollen.

Hali—I must warn them at Hali—

Varzil pulled away, backward through the Tower walls. He glimpsed the mountains for an instant before they faded into mist. For a moment, he feared he had entered the Overworld, that strange realm of mind where neither time nor distance had any meaning. But no, there was no smooth gray footing, no unbroken colorless sky, no directionless watery light, none of the markers he remembered from his brief, guided introduction.

He floated in a world of shifting vapors, curling faintly into eddies and currents . . . like the cloud-waters of the lake.

The Lake at Hali.

Air, heavy with moisture brushed his skin, gaining substance with each passing instant. He felt the stomach-wrenching dislocation of time—

No! I cannot go back, not yet! Not before I warn them!

Hali. Though he had never been inside the ancient Tower, he pictured it in his mind just as he had seen it this morning, a tall slender structure, graceful and adamant. He knew the minds of those who now worked the relays at Hali, but he must not think of them now, least he be drawn even more firmly into the present.

He must concentrate on Hali as it had once been, the age-smoothed stones newly cut, their edges sharp and clean, the translucent panels still fresh from their shaping. A lake of ordinary water skimmed by a morning breeze, motes of reflected light dancing in the sunlight. A city between lake and Tower, white like alabaster splashed with the brilliance of pennants and banners, arbors, gardens, bejeweled fountains. A city of peace and splendor like none he had ever seen, and everywhere the mark of *laran* workmanship, minds harnessed to create a paradise.

The images came to him fresher and stronger now, with an urgency he could not contain. His inner senses came alert, resonating with the tension lying like an invisible pall over the Tower and all the lands around.

Hali! The Tower! Surely there must be *leronyn* awake at this hour who could hear him, even unaided by relay screens.

As his mind reached out in wordless greeting, he slammed against a mental wall so solid, the impact stunned him. Only the concerted action of a full circle could produce so complete a barrier. Not even a hint of presence escaped from within.

Listen to me! He threw all his power into the silent cry. *You are about to be attacked! Watch out! Prepare yourselves!*

For a long moment, he sensed no response. He might as well have been shouting at the wind. There were *laran* workers within, gathered in a circle, minds focused, of that he was certain. They had turned away from the outside world and armored themselves against intrusion. Perhaps they already knew of the imminent attack and were preparing for it.

It came to him that the events which would create the present-day lake had *already* happened. His warnings must go unheeded because they already *had* gone unheeded. There was nothing he could do to change the past.

How easy it would be to give himself over to that thought, to simply imagine himself back in his own place and time. These people were long dead. Why exert himself to save them when they must inevitably perish from age or disease, even if they escaped whatever monstrous weapon Aldaran was even now preparing.

Even now . . .

Varzil could not turn away. He *knew,* and with knowledge came responsibility.

Perhaps his own actions here had saved Hali and all its people from an even greater catastrophe. Perhaps he would have no effect. Whatever the outcome, he would still have his own conscience to deal with . . . if he survived.

He hovered above the lake, the clear waters kissed into the lightest ruffles by the morning breeze. Moment by moment, he sensed a pressure build in its cerulean depths. At first, there was no visible sign, yet he never doubted it.

Pressure . . . imminence . . . The sense of something huge and terrible condensing. Forming, building. He had not realized how dark and cold the depths of the lake were.

Cold . . . but not the brittle burning cold of ice, the familiar cold of winter. It was a cold that no fire could warm. The lake, which had seemed so pleasant, now became a womb for something unspeakable, a thing beyond human imagining, conceived in Zandru's frozen hells.

The morning dimmed, all brightness quenched. The surface of the lake surged, turbulent, like a living thing writhing in the agonies of birth. The Tower itself called to it, summoned it, pulled it forth into day like an unholy midwife.

Varzil strained to make out the shape, vast and murky, on the lake floor. The waters hid it too well.

Suddenly, the sky above crackled to life. Thunder rolled. The heavens went white. Clouds, gray with fury, came boiling out of the north. Though he had no physical form, Varzil quailed with the suddenness and wildness of the storm. He knew thunder and lightning and downpour, the sudden nerve-tearing terror of rockslide and flood. But this, this was another thing entirely.

Focused as they were on the form beneath the lake, would the workers at Hali recognize the imminent danger? Or would they think themselves invulnerable in their Tower of unburnable stone?

Hali! he called again. *HAA-LL-II-II-II!!*

A sound like an avalanche filled the sky. Unlike natural thunder, it did not break and subside, but grew deeper and louder with every passing heartbeat. In the city, people streamed from their homes to throng the wide avenues. Varzil could not hear their cries nor the explosions as wooden structures burst into flame, but he felt them nevertheless.

The waters rose, whipped to froth. The banks of the lake were laid bare, though the depths remained inviolate, a fortress. All around, trees toppled. Stone walls cracked and shattered. The smell of blood and burning rose from the city.

Varzil held his breath, praying for the clouds to break and release their burden of rain, put out the fires, dissipate the awful tension. There would be no downpour of water from this storm, he realized, but something far worse.

Still the Tower stood, mute and inaccessible. And still the thing in the lake grew. Above it, in the belly of the densest, angriest cloud, darkness condensed into a knot.

The sky reached down to the land. Light exploded over the Tower. In an instant, all color fled. The city turned to whitened ashes and nothing moved as the light bled away.

Still no response came from the Tower. The focus of the circle turned frantic, as if racing for time.

They think they can hold out through the attack and complete their own weapon, the thing beneath the lake. And which, Varzil, wondered, would be the worse fate for the entire world?

Thunder crescendoed, but now there came a response. At first, it was only an echo, a resonance. The sky had reached down to the land and now the land itself answered. From all around Tower and city and lake, something rumbled up from the very core of bedrock and even deeper.

The lake began to boil. Steam rose in spurts from the surface. A shape surged through the waves, huge and black as moonless night, misshapen in its hurried birth. It shrieked as it came, the sound rising above the clamor of sky and land. Any creature left alive below would surely be rendered deaf. Flesh was not made to withstand such raging inhuman power, and even Varzil's tenuous mental form reverberated with it.

For a time—a heartbeat, an hour, he couldn't tell—Varzil lost all sense of where and when he was. He shrank to a kernel of himself, form-less and adrift, without bearings or senses.

Invisible winds tore at him, raked across the mote of personality that was Varzil. He no longer witnessed the clash of elemental forces from afar. He was caught up in the maelstrom itself. Battered and tossed, he clung to the tatters of thought. Each moment stripped away some part of him—his name went whipping away in the torrent, echoing as it went, *Varzil, Varzil, Varzil* . . . until the syllables disappeared into chaos.

Memory shredded, bits of images like petals crushed in a landslide—the feel of his arms and legs—food warm in his belly—the gleam in the catman's eyes—Carolin's quick smile—Dyannis prancing through the kitchen, carrying the Midsummer bouquet he'd gathered for her—his father's voice, rough with emotion—

Sound shaped itself into harmonics—a voice—a word—

"Varzil!"

Response stirred from far away. There was something he should know. Should do.

Gray drifted around him, the only world he had ever known, the only world which had ever existed. Timeless, eternal floating. Stillness.

"Varzil, you've got to breathe!"

Tinny and meaningless, the words swept over him, through him. They left little eddies of discord, quickly settling back into calm.

So quiet, so gray . . . All he ever wanted. All he ever was.

"Breathe, damn you!"

Something wet and soft clamped over his mouth. Air forced into his lungs. Gray receded. Pounding shook him—*lub-DUB, lub-DUB*. Then the racket subsided again into blessed stillness. He drifted once more toward the grayness, serene and eternal.

Another breath and then another. Solidness coalesced around him, hands on his shoulders, fingers digging into his flesh. Head and legs and cramping belly. Coughing racked him, wetness sputtering between his lips. He drew another breath, heard the rasp and wheeze in his chest.

Gray . . . yes, there was gray, but beyond him, misty currents that thinned and parted as he passed through them, half-walking, half-floating. A strong arm wrapped around his waist, propelling him forward.

"Come on, you can make it." The voice sounded muddy through the mist-water. "Keep going, that's it. We're almost there."

Varzil nodded, his throat too strange for speech. He staggered up the slope, toward the sunlight. He pushed with his feet, slipped on something, struggled up again. The ground steepened, but the light grew stronger. Long waving grasses gave way to sand pocked with rocks. He stumbled again, landed on hands and knees, and crawled the rest of the way.

Varzil's head broke the surface of the cloud-water just as his strength failed him. He sobbed a breath before sinking down. This time he knew who it was who caught him, who dragged him the rest of the way and laid him out on the shore, who bent over him, gray eyes dark with concern.

Carolin knelt by his side and turned him over. His skin and clothes were dripping, his face flushed except for the paleness around his eyes and mouth. Moisture darkened his red hair, slicking it against his skull. Varzil knew that he himself looked even worse.

When Varzil tried to talk, his teeth chattered. "Did you—see—" The words came out in a jumble of fractured sounds.

"Lie still."

Another man now bent over him as well. Lean, raw-boned, eyes burning. Orain.

"I don't know what happened," Carolin was saying, his voice muffled as if from a distance. "He started screaming and went into convulsions. Then he stopped breathing. I got him out as quick as I could."

"He looks like he's been to Zandru's coldest hell and isn't all back yet," Orain said.

Zandru's coldest hell. Very nearly.

Varzil broke into racking coughs. He felt consumed with weariness, drained in spirit as well as body.

I saw—I saw what happened. The Cataclysm!

". . . soaking wet," said Orain. "Put my cloak around him. Get him up and on the horse . . . take him to the Tower . . . they'll know what to do."

The Tower! No!

But the other Hali Tower lay in the far past, unimaginable years ago, the workers who summoned the thing in the lake long dead, as were their counterparts at Aldaran. Weak as a baby, Varzil allowed himself to be wrapped in Orain's thick dry cloak and hauled onto the back of a horse.

14

By the time Carolin and Orain had gotten Varzil on the rented horse, he was shivering too hard to hold the reins. If anything, Carolin thought, Varzil looked even paler than when he'd pulled him from the lake, with an odd gray-green cast around his mouth and eyes. The horses moved off smoothly, picking their way back along their own tracks in the snow. Varzil slumped over the pommel of the saddle, holding on with both hands.

They had not gone far when Varzil's horse stumbled on a stone hidden beneath the snow. It was only a slight misstep, quickly recovered. Carolin heard the break in the rhythm of the horse's gait and turned to see Varzil swaying in the saddle, making no effort to right himself.

Carolin vaulted off his mount and dashed up just in time to catch Varzil before he toppled to the ground. Orain cried out. Carolin staggered under his friend's weight, for though Varzil was slightly built, his body had gone inert, dense. Carolin feared he had fainted, or worse. A moment later, Orain put his own strong arms beneath Varzil and together they lowered Varzil to the snowy road.

"Varzil! Varzil!" Carolin shook him, feeling the muscles lax beneath the thickness of the borrowed cloak.

Varzil's head rolled with the movement. His eyes remained closed, lashes dark against cheeks barely darker than the snow. Blue veins showed through skin so pale and fine-grained it was almost transparent.

Orain laid his palm flat on Varzil's chest. "He breathes!"

Varzil stirred, though his eyes did not open. Ashen lips shaped words—a name. "Hali . . . Got to warn them . . ."

Warn them? Carolin and Orain exchanged glances. Hali was not under attack, not this deep into Hastur territory. Uneasy peace still held across the Hundred Kingdoms though there were no lack of enemies, but none on the brink of actual war. This much Carolin had ascertained from his uncle's generals.

Varzil! What has happened? If only, Carolin thought, he had the training of a full *laranzu.* Then surely he could reach his friend's mind.

With Orain's help, Carolin heaved Varzil in front of him in the saddle. As quickly as they dared, they made their way to Hali Tower.

✦

When Carolin had first arrived at Arilinn Tower the summer before, he had felt as if he were penetrating a mystery by degrees. The outer courtyards and wooden gate gave way to the arch of the Veil and narrow, enclosed rising-shaft. Like the Tower, the town of Arilinn was walled for defense. In the season he had studied there, he had never quite adjusted to the feeling of living in a series of nested fortresses.

But Hali was an unwalled city, broad and open. A city, he'd always thought, which welcomed the world without fear. A city built upon the presumption of peace. This was not, in fact, true—as he well knew. But the city gave the illusion of such tranquillity that he sometimes wondered, as he did now, what it would be like to live in a time when neither invading armies nor psychic assaults posed any threat.

As they neared the Tower, two men in the familiar, loosely belted working robes emerged. One of them introduced himself as a monitor of the First Circle.

"My friend—" Carolin began.

"What has befallen him?" the other man interrupted. "We sensed a great disturbance from the lake."

"We must get this one inside," the first man said, "where he can be warmed and treated properly."

What was wrong with Varzil was not the cold, Carolin thought. He made no protest as the two *leronyn* carried Varzil within. He followed, feeling the rush of awe as he passed the outer gates. As *Comyn* and Hastur, descended from that Hastur who was the son of Aldones, Lord of Light, he had been granted admittance to the Tower on several occasions, had seen the *rhu fcad* and the holy things. He did not think he would ever take this place for granted. Hali was not the oldest Tower on Darkover or even the most powerful, but it was a place like no other.

Orain stayed in the outer hall, shifting from one foot to the other. If this place was a source of awe to Carolin, who had been bred to it, how much more intimidating it must be to his commoner foster-brother.

They laid Varzil in a guest chamber and placed wrapped, heated stones at his feet and a mustard plaster on his chest. A second monitor, a tall woman whose white-gray hair gave no hint of its original color, came in to assist.

Carolin was dismissed to wait in the hallway outside. Although there was a bench, plain wood with a satiny finish, he preferred to stand, arms crossed over his chest, hands curled into fists and jammed into his armpits. Actually, he would rather have waited downstairs with Orain. Then at least he would have had someone to talk to.

Whatever happened to Varzil, whatever hurt he had taken from the lake, Carolin knew it was his own responsibility. If only he had not insisted on a wild and carefree morning. If only he had stayed in the castle, like anyone of proper sense and decorum. Rakhal or Lyondri would not have gone off on a lark, risking a friend's life if not his sanity. Why, why had he thought it a grand adventure to ride to Hali and the lake?

If you keep thinking like this, we will have two patients to tend to, and what benefit will there be in that?

Stung, Carolin whirled to see a slender robed figure that had come up, noiselessly, to stand beside him. For an instant, the hair and slight build reminded him of Varzil, but this was clearly a young woman, looking up at him with dancing eyes.

"Excuse me—*damisela,* but should I know you?"

She smiled, showing dimples, and tilted her head toward inside the room. "I am Dyannis Ridenow and that's my big brother they've got in there. Whatever did you do to him?"

The words were spoken lightly, without malice, but Carolin flinched. If Varzil died or lived on as an invalid, it would be his doing, his!

"Oh, my dear!" Dyannis said with unusual maturity, for she could not be more than fourteen. She laid one hand lightly on his arm. "I had no intention of distressing you! 'Twas banter, nothing more! Varzil is always getting himself into one scrape after another. Many a time, Father would rant and tear at his hair and say Varzil would put him into an early grave for certain, but no harm ever came of it." She tossed her head, looking very much like the young girl she was. "Varzil's like a cat. He always lands on his feet."

Carolin removed her hand. "This was no childish escapade."

"Whatever it was," she replied, taking no offense, "neither of us can help him by standing out here giving ourselves vapors."

He suppressed a grin as she led him to Hali's common room. This felt very much like the central chamber at Arilinn although it was quite different in furnishings. When Carolin had visited Hali Tower before, he had never penetrated this far into the heart of its community. The place had an air of ancient wealth, of layers of dust and polish, all the precious things brought here over the centuries. It was said that once students donated their entire inheritances to the Tower and pledged themselves to lifelong study there, as if they were *cristoforos* entering Nevarsin. Carolin had never before given any credence to such stories. No one today would think of turning over all his worldly goods, as well as any prospect of future wealth, just to enter a Tower. Except . . . Varzil would.

Now he wondered, just because things were not done in this manner now did not mean that they *might* have been different in the past. What everyone looked at as *the way things are done,* had, in fact, no more true substance than a mayfly. The thought teased him, how might things be even more different still in the future?

A servant brought *jaco* and meat buns. Dyannis refused both, but Carolin ate with a sudden appetite. The hot drink chased the morning's chill from his bones. While he ate, Dyannis talked of inconsequential things. She was clearly making an effort to put him at his ease, playing hostess although she had but lately arrived at Hali. Her chatter was inoffensive, her kindness evident. She had not yet adopted the aloofness of so many *leronyn.* He thought of Maura, and how skillfully she blended the demands of her profession and the Sight with warmth and easy good humor.

A short while later, Carolin's own kinswoman, Liriel Hastur, came to greet him and to prepare Dyannis for the trip to the castle. They, along with several other Hastur cousins from the Tower, were to spend Midwinter Festival and the preceding days of merrymaking at King Felix's court.

Lady Liriel was not only a skilled *leronis* in her own right, but *Comynara*. She was tall for a woman, slender and flame-haired like many of the Hasturs, and wore her rank like a coronet. No one, seeing her hair and her carriage, would have any doubts that she was to be obeyed without hesitation.

At Liriel's words, Carolin recalled his situation. By now, his absence would be noticed. Even without the disaster at the lake, his morning of freedom was over. His uncle would expect him. Yet he could not leave without knowing how Varzil fared.

Without missing a beat of the conversation, Liriel said that the young *laranzu* was recovering well from his unfortunate contact with an object so highly charged with *laran*. The effects were undoubtedly amplified by the cloud-waters of the lake, much as an ordinary water transmitted the energies of lightning. The monitors were clearing his channels and he was expected to make a full recovery. At present, she added in an offhand manner, the young man was too drained to permit even such a short journey, so regrettably he must remain behind and would join the festivities when he was able.

Liriel spoke as if it had already been arranged for Carolin and his man Orain to join her cortège. She made it seem as if nothing could be more natural than the royal heir riding out to the Tower to provide her a suitable escort.

The small party made its way back to the castle. Liriel rode at the head, riding sidesaddle on a beautiful white mare. The horse's trappings were blue-dyed leather with silver medallions fashioned in the Hastur fir tree motif. She wore a cloak of wine-colored velvet lined with silvery rabbit-horn fur. For an instant, the light reflected crimson off the fabric, as if, against all tradition and sense, she wore a Keeper's robes.

Watching Liriel's bearing and utter self-confidence, the thought came to Carolin that she would make an extraordinary queen. It was impossible, of course. Even if he were not betrothed to Alianora Ardais, Liriel was too old for him. Moreover, she had long ago made it clear that one of the prerogatives of her rank was the freedom to choose her own destiny, and that did not include marriage at the whim of her family. She was of the blood of Hastur of Hastur, a *leronis* of Hali Tower, and who was truly worthy of her?

But I, I have no such choice. I must marry and father sons.

Carolin sighed. His would be a union of state. If Evanda smiled on him, he would be granted a bride he could love. He tried to conjure up an image of the young Ardais heiress. He'd never seen her likeness, although his family and hers would exchange miniature portraits so the bride and groom might recognize one another on their wedding day. All he knew of her was that she was a year older and the *Comyn* Council had approved the match. Presumably, she was fertile and capable of bearing sons with *laran*. He had no idea what she was like or what her interests were—probably music, embroidery, and gossip.

"Ride beside me, Carolin," Liriel said, gesturing him forward. "There are matters I would discuss with you."

"Para servirte, vai leronis," he said, nudging his horse to a quicker pace.

"You have very pretty manners, but for the moment, I wish to speak frankly." She glanced back toward Orain.

"He is to be trusted," Carolin said.

"I prefer not to risk intrigue if it is at all avoidable," she said in a tone that did not convince him. She could no more forswear the schemes of power than she could cease breathing. "It is of Hali I would speak, Hali and her sister Towers. I have a favor to ask of you."

"What favor?"

"Ah!" Pale eyebrows lifted. "You have learned well never to give your word without knowing what it entails."

She went on to describe the problems caused by the reduced number of legitimate Towers. "We feel the loss of Neskaya and Tramontana exceedingly. Oh, there are renegade circles operating without either discipline or ethics. Dalereuth now makes *clingfire* for anyone with the copper to pay for it, and as for that nest at Temora, the less said the better." Her voice dripped scorn. "The smaller kingdoms turn to them because they have no choice. They harry one another like bandits."

"What is to be done, then?" What did she have in mind, a war of conquest to bring the internecine fighting to an end? A generation ago, the tyrant Damian Deslucido had tried that, with disastrous consequences.

Liriel kept her gaze straight ahead, as if peering into a future only she could see. When she spoke, the arrogance that had marked her earlier speeches vanished. "We wish—some of us have been talking—we believe it is possible—" She turned to him, swiveling in the saddle so suddenly that the white mare started.

"There is talk of reestablishing a Tower at Tramontana. Not at the old site, but nearby. Doran Alton, who is Second Keeper at Corandolis, has said he might undertake forming a circle, but that is all too soon without an actual Tower. It is for this purpose I travel to the castle, not an evening's silliness. And it is for this I ask your help."

On either side, the snowy hills stretched like mounded fleece. The sun was well overhead, filling the ruts and shadows with light. The tracks where the horses had trod earlier that morning had turned to puddles. A smell arose from the earth, of cold soil and wetness and waiting.

"I thought—there were so many lost at Tramontana and Neskaya, there are not enough *laran*-skilled workers to go around as it is," Carolin said. "How is such a thing to be rebuilt? Where will you find the *leronyn* to staff it afterward?" His eyes widened with a new thought. "You will not strip Hali?"

"No, no!" She raised her free hand, leaving the other one, fingers twisted in the reins, on the pommel of the saddle. "I would never suggest such a thing! Many of the Towers—Hali and Arilinn—have talented youngsters, like your friend. Some at Dalereuth would welcome the chance to do lawful work."

Carolin reflected. Yes, what she said made sense. With both Varzil and Eduin in training, either of whom could become a Keeper, Arilinn's future was assured. Each circle might contribute one worker, plus one or two more from Hali and perhaps the other Towers, Nevarsin or Corandolis or even Hestral, though that Tower had only a single circle. There would be enough.

"Who would go? How would they be chosen?" he asked, and realized that with the question, the idea had gone from conjecture to intention.

Liriel's smile warmed, no longer the thinning of lips but a genuine response. "We will ask no one who does not truly wish to come, who does not share our dream. With a functioning circle at Tramontana, we can extend the relays deep into the Hellers. Messages will no longer have to be routed through the very limits of our ability. There are experiments which are better done in those fastnesses. I—"

Now she laughed outright. "You must have guessed by now that I am to be one of them. Lady Bronwyn and I once talked of this—in fact, it was she who first voiced the idea. I ride now to seek her counsel. So while the rest of you are getting rowdy on Midwinter mead, she and I will be sitting up, huddled together like lady conspirators."

"I? Rowdy on mead? Oh, kinswoman, you have no idea of how dreadful a mistake that would be! Better to go barefoot into a nest of scorpion-ants than to be drunk at my uncle's court at any season!" He sobered. "What favor had you to ask of me?"

She tilted her head, her features still alight with fervor. "That when the time is right and I have presented him with this plan, you ask King Felix to undertake the construction of the new building."

"For Hastur to rebuild the physical Tower?"

"Towers do not rebuild themselves. Stone and mortar cost money, whether assembled by ordinary masons or by *laran*. You must convince him it is a good investment, Carolin. After all, Tramontana fought against Hastur in the last war. What better way to ensure our future benefit than to place the next Tower there under our control?"

Carolin could not argue with this reasoning, and it seemed a worthy cause. Even as he agreed to speak to his uncle, he wondered if Liriel's buoyant certainty were warranted. There was no way to look into the future, the way his illustrious ancestor, Allart Hastur, was said to do, and see which choices led to disaster and which to peace. A Tower was not a toy, that much he had learned at Arilinn. For an instant, he wondered what Varzil had seen in the lake, if it had been the work of *laran* gone wild or harnessed deliberately to some evil purpose.

Or, even worse, some purpose which seemed at the time to be the highest good . . .

Carolin and Liriel fell silent. They went on at a brisk pace, with Dyannis' pony trotting to keep pace with the taller horses. Her laughter rang out, a child's delight in an unexpected holiday. Carolin was glad she'd come along. It would have been cruel to exclude her from this night's festival just because Varzil could not attend.

At dinner that night, Carolin took his place at his uncle's right side, with Rakhal on the other. Others of his family, including his cousin Lyondri and Lady Liriel, sat nearby. Below, with the other kin, sat Maura Elhalyn and beyond her, at yet another table, Orain and Jandria, little Dyannis and Eduin.

Dyannis and Eduin were already deep in conversation, the girl laughing merrily and gesturing with her hands. Eduin smiled, nodding, and Carolin thought he had never seen his friend so relaxed, almost happy.

The banks of candles turned the air thick and golden, like honey, so that every face Carolin looked upon seemed to glow from within. His heart swelled with a feeling he could not name.

If only Varzil were here with me . . .

Even as he thought it, a sense of his friend's presence swept through him. The leagues to Hali Tower vanished. He could almost hear Varzil's voice.

Is it well with you, bredu?

Carolin's *laran* did not run strong in telepathy, yet the words seemed as clear to him as if they were in the same room. It was Varzil's strength, deceptive in his slender, almost effeminate frame, which would carry both of them.

15

After the evening meal came a period of rest and socializing, to be followed by dancing. It was often said that whenever more than two Darkovans gathered together, they held a dance. The tradition held sway for every night until the last guests had departed.

Throughout the next hours, couples circled and wove patterns across the open floor. Carolin, resplendent in supple leather dyed in the Hastur colors of blue and silver, danced with all the older ladies, as was proper for a young man of his station. Later in the evening, when stamina had worn thin and the elders had retired, there would be plenty of time to enjoy himself with his friends. For now, however, propriety must be observed.

The next dance, following a series of sets and reels, was for couples. Orain led his lady wife on to the floor, and rarely had Carolin seen their mutual aversion to one another so clearly displayed. She was of much higher birth, pressed unwillingly into the match by a family eager to curry favor with the king. Orain for his part had not dared refuse the honor bestowed upon him. Gratitude, Carolin reflected, could be the most insidious poison of them all.

Carolin watched Rakhal swing Maura in his arms. Her face flushed with excitement. Her sea-green gown, cut simply and crossed with the

Elhalyn tartan, set off the creamy smoothness of her skin and turned her hair into a glorious sunset.

Carolin frowned. Rakhal did not hold her as if she were his foster-sister and virgin *leronis*. Even in the short time Carolin had been back, he had heard whispers about his cousin's conduct with women, always brushed aside with Hastur charm. Surely Maura would not endanger the Sight, not even for the man who might someday claim her as his bride. Nor would Rakhal be so foolish to deprive Hastur of such a rare Gift. Before Carolin could say anything, however, the dance came to an end.

Rakhal held out his arm to escort Maura back to where the unmarried Hastur ladies sat, but she caught Carolin's eye and beckoned him over. "Carlo is quite as solicitous a partner as you are," she told Rakhal, "and I must have a word with him."

With a smile that stretched his mouth but did not reach his eyes, Rakhal handed her over. She slipped her hand through Carolin's elbow, pulling him aside.

"Is something amiss?" he asked, although clearly she had been enjoying herself. Damp curls had escaped the bejeweled net to frame her face. He caught the faint sweet whiff of mead on her breath, but her step was steady enough and her voice firm.

"Carlo, you have been dancing all evening with aunties who used to change your breechclouts, they've know you that long."

He sighed. "It is a small enough kindness, not to mention my social responsibility." The ladies were either widows or spinsters, and it would have been scandalous for them to dance with anyone but a kinsman.

"And it is your responsibility to make sure your guests have the opportunity to enjoy dancing, as well."

They approached the cluster of chairs occupied by the ladies in question, and for the first time, Carolin noticed Dyannis Ridenow sitting among them. Someone, probably Maura herself, had taken care with the girl's appearance, for her hair was coiled low upon her neck in gleaming braids, interwoven with thin silvery ribbons from which hung a cascade of tiny white bells. Her dress, a bit too big for her, was the shade of silvery-green that Maura loved, and it looked well enough on the girl. She wore no tartan, only a long scarf of white wool, so loosely woven it resembled lace, around her shoulders. While it was warm enough in the center of the dance floor, the perimeter tended to be drafty.

"She has no kinsman here to dance with her," Maura murmured. "I had hoped Ranald Ridenow would be with us, but he has not arrived." She gave Carolina playful push in the direction of the ladies. "Go on, now, and do your duty."

Carolin knew when he was being maneuvered. As host and the friend of her brother, he could dance with Dyannis without any stain upon her reputation. She smiled, recognizing him, even more delightedly as he bowed and held out his hand to her.

"If Varzil were here, he would have the honor of this dance," Carolin said to her. "So I shall just have to fill in as best I can."

They took their position near the edge of the floor for a round of four couples. Rakhal was dancing again, this time with Jandria, in the neighboring set. Unlike the other ladies in their tight-laced silken gowns, Jandria wore a tunic and underdress of muted gold wool. She looked comfortable and warm, and the color set off her dark hair. Carolin had not realized how pretty she was.

As they began the slow opening figures, Rakhal leaned toward Carolin.

"Cousin, wherever did you find that tender little dove? You mustn't keep her all to yourself."

"She's Varzil's sister, and a novice at Hali," Carolin shot back, his words a hiss above the music. Then the movements of the dance took them in different directions.

Dyannis caught Rakhal's parting glance, for she missed a step and the lady dancing on her diagonal had to hurry to keep the figure intact.

"I'm afraid I'm not a very elegant dancer," she said. "At home, we mostly danced the old reels. There was none of this choosing and waiting to be chosen. I danced with whomever I liked, whether it was Father or Kevan or the pot boy."

"Don't trouble yourself," he answered. "I believe some of these figures were devised by dancing masters anxious to prove how indispensable they were. The more insanely complicated, the better, or something like that."

Dyannis giggled, relaxing, and as the dance neared its end, he found himself wishing he could spend another with her. She deserved better than endless conversations about needlework, babies, and people she didn't know, watching everyone else have fun dancing. Nor did he feel entirely sanguine about Rakhal heeding his warning. She was so impressionable, a simple country girl overawed by Tower and court.

Carolin caught sight of Eduin, standing by the table where drinks and dainties were offered. "Come," he said, placing his free hand over hers. "Let me escort you to another of your brother's close friends. Then you will have two dancing partners, neither of whom is a pot boy."

A strange expression passed over Eduin's features as Carolin greeted him, a moment of confusion mixed with gladness as he looked down at Dyannis.

"Carlo assures me it is perfectly proper for us to dance, even though we've just met, since you and Varzil are *bredin*." She used the word meaning, "sworn brothers," with the polite inflection.

"I am sorry, *damisela*—when we spoke at the King's table, I took you for Lady Maura's companion from Hali Tower. I did not realize you, too, have a place there."

Dyannis took no offense at being confused with a genteel companion instead of a *leronis* in her own right. "How could you have known? I have been at Hali but a short time. I have yet to take my place on the relays or do any work besides fetching things for the healers. It was Maura's doing that I join my brother here for the Festival—and now, alas, he is confined in Hali's infirmary and here we are, deprived of his company. Prince Carolin tells me the three of you studied together at Arilinn."

"We are friends, yes," Eduin replied with such an eagerness that Carolin knew whatever lingering resentment he might have harbored toward Varzil had just been erased.

"Oh!" she said, releasing Carolin and slipping her hand into Eduin's. "Perhaps I have been too bold and should have waited for *you* to ask *me*. I have never been to court before, or even in the lowlands, and manners seem to be quite different here. You will think me no better-bred than a banshee!"

Eduin laughed, the happiest sound Carolin had ever heard from him. "I can think of no more delightful fate than to be asked to dance by you!"

As he withdrew to attend to his next duty, Carolin felt immensely pleased with himself to have brought a bit of harmless pleasantry to his friends. They would dance and flirt a little, enjoy themselves much, and in a tenday return to their respective Towers. The only thing that was lacking to complete his sense of contentment was that Varzil was not there to share it with him.

◆

Varzil arrived two days later, looking no worse the wear for his strange adventure. That afternoon, Carolin sat with his friends in the outer chamber of his suite, which had become their accustomed meeting place. He'd been all morning at the *cortes,* taking his uncle's place at the judgment bench.

A knock sounded at the door and then it swung open to admit the guard Sean and Varzil. Varzil wore dark, close-fitting clothing that emphasized both his slenderness and his fair skin. He caught Carolin's gaze and grinned.

Dyannis, who had been bent over a game of castles with Eduin, sprang up and threw her arms around her brother's neck with a whoop of joy. In that instant, she went from demure young *leronis* to ebullient child. He wrapped her in a hug and lifted her off her feet.

"Oooof! Put me down!" She squirmed free and dropped to the floor. "Or I'll tell everyone what you looked like the last time I saw you!"

"Come now, don't tease," Jandria said, eyebrows lifting. "He's put you down, but you must tell us anyway!"

Varzil laughed. "A drowned rat, most likely. Or a frozen drowned rat."

"Or a half-plucked, wall-eyed, drunk-on-Midwinter-mead frozen drowned rat!" Dyannis chimed in.

"Whatever he looked like then, he's back with us now," Carolin said warmly. "And we are glad to have him."

Even Eduin greeted Varzil with unusual warmth. It was as if, Carolin thought, the company had been incomplete without Varzil, only none of them realized it until his return.

It was not until later that Carolin found time for a private word with Varzil. Carolin put in the expected appearance for the royal evening meal and dancing, but slipped away as early as he could do so, unremarked. Varzil excused himself from the dancing, for the Hali monitors forbade such exertion for a few more days.

Carolin made his way to Varzil's rooms and shortly, both of them sat cross-legged on the big bed by the light of a branched candelabrum, talking the way they had back in Arilinn. Their laughter and gestures stirred air currents that sent the flames dancing. For as much as they said to one another, there was even more they didn't say.

Varzil hugged a pillow to his chest, his eyes shadowed. "Carlo—what happened to me down there—"

"What *did* happen? You touched that stone column and went into convulsions. You scared us half to death." *And you look just as scared right now.*

"Yes, I do," Varzil said absently. "I am." He drew a deep breath. "You know that objects can become psychically charged. They can carry mental impressions, particularly of strong emotions. This is especially true if they are used as part of a *laran* spell. Stone and wood and earth don't have channels to carry the energy the way living bodies do, but they have their own patterns of energy, each according to its own nature."

"Just as water carries lightning in a storm," Carolin nodded.

"Yes, that's it. When the energy of the lightning passes through the water, it leaves a faint trace. It's not discernible by ordinary means and it dissipates quickly. But the stone column at the bottom of the Lake had been constructed specifically to draw certain energies to it, *through* it. When I touched it, my own energon fields came into physical contact with it. The pattern of how it had been used entered into me. I saw—" Varzil lowered his eyes, "—I *was* back there, like a ghost with eyes and ears but no voice—and I saw how the lake we know came to be."

Carolin let his breath out. Eyes dark with emotion met his own. "You witnessed the Cataclysm?"

"The beginning of it, anyway. It was no natural catastrophe."

"No, I didn't think it was. It happened during the height of the Ages of Chaos, didn't it?"

"Two Towers made war upon each other, just like in the stories of Tramontana and Neskaya." Varzil hugged the pillow even harder. The knuckles of his hands gleamed white. "Only this time it was Hali—and Aldaran."

"Aldaran!"

In hushed tones, Varzil described how each Tower had prepared to do battle against the other, tapping into the elemental forces of the planet and ancient fears.

"If either side had been truly successful, I don't know whether Darkover would have survived," Varzil said, his voice a shaken whisper. "They were dealing with powers beyond their control. Distance meant nothing, nor did time. No one was safe from these weapons, not even halfway around the world. If Aldaran had time to complete its attack—Carlo, I saw what they were attempting. They would have split open the planetary crust clear to the molten core. Hali, for their part, counted on an even older, more primal force. I didn't get a clear look at its final form, and for that I am grateful." His voice turned inky, hypnotic, and his eyes no longer focused.

And what I did see . . .

"Demon—" Varzil stammered, reeling visibly with the memory, "—from the darkest, coldest hell—the power behind the coming of night—ashes in the black of space—"

"Varzil! What's going on?" Seeing his friend sway, eyes rolling up to show white crescents between half-closed lids, Carolin grabbed his shoulders.

"But Hali was warned—in time—they acted—diverted the attack—into the lake—column like a magnet—changed water and air—"

"Varzil! Can you hear me?"

Varzil shuddered and, to Carolin's relief, drew back, once more in command of himself.

"Carlo, this is important. It was no accident that I, *I* was given this vision from the past. It's happening again, don't you see? Maybe not with those particular weapons, but the conflict is the same. To each age comes its own madness. But the lesson of the Cataclysm was lost."

"What we can't remember, we can't learn from," Carolin said grimly. He thought of the destruction of the two Towers only a few decades ago, of Liriel's dream of rebuilding Tramontana under Hastur control—and for what purpose? For yet another Tower as a tool of warfare?

Carolin sat back, slumping. All his life, he had seen the men of his clan struggle to contain *laran* weapons, only to have new ones spring up like poisonous weeds in a garden of rosalys. If Felix in his prime, and the great King Rafael Hastur and even Allart Hastur could not put an end to the madness, what hope had he? What hope had any of them?

He looked to Varzil, this slender pale lad who had looked upon a disaster which would drive most grown men mad. "Are we doomed to repeat the whole thing again and again until we finally destroy ourselves?"

"As long as men can conceive of such weapons and are willing to use them," Varzil said, "I believe we are."

Carolin had never heard such desolation as now, in the voice of his dearest friend. Something hot and fierce boiled up inside him. "Then we must make it so that men *cannot* conceive of such things!"

"How?" Varzil shook his head. "As long as men are men and time endures, there will be those who must settle their differences with a sword instead of words."

"Then let them use swords on each other, until they have hacked each other into bloody pulp!" Carolin flamed. "At least, he who lands the first blow may well fall beneath the next! Let there be an end to *clingfire* and bonewater dust and matrix spells which strike from afar."

"Aye," Varzil said, inflecting the word in the country style, "that's the problem, isn't it? Lords can sit in their castles and order their Towers to attack their enemies. For each new weapon, another even more terrible must be devised to counter it. *They* risk nothing. If I were king of the world—did you play that game as a child?—I would decree that anyone with a dispute must enter the arena himself and place his own body as surety against his cause."

"Trial by single combat?"

Varzil grinned, a wolfish stretching of the lips.

"No, men will never return to those days, if they ever existed," Carolin said. The heat within him had fallen away, leaving his thoughts preternaturally clear. "I don't believe we will ever do away with armed combat or excuses to engage in it. If I were king of the world, I would forbid any weapon which does not place the user's life in equal jeopardy. I would force all the other kings—indeed, every lordling from the Wall Around the World to the Dry Towns deserts—to sign my pact."

Carolin noticed then that Varzil was staring at him like a blind man gazing at the sun. He gave a little, self-deprecating laugh. "Did I say something stupid?"

"No," Varzil replied, shaking his head, still with that expression of awe. "You said something—I don't know why I didn't see it before. Not merely a pact based on men's consent, a thing which can be as easily taken back as offered, but a true covenant of honor."

"Even if I could enforce such a thing over Hastur lands, I can't see any other lords pledging away their *laran* arsenals," Carolin said practically. He grinned, despite himself. "Still, it's a grand dream, isn't it?"

"One that's worth keeping, even if it may not come about in this lifetime or the next," Varzil said.

Carolin got up and laid one hand upon the door frame. As if touched by some prescience, he shivered. Not because he was afraid, although he knew he would be if he ever tried to put his pact into action, but because the world had *already* changed. Whatever happened now, neither he nor Varzil could return to who they were before those words passed between them.

16

Carolin arrived early at the King's presence chamber for the first audience to be held since his return. The guard admitted him through the private side entrance with a bow. He paused inside the door, studying the room that was to be his one day. It was a pleasantly proportioned, if formal, chamber with a bank of eastward-facing windows, bright and warm enough in the late morning for even a frail old man. Here the king heard pleadings, received written petitions, and decided other issues presented to him by his advisers. Once these audiences had been frequent, sometimes daily, but in the last decade, they had become irregular as more and more matters were left to subordinates.

That, too, will change, now that I have returned.

Carolin remembered coming here as a boy, when he and Rakhal sat with the other nobles in order to learn statecraft. The mingled smells of dust and furniture polish sharpened his memories.

In those days, everything seemed simple—his place in the world, his uncle's reasoned decisions, his notions of what was just and right, what was wrong and how it must be punished. Rakhal was his cousin and playfellow, and would some day be his faithful counselor. If there were darker undercurrents, hidden maneuverings, Carolin had been happily unaware of them. But he could never return to those uncomplicated times. He was a man now, a prince ready to take his place in the world. He must learn to think and act like one. The holiday of Arilinn was over.

The page who followed him everywhere stirred at the doorway. Carolin started to wave the boy about his business, then recovered himself. How quickly he had lost the habit of ever-present servants. He went to the half circle of chairs behind the polished tables and stood behind his usual place at the right side of the king's elevated seat.

Minutes later, petitioners, courtiers, and audience filed into the chamber and took their places according to rank. *Comyn* might sit in their own railed-off section, as Lady Liriel Hastur had, taking the most privileged position. Ordinary people stood. Among them were a judge from the *cortes* and representatives from the city elders of both Hali and Thendara.

A few minutes later, the old Elhalyn lord who had been Felix's chief adviser since before Carolin was born shuffled in and took the place to the king's left. The single remaining seat then was to Carolin's right, one place removed from the King.

With a bustle and tramping footsteps of guards, King Felix entered. He moved stiffly, but with dignity. Rakhal followed a pace behind, trailed by a clerk laden with parchment scrolls and papers. Rakhal placed a hand beneath the King's elbow to help him into his seat. When Felix was comfortably arranged, everyone bowed ceremoniously.

Rakhal's gaze flickered to Carolin, his expression unreadable. Carolin caught the instant of hesitation before his cousin stepped to the vacant place.

"My boy," Felix said, patting Carolin's hand. "So good to have you back with us."

Good, Carolin thought. The king was alert this morning. The vagueness of the other night must have been a passing thing. "It's good to be home."

The remaining introductory pleasantries were soon concluded. Rakhal said, "We must finish in a timely manner so that we do not overtax His Majesty." He motioned for the clerk to set the pile of documents before him.

Carolin glanced at Lord Elhalyn, who as senior counselor had always presented the day's agenda to King Felix. The old lord looked vaguely uncomfortable. Had something happened, some scandal which had cost him the King's special favor?

The sergeant announced the opening of the session and everyone bowed. Rakhal took the scroll bearing the day's agenda and presented it to the King, who nodded his willingness to hear these cases.

The first order of business was the proposal to finance the rebuilding of Tramontana Tower. Carolin did not think that even King Felix would dare keep Liriel waiting through lesser matters, not with her sitting in the front row, back straight, hands precise in her lap. Not a single detail of her appearance or demeanor was less than proper for a lady of her rank, *Comynara* and Hastur. By her very presence, she lent solemnity to the proceedings.

The evening before, as Carolin lingered after the last cup of wine with his uncle and Rakhal, he had broached the subject. Few important decisions were made during public session. Rakhal already knew of the proposal.

"When Tramontana fell, we lost a valuable resource." Carolin made his argument point by point, carefully watching the King for signs of understanding. "Now communications with the Hellers are unreliable. It would not take much to cut us off from them entirely, or reduce the speed of messages to the pace of a fast horse."

"We must have an outpost there," Rakhal said, moving restlessly in his chair. "But the relays are the least of our problems. The more powerful Hastur becomes, the more desperate our enemies. We must expand our defense capabilities, and that means more Towers under our control."

"I don't know what the world is coming to," Felix said, shaking his head. "Old Towers, new Towers with the same name. It's all so confusing. I don't understand why things can't just stay the same."

"That's what we are trying to do, Your Majesty," Rakhal said soothingly. "To put up a new Tower in the same place so that things will be just like they were."

"Oh, yes, well then, that is good."

Afterward, Carolin said, "I do not think the *leronyn* who made the proposal intended a military outpost or a factory for *clingfire,* but a place to train new students, to do peaceful productive work."

"They will do whatever we command," Rakhal answered, smiling. "In the king's name, of course."

"I have lived among Tower folk," Carolin reminded him, "and I would not so lightly dismiss their independence and resourcefulness. Their discipline is as great as any soldier's, nor are they peasants who can

be whipped if they do not obey. I think it unwise to create such expecta-
tions in the King's mind. The Towers are a power in their own right. If
we do not accord them that respect and self-determination, the day may
come when we have no choice."

"What, would you have us go to the expense of rebuilding a Tower
and then demand nothing in return?"

Carolin shook his head. "On the contrary, I would have the Tower
free to do the work it does best."

Now that conversation came back to him. With little discussion, King
Felix read aloud the brief statement approving the project. From the
front row of the *Comyn* section, Liriel met Carolin's gaze and then, very
slightly, inclined her head. She might owe him a favor in return, but he
very much doubted that included blind obedience.

The next several documents appeared to be routine business, matters
which were already settled and required only the consent of the King.
There was some discussion over the next, a tariff dispute between the
cities of Hali and Thendara. The issue was unfamiliar to Carolin, and he
listened with interest as the two representatives put forth their cases. Hali
invoked an obscure legal precedent that Thendara challenged, calling
upon the testimony of the *cortes* judge.

"We must weigh the welfare of the respective parties involved," the
judge said. "Each has an interest here. The point is whether the strength
of this prior verdict is sufficient to counterbalance the compelling arguments for damage."

"The issue is clear," said Thendara, glancing at Rakhal. "We cannot
allow a minority to defy the wishes of so many. We need a new precedent,
one based on today's reality, not the whim of some judge who was probably bribed."

"Bribery is a serious charge," Carolin said.

"This is exactly the type of case where we need protection," Hali
retorted. "Your Majesty, as defender of *all* your subjects, we appeal to
you—" His eyes lifted to the face of King Felix, who had been gazing out
the window for the past five minutes.

"You have all made your points amply clear," Rakhal cut in, "and my
uncle will give them due consideration. Complicated matters such as
these cannot be so quickly decided. Come back next month and we will
discuss it further."

The two representatives, who had only a moment ago been adversaries, exchanged an appalled look. Hali swallowed, visibly choking back a retort.

"Highness," the judge said, his voice taut, "this case has already been continued for an entire season. The parties have compromised upon every aspect except this. Without a ruling on the exact percentage of tariff impounds, the grain will sit in the warehouses for the rest of the winter."

"I don't understand the urgency of the situation," Carolin said. "Surely it won't perish in the cold."

"There is already hunger in Thendara," the representative of that city explained. "The price of wheat has risen past what poor people can pay. Hardest affected are those who depend upon the bounty of the King, for those supplies come from taxes paid in kind."

"We must have a ruling either way," said the judge. "And because the precedent decision was made by His Majesty, only he can determine its relevance."

"Uncle," Carolin said, gently breaking into the old man's reverie, "I think it wise to give these good men a decision. It is our own people who will suffer if this case goes any longer without resolution."

"Then I suppose I must," King Felix said. He shook his thin shoulders, as if recalling himself. "Yes—ah—quite. Let me see the record you are referring to."

Rakhal shot Carolin a furious look and fumbled in the papers, finally producing one. Its edges were discolored and curled with age.

Felix studied the document, lips moving as he ran his finger along each line of text. "Yes, well—ah—Elhalyn? Do you remember this business?"

The old lord straightened in his chair and his eyes brightened. "Majesty, I do. As you will recall, the base tariff was much lower in those times. This ruling was meant to be a temporary increase in order to equalize the relative costs of the different routes of transport, but it has since become permanent. The taxes involved have been raised a number of times for other reasons. Were this ruling to be invoked now, the result would be a far larger burden upon the merchants than was ever originally intended. Than Your Majesty intended at the time, that is."

"Of course," Rakhal said, "Your Majesty is free to reinterpret the ruling in whatever manner you see fit."

Carolin did not like his cousin's oily tone, nor his disrespect for the old lord. Elhalyn might be reduced in royal favor, but he was still the senior member of the council and, what was more important, he was the only one among them who remembered the original circumstances.

The king sighed. His gaze wandered to his right and for a moment he seemed surprised to see Carolin sitting there. "What—what would you advise, my boy?"

Carolin drew a breath. The expedient thing would be to keep with the precedent. The merchants might complain privately about the increased costs, but they would find ways to increase their prices to compensate. One way or another, by impounds or taxes, the price of grain would rise. The people who would pay were those least able to afford the extra burden.

All those years ago, the king had made a bargain with his people, even if it were not written into law. The King was certainly able to proclaim whatever he pleased or rather, whatever his soldiers could enforce. But was it just? Was it honorable? Was there not some implied obligation on the king's part to reconsider a temporary measure when the need had passed?

"I do not agree with the precedent," Carolin said. "His Majesty decreed the original tariff in view of special circumstances. I do not see that these hold true now. The most important thing is to allow the passage of this grain to the people who will need it the most. No one should profit from another's hunger or helplessness."

Rakhal said in a low voice that only Carolin could hear, "If you take that position, Cousin, then your treasuries will be empty in no time. How do you think we arm our soldiers or pay for our dinners, if not by tariffs and taxes?"

"That may be true, but whether it is wise is another matter entirely." Carolin had spent too much time on the streets, both here at Hali and at Arilinn, to so easily dismiss the temper of the people.

"I fear that your season at Arilinn has left you too easily swayed, Cousin," Rakhal said, leaning on one elbow as he turned a smiling face toward the audience. "You should take greater care for the good opinion of the king, and far less for that of the rabble out there. It is their duty to supply our needs, not ours to compromise our goals in consideration of theirs. I refer you to your history lessons. There is a good reason why we *Comyn* rule and those head-blind cattle obey."

Carolin stared at him. Like all educated people of his generation, he had studied the worst excesses of the Ages of Chaos, the *laran* breeding programs and the strange and terrible Gifts they produced. *Comyn* flew wherever they liked in aircars, their homes were heated and lit by *laran,* and whole circles were devoted to shaping beasts for whim or pleasure. Until now, however, he had given little thought to how all this was paid for, and how many people labored so that a few might live in luxury. He had no excuse save ignorance and the heedlessness of youth.

Both can be remedied, he told himself, and wondered if the same could be said for greed.

17

On Midwinter Festival night, the great hall at Hastur Castle glowed with a thousand lights. Garlands of greenery, tied with ribbons and winter-berry, filled the air with pungent sweetness. Since the night before, the delicious aromas of spice bread and nut cakes from the bakeries had mingled with that of the oxen roasting over the open pit in the courtyard.

The feasting began in the early afternoon with the formal blessings of the king. First the royal family, then the other Hastur kin, and finally the assembled noble guests and courtiers took their places beside the feasting tables to hear the time-honored words.

Carolin thought his uncle had not looked so vigorous in years. Perhaps it was because Felix Hastur spoke not merely for himself, but as the incarnation, the descendant of the first Hastur, the son of a god, who had taken on human mortality for the love of a woman.

In some places, the mantle of the Blessed Cassilda was taken by the woman of the castle, standing beside her husband as Lady and Lord of Light. Together they embodied the ancient cycles of light and dark, winter and spring, resting and rejoicing, birth and death. The Towers were said to have their own Year's End Festival, with *kireseth* and all manner of licentiousness. Since he had not yet passed a Midwinter at a Tower, nor was he ever likely to, he would never find out.

No such scandalous behavior would take place here, although there were babes enough born nine months after Midwinter. Still, an aura hung about the old King as he raised his hands and chanted the ancient words. His reedy voice rang out in the hall. Then he clapped three times and the audience broke into wild cheering.

Musicians in the galleries struck up a lively tune. A veritable army of servants issued forth from the corridors where they had been waiting, bearing platters laden with succulent meats, joints and roasts and huge dripping chops, savory pies decorated with stylized emblems, fowl stuffed and glazed, and baskets of holiday breads. More servants brought beakers of wine and hot spiced mead, the drink favored by King Felix.

By the time the dancing hall was prepared, the throng had swelled, with every dignitary from Hali and the surrounding lands joining the castle guests, family, and courtiers.

This evening's program began with King Felix and Lady Liriel partnered for a stately promenade. Watching the king who had been gray and old ever since he could remember, Carolin saw the echoes of a former grace, for the blood of the *chieri* ran in the *Comyn* and especially in his own family. Felix might have outlived his years in human terms, but when the music was sweet and the candlelight soft, his step was as light as any.

Old Lady Bronwyn had come down for the feast and stayed to honor the King's first dance with her presence, then retreated to her chambers. Carolin, as usual, danced with a procession of female relatives, beginning with the highest-ranked, who was Liriel. Like an ice statue in flowing white and silver, she moved flawlessly through the intricate movements of the set. Carolin, like all of his caste and time, had been given dancing lessons as soon as he could walk, but he could not match her cool precision.

Orain was sitting out this part of the evening, claiming he was saving his strength for the more athletic dancing once the older folk had gone to bed and the holiday mead fueled the young. Orain's wife had retired immediately after the ceremony. Carolin suspected he was tired of dancing with his cousin Jandria and much preferred the wild masculine energy of the sword dance.

Carolin caught sight of Eduin and Dyannis together. They circled the room, oblivious of the other couples. On any other night, it would have been unseemly, if not scandalous, for an unmarried couple to dance the *secain* in public. Carolin thought they looked very well together. The girl's pink dress shone like a pearl from the sea beds of Temora against the rich bronze satin doublet and short cape of her partner. Eduin bent his head close to hers, his arm protectively around her.

A slender figure in simple, somber colors stepped onto the dance floor and paused, rigid with tension.

"Varzil!" Carolin called.

Varzil cut like a dark arrow through the glittering throng. As soon as Dyannis saw him, she broke off dancing and gave him an enthusiastic greeting. With an abrupt, jerky movement, he put her off. Carolin couldn't hear the words above the music, but he caught Varzil's stony expression and the sudden reddening of the girl's cheeks.

"I will dance with whomever I please!" Dyannis cried. "And you have no right—"

"We didn't mean—" Eduin began, raising his hands.

"Here now," Carolin said, using his best *cortes* voice. "What's this all about?"

"Nothing worth the breath to tell it," Dyannis snapped. With a toss of her curls, she slipped her hand through Eduin's bent arm. "Please be so kind as to escort me back to the other ladies. I am too fatigued to continue."

With that, she pulled Eduin away. Varzil made as if to follow them, but Carolin restrained him with a touch.

"What's the matter?"

"What's the matter!" Varzil repeated scornfully. "My sister—he's dancing with my *sister!*"

"Eduin? And why shouldn't he?" Carolin said. "She's right, you know. Even here in a lowland court, it's perfectly acceptable for a close friend of her brother to ask her to dance, even if it were not Midwinter. It's no less proper for Eduin than for me, and I did just that while you were convalescing, rather than leave her sitting all forlorn when any blind fool could see how much she wanted to dance. Will you scold me, too? She's having a wonderful time, and so is Eduin. Out here in public, what is the harm in that? Or do you trust her so little that you must guard her honor every waking moment?"

Retreating from the dance floor, Varzil shook his head. "I don't—it wouldn't make sense to you."

"Are you talking about that old feud between you?" Carolin demanded, following him. "Just because he behaved badly when you first came to Arilinn? He's told me a dozen times how much he regrets it, how he's been trying to make up for it ever since. I thought it beyond you to carry on a grudge, Varzil, or to make your sister miserable on Midwinter Festival night."

Varzil turned away, pushing on until he passed the group of older lords and bachelors standing around the perimeter of the room. Here, in the shadowed corners and arched doorways, he halted. His shoulders rose and fell with each heaving breath. Carolin followed at a distance, watching. After a long moment, he went up and laid one hand gently on Varzil's shoulder.

He's been ill, far away from his home. Eventually he and Eduin will put the past to rest, but I can't force it under these conditions.

"I'm sorry," Carolin said. "I came near to provoking an argument between us, and I don't want that. Let's enjoy the holiday in good fellowship."

A shiver ran through Varzil's thin frame. "You're right, as usual. Two days ago, we talked of men finding peaceful ways of settling their quarrels, and here I am, ready to punch Eduin in the nose." He forced a laugh. "I should know better than to try to resolve differences on the dance floor."

"Well, if you must," Carolin said in a lighter tone, "you could challenge him in the sword dance. You know, who can jump farther or kick higher or whirl around more times without falling over."

"In my state, he'd win the first round, even if he were lame and blind. No, I'd best let the matter rest." Despite his words, Varzil looked pensive, his face closed.

Carolin, fearing Varzil might withdraw from the festivities entirely, suggested again they invite Maura and Jandria to dance with them on the next set. To his surprise, Varzil agreed.

The dances had been getting progressively more spirited and less orderly, with plenty of opportunities for the couples to make eye contact or even steal a kiss. By chance, however, the next one was decorous enough to win the approval of the strictest chaperone. Maura tripped through the figures at Carolin's side. Jandria was in an unusually talkative mood. By the time the musicians played the chords which signaled the final courtesies, even Varzil was smiling.

Carolin escorted Maura back to her seat and lingered there for an extra moment. She glanced back to the dance area where Varzil and Jandria still stood in animated conversation.

"Varzil's looking better," Maura said. "For a moment, when he first came down, I wondered . . . Is there some unresolved argument between him and Dyannis? She is what the Venza folk call strong-headed, and I would assume he is the same, from what you have told me of how he got into Arilinn. That doesn't always make for family harmony."

So Maura, too, had sensed the discord across the room. Carolin smiled, thinking there was little privacy to be gained by lowered voices around telepaths. He said, "I think it more a matter of Varzil discovering that his baby sister is a woman grown and capable of pleasing herself."

"To be sure!" Maura said with spirit. "I would expect nothing less, for she has the talent and the ambition to do well in a Tower, instead of sitting home mending socks and making babies." She tilted her head, eyeing Varzil and Jandria. "They're rather a good pair, don't you think? Varzil doesn't know what to make of her, and Jandria has even less patience with receiving instruction from a boy her own age than does Dyannis."

"Shall I rescue him, then?"

"Oh, no!" Maura's eyes twinkled. "I think it's good for both of them. Especially on Midwinter Night!"

✦

When the dance came to an end, Varzil bowed again to Jandria. He could see in her eyes that she would have kept him for another round or three, for although she enjoyed dancing, she did not care much for the usual flirtations. He had no interest in her beyond the mutual enjoyment of stepping to music.

The dance and the brief, light conversation which followed it had given him time to cool down, to decide what to do about Dyannis. Carolin was right, of course. She had committed no social trespass in accepting Eduin's invitation to dance. But she did not need to look at Eduin in that frankly adoring manner. She was too young, too impressionable for such a grand court. She ought to have stayed at Hali for the holidays, or at the very least had her brother present as chaperone and guide.

Carolin's question niggled at the edges of his mind—*Or do you trust her so little that you must guard her honor every waking moment?*

Why did she have to pick Eduin, of all people?

Well, he would put a stop to it. A word or two, and she would come to her senses. In a few days, she would be returning to Hali and her training. Meanwhile, if she wanted to dance, then he himself would dance with her.

He found her sitting beside Maura Elhalyn. As he approached, she lifted her eyes to his. Her thoughts brushed against his, still largely untrained, but sweet and clear.

Varzil, it is so good to see you well.

She was so pleased with herself and her newly-developing abilities, he didn't have the heart to point out the rudeness of speaking mind to mind in a company of nontelepaths. He smiled and held out his hand, palm up, for hers. She looked a bit surprised when he formally requested the next dance.

Unlike the last dance, sedate enough to carry on a conversation, this one was full of jig steps and complicated turns with the corner couple. Varzil tripped over his own feet.

Dyannis giggled at him. "Are you sure you're up for this?"

"I rather think I'm not," he admitted. "But I do want a word with you."

She slipped her hand through the crook of his elbow, comfortable and sure of herself, and led the way off the dance floor. The willful hoyden he had known as a child had given way to a charming young woman. When they were well clear of the other dances, she released him and looked directly in his eyes in a manner he found disconcerting. If he were not her brother, such boldness would surely have been a cause for scandal.

"Well?" she said, one eyebrow lifting in merriment. "Why are you looking so glum?"

"I must speak with you—about dancing with Eduin."

"You apologize for not being here earlier to partner me? Good! I accept. Is that all?"

"No, that is not all!" He wanted to shake her. "I still don't want you dancing with him. It's not a matter of being proper—as Carolin so rightly pointed out, there is no objection there. But I would rather you not form any kind of—" he searched for the word, "—*attachment* to Eduin. Not that such would last more than another tenday, with you returning to Hali and he to Arilinn. But it would not be . . . appropriate."

"And why not?" Colorless brows drew together like pale storm clouds. "Is he not a fully qualified *laranzu* of Arilinn, as worthy of a woman's good opinion as you? Is there some defect of character which you have detected that his Keeper has not? Tell me exactly why it is Eduin you object to, and not Carolin or Orain or even that lecher Rakhal?" Her eyes narrowed. "It's that he is not of sufficiently noble birth, isn't it? You should be ashamed, Varzil, to judge a *laranzu* by his family and not his character and ability!"

Varzil held up his hands at the barrage of her words. "I make no such judgment, sister! Nor have I ever questioned Eduin's talent. I have worked with him in the circle enough to know his skill. His Gift is not an issue here. He is, after all, not offering to marry you, only to dance with you."

"Exactly."

"And I would rather you not. As your brother and closest male relative, I order you—"

"*Order* me? I cannot believe what I am hearing! You would presume— I am not your horse or your dog or even your wife! If you have some reasonable concern, I will give it due consideration, but I do not consider your—your groundless, unfounded –irrational—turnip-brained *whims* to be sufficient reason for anything!"

Dyannis broke off, chest heaving, face and neck flushed with emotion. With a toss of her head and jangling of the tiny white bells in her hair, she shoved him away. Without another word, she pushed her way through the knot of nobles, oblivious to their astonished expressions.

✦

Eduin watched in amazement as Dyannis stalked from the dance floor. Her brother, who ought to have escorted her back to the chairs where the ladies sat, stood as if she'd knifed him. He looked as if he would topple over any moment now.

I don't know what he said to her, but I wouldn't be in his boots for all the gold in Shainsa.

Eduin felt an unexpected surge of empathy for Varzil. Even if he had not been lightly in rapport with Dyannis from their dances together, he would have sensed her fury. The room quivered with it. It was a wonder that every person on the floor who possessed the merest hint of *laran* did not react.

Someone will have to teach her better telepathic control—he caught the edge of Maura's thought as she hurried after Dyannis. With a pang, he wished he could go with her.

He'd never met anyone like Dyannis. It wasn't just her forthright manner. When he'd first come to Arilinn, he'd thought the women there embarrassingly bold. Whether they had come to a Tower for a season or the rest of their lives, they quickly adopted its unspoken rules of behavior. They took lovers as they pleased, but however much pleasure a lover might be, when the sun set and the circles gathered, work was work. They were comrades who held each other's minds—and lives—in their hands.

Dyannis, though she had joined the Tower at Hali, was something else entirely. Behind the sparkle in her gray eyes shone the clearest, purest light he'd ever seen. From that first evening's dance, when he had taken her into his arms, he had felt himself falling into that pellucid radiance. He had felt himself seen, truly and without flinching, right down to the darkest recesses of his secrets, seen and accepted with a simplicity that shook him to his roots.

Eduin's first impulse was to rush after her, to gather her to him, to shield her from whatever had distressed her. He knew this was impossible. His actions would only make matters worse. Besides, Maura, as another woman and her fellow *leronis* at Hali, was far more suitable to sort things out with her.

His next impulse was to stride out onto the floor and ram his fist into her brother's nose. *You've interfered enough! First with Carolin and now Dyannis!* He restrained himself, keeping his *laran* barriers tightly raised to prevent any hint of his true feelings from leaking out. There must be no questions asked about exactly what Varzil had interfered with. Here in this Hastur stronghold, surrounded by so many men and women touched by *laran,* he could not afford the slightest misstep.

And yet . . . even without Varzil's interference, Carolin might not have died back in the Arilinn orchard. Something had caused Eduin to falter at the last instant, had held him frozen as he watched Carolin—Carlo who had befriended him, accepted him, not caring about status—tumble to the ground. By the time Eduin forced himself into action, Varzil was already there, lifting the branch. Under Varzil's vigilant attention, there had been no chance to finish the job. So Eduin had waited . . . and watched . . . and sometimes on a night like this, with music and fine food, warm fires and Dyannis with her radiant eyes, he almost forgot.

But he must never forget. He must always remember why he was here, what he had worked so hard to achieve, how he alone carried the hopes of restoring his family's honor. The old king would soon pass away, and it was Carolin he must deal with. He had not been able to get close enough to either Rakhal or Lyondri to arrange a believable "accident," but that was of lesser importance. As for the second child of Queen Taniquel, he had not been able to discover any trace of such a person. He or she must have perished in adolescence like the young Prince Julian, or else disappeared into ignominy.

Meanwhile, time was running out. Fate and Varzil had foiled his earlier attempts on Carolin. Soon Eduin must return to Arilinn and only Zandru knew when he'd get another chance.

Out on the floor, Carolin stood talking with Varzil, leading him away. Varzil's shoulder sagged minutely.

"He'll be all right," a feminine voice beside him said. Jandria looked up at him with that mixture of friendliness and distance which he found so disconcerting. So might a sister treat him, if he'd had one.

"Varzil? Why does he object to my dancing with Dyannis?"

"Oh?" One dark eyebrow lifted minutely. "I think rather he objects to *her* dancing with *you*. But brothers are like that, as are cousins, as I have had an earful on more than one occasion from my own. Why do men always presume they know better how to manage our lives than we ourselves do?" She smiled, a little ruefully, he thought, and then brightened. "Shall we dance together to console ourselves of the folly of interfering kinsmen? Or would you rather go mope because Varzil has not the sense to keep quiet when he is too ill to behave properly?"

So Eduin danced with Jandria not once but three times, and by then, the younger men had gotten down their swords for the wilder dances. At this point, Jandria pleaded fatigue and a lack of interest, but Eduin rather thought that, for all her acerbic words, she preferred not to watch her cousin make a spectacle of himself. Orain was already three-quarters drunk, as was Rakhal.

Carolin was nowhere to be seen, nor had Varzil reappeared. The thought of any more to drink sent Eduin's stomach into an icy clench. His borrowed clothing, the suit of bronze satin he'd been so delighted with, pinched. He left Jandria with the other ladies, who would arrange a suitable escort back to her chambers, and headed upstairs for his own.

✦

Eduin swung open the door of the outer room. A fire had been lit some time ago, as evidenced by the glowing coals. He stood before the fire, letting it soothe away the chill from the corridor outside and the coiled tension in his shoulders. After all his years at Arilinn, all the months of maneuvering to get close to Carolin Hastur, close enough to do his work without suspicion, he should be inured to pretense. But sometimes the weight of his secrets was almost too much to bear. They haunted his dreams, those formless poisoned shadows. If only he could go home, where he did not need to dissemble every moment—but then he would have to face his father and admit he had failed—

He was not alone in the room.

She had been sitting motionless in the shadows. He had not even heard the whisper of her breath or the rustle of her skirts. Now her mind reached out to his in that silken touch which was like no other—

Dyannis!

Without thought, he turned, crossed the room and knelt before her. It seemed the most natural thing in the world to lay his head on her lap, feel her soft fingers twine through his hair. He did not know whether he heard her murmur aloud, or only felt it in his blood.

"Caryo." My dearest, my heart. Something broke open inside him, and he did not know whether to weep or shout.

They sat like that for what seemed an eternity, he on his knees, she cradling his head in her lap, stroking his hair, whispering words he had never imagined any woman would ever say to him. The logs on the fire shifted, embers crushing with a soft hush.

He raised his face to hers. The fire had dwindled, so that he saw her as a patterning of shadows. She lifted one hand to the table beside her, glanced in that direction. Light flared as the wick of the candle there burst into flame.

So strong a leronis *already,* he thought.

She smiled.

My brother has forbidden me to dance with you. Her thoughts caressed his like tendrils of braided satin, smooth and cool and rich with patterns he longed to explore. *And if he had not done so, I might not have realized . . .*

He held his breath, hardly daring to let his own hopes take shape.

. . . that what began as a pleasantry became much more. She shook her head, so that the tiny white bells in her hair chimed softly. *I never meant—I never thought it could happen—not so soon—*

"Hush, my love," he said aloud. He rose to embrace her properly. Her arms went around his neck, her lips searching for his. Her mind opened to him like rosalys blossoms in the morning sun, each petal unfurling its intimate perfume. Her lips were soft, faintly sweet with wine. Her fingertips caressed the base of his neck. He slipped one hand under the coil of her hair, amazed at the warmth of her skin. Like any well-bred, modest woman, she had kept the nape of her neck covered, for only a lover to see. He felt as if he had just been granted the most sacred of privileges.

The dance of her hands over his skin, the welcoming response of her kiss, the intimacy of touching her neck, all set up a current of excitement, a sweet thrumming through his veins. She was silken heat that set him ablaze. Dimly, he realized that, linked in rapport as they were, their minds and bodies open to each other, his own growing arousal fueled her own. The thought excited him beyond imagining.

He felt himself drowning in the heady sensation of desire and rising pleasure. One of his last coherent thoughts that evening was that he now understood why he had so few liaisons with women before, why they had been so unsatisfying, and that there would never be any woman for him but Dyannis. . . .

18

The weather turned bitterly cold on the morning Maura and Dyannis returned to Hali Tower. Liriel Hastur had gone on ahead, staying only to conclude her negotiations with the King regarding the funding of Tramontana. In the courtyard of Hastur Castle, the ladies' palfreys and the mounts of their armed escort stamped and blew mist from their nostrils.

Varzil had come down to see them off, along with Carolin and Jandria, who rarely seemed to let weather interfere with anything she wanted to do. The ice-edged wind, damp with the promise of more snow, cut through the layers of Varzil's cloak. He shivered, then silently cursed himself for his lingering weakness. His sensitivity to temperature, his lack of stamina, and his fragile sleep, punctuated by nightmares, demonstrated that he had not fully recovered from his ordeal in the Lake. He had determined that his best course was to push himself physically a little farther every day. Jandria fussed over him, saying that he was courting a relapse, and he'd refused to argue with her, only continued as he pleased in a less noticeable way.

Dyannis sat on her horse, wrapped in her fur-lined cloak, the reins loose in her mittened hands, her hood drawn snugly around her head. Though she nodded politely to Carolin, her gaze shifted to the castle beyond him. Eduin waited there, perhaps hidden behind a window, but as clear in her mind as the dawning sun as they said their private farewells.

Varzil had known the night she and Eduin became lovers, and he still blamed himself. Perhaps it would have eased his mind to discuss it with Carolin, but he could not bring himself to say the words aloud. He had acted arrogantly, and she had thrown herself into Eduin's arms. Knowing Dyannis, who was every bit as stubborn and willful as he was, with a temper to match her fiery hair, he should have expected no less.

It was too late to do anything about it now. His only avenue was to let the thing run its course. The enforced physical separation, she returning to Hali and Eduin to Arilinn, plus the demands of their work, would soon dissipate their ardor.

If not, the matter was in the hands of the gods. He scarcely knew what he ought to do in his own life, or he would never have wandered down into the lake or laid his hand on the fallen rock column, so obviously charged with *laran*. Who was he, then, to tell Dyannis or anyone else how to lead hers?

Carolin had finished speaking with Dyannis and now stood at Maura's side. Smiling, she reached down to take one of his hands in her own.

"It's good to have you back at Hali . . ." Her words drifted on, to be answered by Carolin's deeper voice.

Varzil stepped closer to his sister's horse. He searched for the words which would ease the friction between them. Briefly, he'd considered apologizing, but that would have been a lie, and he owed her the truth. He might have been crude and thoughtless in his manner, but he did not believe he had been wrong in his opinion.

To his surprise, she turned to him and smiled. "Dear brother, the way you worry over me, it is a good thing you are not my Keeper!"

"And it is just as well," he found himself answering easily, "that you are not mine."

"A woman Keeper? Even if such a thing were possible, if there were women with the strength of mind to do it, I assure you it will not ever happen at Hali."

Nor, he suspected, at Arilinn. Yet it was not impossible. Liriel Hastur, for example, if she were a man, might well have been chosen for the rigorous training.

A gust of wind, so cold it burned the skin, reminded him that this was hardly the time or place for such philosophical discussions. He stepped back.

"I wish you well, *chiya,* in every path your life leads you. May the blessings of Aldones follow you."

"*Adelandeyo,* my brother. May the grace of the gods lighten your way as well."

With a scuffle of hooves on the packed snow, the party was off. Varzil would have watched them go, but Carolin threw an arm around his shoulders.

"It will not shorten their journey," Carolin said, "if we insist upon standing out here, getting half frozen."

After the shivery dampness of the morning air, the castle felt warm and close. Carolin had little more time to visit that morning. With the conclusion of the holiday merriment, he was taking on more official responsibilities every day. But they stole a few minutes to talk in their usual spot, the sitting room of Carolin's chambers. Rakhal and Eduin were already there, bent over a game of castles. From the look of the board, they had not gone more than a move or two into the game.

"In between all this, I must meet with the stone masons from the city," Carolin said, throwing himself into his favorite chair. "When the weather's better, I may go out to Tramontana myself to take a look."

"Tramontana?" Eduin asked.

"Yes, we're definitely going to rebuild the Tower there," Rakhal said, "one which will be unquestionably loyal to Hastur."

"It's hardly the same thing as rebuilding," Eduin said, "even if the Tower has the same name."

Varzil silently agreed. Felix Hastur clearly intended the new Tower as a tool in warfare. In the days of the late King Rafael II, the Hastur Council had been legendary as a voice of moderation. This project sounded— *felt*—like Rakhal had something very different in mind: restraint for everyone else *except* the Hasturs. But, Varzil thought as he glanced at Rakhal's face and caught the glint of alertness in his eyes, it would not be wise to say so in this company.

"It's not the same." Eduin sat back in his chair, brows drawn together.

"You said that twice," Rakhal commented dryly. "It's putting up a new Tower in place of an old, ruined one. How different can that be?"

"It's quite different," Varzil said, and noticed Eduin's flicker of surprise, "depending on whether you see it from the point of view of the Tower or the castle. We don't have enough Towers to do all the work that's needed. There's no question of that. But to build a Tower with the sole purpose of serving the Lord who commands it—"

"And what else should a Tower do? Legitimately, that is?" Rakhal interrupted. His quickness reminded Varzil of a cat pouncing upon a field mouse.

"Rule itself," Eduin said. Rakhal's jaw dropped. Both Carolin and Varzil stared at him. "Don't you see? Ordinary men, whether they be lordlings or the greatest of kings, play with the *laran* gifts of the Towers as if they were trifles. Toys! They have no experience—no *conception*—of the forces we command. The magnitude, the scope." He turned to Varzil. "Have you tried to explain something as simple as the Overworld to one of them? Or energon rings or matrix lattices or any of the most basic things we use every day?"

Varzil heard the passion and the scorn behind Eduin's words. Without intending it, he dropped into rapport with Eduin.

All this death and destruction has come about because those who wield the power are not those who create it! The great lords sit in their castles and issue orders for newer and ever more powerful weapons, while we of the Towers, we who are the source of that power, are reduced to pawns!

The bitterness of Eduin's thoughts shivered through Varzil's mind. He remembered what he had seen in the lake—the two Towers, Hali and Aldaran, with no focus but each other's destruction, and no limits on what they would do to achieve it. By chance or warning, the devastation had been channeled into the lake. He dared not think what might have happened if the confrontation had progressed, with each weapon fully deployed. Darkover might not fare so well the next time.

Carefully he gathered his words. *The Towers must withdraw from armed conflict, be exempt—*

No! Eduin shot back. *The Towers must rule! We alone possess the power. We alone should decide how it is to be used!*

What was he talking about? The *Comyn* with their telepathic gifts were already the ruling caste on Darkover. But only a few were capable, let alone disciplined enough, to perform the demanding work of the Towers. With a renewed shudder, Varzil realized that Eduin was talking about replacing the *Comyn* with all their traditions of leadership, of

Council, of compromise, with a much smaller ruling body—the Keepers of the Towers.

"I cannot agree with you," he said aloud. "The fewer men who hold the reins of power, the greater the chance for tyranny. For all the faults of the Hundred Kingdoms, there are limits to the harm done by a single bad king."

"And limits to the good which could be accomplished by a single great one," Rakhal said. "I foresee a day when whoever sits in the throne of the Hasturs will hold sway over half the world. This interminable squabbling over every stray cow or unhappy bridegroom will come to an end."

"I share your vision, Cousin," Carolin said with quiet authority. "But I see in it a cause for caution. Perhaps the answer is not to rely solely upon the goodness of any one man, whether he be king or Keeper. It is often our ideals and the honor upon which they are based, not the whims of our nature, which leads us to wise decisions."

"Ideals! Honor!" Eduin said. "Look where they have gotten us!"

Varzil thought of the King who currently warmed the Hastur throne, old beyond the years of ordinary men, because custom and law gave him the right.

"Then we need new ones," Carolin said patiently. "Laws and pacts based upon the best of our nature—upon honor rather than fear."

Rakhal laughed. "You always were too optimistic for your own good, Carlo. You may love honor above all earthly things, but that won't keep you warm at night. Nor will it keep this Kingdom in one piece the next time we go to war. For that, you need *clingfire* and sharp steel, not empty words."

"May the gods grant that such a time not come for many years," Carolin said. "And when it does, would it not be better to have men of honor to stand beside us?"

Varzil looked at Rakhal, as if seeing him for the first time. *He wants the throne. He loves Carlo and wishes him no harm, but in his heart, he believes he is the better king.*

He wondered how long that love would last once Felix Hastur was cold in his grave.

✦

Varzil saw little of Carolin for the rest of the day. Instead, he took his midday meal with Eduin. They found each other in the kitchen, where one of the under-cooks set out bowls of thick bean soup laced with winter greens and accompanied by chunks of yesterday's bread, toasted until crisp and then smeared with fragrant soft cheese. It was the sort of hearty food Lunilla might have plied them with if they'd appeared in her kitchen on a blustery winter afternoon. They sat together at a wooden table, its surface satiny with many scrubbings.

Eduin had set aside his borrowed courtier's garb for the warm, serviceable clothing he usually wore. He looked simpler, more honest, and Varzil found himself warming to him.

As they exchanged their comments over the meal, it seemed that Eduin was exerting himself to be friendly, and Varzil wasn't sure whether it was because he was besotted with Dyannis or wanted Varzil's support on the issue of Tower dominance. This was a dangerous idea, as they both well knew. A Keeper might be above any law but his own, but a lesser worker, even an under-Keeper, was as subject as any man to the king's justice. What Eduin had proposed could easily be interpreted as treason. . . .

"I'll be glad when we're back home," Varzil said. "Banquets are all very well, but I miss Lunilla's cooking."

"It will be good to have real work to do," replied Eduin, blowing across a steaming spoonful. "I've had my holiday among the great and wealthy. I've seen the court in all its grandeur. Frankly, I prefer Arilinn, where I don't have to worry about how fancy my clothes are. Still," he gestured with his spoon, "I'm glad to have seen it once."

They separated after the meal, each to his own activities. With the morning's storm still muttering outside, there was little to do beyond the amusements provided by the court. Varzil, who had little taste for dancing lessons or ladies singing endless ballads about star-crossed lovers, wished he could ride out again to Hali.

Eduin had been right about the value of being useful. Besides the work done in circles and the healing of those sick and injured brought to the Tower, there were the archives. Hali was in constant need of librarians to tend to the ancient documents or transcribe those damaged by age and elements. However, the weather would not permit him to travel to Hali.

In the end, Varzil made his way back to the kitchen and from there, the still room, where a harried herbalist and her assistant welcomed an extra pair of willing hands. He spent a cheerful afternoon with them, trading stories of livestock and folk cures.

That evening, Varzil excused himself early from the evening's modest entertainment to pack the few belongings he had brought. His little bag was heavier than when he'd arrived. The night before, Carolin had given him a parting gift, a cloak pin of silver fashioned in the shape of a running deer. The artisan had shaped the beast's antlers into a semicircle ending at its tail and then filled in the space with a filigree of leafy branches. A tiny ruby glinted in the animal's single visible eye. As a gift from Carolin, the piece was doubly precious. It was just—

Just too much. Too costly, too beautifully wrought, for a simple *laranzu.*

As Varzil held the brooch in his hand, sitting on the edge of the bed in the richly ornamented rooms which had been his, he felt as he had that first night—apart, a stranger. Not even Carolin's love or the easy friendship of Jandria could change the fact that he did not and never would belong here.

I am a laranzu, *not a courtier. I have never wanted to be anything else.*

Meanwhile, he would have to talk to Carolin about the silver pin and find a graceful way of refusing it without giving offense. He wrapped it back up in the lace-trimmed brocade square of Hastur blue and silver in which it had come. Then he opened the door and headed down the hallway in the direction of Carolin's chambers.

Since the morning at the lake, he and Carolin had often been in rapport, sometimes no more than a tenuous awareness of the other's presence somewhere in the castle. Carolin was a weak telepath at best, and his duties, both official and unofficial, dancing attendance upon his uncle and sitting judgment at the *cortes,* occupied the greater portion of his attention. Knowing this could be the last private moments between them for many years at least, Varzil sent out a questing thought.

Carlo? Are you finished with—

The answering jolt of pain ripped through his body and stopped the breath in his lungs. The hallway vanished in the wash of searing fire that blasted through him, obliterating even his awareness of himself.

19

Varzil doubled over, hands clutching his chest. His vision swam and his throat closed up. His heart pounded in his ears, drowning out all other sound.

A second wave of agony swept through him. The world twisted sickeningly. He felt his body, his mind, his very self turn to ashes until only an empty husk remained.

Denial rushed up from some deep, stubborn core. This pain was not his own.

Even as the thought echoed through his mind, he reached out for the image of a wall, the barrier Auster had drilled into him for so many hours. With the first outlines of the stones came a lessening of the tearing pain in his chest.

Not mine—

The wall slammed into place, every seam and gritty mote of dust. He straightened up, grateful for the steadiness of his legs and the air rushing into his lungs. A surge of warmth replaced the pain, except for a lingering throb in his right hand. Looking down at the wrapped pin, he saw that the cloth had somehow come loose and the sharpened tongue of the brooch dug into the flesh of his palm. There was only a drop or two of blood.

With his uninjured hand, he rubbed his chest where only a few moments ago, pain fiercer than a red-hot brand had bored into him. Not
over his heart, but where his wrapped starstone hung. The braided cord
was longer than most, for he preferred to keep his matrix jewel hidden
from not only the casual touch, but the very sight of strangers. His fingers
closed around the pouch of insulating silk, felt the hard edges of the
stone. On impulse, he slipped it out, cupped it in his palm. The blue
jewel instantly came alive, as it always did in direct contact with his flesh.
Deep within its faceted heart, blue fire sprang up, flashing in eye-searing
brilliance. As it subsided, a feeling of warmth remained. The edges of the
cut from the brooch tongue sealed together, as if a week or more had
passed. Varzil hadn't deliberately focused his *laran* for healing, but he
had used the stone in that manner many times.

Varzil gazed into the gem, caught as always in the play and dance of
blue light. He felt himself slip into the crystalline pattern that would
enhance his own natural talent.

Not my pain . . . whose?

An image flashed into his mind—Carolin's face, contorted, eyes
rolled up in his skull, fingers hooked into claws, limbs shaking as in unnatural palsy—

He bolted down the corridor. The guard outside Carolin's door
looked up, his face awash in surprise and then alarm.

"Halt! Stand where you are!" Steel whispered as the guard drew his
sword.

"Sean! It's me, Varzil!"

The guard raised his sword. "Come slowly into the light, so I can see
you. What's your business here?"

Damned explanations! Varzil touched his starstone and sent a burst of
laran through the gem. It flared, searing blue-white across the whole section of corridor.

The guard pawed at his eyes, momentarily blinded. Varzil moved him
aside, murmuring, "It's all right, you know who I am."

He jerked the latch and hurried inside. There was no one in the outer
chamber, where they had all spent so many hours together.

Carlo! He sent out a mental call even as he rushed for the inner door,
leading to the bedroom. Light from a single candle filled the room with a
dim orange haze. A huge bed on a dais dominated the center. Shadows
clung to the dark velvet hangings. The bedclothes were mussed, sheets

like tangled ghosts. A small table lay on its side, with a second candle, visible as no more than an ember-tipped wick, spilled over the carpet. Beside it, half-hidden in the clotted darkness, a man crouched. His back was to Varzil, but he lifted his head.

Eduin!

Carolin lay there, his body contorted and quivering, fingers like claws moving in odd jerks as if trying to grasp something, hold it to his chest. He wore a shirt of fine white cloth, gathered around the sleeves and yoke. The ties had been loosened so that the neckline fell open halfway down his belly. And his starstone, which he had always worn in a pouch of Hastur-blue silk, lay bare on his chest.

"What's going on?" Varzil demanded. "What have you done to him?"

"I—I—"

"Never mind!" Varzil pushed Eduin aside with more roughness than he'd ever used against another Tower worker.

Varzil took Carolin's hands in his own. Carolin was in shock, clearly psychic in origin. His fingers were stiff and cold. They twitched under his touch. Through them, Varzil felt the deep shudders racking Carolin's entire body. Another convulsion was already building.

Varzil wrapped his arms around Carolin. He wasn't prepared for the reaction. It was like trying to hold a dying fish as it bucked and fought. The muscles of Carolin's body had locked in spasm, so that Varzil had to lift the other man's inert weight. They fell over sideways against the chair.

"Carlo!" Varzil cried, praying that somehow he'd get through. "Carlo!"

Varzil strained to reach his friend's mind but met only roiling blackness, as if all coherent thought, all sense of Carolin's personality, had been swallowed up in a mountain storm.

Carlo! Carolin Hastur!

Still clutching his friend's twitching, palsied hands, Varzil threw all the power of his *laran* into the call. Chaos answered him, fragments of thought blown against the raging tumult.

Varzil's own panic receded as he began to make sense of the howling madness of Carolin's mind. Something must have happened to sever Carolin's consciousness from his body, something so traumatic, so unbearable as to tear an otherwise sound mind loose from its moorings. Carolin had *laran,* enhanced by a full season at Arilinn, and if someone other than a Keeper had touched his starstone, even inadvertently . . .

Using his breath to summon his strength, Varzil forced Carolin's hands together around the starstone. Breath burst from Carolin's lungs with a percussive sound, followed by gasping sobs. The iron rigidity of his body gave way. He sprawled, limp except for the grip, hard as rigor, on his starstone.

Varzil heaved himself to a sitting position with Carolin's head and shoulders across his lap. Eduin had set the table to rights and relit the second candle. He bent over Carolin, face taut with concern. Together they lifted Carolin to the bed.

"We had best send for a monitor from Hali," Eduin said. "What happened to him?"

"I thought *you* could tell me that!" Varzil glared at Eduin. "What did you do to him? Did you handle his starstone? Is that what put him in this state?"

Eduin held up both hands in a placating gesture. "No, no, he was like this when I came upon him. I didn't do anything except try to help. You've got to believe me. I love Carlo like a brother, even as you do. I would never—"

Varzil thrust himself against Eduin's mind, determined to learn the truth. Eduin's barriers were as complete and reflective as a mirror of steel.

"I found him like this only moments before you came in," Eduin said. "I didn't know what was wrong, and there was no time to summon anyone from Hali or perform a proper examination. I did what I thought was necessary under the circumstances. It was an emergency."

Varzil managed to rein his own temper under control, enough to see the sense in Eduin's words. There were certain unusual cases, a crisis in threshold sickness, the backlash from certain psychic assaults, in which death was imminent. The only hope the victim had of surviving, or surviving with half a mind, was direct physical contact with his or her matrix stone. The risks were tremendous. Such a shock could stop a man's heart or leave him alive but insane. The only people who could safely handle a starstone, once it had become keyed into the mental patterns of its owner, were the person himself or a trained Keeper.

"You are no Keeper," Varzil said. He had not intended the comment as cruelly blunt as it came out.

Eduin's gaze lowered for a fraction and his color darkened minutely in the light of the two candles. "I hoped that because Carlo and I are close, and I do have the potential to become a Keeper, that I might be able to reach him without harm."

"And did you?"

Eduin met Varzil's gaze, his expression smooth and cool. "I used the lightest possible contact. It made no—it didn't make him any worse. I was about to try again when you interrupted us. Varzil, you must believe me—"

Eduin's next words were cut off by a moan from the other side of the room. As one, they turned and rushed back to the bed. Carolin struggled to sit up. His hair was disheveled, his eyes white and staring like those of a madman. For a stomach-churning instant, Varzil feared that his own action had been too late. Carolin's mental presence had returned, ragged and confused, but resonant with the force of his personality.

"What in the name of all the gods *hit* me?" Groaning again, Carolin raised both hands to the sides of his head.

"What happened?" Varzil asked.

Carolin bent over, his bright red hair falling across his face. His voice was muffled. "I have no idea. I can't remember. One moment I was standing there, getting ready to take off my boots. The next, I'm here on the bed with you two looking as if—as if—Oh, my head hurts."

That's because Eduin's been manhandling your starstone. Varzil clamped down the accusation.

"It's all right," Eduin said. "We'll send for a healer. You'll be fine."

Varzil bent over Carolin, easing him back on the pillows. After searching for a few minutes, he found the embroidered pouch for Carolin's starstone. He held it in his hand for a moment, feeling the lightness of it, the layers of insulating silk, trying to summon a memory of it in Eduin's hand.

Carolin reached for the pouch and slipped it over his starstone. His color brightened visibly, but he looked weary. He lay back with little objection while Eduin departed and Varzil monitored him.

The work gave Varzil something to do, a focus for his own unsettled feelings. Had he interrupted an assassination or a well-meant attempt at help? It made no sense that Eduin would wish to harm Carolin, who had befriended him, included him in these royal festivities, and taken his part with Dyannis.

To his relief, Varzil sensed little lasting damage to Carolin's nervous system and *laran* channels. Carolin was young and healthy, with a mental resilience that allowed him to adapt as easily to being a student at Arilinn as to his duties as the royal heir. He had been disoriented by the short-circuiting of the energy systems of his body and resulting muscle spasms. Carolin was going to have Durraman's own headache.

With his innate strength and a few gentle nudges from Varzil smoothing the disrupted channels, Carolin quickly returned to normal. In a short time, only a Tower-trained monitor would be able to tell he had suffered anything worse than an exhausting holiday season.

At one point, Carolin reached down and took Varzil's hand.

Do not fear, my friend. No evil will befall me as long as we are together.

"We will not be together forever," Varzil murmured aloud. "I hope you did not concoct this episode to delay my leaving."

Carolin's grip tightened. "Listen to me, Varzil. Whatever suspicions you have of Eduin, you must lay them to rest. You cannot go on like this. It will poison your mind."

"You would think the best of every man, Carlo. Not everyone is so trusting. Nor, perhaps, should you be."

Carolin shook his head. "That's the old way of thinking, that every man must be your enemy or your rival. We were brought up on it, like mother's milk. But we have seen beyond the old ways, haven't we? We have dreamed a time when men no longer rain unquenchable fire from the skies on their neighbors, where honor prevails instead of self-interest."

"Carlo, this is no time to be making speeches. I know you mean well, but you're not thinking clearly. You need rest—"

"Then stop arguing with me! If you will not make peace with Eduin for the sake of harmony at Arilinn or for your sister's happiness, then let it be for the dream we share. If that future is to be made real, we must treat all men as our brothers."

Varzil looked away. Truth rang through Carolin's words. He could not dismiss them as the ravings of a man who had just been through a near-fatal ordeal. His instinct was to temporize, to say that after he had wrung the truth out of Eduin, then he would consider this proposal of brotherly love. For Carolin's dream to come to fruition, there could be no exclusions, no matters to be settled first.

"If a crime had been committed, by Eduin or any other man, let him answer for it according to custom and law," Carolin said gently. "And not in the court of *your* opinion. I forbid you to take any action on your own."

With an effort, Varzil nodded. After everything Carolin had done for him, even setting aside their friendship, he owed him no less. Besides, tomorrow he and Eduin would be returning to Arilinn, leaving Carolin safely behind at Hali.

Very shortly thereafter, Eduin arrived with the castle healer. After examining Carolin, he agreed that no lasting harm had been taken, said he thought it unnecessary to summon anyone from the Tower, and prescribed an herbal tonic to be taken in wine at bedtime.

✦

The next morning, Carolin was well enough to bid his farewells in person, although he was still a bit pale around the mouth and eyes. The cold weather held, with rumblings of another storm in the next day or so, and an aircar had been arranged to take them back to Arilinn.

The pilot was a different one this time, a man of few words. Neither Varzil nor Eduin had much to say until the very end of the journey, when Eduin turned to Varzil. His jaw was tight but his gaze steady.

"For the sake of Arilinn and the circles where we must work together, Varzil, there must be an end to your suspicions of me. If you think I have done wrong, you must go to Auster and lay your charges before him. I will submit myself to his judgment."

Varzil heard the certainty behind Eduin's words. Surely a guilty man would not make such an offer. The relationship between each member of a circle and his Keeper was uniquely intimate. With a pang of guilt, Varzil realized that he himself had come perilously close to taking over as guardian of Eduin's conscience, a thing he had no right to do.

What purpose would be gained by humiliating Eduin with accusations?

It is not necessary to like every man personally in order to deal honorably with him. It was something, he realized with a start, that Carolin would have said.

"If I have wronged you, by thought or deed," Varzil said, "then I am truly sorry."

Eduin murmured a few gracious comments and the two fell silent again until the Twin Peaks of Arilinn, framing the gleaming Tower that was their home, came into view.

20

Spring came early with a flurry of rainstorms, each overlapping the one before. In the course of a month, the thick drifts of snow melted into slush. Moisture clung to the stone walls of Hastur Castle, and the smell of boiled laundry and mildew permeated the lower levels. Nothing seemed to dry out properly. Carolin's favorite horse developed a bad case of thrush in its hind hooves. As soon as the roads were open to travel, Jandria left for home and Maura returned to Hali Tower. Carolin missed them more than he expected.

But it was Varzil's absence which cut the keenest. Carolin found himself thinking of Varzil at odd moments, between hearings at the *cortes,* while washing his hands after a morning's ride, when he picked up Roald McInery's *Military Tactics.* Sometimes a feeling would pass over him, like a shadow of warmth, and he knew that across the leagues at Arilinn, Varzil was thinking of him too. He would remember the certainty he felt since their first meeting that somehow their lives were interwoven, that they shared a destiny.

Carolin quickly discovered he had to forge a new place at court amid subtle shifts of power and influence. Perhaps his time at Arilinn, where he had learned to guard his very thoughts, opened his mind to layers of unspoken meaning, to cross-currents of motivation and loyalty. Either his cousins, Rakhal especially, had altered in character, or else he himself was now sensitive to what had always been there. It was not that he distrusted Rakhal, only that he felt he no longer knew him.

Carolin told himself it was unjust to judge his cousin. He himself had changed during his season at Arilinn and here at home, with King Felix's increasing debility, Rakhal had many duties thrust upon him and had borne his burdens nobly. Carolin had no doubt of his cousin's passionate loyalty to the Hastur Kingdom, Carolin was fiercely loyal himself, but they disagreed on exactly what action those feelings of loyalty might inspire. There as no point in provoking a confrontation over things which would possibly never come to crisis. The day was coming when the most powerful lords would force the naming of Regents to prepare for the transition of power to the next King, and then everything would change again.

As for Lyondri, he was no longer a slightly hesitant outsider. He had assumed command of the castle guards and was developing a system of informants throughout the city. The shift imbued him with a sense of importance, and it seemed to Carolin that he thrived on it, although sometimes at the price of kindness. Lyondri seemed to take a particular satisfaction in the exercise of his power.

As the last of the spring showers soaked into the earth, crop plants began to burst forth in abundance. The generous rainfall combined with early warm weather to promise an especially bountiful harvest season. A portrait of Lady Alianora arrived, along with a procession of representatives whose principal responsibility was to oversee preparations for the wedding. King Felix met with them, beaming in approval at their every proposal, and then left them to the *coridom* to make their arrangements.

The portrait, a palm-sized miniature framed in costly copper filigree, was presented to him with great fanfare at the King's court. Later in the evening, in his own quarters, Carolin tried to make out the character and temper of the original. It was skillfully enough executed, showing a young woman in a high-necked white dress. Her straw-colored hair was drawn back in a severe style which did nothing to soften the angular lines of cheek and jaw. Perhaps the artist had intended to render her as a mature, serious lady, worthy of becoming Queen, but instead she looked grim, her mouth a tight line above a stubborn chin. Not a hint of softness or humor showed anywhere in her face.

Carolin set it aside with a sigh, wondering what she thought of the pompous rendition of his own likeness. He hoped she was as skeptical of its accuracy as he was of this one. At least, she looked young and healthy. She might surprise him, once they had gotten through the formal ceremonies and had time to become acquainted. He assumed she came willingly to the marriage, for she would be rich and as secure as anyone in these unsettled times, with powerful connections to benefit her family and friends. Someday she would be Queen and her sons would rule. But could she love him? Could he love her?

It was folly to entertain such questions. Love had nothing to do with it. Love was to be given to his people, his friends—even his favorite horse. Love was not for marriage.

And yet—he had seen couples who were happy with one another, and not all of them were star-crossed lovers sighing after impossible dreams. Varzil had mentioned that his own parents had been devoted to one another until the death of his mother, and they had been joined through family arrangements. It might be possible.

He sighed again and set the portrait in a suitably ostentatious place. Romantic love came at the whim of the gods, but the duty of a Hastur Prince was as constant as the rising of the Bloody Sun.

✦

Lady Alianora's party arrived at Hali a tenday before Midsummer. A festive atmosphere pervaded the entire city. Street vendors cried out their wares, ribbons and ceramic medallions with images of the nuptial couple. The weather had been fine, and the flower wreaths and pennons in the colors of Hastur and Ardais shone brightly in the sun. Within the castle, preparations for the impending ceremony proceeded.

Carolin watched the bridal cortege enter the courtyard with a mixture of detachment, curiosity, and dread. He had been up half the night, thinking about a case he had heard in the *cortes*. A metal smith had claimed that some of Lyondri's men had stolen two valuable daggers. The men, part of the personal guard Lyondri had recently gathered, claimed the daggers had been gifts. It was one man's word against the other, and in the end Rakhal had intervened, arguing privately with Carolin that if he were to rule in favor of the merchant, the entire Hastur family would lose respect. It would become impossible to enforce any law upon the city. Ordinary men could do what they liked and then lie in the *cortes*.

Moreover, Rakhal insisted, Carolin did not properly appreciate the risks he took in rendering these verdicts. Anything Carolin said might be taken as precedent. Was it not wiser to leave decisions to judges?

How else was he to know what was going on in the city? Carolin had wondered. And how would he know if those judges Rakhal had praised so highly were truly impartial, committed only to justice? In the end, however, he had given way to his cousin's arguments. He must keep his mind on princely matters, and no matter how hard he tried, he could not be everything to every man. Although it pained him to admit it, he had human limitations.

As if to demonstrate that very point, here he was, his eyes scratchy with lack of sleep, his nerves frayed, on the very day his bride rode into the city. He straightened his shoulders and went to dress properly to receive her.

It took most of the rest of the day for the lady's entourage to settle into their chambers, for her chests of gowns and jewels, her horses and retainers, lapdogs, maids and sewing women, all to be taken care of. She sent a message, pleading the fatigue of travel and begging to be excused from any appearance that day.

"A bashful bride you've got, Cousin," Rakhal joked.

"All things come in their own season," replied Carolin, and then they both spent the evening in his chambers, along with Lyondri and Orain, the four of them getting thoroughly drunk. It seemed by far the best thing to do, a last raucous fling before the *catenas* bracelet was locked upon his wrist.

Late the next morning, Lady Alianora was presented to the court of the Hastur and met her future husband for the first time. She walked in measured paces down the length of the presence chamber, trailed by her attendant ladies. Her heavy gown of pearl-studded gray satin, crossed by a tartan in the Ardais colors, rustled as she moved. She held her head high, with stiff, unblinking dignity.

Carolin watched from the dais beside his uncle. At least, the pounding in his skull had diminished to a tolerable level. Maura had seen to that, and he had rarely been so grateful for her *laran* skills. He much preferred her gentle teasing than the ministrations of the castle healer. He rose at the appropriate moment and recited his speech, welcoming Alianora to Hali.

She listened with an impassive expression, curtsied, and replied in the same formal tones. Then Carolin escorted her to the seat which had been prepared for her on the dais.

One of her courtiers brought forth the chests containing her dowry, coins and bars of precious copper and silver, along with documents transferring control of the Scaravel borderlands to her husband during her lifetime. Actual ownership of the lands would remain with her, passing to any progeny, but according to law and custom, her husband would have full authority to manage the lands as he saw fit.

The official declarations, couched in the language of legal treaties, went on for some time. Carolin forced himself to pay attention, although he was more interested in studying Alianora herself. She seemed so composed, her features so fixed in profile, that he could not tell what she was feeling. Nor could he catch any hint of her emotions, even with his *laran*. He told himself it was the combination of his own dissolute state and the tension of the situation.

The ceremonies extended well into the afternoon. By then, King Felix had sunk into slumber, occasionally snoring audibly. The court adjourned with a palpable sense of relief. Carolin sent a message to Lady Alianora, requesting a private meeting in the gardens. Each of them would of course be accompanied by the appropriate retainers, but he had hoped that in a less formal setting, they might begin their acquaintanceship.

Alianora replied immediately, using the same messenger, that she was wearied with travel and begged his forgiveness. Her response was perfectly correct. Carolin could find no fault with her desire to rest, to acclimate herself to her new surroundings.

Unreasonably irritable, he put on a soldier's padded, leather-strapped vest and went down to the training yards. Orain was already there, whacking away at a wooden post with a practice sword. Orain brushed lank, damp hair back from his forehead and greeted Carolin with an overly formal bow.

"If you mean to insult me, do it in some other way," Carolin snapped. "I'm sick to death of being reminded of my princely status."

"I hope you're not thinking of running away again," Orain said, referring to the ill-fated expedition to Hali Lake.

Carolin, selecting a wooden blade from the rack, shook his head. The days of careless, impulsive adventures were over, but it would be cruel to say so to Orain. At least, Carolin had some possibility of happiness in his own marriage.

Within a few moments, the two of them had taken up their positions on the marked field, circling and feinting, testing each other's weaknesses. The anxiety and frustration of the last few days fell away. His concentration narrowed to the dusty circle, Orain's eyes, and the sword in his own hands. A fey exhilaration rose in him. They clashed, blocked, sprang apart, and circled again.

Once, when Carolin's attention faltered, Orain caught him across the side with the flat of his sword. Carolin jumped away, his breath momentarily frozen. The next instant, fire spread from the point of impact and he knew he'd have a line of purple along his ribs by nightfall. The pain sent an odd thrill throughout his body.

Blood sang in Carolin's ears. Senses sharpened. The heavy wooden sword grew light. A sheen of sweat dampened his skin and his joints felt oiled. With every breath, he drew in new vigor, clean and uncomplicated. It was as if some god, far less exalted than Aldones, Lord of Light, had shouted in his ear, "Wake up! Pay attention!"

He gave himself over to the moment, watching the shift in Orain's stance, flexing his own muscles, throwing his power into each parry and thrust. Their boots raised clouds of dust and it seemed that time itself hung upon the air.

When at last they halted, lungs heaving, bodies radiating heat, sweat-drenched hair plastered to their skulls, both of them were laughing. Carolin threw his free arm around Orain's shoulders in a spontaneous gesture and felt his friend's response, the instant of relaxation that comes with true acceptance. There was nothing either of them needed to say.

✦

Carolin had rarely felt as drained and yet as wrought up as on the evening of his marriage. The ceremony itself had gone by in a blur, a cavalcade of richly ornamented costumes, flashing jewels, the mingled glare of *laran*-charged glows and banks of ordinary candles, the suffocating clash of perfume and incense. He had stood in a room filled with the dignitaries of his family and Kingdom, people he had known since childhood and many he had worked with since returning to court, and yet he had never felt so utterly alone.

King Felix alternated between napping on his throne and giggling in delight like a child. Rakhal had taken over much of the ceremonial direction, always making it seem as if the King were performing those functions. Orain was somewhere in the throng. Maura waited with the other Hastur ladies, including Liriel, who had returned briefly for the wedding. At one point, she caught his eye and smiled encouragement.

Lady Alianora was resplendent in a gown of silk stiff with embroidered lilies and tiny winking jewels. Under the confection of diadem and veil, her face was unreadable. She walked as if she could hardly breathe. As she took her position, she gave no sign of greeting, no hint that she was aware of any other person.

Carolin stood beside the woman who would be his wife, whose life would be bound to his as long as they both lived. The ancient words rolled over him, and he felt nothing. He wondered what he had expected of this moment. In a flicker of thought, he remembered a hundred comments by older men, who loved and honored their wives but made no pretense of understanding them.

He held out his wrist, as Alianora did, to receive the copper-chased *catenas.* The locks clicked shut. Common folk might take one another as freemates, or follow the country custom of sharing "a bed, a fire and a meal." *Comyn* marriages followed the old irrevocable tradition.

The final phrases completed, Carolin turned to Alianora and lifted her veil. His hands were clumsy, catching in the gauzy stuff, but eventually he got it folded back. Her eyes were pale blue and round, her expression glassy. Her blonde hair had been plaited with care and dressed with tiny jeweled butterflies. Under the faint rouge on cheeks and lips, her skin was very pale. He could see her trembling, and he wanted to take her into his arms and whisper that everything would be all right. Instead, he bent and brushed his lips against hers. Her lips were cold and she made no response, but neither did she pull away.

After a suitably decorous procession, they went out onto the balcony overlooking the courtyard. Under the watchful eyes of Lyondri's handpicked guards, the people of the city waited there with baskets of petals, ready to hurl them into the air. The herald presented their Prince and his new bride.

The crowd went wild with cheering. Carolin waved back. Their joy swept over him. He smiled, at first stiffly, then broadly, then with a laugh that seemed to spring from his very center. This was, he thought, the very best part of being a Prince of Hastur, to know that these people were his, to rejoice in their delight, to serve them with honor. If for no other rea-

son, he accepted this marriage because it gave them cause for such celebration, and an assurance of the peaceful continuation of rulership.

Alianora stood at his side as was her duty, unmoving except for a
slight swaying. She allowed the people below to see her, but whether this
was torment or pleasure, she gave no sign.

✦

Carolin was three-quarters drunk by the time the dancing was over and a
group of his friends, Orain among them, carried him on their shoulders
to the bridal chamber. A little while earlier, a similar group of women,
giggling and blushing at the ribald songs of the men, had taken Alianora
away. They would sing their own songs of the sorrows and delights of the
wedding bed, dress her in a scandalously revealing nightgown, and leave
her to anticipate the coming of her husband.

Carolin remembered this suite of rooms from his visits to Hali when
he was a boy. They had been his father's; his mother had her own. He
had thought nothing of it at the time, nor of his mother's preference for
the country estate at Blue Lake. His parents had always been pleasant to
one another and affectionate to him. Now, standing in the antechamber
which led on one side to a spacious, elegantly proportioned sitting room
and on the other to the bedchamber, he realized he knew very little about
these two people and how they had shared their lives. The thought struck
him with sadness.

That they had loved him, each in their own way, was beyond doubt.
They had left him with images of kindness, honor, loyalty, merriment,
duty. But they had not taught him anything of how a man and a woman
ceased to be strangers. Perhaps they had been more successful in living
their separate lives than in creating a shared one together.

There was no help for it. He would have to make his way as best he
could. He lifted the latch and heard it click open, paused for a moment
so that she might not be surprised, and went in.

The shadowed air smelled of sweet herbs and beeswax. No *laran*-
charged glows lined the walls, only candles, and their light caressed the
polished wood, the soft velvet of curtain and drape, and the cheeks of
the woman who lay on the wide bed, propped up on a mountain of
pillows. She had drawn the covers up to her neck. All Carolin could see
of her was her face, her eyes rimmed with white, and the fingers of one
hand twisted in the sheets. She had been murmuring, too low for him to

understand, but broke off as soon as he stepped through the door. She looked, he thought, as if she were anticipating a rape. He felt sick.

Yet it would have been unthinkable to simply turn around, go back to his old familiar chambers, and forget the whole thing. She had done nothing to deserve such humiliation. Nor could he sleep on the floor or chastely at her side. The marriage had been made for the sake of the Kingdom, and therefore must be consummated.

Moving slowly, so as not to alarm her, he sat on the bed beside her. The only thing he could think of was to talk to her as if she were a mare frozen with terror, perhaps stroke her hair, if she would permit him.

He began awkwardly, reassuring her that he meant no harm. It seemed cruel to point out that she had refused their only brief chance at acquaintance, so he went on to say he hoped they would soon enjoy each other's company and come to care for one another. As he spoke, he felt an easing in the tension of her body.

"Will you not give me your hand?" he said, and reached for hers.

Instead of releasing the covers, she fumbled about with her other hand. As she slipped it free, he caught a glimpse of small polished beads, probably river opal, joined by metal links.

Cristoforo prayer beads. No wonder she was so frightened. The Hasturs worshiped Aldones, Lord of Light. *Cristoforos* were considered by many to be weak and effeminate, unworthy to rule. The scandal of a Hastur heir marrying one of them would be immense.

As he touched her flesh, Carolin felt a fleeting instant of *laran* contact. Many of the Ardais were also Gifted, and she must have gone to great lengths to keep her faith hidden, even from her family. Had she refused this marriage, the reason might have been discovered. If her family had been angry enough, she might even have been killed. So she had agreed, perhaps praying to Holy Saint Christopher, Bearer of the World's Burdens, to show her a way out.

No way had appeared.

"My dear," he spoke as he would to a child and reached out his hands. For a moment she resisted, but allowed him to take her fingers from the sheets and hold both hands in his. "My dear, why did you not tell me?"

"Why, indeed?" The words rushed from her throat with unexpected passion. "What purpose could there have been? How could I, being what I am, bind myself to a son of Hastur, you who claim descent from Aldones, Lord of Light? How could I do otherwise? Disgraced beyond my entire family, beyond redemption? And now that you know, you will have no choice, for my faith is more dear to me than my life. Do your worst. I am prepared."

What does she expect me to do? Rape her on her wedding night? Kill her? With a sickening shiver, he realized that was exactly what she feared.

"I mean you no harm," he repeated, too stunned to think of anything else to say. "Whatever you have heard of us—of me, I am no monster to take a woman unwilling." He referred to the vow of *cristoforos* forbidding all but consensual sexual relations.

Yet . . . the marriage *must* be consummated. For the future of Hastur, for the welfare of his people, the stability of the Kingdom, he must sire sons.

He began stroking her arm. "If—if this were not a problem, would you wish this marriage?"

"What does that matter? I am sworn to it. My wishes have never meant anything."

"That is not true, Alianora." Deliberately, he spoke her name, and watched her involuntary response. "There are many things I cannot change, and the fact of our marriage is one of them." He ran his fingers over the copper *catenas* locked around her wrist. "But to the extent of my power, I wish you happiness."

She stared at him, and when she spoke again, her tone had lost some of its stridency. "I—I would be a good wife to you, a dutiful wife. But I cannot give up my faith."

"I will not ask that of you."

Again she stared, this time in frank disbelief. "It is not possible—"

"Am I a Prince of Hastur or not?" He captured her gaze with his, holding her hands immobile.

She swallowed, mute.

"Then I say that this matter concerns only the two of us, and what we do, how we resolve it, is between us alone." *Do you understand me?*

Eyes huge, she nodded. He couldn't be sure if she'd heard his telepathic thought, or was simply assenting to his proposal.

"Then we will hear no more of this," he continued. "What is secret will continue to be so, within the confines of these rooms."

The knot of tension in his belly relaxed a fraction. He returned to stroking her arms, forcing himself to concentrate on the texture of her skin. She was all softness and fine bone, with no firm muscle. In a sudden, almost frenzied movement, she sat up, threw her arms around his neck, and burst into tears.

He held her, weaving his fingers through her unbound hair. It was thicker than he'd expected, like heavy satin, a small measure of sensual pleasure. That was something, then. Aldones knew how he was going to make love to her like this, a sobbing, quivering stranger.

"It's all right," he murmured. "Everything's going to be all right."

Gradually, she grew quieter, her shudders dying away. He freed his hands from her hair and ran them down the length of her back. The fabric of her night dress was so thin he felt every contour of her body. She leaned into him, burying her face against his chest. By slow degrees, so as not to alarm her, he stroked her sides, her hips, occasionally tracing the curve of breast and buttock. Desire stirred in him and as quickly died.

"Are you—have they told you what to expect?" he asked. "Does it frighten you to lie with a man?"

She made no answer, and she would not open her eyes. Holding her, he lowered himself on the bed, so that they lay together, his arms around her. When he drew back to look at her, she kept her eyes tightly shut. He cupped one breast, noticing that she made no response. Neither did she draw away from him as he pulled off his own clothes and covered them both with the comforter. Her skin was cold through the thin gown, but he would warm them both.

He kept stroking her, more intimately now. She was not unattractive, had been well fed and well tended in life. Her skin was smooth, her breasts round, her belly pleasingly soft. After a long while, he noticed the change in her breathing, the slight inhale as he ran his fingers over her nipples.

She was not unwilling, then. It was his own body which now refused to respond. He tried to focus on her breasts, her hips, the warm triangle of her crotch, all the womanly parts which had sparked his adolescent fantasies. His own body felt tepid, his efforts to stimulate himself mechanical.

I might as well be pleasuring myself, or trying to copulate with an enormous poppet-doll!

Doggedly, he kept on, seizing upon any hint of reaction. At one point, she whimpered and her fingers went around his neck. With that, he was able to achieve an erection, although he didn't know if he could sustain it. He decided that if he were going to finish this business, he had best do it quickly.

She made no protest as he rolled on top and awkwardly slid into her. He felt her flinch as he began thrusting. He tried again to reach her with his mind; she was not barriered, but had simply gone somewhere else, leaving him to do what he pleased with her body.

He closed his eyes and tried to imagine a woman taking pleasure in his movements, welcoming him, yearning for him, embracing his mind as well as his body. He thought of the Castamir lady he had met the season he was presented at *Comyn* Council who had first excited his desire, about Marella, who flirted with him back at Arilinn. His breathing deepened, as his own arousal built. A wave of heat swept over his skin. He thought of Maura dancing, her face glowing, eyes meeting his with that unflinching gaze, the warmth and richness of her trained *laran*. With a rush that took his breath away, spasms tore through him. He thought he cried out, but perhaps it was only within the darkness of his mind.

He rolled off her, leaving one arm across her breasts. His breathing slowed, and the thunder between his ears fell away into stillness. He opened his eyes.

She was staring at him, her lips slightly parted.

"Did—did I hurt you?" Again, the soul-deep sickness threatened to rise up within him.

To his surprise, she shook her head. "I had been warned what to expect. This was not nearly so bad. I—I know you tried to be kind. I am grateful."

Grateful. But it would be unspeakably cruel to throw the word back at her.

He stroked her cheek. "Perhaps a child will come of this night. That would please you, I hope. And from everything I have heard, the first time is the worst."

"Yes, that is what they told me also." She rolled on to one side to study him. "I did not realize—how fortunate I am. You are a kind man, I think, and an honorable one. That is more than any woman can hope for. I will try to be a good and dutiful wife to you."

He leaned forward to kiss her forehead and felt her sigh of relief.

Sleep came reluctantly, although by the change in her breathing, Alianora had dropped off long ago. He lay as still as he could so as not to disturb her, trying to quiet the uneasy vortex of his thoughts. As the first pale glow of dawn seeped through the heavy curtains, he was left with only two certainties.

This woman was his lawful wife, would someday be his Queen, and was deserving of all courtesy, respect and honor. But he did not, nor could he ever, love her.

BOOK II

21

Spring also came early to the Plains of Arilinn. The earth awoke even before the days grew warm, as if bud and seed possessed some secret knowledge of what was to come. Snowdrops and ice daisies in wooden planters burst through the thin shell of frost to unfurl thick petals of yellow and purple in the slanting sun. During the early afternoons, when the great red sun was at its zenith, the drifts of snow in the Tower's outer courtyards fell in upon themselves, melting from within, and though they crusted over each night, no new snow fell, so that each day, the mass of soggy trodden slush dwindled.

Waking after a short day's sleep, as he often did when working through the night, Varzil made his way through the Veil and its courtyard. He paused to appreciate the shoots of green with their clusters of heart-shaped blossoms, stark against the patches of snow and bare dark soil. The air, although still chill, carried the faint damp tang of the new season. Beyond, in the fields, a mist arose from the ground, an exhalation. As yet, town and Tower kept to their winter rhythms, but not for long.

He drew his cloak, with its lining of soft marlet fur, closer around him. Gloved fingers brushed the silver pin that was his sole ornament. He traced the familiar pattern of the stag with its backswept antlers and thought of Carolin. News of his friend had arrived from time to time, mostly carried with other messages along the telepathic relays from Hali Tower. Carolin's first son, named Rafael-Alar, was now a sturdy toddler, and another child was on the way.

As one season followed another, Varzil's own life had settled into a new pattern, a cycle of work and friendship, the slow progression of lessons that brought him further along his path toward becoming a Keeper. There was no longer any doubt that he would. Pride had long since given way to a healthy appreciation of the strenuous dedication involved. Sometimes it seemed he did nothing but work, sleep, and study. Nights melted into tendays, and every once in a while, like today, Lunilla would order him outside.

"You don't see enough of the sun!" she'd scold. "Next thing, they'll be calling you the Hermit of Arilinn, the Keeper no one has ever seen!"

"But there is so much more to do," he'd offer in explanation. He meant not only the routine tasks of the Tower, which all too often these days included receiving and tending those victims of the latest plague, whether poisoning from bonewater dust or some natural illness. Last summer, they had nursed a dozen children from the Lake District, stricken with muscle fever. Beyond the continuing struggle to improve his skills and deepen his knowledge, there was the search for ways to use *laran* to promote peace instead of war. Even if he could not speak to Carolin face-to-face, their dream lived on in his own work.

Lunilla, however, would not be dissuaded. "The work will be there whether you are rested or not. The only difference will be your ability to do it! Out with you, into the fresh air! Go for a walk, look upon a strange face, think of something besides matrix lattices and channel balancing for a few hours!"

He walked toward the city, noticing the stiffness in his legs. Lunilla was right; he wasn't getting enough exercise. His body was young enough to be forgiving, but the long hours of immobility, combined with the intense concentration and energy drain of circle work, would eventually take their toll. He had been putting off attending to such things. There would be time for them later.

At least until the next war breaks out. In a way, it already had. Isoldir and Valeron had clashed, and even Arilinn was now called upon to make *clingfire* from time to time. At home, Serrais was beset with Dry Towns bandits on one quarter and ambitious neighbors on the other. Kevan and several other men had been killed in a border raid, following the death of old *Dom* Felix. Varzil had not returned home for the funeral because travel was too dangerous. His brother Harald now ruled as Lord of Sweetwater.

Varzil set a brisk pace into the city, stretching and warming his muscles. He lifted his arms, making circles with his shoulders. The joints in his upper back crackled.

The morning market was almost empty, the winter crops sold. At this season, there remained only hard-shelled squashes and root vegetables, a few hothouse herbs, things that could be stored in cellars over the frozen months. It would be a few tendays still before the first of the spring greens appeared.

Greens and tonic, Varzil thought wryly, *that's exactly what I need.*

"*Dom* Varzil!" came a woman's voice from one of the shops bordering the square. He recognized the baker's wife, her hair tied back under a white kerchief, sleeves rolled to the elbow and a dusting of flour on hands and across one cheek. She grinned as he strolled over.

"And a fine afternoon it is to you, too," he answered in the same lilting tone.

She flushed a shade redder as he stepped inside the shop. The warm air swept over him, laden with the yeasty smell of bread and the sweetness of honey and spicebark. Behind the worn but freshly scrubbed counter, the shelves were three parts bare. A slatted wooden tray bore only a single spiral bun. The sight of the pastry, glistening under a light honey glaze and studded with nuts and candied pear, made his mouth water.

Before Varzil could protest, she snatched up the bun and placed it in his hand. "You're much too thin," she said, sounding just like Lunilla. "Don't they feed you up there?"

Varzil ignored her question and bit into the bun. Though not as heavily sweetened as Lunilla's, there was a perfect balance of the light, chewy bread and the concentrated flavors of nut, fruit, and spice. Wishing there were another for him to purchase, he dug into his belt pouch for a coin.

"Put that away!" the baker's wife snapped. "I'll none of it! After what you did for my sister's boy when he was took so bad, you should have a thousand buns and still not be owing!"

She was so vehement, he dared not contradict her. Some of the Tower workers accepted gifts or ordered things specially made without paying for them, as their due, but Varzil didn't like to do so. His tastes were simple, and between the little money he had of his own and the stipend he received for certain kinds of dangerous work—making *cling-fire*, for instance—he could buy whatever he needed. He wondered irritably why he should be treated like a demigod because he had one talent and not another, *laran* instead of horsebreaking or metalsmithing or baking like this woman's husband. But it would have been ungracious to say so or to refuse her gratitude.

He kept his eyes from the racks of bread, least she press more upon him, and asked about the news of the town.

"Ah, the usual!" she said, clucking her disapproval, but whether it was of the gossip itself or the doings being gossiped about, he could not tell. "Looks to be an early spring, which means late summer storms and half the harvest ruined if it's left too late." At his quizzical expression, she added, "My da still farms wheat and oats away south. He'll keep out extra for us, though, so there'll be no lack of good bread for you. We take care of our own."

Just then, another customer came into the shop, a harried-looking woman wrapped in three threadbare shawls, one layered on top of the other. She asked in a low voice if there were any bread left over from yesterday's baking, and while the two were discussing the price, Varzil slipped out the door.

He spent the next hour contentedly strolling Arilinn's twisted lanes, watching people scurrying out on errands during the few hours of relative warmth, packs of children darting here and there to shrieks of delight. He took the coin he would have given to the baker's wife and left it in the hand of a beggar, wondering where the man went at night. Now and again, he picked up snatches of conversation or quickly-masked scowls. While the baker's wife, whose nephew had been saved during a bout of lung fever, greeted him happily, not all the inhabitants of Arilinn felt that way. Sometimes, he caught phrases like, "damned sorcery" or "mind tricks," and those not spoken kindly.

Why do they fear us? he had asked Auster after one such disturbing episode.

They do not know us, was the answer.

How can they? With the exception of those sick who are brought to us, all they know of us is superstition and tales of battle! They think we have nothing better to do with our time than make terrible weapons or sneak into other men's minds!

You will get used to it, Auster had said serenely. *Our work requires us to live apart; there is no cure for that. The Tower can be a necessary refuge.*

A refuge or a prison? Varzil still wondered. Was it possible, or even desirable, for people of talent and power to separate themselves from the rest of humanity?

Varzil was still lost in thought as he turned his steps toward the Tower. He was drawn back to reality by a mounted party approaching the gates. There were four armed men on good horses, bearing a pennant he did not recognize. They surrounded two ladies, one of them a person of some importance by her bearing, the quality of her long cloak and her palfrey's beautifully ornamented gear. Varzil caught up with them just as the guards were helping the lady to dismount.

As he lifted his eyes to hers, his first impression was one of merriment. She was veiled as befitted a proper *Comynara,* but lace could not hide the sparkle in her eyes. They were green, slightly tilted, and alight with interest in everything around her. She met his gaze boldly.

"I'm Felicia of Nevarsin."

"I'm—Varzil Ridenow." He stared at her, feeling slow-witted. With a flicker of his gaze back in the direction of the Tower, he added lamely, "Under-Keeper, First Circle, Arilinn."

Her smile deepened, revealing a small dimple at the left corner of her mouth. She tucked a stray auburn curl behind her ear. "You correct me so tactfully, Varzil of Arilinn. I was and suppose I still am, until matters are arranged otherwise, matrix mechanic of the Second Circle at Nevarsin. We'll see what use your Keepers can make of me."

Without waiting for assistance, she kicked her feet free from the stirrups and dropped lightly to the ground. She had, he noticed, been riding astride, and she handled herself in an easy, graceful way. Once on her feet, however, her color paled. She clutched the saddle with one hand, covering her mouth with the other to smother a cascade of coughing.

Are you ill, domna?

"I *was* ill," she replied aloud, "and if I stand out here for much longer, perhaps I will be again. Would you please give instructions for my escort?" She turned toward the inner courtyard and the Veil. "And Varzil, as soon as I am able, I intend to take my place in the circle like everyone else. It is hardly seemly for you to call me *domna* as if I were some over-dressed plaything and not a trained *leronis.*"

Her words stung him into action. In short order, he arranged for quarters outside the Tower for her men, stabling for their mounts, and *kyrri* to carry her belongings aloft. He remembered that a new *leronis* was due to arrive from the Tower at Nevarsin, but not for a tenday or so. He didn't know anything about her, other than she had suffered some lingering damage to her lungs from a fever last winter and it was thought the milder climate of the Plains would do her good. The winters at Nevarsin were legendary for their brutal cold.

When all was settled below, Varzil came up by the rising-shaft to the common room that now formed the heart of his Tower family. Felicia perched on the very divan where he had sat, with Lunilla clucking over her and plying her with a hot drink. Varzil grinned, remembering.

Felicia looked up, caught his expression, and grinned back. Afterward, when she had finished her interview with Auster and been assigned quarters, she remarked to Varzil, "I do not understand why everyone assumes that because my body has been weakened, my mind is not capable of work. There are few things more tedious than being forced to lie still when you are already bored past reason, or being restricted to only the simplest tasks, as if your intelligence were somehow linked to the muscles of your legs!"

Varzil caught the image of a bedchamber with bare, featureless walls, looking across an immaculately smooth comforter, and seeing little pairs of legs, detached from the rest of their bodies, cavorting about. The notion was so fanciful, he chuckled.

"I suppose they are right, and I should rest after my journey," she sighed. "I hoped to be given real work, and not just drilling novices in basic theory! Where is it written that all women must enjoy teaching children?" She wrinkled her nose.

"I don't know," he said lightly. "Perhaps we could comb the archives and find out. That's what Auster puts me to doing when he decides I've been working too hard."

"No dust for me," Felicia said, making a face. "Bad lungs, remember?" By the time Cerriana came to join them, they had discovered half a dozen mutual friends.

◆

Arilinn Tower bustled with the excitement generated by its newest arrival. All three circles were curious about the new *leronis,* a trained technician,

and there were the inevitable social overtures and shuffling of relationships as she settled into their midst. Fidelis fussed over her like a mother
hen until Eduin suspected that he, like half the Tower, was smitten with
her.

Eduin himself had little energy to indulge in the novelty of the new
worker. Felicia had brought not only herself, but news from Nevarsin,
the Tower and *cristoforo* monastery there, as well as the territories she
had passed through, and a pouch of letters. Among these, there had been
a message for Eduin.

Eduin took it to his chambers to read in private. By the time he had
climbed the stairs, made his way down the corridor and barred the door
behind him, his hands were shaking. Pausing, he turned on the telepathic
damper that would prevent any inadvertent psychic eavesdropping. He'd
convinced Gavin Elhalyn on his very first day at Arilinn that he was so
sensitive to stray telepathic thoughts that he needed it to maintain his
sanity. Thus, he ensured that no dream image or unguarded thought
could betray him, here in his own room. The weight of his childhood
oath, of the things he had done and more importantly, the things he had
not yet done, dragged on him. He could not have endured it without this
safe haven.

With a gesture, he summoned the blue fire to light a glow-globe. Dry-
mouthed, he lowered himself to the edge of his bed.

The folded paper was of poor quality, ragged around the edges from
rubbing inside the letter pouch. The handwriting was not his father's. He
did not know whether to be anxious or relieved. Yet, he could think of
no one else who would have cause to write to him. Dyannis certainly
would not.

The letter had been handled by so many people that no psychic trace
of its writer remained, not in the outer wrapping anyway. He knew that
to open it would change his world.

Shaking, he ran his thumbnail under the plain wax seal, no more than
a drop to hold the edges of the letter closed, devoid of any signet. Then
he unfolded the paper and began to read.

The hand seemed childish, the letters ill-formed and lines slanting as
if drunken. He realized after a word or two that the writer was barely
literate.

The letter wasn't long, three or four unembellished sentences. It was
enough.

"*To* Dom *Eduin of Arilinn—*

Rumail of Keycroft says to tell you he was took bad with the lungs this last winter. He would of writ this himself except he can't sit up no more. He says to tell you he doesn't know how long he can hold out and you will know what to do.

Your respeckful servant,

Esteban, cowman at Keycroft. I learnt to writ from the cristoforos."

Eduin closed his eyes to suspend the present moment, that breath of numbness before realization descended upon him. There was only one reason his father would send such a message, only one cause desperate enough to entrust to writing.

His father was dying.

The letter was undated. He had no idea how long it might have lain at some waypost, waiting for a traveler going in the direction of Arilinn to carry it. As he reread it, he dared to hope. This cowman, this Esteban, mentioned *last winter* and it was now barely spring. Assuming it had not been a year ago, not too much time had elapsed. His father had weathered bouts of lung sickness before; he might well hold on for months, until Eduin arrived. If it were possible for any man to cling to life for the sake of a greater purpose, his father would.

As Eduin made his way along the corridor toward Auster's chambers, he gathered his thoughts. He prepared a speech, including the mental impressions that would convey the urgency of his request without leading to any deeper questions. The social rules of the Tower would work in his favor; part of living closely with other telepaths was knowing when *not* to pry.

Auster, however, was not in his quarters. In the course of searching for the Keeper, Eduin passed through the common room, where trays of the concentrated foods needed for matrix work had been laid out. The faint, enticing smell reached him across the room. His stomach grumbled; he had not eaten that day. As he started toward the table, he realized the room was not empty. He had kept his own mental barriers raised, so he had not sensed the two people sitting on the divan. They sat in wordless stillness, but immediately he sensed the communion of their minds.

The new *leronis,* Felicia of Nevarsin, sat beside the person Eduin wanted least to encounter—Varzil Ridenow.

Varzil broke the silence, half rising. "Eduin! Please come, talk with us."

"Yes," Felicia added. "I've had two words with just about everyone else. In a few minutes, Fidelis is going to appear and order me off to bed, so quickly, say something amusing about life at Arilinn."

Eduin hesitated. "I've got to find Auster."

"You might as well eat something first," Varzil said. "He's in private session with Valentina and Ruthelle."

"Valentina?" Felicia said, raising one slender eyebrow. "The Aillard girl you told me about?"

Varzil nodded, and Eduin sensed the light, easy rapport between them. They spoke aloud from courtesy and to maintain the personal distance necessary in the Towers. "She's still fragile," Varzil said, "as are many of her line, but Auster thinks she has great potential."

Eduin, lulled by the innocent-sounding chatter, took a plateful of pickled fish and carrots, finger cakes, and sugared nuts. He ate quickly, hardly tasting the food. If he were to make any distance today, he could not wait for Auster's permission before he began packing. But he had no horse, nor any funds to rent one, and Arilinn kept none of its own.

"Excuse me," Felicia broke in. "I truly don't intend any rudeness, but is there anything I can do for you?"

Eduin's head jerked up, facial muscles tightening. He knew he was not as good at masking his expressions as he was at hiding his thoughts. Now Varzil was looking intently at him, too, with those knowing eyes, and he could not talk his way out of this one. Ever since their season at Hali, Varzil had treated him with impeccable courtesy, yet Eduin did not believe his suspicions had abated.

He'd been a fool to try stopping Carolin's heart by taking his starstone from him. Only the looming fact that the next day they must follow separate paths, putting Carolin beyond his reach, had spurred him into such precipitous action. Even then, he had planned badly, choosing a time when Carolin was alert and able to resist. At the fateful moment, he had paused and then Varzil had burst into the room.

Perhaps . . . he had wanted to fail.

Tell the truth, he urged himself silently. *Tell them what they want to hear.*

He let his face reflect the emotions that roiled inside him. Pain, loss, anxiety . . .

"There was a letter for me—in the packet you brought." His words stumbled of their own accord.

"Bad news?"

"I'm afraid so." He paused, swallowed hard. The sympathy on their faces deepened. "My father's been taken seriously ill. I must go home. As soon as possible."

"It's a shame there's no aircar available."

Eduin shook his head. "My father lives in a small village across the Kadarin. It's too rugged up there for aircar travel."

"The Hellers are like that, too, particularly around Nevarsin," Felicia said, nodding. "The cars can't navigate in the air currents. People say they're too unreliable, anyway."

"What can I do to help?" Varzil said, getting to his feet. "Shall I arrange for a horse?"

Looking now at Varzil's face, relaxed and eager to help, Eduin wondered how they had each misjudged the other. True, he'd felt a spasm of jealousy when Varzil had been chosen for a Keeper's training before he had. But there was no hint of malice or triumph in Varzil.

With as much courtesy as he could manage, he accepted Varzil's offer of help.

22

Eduin's borrowed horse was stumbling with fatigue, its breath hoarse
and ragged, by the time he reached the little village where he had passed
his early years. He had not been home since he had been taken away as
a child to begin his training as *laranzu* and instrument of revenge. Since
leaving the open fields, he had been obliged to ask directions several
times. The road was often little more than a goat trail through the ragged
hills. The pastureland was broken and poor, the hillsides marked by ero-
sion gullies, jumbled stones, and the skeletons of lightning-struck trees.
Even the sheep looked tattered.

Yet memories stirred, more powerful the closer he came. He was
struck by how familiar and yet how altered the huddle of buildings
looked. Had the village fallen on hard times, to look so gray and bleak,
or had it always been that way? A child's memory could paint even the
most desolate scene in glowing colors.

He brushed away the thought, as well as the disgust that rose with
each new sight and smell. Heads emerged from the doorways, and two
boys and a puppy ran out to stare at him. Smiling, he allowed his horse
to slow its pace so they could get a good look at him. Few strangers found
business this far along the Kadarin, certainly none so finely-dressed as he.
His cloak was of fine wool, thick and warm, the brooch real copper; his

boots and saddle gleamed with polish. His horse was far better than any-thing these villagers could afford.

A woman rushed out after the boys and gathered them against her patched skirts. Fear radiated from her. Worry and exhaustion muddied her thoughts, but Eduin caught a memory of men with knives and of blood spattered across the muddy street.

At this hour, the men were still out in the fields, but the woman drew herself up, a mother defending her children. She looked to be Lunilla's age, but in an instant he recognized her.

Fiona, that was her name. She was two or three years older than he. He remembered her as a sweet-natured girl, always happy to follow his lead. They had been playfellows, and she was to have his dog when he left. Had he stayed in the village, they might well have married. He hardly knew her now, nor did he want to. Poverty and early motherhood had bled the color from her cheeks, turned her breasts flat and pendulous, her body a shapeless bulk under layers of homespun.

She glared at him before hurrying her children inside. Happy to avoid an awkward conversation, Eduin clapped his heels to the horse's sides. The beast lurched forward.

It took only a few minutes to traverse the village that had once com-prised his entire world. His father's cottage was tucked behind a hedge that had grown wild and then died off around the trunks, leaving a core of dead branches. A mule and an elderly, antler-cropped *chervine* shared the split-rail corral with two cows. The mule pricked its long ears at his approach. He looped his horse's reins around the rails and went up to the house.

The thatched roof had seen better days, as had the walls, but some repairs had recently been made. The garden, which he remembered as a strip of flowers and, beyond them, onions, redroot, and summer greens had degenerated into a tangle of dry weeds. The rough-cut threshold creaked under his weight. He put one hand on the wooden latch and the door swung open.

The first thing he saw was the knife, its point inches from his throat. The man who held it glared at him. Tangled black hair and beard framed blue eyes, a crooked nose, and lips full and ruddy.

The stranger wore a leather vest, stained and worn, but thick enough to turn a casual blow. Eduin had no doubt that he knew exactly how to use the knife and the other weapons which were doubtless ready to hand.

Eduin was a Tower-trained *laranzu*. He had little to fear from mere steel. Without bothering to deflect the knife point, he reached out to the other man's mind—and found a kernel of *laran*.

The beard and belligerent expression masked a face that was hauntingly familiar. He had not seen his older brother since he was a child and Gwynn already a grown man.

"What—" Gwynn drew back, clearly stung by the unexpected mental contact.

Eduin opened his arms. "It's me, Eduin! Don't you know your own baby brother?"

The blue eyes narrowed. With an expert flip, Gwynn reversed the knife and slipped it into a sheath at his belt. He caught Eduin in a rough embrace.

"Little Eduin! Now a grown man—I'd never have known you!"

Gwynn pounded Eduin's back hard enough to start a coughing fit. The leather vest rasped Eduin's face and the stench of a body too long on the trail brought bile to his mouth. Eduin pushed himself away as soon as he decently could.

"Father sent word to me at Arilinn. Is he—"

"He's still with us, lad." Gwynn drew Eduin into the cottage. The closeness of the central room enfolded them. The little fire which danced in the grate could not dispel the dank, oppressive atmosphere.

"I just arrived myself two nights ago—" Gwynn said.

And clearly haven't thought to bathe since.

"—the lass from the village had been nursing him and at least doing no harm. He roused after I'd gotten some decent ale into him, but I still fear—Arilinn, you say?" The blue eyes, shadowed now in the subdued light, shifted. "The Tower there? You—a sorcerer?"

"Yes, I am a *laranzu*, a matrix technician," Eduin cut him off. "And I also trained as a monitor, a healer. I must see him at once."

He pushed past Gwynn and into the room his father used. It was scarcely large enough for a bed and a clothes chest, but a stool had been drawn up alongside. The window on the opposite side, old and thick, admitted a watery light.

The old man lay with one hand at his side, the other on his chest. The bedding, worn though it was, had been smoothed and tucked neatly about him, and several layers of thin pillows supported his head. His beard had been recently combed, for it lay like a fall of snow over his chest. On the floor, a cup held some dark liquid, still steaming lightly, and a wooden spoon.

Eduin, lowering himself to the stool, felt a pang of regret for his judgment of his brother. Hard though Gwynn might be, he had tended their father lovingly. If he had not bathed himself, clearly it was because he had devoted himself to the old man's welfare.

Gently, Eduin laid one hand on top of his father's. There was no response. The skin felt hot and brittle, although not dehydrated. The chest rose and fell in stutters. He slipped his fingertips around the bony wrist to feel the pulse. It was thready, but regular.

Pray Avarra I have come in time.

Smoke from the fire must have gotten into his eyes, for they stung as he turned to look up at his brother. "Tend to my horse and bring my saddlebags inside. I will do what I can for him."

Without a word, Gwynn departed. Eduin arranged himself so that he could skim his hands over his father's body. He closed his eyes and took a series of deep breaths. Each one took him deeper into the state of proper mental sensitivity. It had been some years since he had done a monitor's work; he had never been particularly interested in healing. But he had mastered the basics, if only to learn how *laran* could be used to stop a man's heart.

Now that he was sitting very still, he could hear the rasp and wheeze of the old man's breathing. After a cursory scan, he settled his attention upon the lungs.

The old injuries had left extensive scarring. In many areas, the delicate air sacs were torn, but that had happened long ago. The body had adapted as best it could to the compromised air flow. Now, fluid choked most of one lung and the lower lobes of the other. Gwynn's care, excellent though it had been, was too little and too late. Eduin was not sure that even *laran* healing would be enough.

He must go deep into the lung tissue, right down to the cellular level. Drop by drop, molecule by molecule, he must relieve the congestion and increase the blood flow.

Eduin visualized each air sac, each blood vessel, like motes of palest rose enclosed in a webwork of membranes. Everywhere he looked, burgeoning clusters of microbes fed upon the dying tissues. The fever generated by the body in an attempt to save itself was already falling, the battle lost.

His heart quailed within him. He had not realized how extensive the damage was, how far-reaching the infection. His father's illness was hopeless by any standard he knew. In the cases of pneumonia he had assisted in, the patients' bodies had been strong enough to fight it off, given the chance. Moment by moment, he watched his father's immune system falter.

Denial shocked through Eduin. He had not ridden all those leagues to have his hopes fulfilled and shattered, to find his father still alive and then to lose him, not if it were within his power to save him.

Heedless of caution, he threw himself into the task. He shaped his will like a spear point, like a bolt of fire. Before his onslaught, pockets of infection withered. Sodden, swollen tissues shrank to normal size. He sensed the rush of air into clogged passages and the minute rise in life energy.

The process was too slow, moving layer by layer through the lungs. His father was failing too fast. If Fidelis had been there, or even Cerriana, one of them could have supported the old man's systems while the other dealt with the infection.

He could not do it alone, and for this his father must die.

Eduin raged in soundless frustration at the gods who would let this happen. He had been sent away so young, had spent his entire life in obedience to his father's dream, setting aside friendship and even honor. He had betrayed Carolin, whom he loved as a sworn brother. And now to lose his father, without even a chance to say farewell, to make some sense of his sacrifice . . .

Eduin's mental vision blurred. His concentration shredded. The arrangement of tissues, the flow and ebb of blood and lymph, faded in his inner sight. As he struggled to regain his focus, he noticed something he had not seen before. Energy patterns overlaid the physical structures. Shifting his mental vision, Eduin saw them as streams and nodes of color. Excitement rose in him as he recognized *laran* channels.

How could he have forgotten that his father was Rumail of Neskaya, once the mightiest *laranzu* of his age? He, Eduin, was *not* alone. If he could but reach his father's mind, together they could cleanse his physical body.

Father! He called with all the power of his skill and love. Then, thinking that perhaps the old man's cognitive functions might be impaired by the fever, he added, *Rumail! Rumail!*

A whispered mental voice, reedy as if long disused, answered him. *Who is it—who calls—Rumail Deslucido?*

Eduin, your son.

A pause, then the reply, weak and distant: *My Eduin? I sent him away, into the hands of the enemy. Ah, my Eduin! Are you dead, too, and do you call me now from the Overworld?*

"No, Father," he said aloud, for the spoken words would help anchor the old man's spirit in his body. "I am here, beside you. I did not come too late."

Eduin shifted once more into telepathic speech. *We must heal your lungs. Together, I know we can do this.*

Ah no. My time has passed. I am weary—so weary—

NO! Eduin cried. *You cannot die, not now!*

For a heartrending moment, there was no answer. Had he truly come too late? Had his father's spirit gone so far into the Overworld that he could not turn back?

Don't leave me! tore from the depths of his soul.

Silence answered him.

Was this all the reunion he was to have—a fleeting moment of contact? Nothing more?

In a flood of anguish, Eduin saw his own life fade as if it had never happened. Again, he was a child in this very room. Together with the cottage garden, it was all the world he had ever known. His father was as tall and stern as a god. He was his father's pride, his hope. He knew nothing of justice or revenge.

A hundred times, he had set aside his liking for Carolin Hastur, his own desires, the path his *laran* Gifts would have taken him, all for the promise he had given. The one thought he clung to when it seemed he must give up all else was returning here to see his father smile, to hear the words that he had done well, that all was made right, that he had not failed.

But he *had* failed. Carolin Hastur lived and prospered. Nor had he discovered so much as the name of the second child of Taniquel Hastur-Acosta.

He had thought he still had time to accomplish his quest and return triumphantly to his father.

It can't be too late! Father, please!

Even as he pleaded, Eduin felt his father's mind sink deeper into oblivion.

Fight! You must fight to live!

Like a last breath, bleak surrender answered him.

In desperation, Eduin searched for a reason—any reason—compelling enough to reach his father's fading consciousness. If not for love, then perhaps for hatred—

Father, no! You must live, if only to see yourself avenged upon the Hasturs!

The answer came as a breath from his father's lips. "Ye-e-s-s-s. Revenge."

Where once there had been only the gossamer remnant of consciousness, now Rumail's mind flared. *Laran* pathways surged with power. Even dying, his talent shone.

Eduin reached out to his father's rising response, like two pairs of hands clasping, fingers lacing, strength wedded to skill.

Rumail's mind was powerful, but complex and strange. Eduin recognized the patterns of discipline and native talent. The basic training had been similar to his, but decades of bitterness had taken him in unexpected directions. Now Rumail seized Eduin's mental energy as a Keeper might, to shape and use according to his own will.

Eduin felt his *laran* energies being sucked out of him, faster with each passing heartbeat. Panic clawed at him. The more he fought, the sharper the pain. He struggled, but found himself held fast by invisible claws. Dimly, he felt his chest heave, his hands move. His heart hammered in his ears. An image came to him—the expression on Carolin's face as his own fingers had closed around the starstone, the white as his eyes rolled up, the catch and stutter of his heart—

Insolent boy, how dare you resist me? Submit, or I will take what I need! The words thundered through Eduin's skull. *Give over, or we both shall perish!*

Something inside Eduin broke, a bulwark collapsing, a wall of straw shattering in a whirlwind. He lost all sense of his separate self. There was no difference between he who took and he who gave. Two minds became one, swept up in a psychic maelstrom.

Gradually, as the sky above the Hellers cleared after a winter storm, the tumult grew less chaotic. Order emerged under his father's relentless control. Eduin could not tell what was being accomplished; at moments, he had the faint impression of fluids—lymph, plasma, blood—pulsing through tissues, of nodes of colors that surged and then subsided. But whether these things happened in his own body or another's, he could not tell. Once, he heard someone cry out. Another time, he felt a gust of cold air.

There came a moment when Eduin sensed his father's returning vigor as separate from his own. At first, he felt himself buoyed up by it, as if on a current of rising steam. The image shifted, darkening and growing more solid. Pressure, like a fist of granite, surrounded him. He struggled as it closed him in an ever-tightening grip. Pain, like lightning, jolted through him.

Father, no! Please, help me!

For what seemed an eon, he hung suspended between crushing agony and desperate hope. Suddenly, the sensation vanished. He was free—

No, not free, for the terrible pressure was now *inside* him. Its relentless force laid bare every secret thought, every instant of self-doubt and shame.

Memories flashed behind his eyes—Carolin's warm smile—the delicious abandon of striding through a sun-warmed field at the side of his friend—

Carolin climbing the apple tree, stretching out with that unconscious grace—seeing the weakness in the branch, knowing he had but to nudge the wood fibers apart and Carolin's weight would do the rest . . . and hesitating—Carolin's face ashen as he lay unmoving—Varzil bending over him, radiating concern—the roil of guilt and love in his own belly—

Carolin's eyes wide in shock and confusion as Eduin's fingers tore away the silk wrappings and closed around his starstone—his mind touching Carolin's—

Carolin's thoughts like a flood of sunlight—Towers gleaming against crystalline skies, fields golden under the wind, a woman's laughter, a black horse galloping, wine goblets raised, men singing—fading now in the white electric overload—his own body wrenching away—

Praying: *No, let it not be too late!*

Carolin's eyes opening—his own relief and shame—

The dozen other times he had seen an opportunity too late because he had been distracted by the simple pleasures of Tower fellowship, the growing pride in his work—

Like dried leaves in a wintry blast, the images shredded into dust. Pressure condensed into wrath.

You failed me! You gave your oath and then betrayed it—you betrayed all of us—

No, Father, please! Give me another chance. I'll do better, I swear I will! I won't let you down again!

You will not.

Something in Eduin's innermost core *twisted,* as if a gigantic fist had reached inside him, wrenched his heart free from its moorings and replaced it with ice. Eduin had neither the power nor the will to resist. He could only watch in sick horror as the new heart began beating, as its chill, bitter blood flowed into every part of his being.

And then, he felt nothing, no pang of loss, no shadowed guilt, no torment, no joy. Nothing but emptiness and purpose.

◆

Eduin came back into his own body slowly, as if he had been absent for a long time. He was sitting hunched over, his head almost resting upon his knees. His spine creaked as he lifted his head. His brother Gwynn stood in the doorway.

From the bed, his father gazed back at him. A healthy flush replaced his former pallor. His eyes were calm and alert. He lifted one hand to Eduin.

"Now I have both my remaining sons with me. Now we cannot fail."

Gwynn brought soup, thick with stewed minced jerky, rye groats, and shredded cabbage. It wasn't the concentrated food Eduin had become used to following intense *laran* work, but it warmed his belly. Rumail laid his bowl aside and slipped back into sleep.

One glance told Eduin that this was nothing to fear, but healing rest. He himself staggered as he got to his feet. Though he could remember little of what happened, his father was well. That was all that mattered. He felt more drained than he had after the most exhausting circle work. Auster had never asked so much for so long.

Auster, he reminded himself, was a weakling and a pawn of the Hasturs.

◆

Two days later, Rumail had recovered sufficiently to leave his bed for short periods of time. Eduin, after sleeping through the rest of that day and the following night, helped Gwynn with the continuing repairs. Working side by side, he became a little better acquainted with his older brother, whom he barely remembered.

Gwynn had been in his teens, older than Eduin, when he was sent away. He had *laran,* but not enough to win him a place at a Tower. Therefore, he set about learning fighting skills, working his way up the ranks. On the way to Thendara, he had killed a man in a drunken brawl, and now there was a price on his head in the lowlands.

"It seems that none of us has succeeded," Eduin lamented as he and Gwynn lifted a new split-rail into place around the livestock pen. The very thought brought a pain like burning ice deep in his guts.

"'Tis true enough we're not yet done with the filthy Hastur brood," Gwynn replied. "But the cause is not lost, not while there's strength in my arms or magic in your head. The easy part's been done; best be patient for the harder."

"Done? What do you mean?" Eduin paused in wrapping the rail to the post.

"You'd be too young to remember, and the Hasturs sure enough kept it quiet." Gwynn's blue eyes glowed in his dark-bearded face. "Did you never wonder how the throne came to Old Felix, when it was King Rafael who ordered Uncle Damian's execution?"

Eduin shrugged. Rafael II had died childless although he had not heard why, and so the throne had passed to the collateral branch, bringing Carolin into the line of succession. "You mean—*you*—"

Gwynn shook his head. "Not that I wouldn't. But Karlis, who was better than I'll ever be, as wily as an Aldaran assassin—aye, that was his doing, his triumph, for all he was caught and killed for it. Which leaves the rest—" he grunted as he lifted the last rail by himself, "—to you and me, baby brother."

After a time of concentration on the work, Eduin asked, "Did you ever think—what it will be like when we get them all? The royal line, the children of Queen Taniquel? What then?"

"To see the world made right, justice finally done? Karlis and Ewen avenged? Father free to die in peace? Lad, I would give my right arm, no—I would give my life—to see that day."

Eduin, seeing himself reflected in the fierce blue light of his brother's eyes, looked away. It was a long time before he could speak again.

◆

Rumail listened gravely as Gwynn told his story, all three of them sitting in front of the fire in the main room. The scowl lines in the old man's face deepened further with Eduin's news.

Eduin braced himself for Rumail's censure, but the old man only nodded and said, "I dared not hope it would be that easy. They are more devious than thieves, these Hasturs, and have good reason to fear the slightest shadow. Their evil deeds pursue them everywhere."

"Father, what would you have us do?" Gwynn said.

"Do not berate yourselves. You, Gwynn, have survived where your brothers have not and now are a skilled swordsman and tracker. You, Eduin, have done far more than I ever dreamed possible. To have advanced so far, and at Arilinn!"

"Yes, Father," Eduin burst out, "but they have not chosen me for a Keeper, nor are they likely to."

"Better men than you have been denied that training," Rumail said. "You have bought me something more valuable."

"What is that?" Eduin blinked.

"You cannot guess?" Rumail's grimace spread into a mirthless grin. "You have been the bosom friend to Carolin Hastur. You have held his starstone in your hand—"

Instantly, Eduin understood his father's intent. "I have even more!" he cried, and hurried to bring his saddlebags. He drew out a comb of tortoiseshell and silver filigree. It had been Carolin's Midwinter gift to him.

Rumail held the comb between his clasped hands and closed his eyes. Eduin felt his father's concentration like a shimmering in the air. "Yes," Rumail murmured. "Carolin, this Prince of Hasturs, has handled this more than once. There—in the metal, the imprint of his thoughts."

The old man took a deep breath. His lips moved silently, as if giving thanks. "With this, I can construct a weapon designed exactly to his mind. I will have to send to the Nest at Temora for the housing, but it can be done. Oh, yes—it can be done. And you, Gwynn, who can shadow a man without rousing the least suspicion, you shall be the archer to loose ⸱ this lethal arrow."

So that would be the end of Carolin Hastur. A trap-matrix, keyed to Carolin's mental signature, was as deadly as it was illegal.

"But what of the children of Queen Taniquel? Carolin is a Hastur, true, and the next King when old Felix finally passes to his well-deserved grave."

"You speak rightly, Eduin. I mean to destroy the Hasturs, most especially the spawn of that hell-bitch. So far as we know, she had but two, and the older one, a boy, died of threshold sickness thereby saving us the trouble of snuffing him out. Yet we must not spread ourselves too thin in our search. Gwynn will dispatch the young Hastur, and you will return to the Tower work for which you are so well suited. The genealogy archives are kept at Hali. From there, you must discover the fate of the second child. It was a daughter, I believe, though that makes no difference. Her sex cannot mitigate the guilt of her blood."

Hali! Dyannis . . .

"And perhaps I will have another chance with Carolin's cousins," Eduin said.

"Do nothing to endanger your position," Rumail said, his voice suddenly stern. "But in case you do fall under suspicion, you must have the full benefit of the Deslucido Gift. Of all my sons, you are the only one with sufficient *laran.*"

Rumail communicated directly to Eduin's mind, fully aware that Gwynn could have only the sketchiest idea of what followed.

Now that I am completely sure of your loyalty, I will teach you how to defeat truthspell. You will be able to swear to whatever serves our higher purpose, and no laranzu *on Darkover will be able to tell the difference.*

23

Varzil started awake to the sound of gentle tapping on his door. The milky haze of the stars suffused his room. He'd forgotten to draw the shutters and the night, on the crisp edge of autumn, was preternaturally clear. He had been asleep for only a few hours.

The tapping came again, soft but insistent. Felicia stood outside his door wearing a long, thick shawl over her usual woolen robe. Light from her candle fell across her face. Aside from the redness of her eyes, her appearance was tidy and proper, from the felt boots on her feet to the shawl wrapped around her shoulders.

"I am sorry to disturb you," she said.

He stepped back to invite her to enter. She went to the fireplace where last night's embers still glowed softly. Varzil bent to add another log to the pile.

Feeling a little self-conscious, he bade her sit and drew up the second chair. At Arilinn, men and women visited each other's quarters freely. Work in the circles enforced periodic celibacy for both sexes, and it was assumed that every adult was capable of managing his or her own affairs. But sitting here in his night shirt with Felicia, with her erect posture and serious demeanor, hands folded neatly on her lap, he felt awkward. With a rueful inner smile, he wondered if they ought to have a chaperon.

"Would you—can I offer you wine? Or send a *kyrri* for some hot *jaco?*"

"I have a favor to ask of you," she began. Her voice, though steady, was lower than usual in pitch.

Of course—

"No." She shook her head, insisting upon words. "It's complicated. Hear me out."

"All right," he said aloud, settling back into the chair to indicate that she should proceed in her own way and pace.

"Tonight was my rotation on the relays," she began. "I received news of rather more personal importance than the senders at Hali intended. Queen Taniquel Hastur-Acosta has died."

Varzil blinked. "*The* Queen Taniquel? The one from the ballads? I didn't realize she was still alive." Those tragic events were but a generation past. The glamour of legend had made them seem far more distant.

Felicia smiled, a little sadly. "She didn't want— After everything that happened, she withdrew from public life."

Varzil waited for her to continue. This news clearly affected Felicia more deeply than the passing of a famous queen.

"She'll be buried at Hali, at the *rhu fead* with her illustrious ancestors. It will be a private affair, but I will have to attend." She paused, looking away, into a distance that only she could see. The fire crackled and the flickering lights burnished the smoothness of her cheek. An unshed tear glistened at the corner of one eye.

So softly, he could barely make out the words, she said, "She was my mother."

For a long moment, he could not be sure he'd heard correctly. His first impulse was to suspect a metaphorical reference, as if she had claimed the Blessed Cassilda, or Naotalba the Accursed as her parent. Suddenly, he understood her modesty and her insistence upon proving herself.

He smiled gently. "I never knew your mother except as the heroine of song. I am sorry to never have had that privilege."

She sighed and some of the iron poise melted from her posture. "There's something so comforting in talking to you. You're the one person I could count on not to run down the halls, screaming out the news. I would rather my parentage not be generally known, even now. You can, I hope, understand why."

He saw her walking down a street in Hali, in Arilinn, saw people crowding around, crying out her name and then, "Taniquel! Queen Taniquel!" reaching out to her with their hands, not ten or twenty but hundreds, hands and eyes and shouting everywhere she turned. He saw her eyes white and strained, watched her struggle to keep her *laran* barriers up against the battering adoration, the hunger for a hero.

It's impossible, he thought. *No human can live up to a legend. Not Queen Taniquel. Not you.*

You have been on the streets, she answered silently. *You know how desperately these people want someone to save them. And not just in Arilinn, but in Dalereuth, in Temora . . . in Thendara . . . everywhere.*

"Does anyone else know?" *Who you really are?*

"Here? Only Auster and now, you. Were I a man, I could travel to Thendara and no one would ask my business. Alas, that is not the case. So, Auster has made arrangements for me to go as part of the entourage of Lady Liriel Hastur. She knows me only as a distant cousin of a minor branch of the family, a *leronis* of Arilinn."

Liriel Hastur had been at Tramontana this last year, lending the prestige of her rank to the newly rebuilt Tower there. She had arrived in Arilinn only a tenday earlier, on some private business in the Hidden City.

"So you will travel in disguise?"

"Oh!" she said, with a little gesture as if that part were obvious. "I'll be her attendant."

"But you—" *far outrank her.*

No, it's Felicia Hastur-Acosta who outranks her. I am Felicia of Arilinn, Felicia Leynier. Nothing more.

Oh, a great deal more.

Don't flatter me. "Varzil, listen. I—I have been long alone and in hiding. If my brother had survived, I would have had some consolation there. As it is, the few Hastur relatives who are even aware of my existence are strangers to me." She paused, eyes downcast and blinking hard. "This will be the hardest thing I have ever had to do, to stand at my mother's grave and say nothing, just as if I never knew her."

Varzil, already in rapport, caught a ripple of her fear. The funeral might be open to only family and a few select close friends, but it was impossible to disguise that it was Queen Taniquel being honored. Rumors would spring up like wildflowers after the last frost. The very assemblage of Hastur dignitaries would generate questions. Lady Liriel might speak as befitted a *Comynara* and Hastur. Carolin also had the right. But anything at all Felicia said would attract the very attention she feared, for why should an unknown *leronis,* even if distantly related, share that privilege?

"I will serve you in any way I can," he said. *Would you have me speak for you?*

For a moment, Felicia retreated into herself. Then she touched the back of his hand with her fingertips. "You—it is known that you are a friend of Carolin Hastur. It would not be unseemly for you to go to Thendara. Will you come with me, so that I am not alone? Will you do this, and keep my secret?"

For a long moment, her eyes held his in wordless communion. Their heartbeats echoed one another.

"Considering the number of lords and kings on Darkover who *want* to be famous, the opposite strikes me as a reasonable enough request," he said, forcing a lighter tone. "It will be good to see Carlo again, although I would wish for happier circumstances. I will have to ask permission of Auster, as my Keeper."

She nodded. "I've already done so. I would not have approached you without his leave."

Varzil wondered what Queen Taniquel had been like, the real person and not the stuff of legends. It did not seem a kind thing to ask now. In bereavement as in every other aspect of life, there was a time when words flowed and memory became a gift, and a time to keep silent.

◆

Varzil set off as part of Liriel's entourage the next day. They traveled together across the Arilinn Plains and up into the Venza Hills. From here, they would descend into Thendara and the true lowlands.

Varzil remembered Liriel from his Midwinter season at Hali, tall and reserved. She wore ordinary clothing, although of superb quality, but there was no question that she was a Tower-trained *leronis.* She spoke little, and then primarily to Felicia, treating her with impeccable, if distant, courtesy. Beyond greeting Varzil with a nod and an acknowledgment of his rank, she had little to say to him. Her reticence bothered him very little. She would be a difficult coworker, should they ever find themselves at the same Tower, with her combination of Hastur arrogance and natural reserve. But there was no malice in her.

Felicia often rode at Varzil's side, sitting easily upon the same horse she had ridden to Arilinn. The guards were all Lady Liriel's own, having accompanied her from Tramontana. As the days stretched on, Felicia began to talk about her mother.

"I was born at Acosta and spent my childhood there," she said in a voice so low that only Varzil could hear. "After the destruction of the two Towers—Tramontana and Neskaya, you know—my parents opened their home to the survivors. *Tio* Aran, who had been my father's dearest friend, stayed with us the longest. He taught me how to ride and when I was very little, he laughed a lot. Then he stopped laughing. After that, my father died. I must have been about eight or nine, so I don't remember much. My mother was never the same. After my brother Julian died of threshold sickness, she took me away from Acosta. It must have been too painful for her, with all those memories. I don't know."

She fell quiet, looking into the distance. Her mind, usually as clear as a running spring, turned opaque. After a while, she came back to herself.

She spoke again of her childhood, of the nightmares that plagued her. ". . . and when I woke frightened from those dreams, she would sing me back to sleep, no matter how weary or sad she felt. I always knew I was safe in her arms . . . And when the time came, she blessed my leaving, so that I might never regret my own choices or fear to follow my own destiny. I think the greatest gift she gave me was the absence of her shadow."

Once he asked about her father, and she shook her head. "His gift to me was his name, so that I could live out in the world like an ordinary person."

"Leynier?"

"Yes, Coryn Leynier."

The Coryn, the Coryn of Coryn and Taniquel.

"I have never known whether to love him for the life he gave me or to hate him for taking my mother away with his death," she said softly. "All I know is that I want to live my own life, to be Felicia, myself, and neither an echo nor a sacrifice."

He nudged his horse closer to hers, so that he could reach out and take her free hand where it lay on the saddle pommel. Her fingers, cool through the thin gloves, closed around his.

"There is very little certain in this world of ours, except for death and next winter's snow," he said. "But as long as I have breath and mind, you will be only Felicia to me."

24

The *rhu fead* at Hali, holiest place of the *Comyn*, lay an hour's ride north from Thendara. The high white haze of the early hours turned into an intermittent drizzle, as if the sky could not make up its mind whether to rain or not. The horses shook beads of water from their ears and plodded on.

Felicia, like Liriel, wore the drab formal attire of the morning, but the subdued colors only served to heighten her dignity. She went veiled, a cloud of black gauze obscuring her features. Though she kept to herself and spoke little, her mind touched Varzil's from time to time. She asked nothing of him, only his presence.

The funeral party was small, much smaller than befitted a Hastur Queen. Carolin arrived with a single attendant, but no other member of the ruling family. There were a only few people Varzil did not know, including one elderly kinsman, an Elhalyn lord, who spoke little but wept silently.

In the sight of that assembly, the body of Taniquel Hastur-Acosta was laid to rest in an unmarked grave, according to custom. Here she would join countless generations of *Comyn*, her resting place indistinguishable except for a slight mounding of earth that would disappear in a few seasons.

Liriel Hastur walked slowly to the open grave. "I speak not only for myself, but for Lady Bronwyn Hastur, who knew and loved her. She said—" Liriel's voice broke, though she quickly recovered her composure, "—she said that all the gifts of the mind, of *laran* itself, counted as nothing without a generous heart and a noble spirit."

When she ended her message with the formal phrase, "Let that memory lighten grief," her shoulders sagged in relief.

One by one, the others took her place. Each had some personal memory of Queen Taniquel to offer, not the legendary image, but the woman—human, fallible, and loved.

Can any of us ask for more, than to be remembered like this? Varzil wondered.

Without conscious intention, he stepped forward to stand beside Taniquel's grave. "I never had the privilege of knowing her, yet she has touched my life. In being remembered here, by the people who did know her, she has given me the knowledge that within every legend is an ordinary person who has found herself faced with extraordinary trials and has risen to them. That how the world and history see us is very different from how we see ourselves. In her memory, I am reminded it is not fame but inner truth that makes us who we are. Let that memory lighten grief."

He moved back, to find himself at Felicia's side. Her eyes, green like spring, like the sea he had never seen, met his own. His mind reached out to hers and for a trembling moment, there was no separation, no difference between them. Then the sounds of the funeral assembly reached him.

"Forgive me, I have been rude in staring at you," he said, holding out his arm for her to take.

"There is no lapse of courtesy." She placed her fingertips on his sleeve so lightly that he felt only a featherweight of pressure. "Not between *bredin*." She used the plural form of the word which might mean *sibling* but also *beloved*.

Have we not spoken mind to mind? she asked. *And have there not been times when we have been of one mind?*

He choked off the response, for Carolin had come up to him. With a nod, Felicia left them to walk in Liriel's shadow.

"My friend," Carolin said, "I cannot return with you to Thendara, but I would very much like to arrange a proper visit. I hope you do not need to return immediately to Arilinn?"

"I am not expected back at Arilinn for some while," Varzil said. "We cannot return immediately, for even with fresh mounts, the ladies will need to rest." He did not add that Felicia had business to conduct regarding her mother's estate.

"A tenday or two, at the least, knowing Liriel," Carolin said. "Times have changed since we could send an aircar for such a purpose."

"Serrais has now reserved aircars for military use only," Varzil said. "Arilinn's airfield is closed now, did you know?"

"Yes, we'd heard."

They walked together toward the area where servants held the reins of their mounts. Carolin said, "If you have the time, perhaps you can ride with me out to Blue Lake. It's the country estate where I was raised. I've business there and I'd welcome the company for the journey. It's been too many years since we were at Arilinn together."

✦

Returning to Hastur Castle, Carolin went first to his uncle's chambers. Rakhal was there, sitting across the beautifully inlaid game table, now spread with a few scattered castles. Rakhal was clearly playing to lose, to prolong the game, to keep the King amused.

King Felix looked up. The late afternoon light fell across his features, bleaching his eyes colorless and turning his cheeks into a myriad of tiny creases. "Sit down, my boy."

Carolin sat, exchanged a few pleasantries, and delivered Lady Liriel's respects as she had asked. The King remembered little of the morning's business, for the funeral had been private and quiet.

As soon as he could do so with decorum, Carolin took his leave. He would be up half the night, catching up on the day's work which he had put aside for the funeral, not to mention this overlong and pointless interview. Blue Lake called to him; he missed its simplicity and freedom. He longed equally for time with Varzil. He had never lost the sense of connection with his friend, although their lives had taken very different directions.

He worked well into the evening, stopping only for a private dinner in his chambers, together with Alianora and their two boys. Rafael, the older, ran to him with delight. Alianora carried little Alaric with an ease which spoke of both deep affection and custom. She had long since moved to her own suite of rooms, but often met with Carolin at times like this. Carolin suspected, from the obvious attachment of the boys, that she spent as much time in the nursery as in her own sitting room.

Motherhood had rounded Alianora's curves and bestowed upon her an air of gentle contentment. She remained reserved, an essentially private person. Only her children, two fine, healthy sons and another on the way, evoked any spark of passion. She did not ask about the funeral, nor about any of Carolin's other business; he could never be sure if she felt it improper to inquire, or simply had no curiosity. The children sufficed for her; they comprised her entire world.

Carolin sat back in his chair, finishing the last of his single cup of wine, and regarded his family. Fatherhood had surprised him; the memory of the first time he had held Rafael in his arms still brought a rush of tenderness. Watching his son play in front of the fireplace and Alaric in his mother's arms, he tried to etch their images into his mind. Outside the fragile haven of these walls, untold dangers stalked their world. He knew it was foolish to become too attached to children who might die of any of a hundred causes, from lung fever to threshold sickness, and in the case of little princes, deliberate assault.

No, he would not think of that. He must go on as if all would be well, must hold to the dream of a world in which children like Rafael and Alaric had no need to fear being seized as a hostage or having poison slipped into their milk, face hostile armies at their gates, or *clingfire* raining from heaven.

In this world, the love which welled up in his heart was so very precious. . . .

He thought of other kinds of love, too. The love he had felt for his own parents. The love for his friends, for Orain and Jandria and Maura. For Varzil.

Now, a gentle sadness crept over him. Undoubtedly it was the influence of the day's events, the intense, unexpressed emotions of the funeral, what was said and what left unsaid. He had seen the way Varzil looked at Felicia Leynier, had felt their moment of mental communion. It did not take a telepath to realize that they were in love, or would be very soon.

He would say nothing of it; some things were not discussed, and besides what would he say? That he was happy for his friend, that he feared such an alliance could never end in happiness, that against all sense, some secret part of him wished that he might have known such a love?

"You look tired," Alianora said, "and it is time for the boys to be in bed. Shall we see you again before you leave for Blue Lake?"

Carolin roused from his melancholy; the woman before him was his lawful wife *di catenas,* the mother of his children, who had kept her own promise to be a good and dutiful wife to him. How could he insult her by wishing she were someone else?

The world went as it would, and not as any one man would have it, Carolin reminded himself of the old proverb. He would be a loyal prince, a faithful husband, a loving father. Someday, as King, he would have the chance to do more.

◆

Two days later, Varzil and Carolin set off on horseback, leading a *chervine* laden with supplies, into the Venza Hills headed for Blue Lake. There really *was* a lake, Carolin assured him, and most of the time it *was* blue. If the weather cleared, as it looked likely, they would have fine fishing.

They let their horses set an easy pace. The road dwindled and the land grew steeper and more rugged. First Hali and then Thendara, with all its noise and color, fell behind. As hours stretched into days of easy companionship, fellow travelers became even fewer. They stayed in simple but comfortable travel shelters that were placed a day's journey from one another along the major mountain roads. Under strict truce, no man might draw a weapon upon another in a shelter, no matter how dire the cause. No sane man dared risk exposure to the Venza's killing storms.

Toward afternoon on the fifth day, the clouds lifted altogether. They halted at the crest of a pass to let their horses breathe. Above them, a lonely hawk hovered against the sky. Varzil spotted what looked like a shadow across the distant hills. He pointed it out to Carolin, for the day was clear.

"Yes, that's recent *clingfire* burn. See how it stops at the rock seam?"

Varzil, searching with *laran* as well as vision, shuddered. Now that he knew what it was, he smelled it across the leagues.

"Sometimes I fear that you and I will see no end to such things," Carolin said.

"I pray we are both wrong about that. I'm always being told, *Wait.*

Be patient. Let things develop in their own manner, until I'm sick of it. I expect you hear the same things, too."

"That I do, but I won't give up and neither should you. Just because a pack of old donkeys can't see past their own noses doesn't mean the rest of us have to live that way. I have a whole court full of them to deal with! Not to mention the aunties of both sexes who think that nothing should ever be done for the first time!"

Varzil chuckled. Arilinn, too, had its share of conservatives. While few Towers were more prestigious, none were less likely to experiment. Sometimes Barak, the younger Keeper, acted as if preserving the past was so important, it overshadowed any other concerns.

"I agree," Varzil said. "Whether it's your pact or something else, we must never give up trying to change things for the better. Perhaps what's wrong is that although people suffer the way things are, they don't suffer enough. They fear what they don't know far more than what they do."

Carolin nudged his horse down the pass, loosening the reins so the animal could lower its head and set its own balance. "Maybe true change requires desperation. I hope it will not come to that. I cannot imagine anything more horrendous than what happened at Neskaya and Tramontana, and that didn't have any lasting effect. The new Tower at Tramontana serves Hastur alone. There will be no shortage of *clingfire* when the next war comes. If the rumblings out of Asturias continue, that won't be long."

Varzil heard the disappointment in his friend's voice that the new Tower at Tramontana had only increased the potential for destruction. "Someday," he said, "when I am Keeper and you are king, we won't have to do things as they have always been done."

"We will rebuild Neskaya Tower," Carolin replied. "Not as yet another source of dreadful *laran* weaponry, but as a symbol of peace and hope. Upon my honor, I swear it."

✦

"Look!" Carolin pointed. "Can you see the lake?"

This morning, they had come down from the hills into rolling pastures. Graceful, water-loving willows lined the many streams. The land itself smelled fresh. Varzil spied an oval of blue, like sky made liquid and collected in a cup, a sprawling manor house, lawns dotted with shade trees, gardens with low rock walls, and the rows of a small orchard.

"It's not as exciting as court, but it was a grand place to grow up in," Carolin said.

Varzil thought of his own home at Sweetwater, the rugged land, the herds of cattle and horses. In comparison, Blue Lake was a princely estate. It did not have to support itself, although it looked as if it could easily do so.

As they went down toward the river and denser woods on either side, Varzil began to grow uneasy. The day was fair, the birds trilling to each other in the branches. Carolin talked on, sharing memories from his boyhood, the little stag pony which had been his first mount, the red leather belt he and Orain had come to blows over, stealing berry scones from the kitchen without getting caught and then finding out Cook had left them out for him. Varzil heard the happiness shine through Carolin's words.

With a cry, a rainbird took wing from the undergrowth in front of them. Varzil's horse snorted and pranced as if the tiny bird were a giant carnivorous banshee on the hunt. He kept his seat with an effort. A faint prickle crept up his spine.

"What's the matter?" Carolin asked.

Varzil shook his head, but he was already scanning the open sky. With the river gleaming through the bushes, the air felt heavy and damp. He'd be happier once they were in the open, though he could not explain why. These were not wild woods. There would be no wolves or Trailmen lying in wait. This deep into Hastur territory, they had little to fear from an armed assault. The most dangerous part of their journey had been the passage through the Venza Hills. The road had been peaceful and until now, Varzil had felt perfectly at ease.

Settling himself again in the saddle, Varzil reached out with his *laran*. He touched the curling river currents, the sleepy green peace of the woods and surrounding pasture land. Bits of brightness marked livelier minds—silvertrout, fox, rabbit-horn, the rainbird's nesting mate. . . .

Something mechanical . . . the hard bitter edge of a starstone shield—

Just a little farther and I'll have you, Hastur scum . . .

The edge of the thought trailed across Varzil's mind like a molten brand. He jerked alert.

—Carolin spinning through the air, his back arched, arms flung wide, a blossom of crimson unfolding across his blue-and-silver jacket—

In front of him, Carolin rode easily, now glancing back over his shoulder. His black mare bobbed her head, ears relaxed, tail swishing an errant fly.

Varzil clamped his heels into the sides of his horse. The animal surged forward. Its hindquarters bunched, ears flattening against its skull. He lashed it with his mind as well as his heels. Within a stride or two, it was at full gallop and even with the rump of Carolin's horse. Varzil caught the expression of amazement on Carolin's face, the quick movement as the black mare threw up her head.

A slender shape like a splinter of silvery metal burst from the tangle of brush ahead of them. If Varzil's horse were not already at a gallop, he could never have reached it in time. It pierced the air, emitting a thin whine. He grabbed a handful of his cloak and thrust it in front of the sliver. At the same time, he gathered his *laran* like a battle hammer and brought it smashing down. Something within the device shattered.

The lined wool of Varzil's cloak slowed the sliver's progress. Momentum pulled him from his horse. He hit the road in a snarl of cloak and legs, but he had the thing wrapped.

"*Aldones!*" Carolin dropped to the ground and rushed over.

The impact of Varzil's fall knocked the breath from him. His cloak twisted sideways around his shoulders, much of it bunched up in his hands. He didn't dare loosen his physical grip until he was certain that the thing—whatever it was—was truly inert.

Carolin reached for the bundle.

"No, don't touch it! It isn't safe!" Varzil said.

With his mind, Varzil explored the device. It reeked of *laran* technology, glass and metal, though he had never encountered its like before. He'd heard of mechanical birds in which a *laranzu* could send forth his consciousness over great distances, akin to the link with sentry birds but without their fleshly limitations.

This one was too small for such a task. It did, however, contain a starstone chip.

Varzil told Carolin to stand back while he slowly unwrapped his cloak. The gleaming dart was perhaps a hand's length from tip to slightly rounded belly. Fins of metal ran its length for balance and guidance. A tiny starstone winked at its tapering head like a malevolent eye.

"That *thing*—" Carolin began.

Varzil did not respond, for at the sound of Carolin's voice, the dart began vibrating. He tightened his grip to hold it fast. He felt rather than heard a faint, ominous humming from its core. The sensible thing to do would be to take something solid—a rock if there was one to hand, or the hilt of a dagger—and smash the starstone. The thing had been aimed at Carolin, and might yet prove deadly if it pierced his flesh. Yet some instinct held him back. Destroyed, its secrets would perish with it.

He thrust deeper into the thing with his mind. The starstone was a guidance device, of that he was certain, but it did more. In a flash, he realized that it generated an energy field that masked the contents of the body. The barrier gave way under his determined probing.

Clingfire!

A mote of the caustic burning stuff lay within a fragile glass bubble. Even the lightest impact would crack the vessel, releasing its contents into the flesh of its victim. There it would ignite, burning away vital organs, muscle and bone until there was nothing left to be consumed. Neither water nor smothering blankets could extinguish it, and it would spread to anything combustible that came into contact with it.

It would be a death of screaming torment. Men had been known to slit their own throats rather than endure the pain of *clingfire.* A victim's only hope was to cut away all the flesh around the burning area.

Varzil recoiled in horror. The dart was designed to place the *clingfire* deep within the victim's body—within *Carolin's* body—where there would be not the slightest hope of rescue.

Carolin bent over Varzil's shoulder. "It's some kind of killer device. I don't recognize the exact type. There was a report of such things at the *Comyn* Council last season."

"Someone is making these—these—?" Varzil's mouth filled with bile.

"No legitimate Tower, at least none that will admit to it," Carolin said. He reached one hand toward the dart, which quivered even more strongly. Reflexively, he drew back. His face paled.

"It's keyed to *me.*"

"Yes, and whoever sent it is still here . . . nearby."

Varzil tightened his grip on the device. Even through the folds of his cloak, he felt its thrumming as a sickness in his blood. It was not alive, but it carried the intent of its master. With one hand, Varzil freed his own starstone and focused on it. Within moments, he overshadowed the vibrational pattern of the chip. The humming ceased, although the linkage to the guiding mind remained. Whoever had sent this thing would believe it still active, at least for the next crucial minutes. . . .

Varzil cast his telepathic sense like a net over the surrounding woods. He felt Carolin link with him and used the stamp of Carolin's personality as a resonance, a lure. The killer would be thinking of Carolin—

There, in the brush beside the river!

Moving silently, Varzil and Carolin crept along the road. Carolin slipped his short sword free from its scabbard, slow and easy, almost soundless. Varzil felt the killer's mind, knew exactly where the man crouched. Aside from the river itself, there was only one path of escape. He pointed for Carolin to position himself there.

Varzil took out his small traveling knife and pried the starstone chip loose from the dart. The *clingfire* would have to be disposed of later, preferably in a Tower. He placed the chip on a rock and, using the hilt of his knife, smashed it.

There was a sudden rustling in the brush along the bank, a body thrashing. Varzil felt the man's mind reel in shock and surprise. Shouting, Carolin rushed forward. Varzil left the dart, still wrapped in his cloak, and pushed his way to the river.

A man in a worn leather vest lunged into the water, splashing wildly. His movements were uncoordinated, the river current strong. He lost his footing and went down just as Carolin jumped into the water.

They floundered in the hip-deep water. Carolin hauled the other man upright, one hand twisted in the man's collar, the other holding the short sword to his throat. He half-dragged, half-prodded the man toward the bank where Varzil waited. The man struggled, arms and legs flailing, but he could not resist Carolin's expert hold.

Carolin threw the man down on the rocky bank of the river. Panting heavily, the man lay against the crushed reeds and moss-laced stones. Varzil knelt and peered closely at the man. Blue eyes glinted in a darkly bearded face like chips of cloudless sky. The man's mouth worked soundlessly. A mixture of rage and terror emanated from him.

"Who sent you?" Carolin snarled. "Where did you get that thing?"

"Let me do this." Varzil placed one hand on Carolin's arm. He had not the Alton Gift of forced rapport, but he could do far more, mind to mind. He reached out with his *laran,* only to meet a shield like twisted clouds. It wouldn't be hard to penetrate, given the man's fear and confusion.

The man had *laran* enough to guide the killer dart, but he could not have created it. Despite the hatred emanating from the man's mind, Varzil did not think he was the one to plan this attack. He had acted for someone else.

Varzil pressed deeper, and the man's psychic shields began to give way.

"No! Ye'll ne'er trap me that way!" The man spat in Varzil's face.

For a moment, Varzil was blinded by the man's spittle. He felt Carolin's recoil of shock, heard the scuffle of the man scrambling to his feet, slipping in the mud, the scrape of wet boot leather on rock. By the time he'd wiped his eyes, Carolin had pinned the man against the knotted roots of an ancient willow. The smell of churned mud and the sweat of fear stained the air.

Varzil caught only a glimpse of the man's eyes, the instant of wide white despair.

The man's body stiffened, an arc of agony before he crumbled. He lay against the tree, twisted to one side. The angle of his lolling head and splayed arms gave him the look of a doll tossed carelessly aside.

Varzil did not need to touch the man to know he was dead. The sudden tearing away of the man's life energy left a fading clamor, like an ill-tuned bell struck but once and then forevermore still. Nausea rose, a noxious river swell in Varzil's throat. He turned to the water, retching.

"Bredu!" Carolin's voice pierced the waves of sickness.

"I'm all right," he managed to speak. "Are we far from Blue Lake? I need a secure place where I can examine this man more closely. We must find out who sent him to kill you . . . and why."

25

Varzil would have wished for a different introduction to Blue Lake. The house and grounds held all the charm and tranquility he had seen at a distance. It was the perfect place for an active, imaginative boy to grow up, and in later years, it would offer a sanctuary against the intrigues of the court.

The *coridom* of Blue Lake and the servants who rushed out at Carolin's arrival stared open-mouthed at the limp body slung over the pack animal. Varzil could tell from the ease and speed with which Carolin's orders were obeyed how greatly he was loved. These people remembered him as a child, as a youth; nothing he did as a man could shake their trust. They needed no explanations, although it must have been unusual for their master to arrive with a dripping corpse.

Varzil refused to perform his *laran* examination inside the house, where people lived and slept, nor the barn with its flammable materials. The little stone-walled building used for making ale and cider was lined with racks of bottles, empty barrels, and glass containers. It smelled of apples and its clean dirt floor. A burly man in a farrier's leather apron picked up the dead man as if he weighed no more than an empty saddle and carried him inside.

It was a simply matter to clear off one of the worktables and lay the corpse upon it. His clothing and hair were still damp. Varzil opened the shutters to admit more light, happy that he would not need a candle.

Carolin stood in the doorway. "I don't like leaving you alone with him."

"It's safer this way," Varzil said. He did not want to add that any distraction, no matter how inadvertent, could risk his own life, if not his sanity. "Go and greet your people. I'll be along as soon as may be. The longer I delay, the less information I can recover."

And the farther into the Overworld I must search . . .

Varzil drew up one of the three-legged stools so that he sat level with the man's head. He unwrapped the dart, inert now, and laid it where he could easily reach it.

The man's body was almost cold and had begun to stiffen. His face was purpled with blood from having been carried face-down across the *chervine's* saddle. Nothing could be read in his features, no clues as to what sort of man he had been in life. His hands and forearms bore the pattern of calluses and scars typical of a mercenary or adventurer. He wore no amulet or other jewelry, nor any identification papers in his folded belt. Varzil and Carolin had searched the river area briefly for some trace of a horse, but found nothing. The man might have been waiting there for days. As Carolin had pointed out, he had made no secret of his intention to visit Blue Lake. His departure had been delayed a few days by the funeral.

Varzil took out his starstone, holding it in his cupped hands. Closing his eyes, he focused his attention through the stone. Within a few minutes, its familiar pulsating warmth spread through his mind.

He laid his fingertips on the man's exposed wrist, where once he would have felt a living pulse. The flesh still retained the imprint of that rhythm, leading inexorably to the man's heart. Just as a physician might trace the physical vessels, now Varzil used the same pathways to follow the dead man's mental energy.

Fleshly decay had hardly begun. The chill of the river had delayed its onset. The man's energon nodes and channels had shut down, but their structure as yet remained intact. Sometimes, Varzil knew, when a person died suddenly, the spirit often lingered for a time. He had hoped such would be the case, but now, as he went deeper and farther along the pattern of energy channels, he felt no trace of any consciousness. The utter absence struck him as unusual. The man had been dead some hours, true. In even a natural death, there should be some imprint of personality, some persistent attachment to living. Unless . . .

Unless the man knew he was going to die. Unless he *meant* to die.

Varzil wondered if he were looking at one of the fabled Aldaran assassins, mentally implanted with a suicide command should their mission fail. He wasn't even sure whether they existed or were a product of the distorted legends from the Ages of Chaos. Stranger things had been proven true.

Varzil did not think this man was one of them. The man had directed the *clingfire* dart and died before he could be questioned, but he didn't seem skillful or ruthless enough. Thoughtfully, Varzil touched the dart. It had been made by other hands. Dalereuth, perhaps, or some renegade Tower. This man had enough *laran* to guide it to a target, but nothing more.

Closing his eyes again, Varzil slipped into the Overworld. He had always found the transition disorienting, though his teachers assured him he did it more smoothly than most. Now he stood on a featureless gray plain, blinking in the diffuse unchanging light.

The Overworld was composed of mental material, not ordinary, familiar earthly components. As such, this mind stuff could be shaped by thought. Now Varzil gathered it up, forming a tall obelisk like a finger pointing to the pallid sky. On each of its four sides, he visualized an incised picture—the manor house here at Blue Lake, a grazing horse, the ancient gnarled willow by the river, Carolin's sword. These symbols, images of real things, would create an anchor here in this place where time and space lost all meaning.

The form which Varzil took in the Overworld resembled his actual physical body. As usual, he clothed himself in the loose robe he wore for Tower work. He clasped his starstone and used it to call up the pattern from the chip in the *clingfire* dart. It wasn't a complicated pattern, nothing like a functional matrix stone. Yet because the dead man had been in some way linked with it, it resonated with his own personality.

Working carefully, Varzil was able to tease out the impression of the dead man's mind. Some instinct held him back from calling out directly. It was never entirely safe to have dealings with the dead.

Instead, Varzil used the trace as a guide. He slowly turned in each direction, making a complete circle. Searching . . .

Toward the end of his circuit, he sensed a ripple of invisible colors.

Once, on the edge of the Dry Towns, he had seen distortions caused by heat rising above the wind-smoothed sand. It had looked like water, but Kevan called it a mirage.

Grayness flickered, beckoning. He willed it to come closer, knowing the futility of trying to approach anything so evanescent here in the Overworld. Even things that appeared solid might retreat, tantalizingly just beyond reach. He had heard tales of the unwary, rushing about after departed loved ones, lost and desperate, until their physical bodies withered to lifeless husks.

The twist of colorless light steadied, separating into black and white. Varzil held the images firmly and waited for more detail to emerge . . . diamond shapes upon a hanging banner and beyond it, the ghostly lineaments of a wall. A fort or castle, he thought, or the remnants of one. The tracery of stone and wood felt like memory rather than dream.

Something which had once existed?

He raised his starstone to eye level and peered through it at the shadowy form. The castle solidified and seemed larger as well. A man stood before the wooden gate, wearing the battered leather vest of the assassin. He looked very much as Varzil had seen him. As if sensing Varzil's presence, he turned to glance behind. The door swung open.

The man raised a fist and shook it in Varzil's direction. "I may have failed, but the cause lives on. Death to the Hasturs! We will be avenged!"

Varzil leaped forward. He was too late, for the man darted into the opening just before the wooden gate slammed shut. The castle vanished instantly.

Panting, sweating, Varzil found himself back in the stone hut at Blue Lake, with no more idea of who had sent the assassin than before.

✦

The *coridom* took care of disposing of the assassin's body. Varzil sat up with Carolin long into the evening, talking about what had happened. A fire had been laid in the comfortable sitting room, though the night was mild. The household had gone to great lengths to welcome its master, and it had taken most of the evening to find a moment of quiet. Even so, Carolin had had to kindly ask the *coridom's* wife, who remembered him as a lad, to please leave them to their talk.

Carolin was clearly bent on dismissing the attack as the actions of a madman. Varzil fought his rising anxiety, trying not to say, *Someone tried to kill you. It is not the first attempt. Next time, they might succeed.*

"If you're thinking about Eduin, I won't hear of it," Carolin responded to Varzil's unvoiced thought. "The incident with the starstone was an accident, a misunderstanding. I said once that the two of you were going to have to work out your grievances, but I didn't mean using me as the battleground." He sat back in the huge, upholstered chair that clearly had seen better days, one hand unconsciously tracing the embroidered pattern of castles, sword ivy, and rosalys.

Varzil bent forward, resting his elbows on his knees. Deliberately, he avoided mentioning the fall in the orchard at Arilinn. It had been a long time ago. Perhaps Carolin was right about Eduin after all. . . .

"What about the black-and-white banner?" he said, unable to give it up entirely. "And the words, *We will be avenged?* This attack was aimed at you, the next Hastur King. Who feels themselves wronged by your family? Who harbors such bitter hatred?"

"Let go of it, Varzil, before you drive both of us mad!" Carolin straightened in his chair. "Don't you understand? Even a King who is loved has enemies. It's one thing to exercise prudent care, and quite another to see evildoers in every shadow. If I insisted on tracing every possible threat to its very end, I'd never do anything else!"

"Carlo, if anything happened to you—"

"Bredu." In a lightning move, Carolin reached out and captured one of Varzil's hands between his own. Varzil, who knew only the rudiments of swordsmanship and had spent little time around fighting men, had not realized just how quick or powerful his friend was.

"Would you have me cripple myself trying to prevent every conceivable catastrophe?" Carolin said. "Life must be lived on its own terms, and part of being a Hastur, let alone a king, is the ongoing risk. Not what you face in the circle—" Here he gave a quick grimace that brought an answering smile from Varzil. "—but others. I have been born and trained to those risks."

Don't ask me to be less than I am.

Varzil caught the unspoken thought. How would he react if Carolin fretted every time he joined a circle or linked with one of the matrix screens that made possible the complex, sophisticated work of the Towers?

I would say that such risks are mine to take. I would not live my life walled in by imagined terrors. I cannot ask my friend to do what I myself would not.

Relenting, Varzil slid his hand free and placed it on top of Carolin's. "Once you said there were two kinds of power—that of the world and that of the Tower. I fear I have been guilty of attempting to judge one from the vantage point of the other. Yet we must have both, if we are to succeed with our dream of a new Darkover."

26

Despite Varzil's lingering misgivings, the journey from Blue Lake to Hali and then back to Arilinn was one of the most joyous times of his life. Without the urgency of the funeral, he and Felicia enjoyed a leisurely pace. He did not speak of the assassination attempt or his venture into the Overworld, although they weighed heavily upon his thoughts. Felicia had her own burdens; he would not add to them.

"I was glad of the chance to see Lady Bronwyn again," Felicia said as they let their horses walk on easy reins. "I doubt I'll get another chance, she's so frail. In a few years, there will be no one left who remembers my parents." She sighed lightly, without any trace of self-pity. "She swears I took my first toddling steps into her arms."

She glanced at him, green eyes dancing. "Do you miss your family?"

"Only Dyannis, and she's at Hali now, so we speak regularly across the relays," he answered. "Once my father reconciled himself to my being in a Tower, he started referring to me as *my son at Arilinn*. I rather think he was as glad to find some place to put me as I was to get away."

"Yes, there is that," she said. "Carolin has offered to find me a nice husband, but I think he's relieved at how adamantly I've refused."

Varzil looked out over the sloping pastures. He felt absurdly happy that Felicia should be so firm in her refusal of marriage. She was far too talented to resign herself to a life of babies and fancy embroidery. He supposed her *nedestra* status added to the difficulty of a suitable match, but posed no problem in the Towers.

Varzil thought of Eduin, who for all his faults and obscure birth had become a skilled *laranzu,* a valuable asset to any Tower. Eduin had not yet returned to Arilinn from his journey home. Before Varzil and Felicia left for Hali, there had been some speculation that Eduin might wish to transfer to another Tower. Indeed, on the eve of their departure, a message had come over the relays from Hali Tower, requesting Arilinn to release him so that Eduin might join them.

In these unsettled times, few *leronyn* spent their entire lives at the Tower where they had first trained. Some, like Eduin, found one reason or another to start afresh; others, like Carolin, came for a short time only, whether a single season or a few years.

Carlo . . .

The memory of the riverside attack returned. The man in the leather vest had been fanatic in purpose, carefully prepared, armed with a sophisticated weapon attuned to Carolin alone. Whoever had planned it would not be deterred by a single failure. Carolin might not be so lucky next time. Varzil could not help thinking that he had missed some vital clue, had not pursued the matter to its end. . . .

"Varzil, that thought has been nagging at you all morning," Felicia said with a trace of acerbity. "Whatever is it?"

He realized he had been shielding his thoughts imperfectly and was about to apologize when her mind brushed against his.

If we are to work together, there can be no such secrets. Privacy, certainly, but nothing that might distract us and thus place the entire circle at risk.

So might a Keeper speak, he thought.

Felicia was right. Working in a circle was like living without a skin. Matters normally considered exempt from polite conversation could not be concealed. A thought was as potent as a deed and few topics were taboo. It was the duty of Keeper and monitor to make sure each member was fit to work.

Speaking mind to mind, Varzil told Felicia what had happened on the road to Blue Lake. She kept her eyes downcast, her gaze somewhere in the direction of her horse's ears, listening intently. Once or twice, she raised her eyes to his and he sensed the turmoil behind her quietness.

"This sad world of ours has more than its share of wickedness," she said when he had finished. "Yet Carolin is a good man who has done nothing to deserve such a fate."

"No, these men, whoever they are, hunt him for what he is—a Hastur."

Felicia sighed. "Imagine them, Varzil, so consumed with the evil of their deeds, the dark malice of their thoughts. To nurture such hatred is to suckle a scorpion-ant at one's breast." *It is Evanda's own grace that I am not such a one!*

Varzil stared at her. Felicia had always seemed so gentle, so compassionate. Yet who was immune from the call of justice, given sufficient cause? Every man had his weakness, and even the strongest sword its breaking point.

"You are thinking of the great battle of the ballads?" he asked aloud. "The one which destroyed Neskaya and Tramontana Towers?"

She shook her head. "Even before that, King Damian Deslucido conquered Acosta and killed King Padrik, who was father to my brother Julian."

Varzil heard the bitterness in her voice and knew it was not hers alone. It was something she inherited along with the color of her hair and shape of her hands. Just as he had been fed on suspicion of the Hasturs, from before he knew who they were.

"I had heard the family was extinct," Varzil said. *And therefore you are free of the burden of hating them.*

"They are, and I am. But my mother was not. If any had by some chance survived, I believe she would have hunted them down herself. She was adamant that no trace of them remain. It's understandable, of course. She was very young when Acosta was overrun. And newly pregnant with Julian. It must have been horrible to see her husband cut down, to find herself a prisoner facing a forced remarriage."

Another reason why Carlo's pact or something like it is so important.

"It is something Carlo—Carolin Hastur—and I have talked of over the years," Varzil said. He hesitated to say more, but under her gentle prodding, he found himself pouring out his dreams. He ended with the promise to rebuild Neskaya Tower as a symbol of hope.

"A hope of a new Darkover, one free of these incessant wars," she murmured. "I pray I might live to see such a time."

On impulse, he said, *You will see it. I promise you. You will be part of its birthing.*

She pulled away from his mental touch with a sad little shrug. *Do not offer me empty promises, Varzil Ridenow. We may be blessed in our times, or cursed, and nothing we can do will change the will of the gods in this respect.*

✦

With a feeling of deep contentment, Varzil entered the matrix laboratory and studied the assembled members of the First Circle at Arilinn. Auster was turning over more responsibility to him as under-Keeper, although the older man would direct this night's work. Varzil knew and loved every person in the circle, from Valentina Aillard to Gavin Elhalyn. They were his family, a family of the heart in ways that old *Dom* Felix Ridenow and Lord Harald could never be.

I have found the place where I belong.

Felicia had joined the circle this evening. Since coming to Arilinn and proving to Fidelis' satisfaction that she had truly recovered from her lung fever, she had been training with the higher-level matrices and had easily mastered the work.

She sat in her place around the low, round table, quietly preparing herself for the task ahead. This night, the laboratory had been set up for one of the most demanding tasks, the refining of raw materials for *clingfire*. Varzil was not happy about making the incendiary weapon and had urged Auster and the other Keepers to refuse.

"We are not willful children, to pick and choose what lawful work we will do," Auster had replied. "Arilinn's strength lies in our adherence to tradition, to those techniques which have proven themselves over the centuries. Dissension and rebellion are the surest way to disaster, and our world has seen more than its share in this last generation. I will not permit another such catastrophe under my authority."

In the end, Auster's word as Keeper was law. Just as a circle could not function as a conglomeration of individual talents, so a Tower could not continue with disparate voices. Barak, Keeper of the Second Circle, was even more conservative.

Now Auster would weave together the *laran* of the circle into a coherent whole, channeled and amplified through the enormous artificial matrix screens. They were working with a seventh-level matrix, which technically required seven qualified workers to control. Other Towers might have used six upon occasion, but Auster insisted upon things being done properly.

Cerriana took her place outside the circle, wearing the white robe of a monitor. The basic elements for the *clingfire* had already been mined and lay ready in their glass containers. The next step required distillation at high heat. Sometimes the glass vessels exploded, spewing bits of burning material. Even with protective clothing, workers were sometimes horribly injured. Iron or steel containers would have been more stable, but vulnerable to corrosion.

Varzil, in his capacity as under-Keeper, had already ensured that the chamber was shielded. He made one last check, for a distraction at a crucial time could prove disastrous, and then settled himself on his bench.

"Let us begin," Auster said.

As one, the members of the circle reached out hands and minds to one another. Varzil slipped into the familiar stream of mental energy as each person bent his concentration toward the Keeper. With the confidence born of his decades of experience, Auster attuned the individual psychic signatures into a harmonious unity.

As an ordinary circle worker, Varzil had happily accepted the loss of personal separateness under his Keeper's control, one note in a symphony, one color in an ever-changing rainbow, one droplet in a river of dancing light. Since he had begun his Keeper's training, however, a shift had taken place. The relentless rigor of the exercises had altered his consciousness so that, while part of him floated, serene and blissful, in the energy nets, another part remained aware and separate. Later, as he progressed in skill, he would be able to control and direct the focused *laran* of the circle while still remaining an integral part of it.

Auster, a magnet of power, glowing like a sun . . .

Felicia, bright and shining like sunlight on new steel . . .

Gavin, immovable as a rock . . .

Valentina . . . Richardo . . .

Lorens, who had helped to build this matrix lattice, holding the pattern in his mind like a map . . .

From outside the circle itself, Varzil felt Cerriana's subtle presence. Her mind moved constantly around the circle, checking each person, testing breathing, pulse, the rhythmic blinking of eyes, the tension in back and neck muscles, the temperature of extremities. Wherever she found discomfort, no matter how minor, she eased it. Even something as trivial as a toe cramp could mar the perfect concentration necessary for circle work. For this reason, she had not linked in the circle itself, but remained apart so that she could devote her entire attention to the others.

As if from a distance, Varzil felt a gentle warmth through his lower back as Cerriana relaxed the muscles there. He reminded himself to thank her afterward.

Auster had completed the work of weaving the minds of the circle together. The raw elements of the *clingfire* in their glass vessels stood ready. Using the artificial matrix crystals to amplify their already powerful *laran,* he began the next phase, raising the temperature to distillation levels.

Varzil felt the shift as Auster tightened his control. This work was doubly dangerous, first because of the power of the matrix lattice, secondly from the physical effects of the *clingfire* itself.

Something was not right.

Varzil could sense no disturbance in the energy net, no discord in the psychic resonances. Auster had done this work many times. The circle was more than able to manage the matrix. Cerriana had checked them all carefully before they began work, to make sure neither of the women was approaching her cycle, and no one was too tired for the demands of the work.

What, then? he asked. *Cerriana?*

I can find nothing amiss, only the trouble in your own thoughts. This was a polite way of telling him to attend to the business at hand.

Time lost its meaning, moments or hours passing as the circle continued to pour their focused thoughts toward their Keeper. The first container grew hotter. The more volatile elements began to evaporate and pass through the distillation apparatus.

One mote, one fragment at a time, the process of separation and purification continued. The circle finished one vessel and began the next. Through his closed eyes, Varzil envisioned the corrosive stuff as glowing, molten orange-red particles which possessed their own eerie beauty.

The colors wavered in Varzil's mental sight, the outlines of the containers vibrating. When he was six, he had fallen from his pony and struck his head against a stone. His eyes had fractured a single image into three, five, a dozen, all jerking erratically. His nurse fussed and his father had forbidden him to ride for a week. But there was nothing wrong with his skull now.

He felt rather than saw the first crack in the thin-walled distillation tube, waited for a horrified second for Auster to reinforce it. The massed *laran* of the group was more than enough to stabilize a minor flaw and continue working.

Instead, the circle wavered, its unity unraveling. Strands of mental bonds tore free, whipped by invisible winds. At first, only a few, then more and more with each passing heartbeat. The circle faltered.

A worldless scream pierced the circle. It came from Auster.

On pure instinct, Varzil wrenched his focus free from the disintegrating net. His own mind shrilled in protest at the rupture, but he shoved the pain aside. With all his might, he plunged into Auster's mind.

And found chaos. Darkness ravened through the orderly patterns of the Keeper's consciousness, leaving howling emptiness in its wake. Thoughts formed, only to shred away into incoherent syllables, fragments of sound and color and taste. The mote that was Auster's personality flailed against it. The more Auster struggled for control, the weaker and less coherent his efforts. His attempts to make sense of his own thoughts fueled the panic within him.

Varzil recoiled, caught between horror and paralysis. Like everyone else, he had trained first as a monitor. Working in the healing circles, he had treated both fleshly and mental wounds, the nightmarish aftermath of madness or pain too great for sanity, but never these gaping wounds, psychic as well as physical, never this numbing confusion.

Precious moments slipped by. A new pattern emerged in Auster's mind, a stalemate of sorts. The damage—the gaps of emptiness—ceased to spread, and their movement slowed. Auster's own thoughts strengthened, although the edge of desperation remained.

Auster!

I . . . I don't know what happened . . .

Images of searing light flooded Auster's consciousness, jagged echoes behind his eyes. He looked out upon a circle of blank-eyed people, knowing he *should* recognize them. To one side, a woman in a white gown jerked upright, loose hair like a veil about her bloodless face.

Varzil! came Cerriana's anguished mental cry. *You must do something! He'll break the circle—*

What's wrong with him?

Stroke . . . we must clear the blood vessels to his brain . . . there is bleeding inside his skull . . .

Varzil deepened his rapport with Cerriana and together they shifted to the physical level.

Cerriana traced the network of arteries in Auster's brain as they branched and narrowed. In many places, the usually smooth linings were thick and roughened. In others, Varzil saw crooked, tortuous paths instead of gentle curves.

There!

Where Cerriana indicated, the overlay of energy pulsed red and congested, involuting upon itself into blackness. Here an artery twisted and broke off into two smaller branches. Caught in the narrowed opening, fragments of shredded tissue tangled with rust-colored clots and fatty plaque. Beyond it, brain cells stuttered. One wall of the larger artery, weakened by pressure and layered scarring, had ruptured. Blood pooled, pressing against the delicate nerve tissues.

In horror, Varzil realized that the hemorrhage was perilously close to the *laran* centers of Auster's brain.

Varzil dove into the pattern of cell and membrane. Working as quickly as he dared, he reinforced and stimulated fibrous cells to span the tear in the artery. This natural process was driven at a greatly accelerated rate by Varzil's mental energy.

As soon as the breach was sealed off to prevent any new bleeding, Varzil began reabsorbing the clotted blood pressing on Auster's brain tissue. He teased cells free from the matting of fibers, and sent a flood of scavenger cells and fluids to carry away waste and bring in nutrients. The work was not very different from healing tissues damaged by frostbite or gangrene, but here he was working inside a man's brain.

Not any man's, but a Keeper's. A man could live without a toe or even a foot. For anyone Gifted with *laran,* the loss would be far more devastating. And for a Keeper . . . As a novice, Varzil had heard stories, whispered when their teachers could not hear, of *leronyn* who had taken their own lives, rather than live on as psychic cripples.

Moments passed with aching slowness, as Varzil rebuilt and cleared, cell by cell. He dared not push too hard or risk starting the bleeding afresh.

The crushing pressure on the brain eased. Like embers springing to life in a freshening wind, the cells recovered. If he had been in his physical body, Varzil would have wept.

Cerriana, meanwhile, had been restoring the blood flow inside the artery. She could not simply break up the clot, lest it be carried farther along and close off even smaller vessels. Instead, she had gone down, below the level of the cells, shifting the energy between elemental particles. Solid material softened, became liquid. She filtered the fragments, passing only those smaller than blood cells. The tiny trickle of blood became stronger with each passing moment.

Varzil soared with relief when he realized Auster would survive. Already the last resonances of the pain faded. Auster had regained enough alertness to remain quiet and cooperate with the healing. He might recover enough to have years more of active work.

Work—*the circle!* Varzil had been so narrowly, so desperately focused on saving Auster's life that he had blocked out all everything else.

The *clingfire!*

27

In a flash, Varzil reached out with his mind to the circle. The psychic bonds resonated with the cracking vessel and the fracture of the melded minds. But, miraculously, the circle held. The *clingfire* sat on the work-table, safely contained.

The circle was no longer a tapestry of mental energies patterned by Auster's signature technique. Instead, it had been transformed into a sphere of gossamer iridescence that bore the unmistakable imprint of Felicia's *laran*.

It was not possible! From his first days at Arilinn, Varzil had been taught that women simply did not have the strength to do a Keeper's work, that they lacked the psychic dexterity to produce a coordinated unity from disparate minds, to focus and channel those immense energies to the designated task.

Yet the circle had held. Held under Felicia's sure control.

Felicia—a woman—had taken over as Keeper, against all the limitations of her sex, contrary to all tradition.

She was at the very limits of her abilities, holding a circle of only five minds linked through a seventh-level matrix. No Keeper in living memory had done such a thing. The slightest distraction might fracture that fragile unity.

He must do something. If he forced his way into the circle, he would increase their number to six. He had sufficient training as Keeper to assume the centripolar role and stabilize the new configuration. As soon as the thought arose, he knew it was impossible. The circle now belonged to Felicia as surely as if she had brought it together in the beginning. She had gathered up the unraveling strands of *laran* and reshaped them in her own way. He could not simply step into her position.

He would have to rebuild the circle entirely. That would take time, if only a few instants, but time he did not have. In the chaotic breach, he would risk damage to the entire circle, not only from the sudden, unprepared psychic dissolution, but from the *clingfire* itself. In its half-processed state, with the cracked container held intact only by *laran* forces, it could ignite or explode at the slightest lapse.

Between one heartbeat and the next, he knew what he must do. It would take every mote of skill he possessed. All of his training as under-Keeper was in how to control the collective minds of the circle, not how to submerge himself in another's personality. Yet this was exactly what he must do.

Fighting his instincts, Varzil opened himself to Felicia's mind. He could not afford even a hint of imposing his own pattern upon hers.

He felt as if he were gliding through layers of iridescent mist, like passing through the Veil of Arilinn Tower. The cool of a spring evening alternated with the kiss of autumn sun. Perfume swept through him, now the tang of wet earth stirring with green shoots, now the heavy must of grain ready for harvest, now the metallic cold of impending snow. Smell, temperature, color—the pattern lay not in any individual factor, but in the rhythm of their change. He sensed the others not as disparate minds, but a blending of congruent elements. Somehow, Felicia evoked a resonant strain in each one and catalyzed a harmony which already existed, so that their energies amplified one another, building naturally in the direction of her guidance.

Let sun be warm and shade be cool, red be red and green be green, the thought came to him. He did not need to force any kind of change, only bend his will toward things being exactly as they were.

Felicia shifted the energies to include Varzil. Her mental control was rough-edged with inexperience, but sure. She knew exactly what she was doing, even if she had never done it before; the patterns of mental energy made deep, intuitive sense to her.

She gathered up their focused *laran,* intensified by the matrix, and bridged the crack in the *clingfire* vessel. Her surge of triumph spread through the joined minds of the circle.

Auster moaned, a low wordless sound. Varzil came instantly alert and felt the others in the circle do otherwise. Had Auster been a stranger, he could not have affected their concentration, but each of them had, over the years, given his mind into Auster's keeping, and the roots of that deep synergy remained. One by one, they dropped out of rapport.

One moment ago, Varzil had hardly been aware of his physical sur-roundings. Now, the air felt still and cold. Nausea swept through him. He took a shuddering breath.

The chamber erupted into movement and sound, the rustle of cloth-ing, a gasp, a murmured exclamation. Gavin and Lorenz rushed to Aus-ter's side. Valentina jumped to her feet, toppling her bench, then wavered and crumpled into Richardo's arms.

Beside the door, Cerriana bent over the telepathic damper. The field died.

Fidelis! Varzil called silently. *Come quickly! Auster's had a stroke!*

How bad? came the muffled reply.

Cerriana and I stabilized him. He's weak, but awake. I don't think he can walk on his own.

The circle?

The rest of us are fine.

Footsteps pounded on the stairway below. Fidelis burst into the chamber, hair awry, still in his casual clothing. Auster protested weakly as Fidelis bent over him.

"Lie still, old friend," Fidelis murmured. "Let us do our work."

Cerriana outlined what had been done, using speech rather than communicating with *laran* to avoid distracting him. "I think we should get him out of here. It's so cold, he could easily go into shock."

"I'm all right, " Auster grumbled, slurring his words. "Just tired. What's all the fuss?"

"You've had a stroke," Fidelis said. "Gavin, Lorenz, make a chair carry to take him down to the infirmary."

As they moved Auster from the room, Varzil took a quick measure of what else needed to be done. The *clingfire* was safe enough now and could stay where it was for the time being. The huge matrix still hummed with power. Valentina was recovering from her faint, in need of hot food and rest, but nothing more. Richardo would help her downstairs.

Only Felicia had not moved from her place at the table. Her face was very pale, her chest rising and falling like the fluttering wings of a bird. She stared straight ahead.

Varzil knelt beside her and took one of her hands between his. The slender fingers were stiff, almost icy. She made no response.

Felicia . . .

Without thinking, he gathered her into his arms, wrapping her in flesh as well as mind. For a heartbeat, she relaxed against him.

It's all right . . . he told her. *I'm here.*

She stirred, pushing away. "Please, don't fuss over me." The psychic contact faded as she drew away. Barriers, thin and patchy, rose in her mind. She kept her gaze downcast.

"Don't fuss—after what you did?"

"What I—I don't know—Auster—he was taken ill—and the circle— the *clingfire*—" Felicia tore away, scrambling to her feet, and backed up almost to the far wall. Shivering visibly, she wrapped her arms around her body. Her breath came in gasps. "No, I didn't—I couldn't have—"

White-rimmed eyes met his. "It was *you*—" she stammered. "You're a trained under-Keeper. You mended the vessel, you kept the circle together. That's it, that's the way it happened—it must have!"

"Felicia, stop!" Varzil grabbed her shoulders. The physical contact jolted through both of them. Her words fell away, along with the shreds of her barriers.

They had been so closely linked in the circle, their minds so finely attuned, that now the rapport remained. In some ways, she was as unlike him as he could imagine. Each of them had their own story, private and hidden, that no other could ever fully share. But in other ways, embracing her mind was akin to looking into a mirror.

At last, Varzil became aware of her trembling, that she once more leaned against him. Her fingertips pressed into the muscles of his arms. To his mental question, she murmured, "I am cold . . . and hungry. But I do not want to go down and be among the others."

"I'll bring you a meal in your room."

Felicia sighed and nodded. He helped her down the stairs, steadying her when her balance wavered.

By the time they reached Felicia's chamber in the women's section,

Varzil, too, was shaking with hunger and exhaustion. Felicia could barely talk.

She sank down on her bed. The quilts were thick down, decorated in appliqué with a Tree-of-Life pattern. Birds spread their satin wings and nestled in the patchwork branches. He took a moment to stir the embers in the grate and add kindling. The temperature in the room was rising noticeably by the time he left.

◆

When Varzil returned, he found Felicia wrapped in the Tree-of-Life quilt. She'd brought out a small folding table and placed it within easy reach. He set down the tray with its beaker of steaming *jaco,* honeyed nut rolls, and covered dishes of soup and barn fowl stewed with fruit. She lifted the cover of the tureen and sniffed appreciatively.

"Ah, Lunilla's good bean soup. I feel better already." She moved over, making room for him on the bed.

With the first spoonful, Varzil's hunger awoke in force. For a time they ate in companionable silence, each bent on replenishing the energies drained during the last hours. The warm food filled his body. Lassitude filled his muscles. His head seemed to weigh as much as a mountain.

Varzil was acutely aware of Felicia's nearness, both her body sitting beside him and her mind, still in rapport with his. There was much to say, and even more that needed no words. This was a good thing, he thought, because he wasn't sure he could form a coherent sentence. Getting back to his own chambers would be a monumental task. He gathered himself, taking a breath to fuel the effort.

Felicia laid one hand upon his shoulder, no more than a feather's weight. He felt it as a shimmering bolt down the center of his body, through all the depleted *laran* channels. She slipped her arms around him and he felt himself sinking slowly, as if moving through honey. The bed seemed to rise up to greet him. She pulled the Tree-of-Life quilt over them both. Warmth surrounded him, seeped into him.

He brushed his lips against hers and she sighed in pleasure. Her breath was sweet against his face. Neither of them could do more, between exhaustion and the lack of sexual desire that accompanied active matrix work. Lying in each other's arms, still in their working robes, slipping into sleep, Varzil felt an intimacy he had not dreamed possible. They were part of one another, as much as the breath they shared.

✦

When he awoke, she was standing at the window. The night was almost over. Pale light illuminated her features, taut and still. He slid from the bed, using the quilt like a cape, and wrapped them both in it. Her posture softened, but only a little.

"What is it, *preciosa?*"

I fear what has been set in motion. Oh, Varzil, I greatly fear it.

You have done something amazing. You are *amazing.*

She pulled away, turning so that her eyes caught the gray light. "Don't patronize me."

"I'm not—"

"We must think of what to say." She began pacing, absently pushing back her coppery curls. "If we convince them *you* were responsible, that I was only a member of the circle, just a technician doing my own work—"

"Felicia! What are you talking about?" His voice rose in pitch without his intention. "Are you suggesting we should try to hide what happened—that *you* held the circle—that *you* acted as Keeper? I will not—I cannot—claim credit for what you accomplished last night."

Now she faced him full on, her face such a mixture of warring emotions as to wring his heart. In that brief time when she had seized control of the circle, remaking it to the pattern of her mind, some part of her had leaped to life, as hot and eager as any flame. And yet—

It was not modesty which held her back, nor any ingrained belief that she as a woman could not do what she had done.

It was fear.

There will be opposition, of course, he said reassuringly. *People will believe only what they want to. But there are enough open-minded Keepers and matrix workers, people willing to defy the strictures of tradition.* And if the world could change enough for a woman could become a Keeper, then Carolin's pact might also come into reality. *In the end, the Towers will stand with you.*

She waved him silent. Her voice came thick, as if each word were torn from her heart. "But at what cost? Varzil, I have spent my whole life hiding who I am. The only reason I *have* a life is that I have succeeded. I am Felicia of Arilinn—only that. But if I become Felicia the Keeper, Felicia the Freak, if every scheming busybody in the entire *Comyn* focuses on me because of this, how long will I be able to live as myself? How long before I become *Taniquel's daughter? Coryn's daughter?* A thing of legend instead of flesh?" She broke off, smearing tears from her eyes with the back of one hand.

"I think you cannot be any less than you are," he answered. "Neither falsehood nor silence can change what has already happened."

Felicia gazed out the window, rocking with her silent tears.

Even if he lied for her, which he would not do, it would be no use. Everyone in the circle knew what she had done. Despite attempts to keep it secret, word would leak out. It wouldn't be the first time such rumors had been passed along the relays. If she herself denied what she had done, the matter might well go no further. But at what price to her integrity? To women in Towers everywhere? To Darkover?

She must decide for herself. If he tried to tell her what to do, he would become her adversary instead of her ally. She would make the right choice, in her own way and time. He had no doubt of her courage or her ability to face the truth.

He went to her, put the quilt around her shoulders, and kissed her brow.

"It is for you alone to decide." He closed the door softly and headed for his own chamber.

✦

Varzil did not have another occasion to speak privately with Felicia for almost a tenday. Barak's circle took over the completion of the *clingfire* processing, and Varzil and the others from Auster's circle assumed their less dangerous tasks. It was not the first time Varzil had worked as Keeper. Always before, Auster had been there, sometimes actively advising, sometimes only lending his silent encouragement. Although the projects were not exacting, Varzil executed each one with meticulous care. Sometimes he was so drained afterward, he barely had the energy to haul himself upstairs to his chamber.

Felicia did her share as soon as Fidelis released her back to work. "I'm no more tired than anyone else in the circle," she told Varzil as they sat before the fire in the common room, each with a mug of Lunilla's steaming herbal tonic. "Fidelis had to satisfy Barak I'd taken no harm from what I did. If I were a man, the question wouldn't have arisen. If I go on with this, every busybody from here to Temora will be watching over my shoulder, probing my channels, probably clucking like old hens over my laundry."

"Have I told you what happened the first time I tried to get into Arilinn?" Varzil said with a smile. "They wouldn't have me."

"You? I can't believe it!"

"Oh, indeed. It didn't help that my father was dead set against it. I think their real fear is that I'd die on them—I was that sickly-looking— and start a war."

Felicia lowered her mug. "You're not exactly a farmer—*strong as an ox and half as smart*—but, Varzil, you have such a powerful Gift. How could they miss it?"

"Auster didn't, but my father had to be convinced first. To do that, I had to rescue my brother Harald from catmen. You've probably heard the story. The point is that there are always obstacles, whether they seem insurmountable or merely bothersome. The question is not how difficult the path, but whether in your heart, you wish to undertake the journey."

I do . . . and yet I do not . . .

She looked away, biting her lower lip. He'd rarely seen her this troubled.

"What troubles you? It cannot be these petty annoyances. You are not a person to shrink from doing what is right for mere personal convenience, even risking the loss of your anonymity. What truly holds you back?"

She was silent for a long moment. "I—I am not sure. I have been trying to reason things out. I tell myself how difficult it is to go against tradition and everything I have been taught to expect from myself. A certain amount of anxiety is to be expected whenever anything new is attempted. I think what it was like for my mother. She rode with the army to take back Acosta, you know, and that was unheard of. I have this feeling—I don't know—that once I start upon this road, there will be no turning back. I cannot see the end. I do not have the prescient talent of Allart Hastur. All I can see is darkness, darkness and fire."

Varzil had dropped into rapport with her, so that her dread shivered through them both. He saw that he had been right. Felicia would not let fear stop her.

He set aside his own mug, now grown cold, and took her hands in his. "I have said that it is your choice, and I stand by that. I believe your 'darkness and fire' is no more than what we all worry about in these times. War and its companions, famine and plague, haunt all our dreams. Were we not engaged in making *clingfire,* surely one of the most terrible weapons imaginable, when Auster suffered his stroke? If we allow ourselves to be paralyzed by all the disasters which *could* happen, if we turn away from the chance to make a real change, then we are as guilty of those horrors as if we had committed them ourselves."

Felicia's chin lifted. "Do you lay that responsibility on me? I did not ask for this, only to live a private life."

"Is that possible for any of us?" he countered.

Her shoulders sagged. "You are right. Had I been born a head-blind fool, I would never have known the difference. But I am as the gods made me, even as my mother was, and I have seen the path which has been set before me."

For a moment, Felicia looked so desolate, so fragile and vulnerable that Varzil wished he could take back his harsh words. She would never give in for the sake of peace, but would consider her decision carefully, weighing what she would lose against what she—and Darkover—would gain.

Later that day, Felicia presented herself to the remaining Keeper of Arilinn and requested to be trained as one of them.

✦

"It is impossible for a woman to become a Keeper," Barak repeated. He swept the air with his hands to emphasize his point.

The entire population of Arilinn, down to the lowliest novice, had gathered in the common room. Auster sat in front of the empty fireplace, facing the assembly. A month had passed since the fateful incident, and his voice still carried a faint slur. A tiny bubble of spittle had formed at the right corner of his mouth.

The events of the last month—Auster's stroke, the immediate intervention by Cerriana and Varzil, and most of all, Felicia's astonishing feat of maintaining the circle and stabilizing the *clingfire* had been told and retold, with the same question, *Was it true? Had a woman functioned as a Keeper?*

"Barak," Lunilla said with the respect due his rank. "We accept that there has never been a woman Keeper at Arilinn, or one acknowledged at any other Tower within recorded history. But the fact is that something *did* happen on that night, something which demands an explanation. If not for our community here, then for our fellow circles at the other Towers."

Gavin Elhalyn stood up. "As a member of that circle, I believe Varzil's testimony that when he had finished the immediate care necessary to save Auster's life, Felicia had already stabilized the circle under her own control. For myself, I am not sure. Things happened so quickly—we were all in deep rapport. If Varzil says this is what happened, then it must be so. When I could perceive things clearly once more, it was Felicia alone who held us in a circle."

Varzil had not expected such a strong statement from Gavin, who had served loyally under Auster for many years. Such was the man's integrity that he would not retreat from the truth. He had been there, had felt Felicia's silken touch spin them into a single unity. He would not deny it.

Felicia kept to herself, chin lifted, back straight. She reminded Varzil of steel, bright in the sun. He wished he could take her hand. That would be an unforgivable breach of Tower etiquette, but more than that, it would compromise the poise, the pride that she wore as a mantle.

"That is as it may be," one of the other men said. "People—including women—can do extraordinary things in an emergency. This is not at all the same thing as a reliable talent. This is why we insist upon discipline and tradition. From the newest novice to the most revered Keeper, we are all bound by the same standards. We do not make promises we cannot fulfill. No one may work in a circle, with the minds of others dependent upon his skill and competence, unless he is fully trained and fit."

"A single incident does not make a Keeper," Gavin conceded.

Heads nodded in agreement.

Varzil got to his feet and the murmurs died. All eyes shifted to him. He was, after all, Auster's chosen successor, under-Keeper of Arilinn.

"We live in extraordinary times," he reminded them, "times of both disaster and promise, hope and trial. Our fathers saw the destruction of two great Towers. They lived their lives in a world gone mad, teetering on the brink of conflagration. We have the chance to make a new world, to envision new possibilities. Who is to say that a woman Keeper is not one of them?

"What is really at stake here?" he demanded, pacing now, for the energy coursing through him would not allow him to stand still. "If we are right, if Felicia's actions in maintaining the circle are an indication of her true talent—why, then, we will be hailed as pioneers, as visionaries. The Towers are too few and too distant as it is. Rebuilding Tramontana stretched our resources even thinner. Can you imagine what a difference it would make if we could draw upon our *laran*-Gifted women as well as men for Keeper training?"

They were far fewer than when Varzil had first come to Arilinn. Barak's circle was at a bare minimum. Others, including an extremely promising lad from Marenji, had left for the usual reasons, marriage, war, shifts in power in the small kingdoms. It was the same everywhere. Hali's Second Keeper had gone to the new Tower at Tramontana, taking some of the most experienced workers with him.

Several of the older folk, Lunilla and Richardo, drew back with horrified expressions. Only Auster listened impassively. Varzil feared he had pushed them too far and in doing so, lost his own argument.

He lifted his hands in conciliation. "All I am saying is that we have nothing to lose by giving Felicia a chance. If you are right and what happened was an aberration, a short-lived bridge until I could take over the circle, then we are no worse off than we were before."

"Let the others break with tradition at their peril," Barak said. "Arilinn will hold to the ancient truths, the time-honored principles that have made us great. There has never been a woman trained as Keeper here. There never will be."

The fools! Varzil thought with a burst of anger. Here was a treasure at their feet and they chose to retreat behind tradition.

Tradition be damned! Half the room flinched visibly.

Felicia rose to her feet. She regarded Barak, Arilinn's sole remaining functional Keeper, with calm eyes. "*Vai dom,* do not trouble yourself on my account. I would not be a source of dissension in this Tower. I am, as always, at the service of Arilinn. As long as I remain here, I will do my best in whatever capacity my Keeper deems suitable."

Liriel Hastur could not have spoken more graciously. Felicia sat down amid a ripple of approval. Auster smiled and nodded to her.

Varzil could find no fault with Felicia's words. He envied her ability to say what was so clearly expected, to appear less than she was. Perhaps this was because it was a skill he had practiced himself for so many years.

Carlo, me, and now Felicia . . . all of us lying quiet, waiting. Waiting for what?

28

A tapping at the door startled Varzil awake. He'd fallen asleep with Felicia in his arms, the covers thrown over both of them.

The meeting had left everyone overwrought. Felicia had gone with Varzil to his chambers after a brief evening meal, for neither of them were to work that night, not even in the relays. He'd touched her lightly on the back of the wrist, in the manner of telepaths. She'd surprised him with a smile.

"It is no more than what I—you and I—expected," she had said. "But I think you were right all along, Varzil. We of the Towers are not so many that we can afford to throw away half of those with the talent to become Keepers. Certainly not just because superstition and tradition say women aren't capable of the work. I know what I did—I *was* a Keeper."

Her eyes met his, luminous even in the muted light of the *laran*-charged glow-globe. "I *am* a Keeper. And if Arilinn will not give me the training I need to use my talents, I must find another Tower that will."

He had drawn her close to him, torn between pride and the heart-tearing knowledge that to do so, she would have to leave him. He thought of the brief romance between Dyannis, his sister, and Eduin. In the end, the distance and the demands upon them in their separate lives had worn away their hope, or so it had seemed to Dyannis. He did not want that to happen to him and Felicia. He thought of going with her wherever she went; surely someone with his training could find a place at another Tower.

"*Caryo mio,*" she had whispered into the curve of his shoulder. "What we have can only be enriched by time. Distance is no consideration." Once again, they had slept in each other's arms, too drained of *laran* energy to have any sexual desire. They bathed in the intimacy of each other's body heat and breath, the rhythms of each other's minds.

Now he sat bolt upright at the tapping at the door. Felicia stirred at his side. "Come in."

Gavin's head appeared in the opening. "Come quickly, Varzil. And you, too, Felicia. Auster's had another stroke."

Varzil reached for his fleece-lined indoor boots. Felicia was already pulling on a shawl over her night dress. "Shouldn't Fidelis—Cerriana—"

"They have already been summoned," Gavin replied, holding the door open for them. "This is more than a matter of healing. He's asking for you by name, Varzil."

Despite the quiet of the hour, few others were asleep. Varzil quested outward with his mind. The matrix laboratories sat vacant, their telepathic dampers idle. Even the relays had fallen silent. Cerriana stood at the door of the infirmary, explaining to Valentina that her presence would serve no purpose, but only interfere with the work at hand.

"Good, you're here." She stepped back for Varzil to enter. He took Felicia's hand and drew her inside with him.

Auster's face was almost as pale as the sheets of unbleached *linex.* The lines of his face, once deeply incised, had faded into a webwork of tiny wrinkles. His eyebrows and lashes were likewise colorless, shades of white upon white. But for the hesitant rise and fall of his chest and the faint irregular pulse at his throat, he might have already passed from the living.

Fidelis sat to one side of the bed. He held two fingertips against the inside of Auster's wrist, eyes downcast, all his concentration inward.

Varzil lowered himself to an empty stool. He knew better than to speak. Auster must have sensed his presence, however. Pale lashes fluttered open. At first, his gaze was unfocused, his once-keen thoughts now hesitant.

I am here, Auster.

"What's that? Don't mumble, young man. I can't hear you." Auster's lips twisted around the words, for the left side of his body was clearly paralyzed.

Varzil probed deeper, something he would have never dared to do in the days of Auster's strength. Any monitor could have assessed the neurological damage. The hurt done to the *laran* centers of Auster's brain was far more profound. The old man might live on if his body were tough enough, the lungs taking in air, the heart continuing its relentless rhythm. A stroke patient might, with patience and skillful healers, learn to speak or walk again. For this deeper loss, there was no cure. What made the man, what made the Keeper, was already gone.

Varzil swept one hand across his eyes, praying he would not weep. When he had come to Arilinn so many years ago, a rebellious, terrified adolescent, Auster had seemed as a god, Keeper and *laranzu,* surely one of the most powerful men on Darkover. His mental abilities had been legendary.

"Varzil? Varzil lad, is it you?" Auster asked in a voice that was even more potent for its weakness. Every syllable expressed his determination to complete this one last task.

Gently, Varzil brushed his fingertips against the papery skin on Auster's wrist. "I am here, beloved teacher."

Auster's hand fumbled free to catch Varzil's. The fingers with their bony joints felt like the bars of a decrepit cage, barely able to contain a feather.

"Varzil . . ." Slow and thin, the voice continued. "I want . . . there must be no question . . . as to who . . . will take my place."

Fidelis met Varzil's eyes. Neither of them spoke of false hope. "Auster, you have trained Varzil yourself for all these years," Fidelis said. "Surely everyone at Arilinn knows you intended him to be Keeper after you."

One hand waved. The thin chest shook with the effort of yet another breath. "Everyone here . . . yes. But those arrogant—" Auster broke off into coughing, soothed only when Fidelis brought his monitor's skills to clear his breathing passages. The stroke clearly had compromised his body's ability to keep his lungs clear. Already Varzil sensed the first intimations of the pneumonia that would surely end his life.

"—those arrogant nine-fathered banshees . . . think you're either too dangerous . . . or of no consequence . . . want the Towers biddable . . .

Promise me, you will serve no king's private . . . purposes . . . only Arilinn . . . only the highest good . . ."

"I will be pawn to no king," Varzil promised, thinking of Carolin and of Felix Hastur, who still occupied the throne at Hali.

Ally and friend, he vowed, *but never servant.*

Until that moment, Varzil realized, there had always been the possibility that Carolin might ask of him something which ran counter to his own conscience. He had never seriously considered it, for he could not imagine anything which Carolin wanted that he could not agree to. But Carolin was not yet King.

". . . answer to your own conscience . . ."

Varzil bent over until his cheek brushed the aged hands. His tears wet the clasped fingers. From this time onward, he must look to no other man as the Keeper of his conscience. He would be responsible not only for himself, but for the men and women who served under him.

Auster's voice was now very low, so that only Varzil could hear his whispered syllables.

". . . name you . . . *tenerézu* . . ."

Varzil held his breath, waiting. Listening with his *laran,* with his heart, praying there would be one more word, one more moment of communion. Silence and stillness answered him. Then came a shimmering at the very edges of his senses, both physical and mental. He knew it for the very moment when life extinguished, leaving only a frail husk.

◆

It seemed that the heavens themselves mourned the passing of Auster Syrtis, Keeper of Arilinn Tower. As the year hastened to its end, the weather, which had been unseasonably mild, turned bitterly cold. Auster's family had sent a message requesting that he be buried in the small plot Arilinn kept for its own. Here, in an unmarked grave just as at the *rhu fead,* he would join generations of nameless Keepers before him.

Almost overnight, however, the ground froze so hard that no wooden tool could scratch its surface. Gavin went out with one of the precious metal spades and came back shaking his head.

"My uncle Aran said this often happens in the Hellers," Felicia remarked, looking at the dented tip. "The poor pack the bodies in the snow banks, where they stay frozen solid until the spring thaws. At Tramontana, it is said, they had other ways."

The farewell service for Auster was even simpler than the one Varzil attended for Taniquel Hastur. The Tower community gathered in their own common room, instead of the gravesite, to share their memories and comfort one another. They began just as the brilliance of the day, hard-edged with cold, began to seep from the sky. Sunset colors streamed in through the windows. By the time they were finished, a dense and velvety darkness surrounded them.

As if, Varzil thought, *a night of the spirit as well as the body had fallen.*

Immediately afterward, Barak, as sole remaining Keeper, ordered the body brought into the laboratory which had been Auster's favorite. Here he gathered a circle. Varzil was included, along with those who had worked most closely with Auster. Together, they created a protective field around Auster's body, a sphere of mental space in which time itself was held in suspension.

Afterward, Barak summoned Felicia for a private meeting. Varzil felt uneasy, for Barak had been the staunchest opponent of any expanded training for Felicia.

Making his way down to the Tower kitchen, Varzil found Lunilla pulling trays of seed buns from the oven. The familiar smells wafted through him. With a sigh, he poured out a mug of *jaco* and took his place at the battered worktable beside Valentina. Across the table, two of the new arrivals, one just qualified as monitor, stared at him with rounded eyes. A smile twisted Varzil's mouth. Here he was, Auster's chosen successor, down in the kitchen along with the youngsters.

"Just like old times." Smiling, Lunilla slid the buns on to a wooden platter and placed it in the center of the table. Seeing the novices hesitate, she said, "Go on, before Varzil snatches them all!"

"And don't think I wouldn't," Varzil said, reaching for one. He dropped it, blowing on his fingertips.

With an elegant toss of her head, Valentina used the edge of her shawl to pick up her own bun. She tore off one tiny morsel after another blew on them and lifted them delicately to her mouth.

They ate in companionable silence for the next few minutes. Only when she'd refilled everyone's hot drinks did Lunilla sit down herself. She reminded Varzil of a mother barnfowl clucking over her chicks. He was no longer the stripling lad who'd spent a night half-frozen at Arilinn's gates. Nor could *jaco* and seed-buns, no matter how filling, solve the problems before him.

Barak meant to rule Arilinn, an Arilinn bound by tradition. An Arilinn in which there was no place for a woman Keeper.

Or, perhaps, came the chilling thought, *Tower neutrality.*

Varzil! I have news!

The corridor door swung open and Felicia burst in. High color stained her cheeks and her breath came quick and light, as if she'd been running. Her excitement, like a freshening breeze, swept through the room.

"What is it?" Varzil asked as his pulse quickened. "Has Barak changed his mind?"

"About training me?" She shook her head. A few tendrils had come free from the braid coiled low on her neck and framed her face like a coppery aureole. "No, he's as unmovable as the Twin Peaks. But not everyone on Darkover thinks like him, thank all the gods at once!"

"What happened?" Varzil demanded.

Other voices joined his in a murmur. "What is it, child?" Lunilla asked.

"Hestral Tower has asked for me. They want to train me as a Keeper!" Felicia threw her arms wide, dancing like a child. Triumph rang in her voice.

Varzil caught her in an embrace. For a moment, as their bodies pressed together, he felt that silken oneness of mind. Joy suffused him; his body quivered with its delirium.

"This is news indeed," Lunilla said in measured tones. "I don't pretend to know where this will lead to, or that I'm not glad Arilinn's out of it. Even Durraman's fabled donkey can see that the world is changing."

Felicia sobered for a moment. "Perhaps Barak and the others are right and I shall fail. But, oh Lunilla! I will have had a chance to *try!*"

"You won't fail," Varzil said. At the back of his mind, he glimpsed a woman in the crimson robes of a Keeper, lightning bursting from her upraised hands.

Then the image was gone, leaving a sense of disquiet. Had it been Felicia she saw, or some other woman, perhaps in the future? And why did she call up such power? What need had she of lightning?

"The blessings of the gods go with you, child," Lunilla was saying in her kind, gentle voice. No matter what her personal opinion of women as Keepers, she genuinely cared for every person in Arilinn.

"When will you go?" Valentina asked. "Next spring?"

The hectic color seeped from Felicia's cheeks, though her eyes still shone. "I think so, when the weather permits." Her glance sought Varzil. "At least, I'll be here for Year's End."

29

All the way back from Thendara, whipping his horse into a lather, Carolin heard his wife screaming in his mind. With his paxman at his heels, he galloped into the courtyard and jumped to the ground before his horse slid to a stop. His spurs clanged against the stones as he raced through the outer halls and up the stairs to the royal quarters. Ignoring the protests of the waiting-women, he rushed to her bedchamber. Even if he had no shred of *laran,* no awareness of her, he would have seen the frantic expressions of the maidservants rushing down the corridor. His paxman remained outside, brow furrowed in concern but asking no questions.

Common men might leave the mysteries of the birthing bed to the women, but Carolin was *Comyn* as well as Prince. Where else should he be, but by the side of his wife, lending her his strength, sharing her suffering? Was he not half the parentage of this child?

The room felt closed in, drenched with fear and sweat, curtains drawn against the brightness of the day, candles and oil lamps flickering. A woman moaned and writhed on the high, wide bed. Midwives on either side tried to soothe her. One held her hand, murmuring words of encouragement, while the other sponged her forehead.

Carolin hardly recognized Alianora, who had always seemed so composed, so formal. Heat flushed her cheeks; her unbound hair hung in damp, lank strands. Through the thin gown stretched across her belly, her muscles tensed. She tore her hands away from the midwives and clawed at the roundness. Her breathing became hoarse. Convulsing, she shrieked like an animal.

He went to her side and gently took one hand. There was no response. She was locked away from him, her mind engulfed in the demanding urgency of each moment.

Alianora. I'm here with you. You're not alone.

The older midwife, her gray hair bound neatly under a head scarf, bent over the laboring woman. "Just keep breathing through the pains, that's a love, there now, it will pass in a moment, don't fight it, just breathe."

Carolin felt the pains peak and then subside, leaving a cold, boring ache. He felt it shiver through his own body and knew something was wrong. Childbirth was painful, that was the way of the world, but not this icy grip, this touch of Zandru's deepest frozen hell.

Alianora turned toward him. The crazed fear in her eyes diminished for an instant. Her features softened in recognition.

"I am here," he said, tightening his grasp on her hand.

She rolled away, her eyes squeezing shut. "Ahhh! Ahhh!" came once again, that cry of mindless agony.

The midwife met his eyes, and he saw her own fears.

"Have you sent to Hali Tower for a healer?" he asked.

"Aye, there's one on the way," she said, not adding any honorific, for this was her realm and no time for courtly manners. *For all the good it'll do the lass and her wee bairn.*

She rose and led him back to the door, out of Alianora's hearing. "The child's placed wrong and for all that it's early, willna be turned. There's little ye can do here—"

Women had said those very words to husbands since Hastur, Lord of Light, first courted Cassilda.

Carolin drew himself up. The midwife swallowed the rest of her words. He said, "I will wait."

The other women exchanged glances, but made no further protest. One brought a chair for him, so that he might sit at the side of the bed. His presence seemed to calm Alianora during those times when her screams died down. He spoke to her, but could never be sure she understood.

How could a woman, so small and weak, bear such pain? A man would have been exhausted—or driven mad—by what she endured. Yet the pains came in wave after unrelenting wave.

After what seemed an age, the door swung open and a woman in a green riding cape burst in. She carried with her the smells of fresh air, saddle leather, and wildflowers. Her hair, as red as his own, had come loose from its single long braid, curling in tendrils around her wind-whipped face. She nodded once to Carolin and went directly to Alianora. He did not know her, but he recognized what she was—a trained monitor, a healer, a *leronis* of skill and power.

She bent over the laboring woman and laid the back of one hand gently against the fevered cheek. Alianora lay quiet except for the rapid rise and fall of her chest.

The monitor looked up, raking the room in a single glance. "I must have a secure place to work. You—" indicating the head midwife with a tilt of her head, "—bring me these things," and then she rattled off supplies, linens, boiled water, herbal infusions, and yet more clean linens.

"Will she—" Carolin was surprised at the unsteadiness of his own voice, "is she—"

"I do not know!" the *leronis* snapped. "And I cannot find out if you keep interrupting me!"

"Husha!" one of the maids cried. "Do you not know who this is? It is Prince Carolin, her husband!"

"I don't care if it's Aldones himself, he and you are to leave immediately." At her words, midwife and maid retreated toward the door.

"Val leronis," Carolin said respectfully. "I passed a season at Arilinn. Please allow me to help."

"Yes, you may have some small measure of skill. Certainly you have *laran*. But this woman's life hangs by a thread and I do not have time to instruct an apprentice. If you care at all for her, leave me to do my work!"

There was nothing for it but to obey. He paused once at the door, seized by the fear that he would never see her again alive. The healer's starstone flared in a burst of blue-white radiance. *Laran* power surged, filling the room. He glimpsed Alianora's face, her eyes rimmed with white. Then the door closed behind him.

"Sir?" His paxman was still waiting, holding the riding crop Carolin had shoved into his hands.

Carolin hesitated, irresolute. The light was stronger here, and the familiar carpeted hallway and furnishings struck him as outlandish.

The head midwife had lingered a few paces away. She nodded to him. "Ye might comfort the bairns."

Avarra's sweet grace! The boys! Young though they were, and not yet come into their *laran* Gifts, they might have sensed something was wrong. This was the time Alianora usually played with them.

"Sir?" the paxman repeated.

"Go on, tend to the horses. I'll send if I need you."

What can you, or I, or any man do here?

Carolin took a few moments to compose himself before entering the nursery. Rafael and little Alaric were playing with a puzzle spread over the fine-woven carpet while their nurse watched from a corner chair, her fingers flying over her needlework. They ran to him, but silently, not with their usual clamor. He threw himself to his knees, heedless of boot and spur, and caught them up in his arms. They smelled of herb-scented soap and that unmistakable sweetness of children's skin. Joy, so unexpected it was almost a physical pain, swept through him.

"Hush, hush," he found himself saying, as much for himself as for them. After a long moment, he rose and settled them all upon the cushioned divan.

"Tell us a story, Papa," Rafael pleaded.

"A story?" What would Alianora have told? A comical tale of Durraman and his ancient but always resourceful donkey? A jingle about the notorious monk Fra' Domenic and the contents of his many pockets?

No, she would not have jested about a *cristoforo* monk. Gods, was he going to cry?

"Carlo." The voice was low, yet feminine. *Maura.*

She stood just inside the door, having slipped through it so quietly he had not noticed. Like the healer now tending to Alianora, she must have ridden hard from Hali Tower, for her cheeks were bright, her hair an aureole of curls.

Looking at her, with her gray eyes brimming with tears, he could not speak. She went to him. He reached out to her, thinking to take her hands, but instead his arms went around her. The divan was of such a height that his head rested naturally between her breasts. He felt her hands tighten about him.

Dear heart, I am so sorry. Her words rang like a bell in his mind. So clear, so simple, with such undemanding love.

Stripped bare by the moment, by worry and frustration, he had no defenses against her. She had slipped, gentle as dew, past the barriers of rank and history. Without judgment, without expectation, she seemed to peer directly into his heart. She saw everything that he was, everything that he thought and felt and dreamed, and accepted it all. The moment shook him to the core.

Gently, Carolin pushed her away and clambered to his feet, lest in a moment of weakness he betray his own response. What honor could come of it? She was a pledged virgin and he—his own wife lay dying just a short distance away.

✦

When Carolin returned to Alianora's chambers, the healer had just finished straightening the covers. Buckets overflowing with blood-soaked linens sat just inside the door. Their smell hung in the air. The healer went to the curtains and pulled them open.

So that she may look her last upon the glory of the day. Our poor child never even had the chance.

She bowed and slipped out the door, leaving Carolin alone with his wife.

For a terrible moment, he feared she had already slipped away, she lay so pale and still. When he lifted one hand, he was surprised at how cool it felt. The copper *catenas* bracelet lay loose around the fragile wrist.

Her eyes fluttered open. Pale, bloodless lips moved, shaped his name, but only a whisper of breath emerged. A film had fallen over the blue eyes, giving her the appearance of blindness.

He pressed his lips to the back of her hand. "Alianora. My good and dutiful wife."

"My . . . husband."

By the grace of Evanda, there was time for one last gesture, one last farewell. What could he say to her? Nothing, he realized, that had not already been said in those few words. He remembered the first night they had lain together. In a moment of mental intimacy such as they had not shared in all the years together, he saw what was in her mind, the one thing she wished for above all else.

Yes, they were there, hidden in the toe of an old pair of boots. Not in her jewelry case or in any other place where they might be easily discovered.

He placed the *cristoforo* beads into her hands, closed her fingers around them, and felt the answering pulse of relief and joy. Though he did not know more than a phrase or two, he sensed her own thoughts rising and falling in the ancient rhythms of prayer. When the final echoes had grown still, he realized that she was gone.

He leaned over and pressed his lips to her brow. She looked more at peace than she ever had in life. "May Holy St. Christopher, Bearer of the World's Burdens, sustain your spirit." Perhaps the words were wrong, for he knew little of her faith, but he spoke them with reverence. Surely, her god would understand. Surely her god would embrace her and their unborn child.

Sounds outside the door returned him to the present moment. He must go inform the King, and Rakhal and Lyondri. Maura would keep the children safe. Sustained by her gentle wisdom, he would find a way to tell them, too.

First, though, Carolin slipped the prayer beads from between Alianora's limp fingers. He could not leave them here, where her secret would surely be revealed. To bury or destroy them was abhorrent, a negation of her entire life. There was one place, though, where he could take them—the monastery of Saint Valentine of the Snows at Nevarsin. They had planned to send the boys when they were older, as royal children often were, for the superb education and training in self-discipline. When the time was right, he would go with them, on an errand of his own.

As he opened the door to let in the world with all its cares and bustle, Carolin thought Alianora's departing spirit smiled upon him.

30

Storms swept the Plains of Arilinn, burying the city in a blizzard. Winds howled and hail battered stone. Behind the Tower walls, the community of Arilinn gathered to celebrate. Warmth and light filled the common room, not only from the immense fire but also the banks of *laran*-charged lights and heaters. Once, the entire city had glowed with the blue-white illumination produced by the circles. Now, there was only enough for special occasions in the Hidden City and the Tower itself.

"Perhaps a time will come when all of Darkover can enjoy such luxury," Varzil said, sipping the rich Acosta wine Carolin sent as a holiday gift. The vintage was dark and heady, filled with subtle, complex flavors.

The news of Alianora's death and of her lost child lent a sad poignancy to the gift. Carolin was generous, even in sorrow. Yet wine itself was like life—ordinary grapes transformed into a potion to ease old wounds or open them, a bearer of joy as well as despair.

Felicia, at Varzil's side, lifted her goblet. "To the new days ahead. To seeing dreams become reality."

"Let us hope they are dreams of peace and prosperity," Cerriana said, "and not other dreams."

Across the table, Fidelis said, "Do not all men wish for an end to strife and want?"

"Of course they do," she replied. "It's just that—well, this is a time for hope, for renewal, is it not? Then let us not speak otherwise, least we give power to our own fears."

Varzil's mood, which had been effervescent with Felicia's nearness, the coming Year's End ritual, and the fellowship of the evening, darkened. Recent relay messages had hinted of unrest in the city of Hali, a proliferation of outlawed weapons, dissension among the Hasturs, and rumors of escalating conflict through the Kilghard Hills.

Despite his personal grief, Carolin's letters had been hopeful, full of confidence in the ability of honorable men to work together. Varzil prayed his friend was not mistaken in his trust.

He put the thought from him. There would be time enough to deal with such worries. For tonight, all who dwelt within the Tower would celebrate the turning of the seasons.

The meal ended, and the table was moved to clear a space for dancing. Barak and Lunilla, as senior members of the community, took up the symbols of the ancient rite. He lifted a sword, not the true Sword of Aldones, but a lightweight imitation, its edges carefully dulled so as not to wound through accident. The metal had been shaped to collect and reflect light, and a starstone chip glittered in its hilt. The effect was a dramatic halo of blue light around the blade and whoever wielded it.

Lunilla had set aside her usual brown and gray for a robe of shimmering white. Though she was old enough to be a grandmother, when she took up the garland of *kireseth* flowers, an aura hung about her, of youth and sweetness and springtime.

Valentina began singing in her clear, light voice. The melody was simple, the words ones they all knew by heart. Together, Barak and Lunilla moved through the dance-like reenactment.

"The stars were mirrored on the shore,
dark was the vast enchanted moor . . .
Robardin's daughter walked alone . . .
when Hastur left the Sphere of Light . . ."

Varzil took Felicia's hand, even as Barak took Lunilla's and couples formed throughout the room. The air turned golden and thick, like honeyed wine. His head swam with it, and with her nearness. He felt her warmth even through the layers of their festival clothing.

"Then singing like a hidden bird,
Cassilda cast a secret word,
beside the waters clear and cold;
he heard her as he downward spun
and through the fields of stars he came."

The men moved apart from the women and came together again.
Apart . . . together . . . Each time, the lines drew nearer.

"Cassilda left her shining loom;
a starflower in his hand she laid . . ."

Apart . . . together . . .
Lunilla went down the line of women, giving each a blue *kireseth*
blossom. Golden particles glittered on the stamens. Normally, the flowers
were forbidden in the Towers and only careful distillations of the active
components used. *Kirian,* invaluable in the treatment of threshold sickness, was one of these. Anyone unfortunate enough to be caught in a
Ghost Wind, when winds blew the raw pollen down from the mountain
heights, might suffer hallucinations, the breakdown of all normal mental
barriers, even madness.

"They wandered in the shining wood
and in the mortal sun they stood . . .
a glory mirrored in each face . . ."

The circles of men and women had come around so that Varzil now
faced Felicia. It seemed to him that glory was indeed mirrored in her
face. He saw her with his heart as well as his eyes, saw the shining light
within her, the beauty of her features and the silken touch of her *laran.*
Even as the Cassilda of legend had offered *kireseth,* the starflower, to
Hastur, so now Felicia, along with every other woman in the room, offered it to her partner. Many of the couples would complete only a ritual
acceptance. They might remain together for a time, then leave for their
own chambers. Every other time at Year's End, this was what Varzil had
done. He'd had no need of anything more.
Varzil bent over the five-petaled blossom. The distinctive scent of the
pollen rushed through him. He ran one finger along the waxy petal, then

held it for Felicia to inhale. The gold-dusted stamen cast a gentle radiance on her face. When she raised her eyes to his, he could see the Blessed Cassilda smile through her.

The song continued, carried by its own momentum, the force behind the ritual growing even more insistent. Voices blended so that sometimes he heard each distinct word and the next moment, only the rise and fall of the melody. At one point, he became aware of the first effects of the *kireseth;* the singing had stopped and yet the sense of being caught up in something wildly joyous, dangerous and inexorable carried him along. He had been exposed to small amounts of the pollen as part of his training and so, he thought, he knew what to expect. *Kireseth* lowered mental boundaries and acted as a psychic catalyst.

Nothing, he realized, could have prepared him. One moment, he was drowning in the lights reflected in Felicia's eyes, filled with a growing excitement he could not name. The next, he *was* the lights, the fire, the translucent blue stone walls, the softness of her lips. He did not know where he was, because he was everywhere at once—in the common room at Arilinn Tower, at the bottom of Hali Lake, soaring above the Twin Peaks, howling with the Ya-men in the hills beyond Sweetwater.

Liquid fire rushed through his body, energy surging through his *laran* channels. Dimly, the thought came to him that the purpose of this ancient rite was just this, to clear out the blockage and stagnation of the year's work.

The same channels carried sexual energy and *laran,* which was why threshold sickness often came about with the awakening of adolescence. Both men and women became sexually unresponsive while actively working in a circle. Even with the careful attention of the monitors, there were times when the body could not handle the energy flows. *Laran* nodes shut down; energy accumulated.

He bent to Felicia. Her arms went around him, pulling him closer. Her lips on his were at once yielding and demanding.

Varzil was no longer in the common room; he felt Felicia's hand in his, saw the walls of the corridor to her chambers kaleidoscoping by. The edges of his body were dissolving into particles of brilliance. Each tiny piece vibrated, expanding and overlapping until his entire body became a vessel of light. The light coalesced into a node of heat, centered deep within his belly and reaching—exploding—out through his genitals. His skin flamed with it.

Desire engulfed him, sweeping through every fiber, every cell of organ and nerve and skin, not only his own arousal but Felicia's, each catalyzing and feeding upon the other. He felt her passion as his own and it excited him even more.

As he stretched his body on top of hers, she softened and opened herself to him. He felt himself surrender along with her, both of them yielding to something greater. She cried out in pleasure as their bodies began to rock in primal rhythm. His own climax built slowly, in wave upon growing wave of intensity.

All sense of his separate self fell away. Neither body nor mind retained any boundaries. He was man and woman, sun and stars, night and day. Joy swept through him and the world reeled with it. Gradually, he slipped back into himself and darkness took him.

✦

He felt the dawn approach. The *kireseth* had worn off some hours ago, but he had not slept. Neither had Felicia, lying naked in his arms under layers of quilts. The psychedelic-fueled sense of oneness had faded, but the contentment and joy remained. How warm she was, how delicious her scent, her velvety skin, her unbound curls. She stirred, shifting her hips, and traced a spiral pattern on his chest with a fingertip.

How can we be parted, after this night?

"It wouldn't always be like this," she murmured aloud. Her breath teased the hairs on his chest. "Even if one of us sacrificed our training so that we could be together, we would be working most of the time. And we would in time come to resent the price we paid."

I know that, beloved. It was a wish, nothing more. This time together is a gift. I would not lessen it by ungratefully demanding what cannot be.

A flicker of presence in the corridor brought him alert. Gathering the Tree-of-Life quilt around his shoulders, he tiptoed to the door and opened it. A tray with covered dishes and a pitcher of steaming *jaco* sat on the floor. He caught a hint of Lunilla's touch.

Felicia wrapped herself in a warm robe and sparked the embers in the fireplace to life. They sat cross-legged on the square of hearth carpet, knees touching, and ate in companionable silence. They had remained in light rapport, each responsive to the other's shifting emotions. Echoes of their deeper connection remained.

And, Varzil thought as he reached out to stroke her cheek, would always remain. He felt the impulse to make a pledge of some kind, a statement of the bond between them.

You have already given me something of infinitely more value than words, she thought.

He understood. Without his belief in her, she would have faded into obscurity. Now she had a chance to become the first woman Keeper in recorded history. He had no doubt that she would.

Quicksilver, her mood sobered. He often forgot how small she was, silk and steel. She shivered and her eyes lost their focus, as if she looked upon some private desolation. Her mind turned opaque, barriered.

Another touch of apprehension? Was it the natural anxiety of embarking upon such a mission, a glimpse into a dire future, or sadness at their parting? Respecting her silence, Varzil made no attempt to reach past her *laran* shields.

"It is not lily days which shape our souls," she said, as much to herself as to him, "but the frozen winter nights, when we find ourselves in the pit of Zandru's Forge and there discover who we truly are."

"I would not have you walk such a path, beloved," he said, touching her cheek.

"Nor I, you. But the world goes as it will, not as you or I would have it."

Felicia went to the free-standing cupboard that held her personal belongings. She took out a wooden box, its fine carvings smoothed with age, and set it on the carpet between them. From a wrapping of white silk, she drew out a ring, a curve of silver set with a faceted stone.

At first, Varzil thought it a starstone by its brilliance, the way it sparkled with inner light. But the color was white, not blue. She held it out and he looked into it. No, not a starstone. When he touched it with his mind, it hummed, clearly sensitive to his *laran*. He probed deeper into the crystalline structure. No single person had keyed into the stone, yet it bore the imprint of layers of personalities, just as the stones at the *rhu fead* had been worn away by generations of *Comyn*.

"Where did this come from?" Varzil asked. "I've never seen anything like it."

"It belonged to my great-uncle, I think, although my mother never said for sure. She gave it to me with a whole boxful of trinkets, everything from a huge Temora pearl to a string of beads of atrociously badly carved *chervine* horn. She had only a little *laran* and was never trained in its use. I suppose that to her, it was nothing more than a pretty crystal."

"It's not a matrix. More like second cousin to one."

"Yes, that's what I thought."

She took the ring back again and cupped it in her hand. Eyes closed, she focused her mind upon it. When she handed it back to Varzil, it sang with her presence. "That's to remember me by."

He tried the ring on several fingers before settling on one. The ring had probably been made for a woman, but his hands had always been small. It no longer looked ostentatious, even for his modest tastes.

Soon they would follow their separate destinies, she to Hestral, he remaining here at Arilinn, and Carolin soon to be King at Hali. If they succeeded, they would change the world. What would Darkover be like, with women Keepers and a pact of honor between kings, without the terrible *laran* weapons and constant welfare? He could not picture it clearly, and perhaps that was just as well. For the moment, with Felicia by his side, he was content.

✦

Half a continent away, in Hali Tower, Eduin looked up from the archives as Dyannis entered. She had welcomed him to Hali, at first joyfully, then with growing puzzlement at his refusal to reciprocate. His post here as archivist was temporary. Once he'd found what he was looking for, he would have no reason to linger. He could not afford any entanglements.

Eduin had thought to make another attempt at Carolin, now that the interfering Varzil Ridenow was out of the way. But Carolin was not at Hali; he'd taken his sons to study at Nevarsin, among the monks. Eduin's efforts to seek an audience with his cousins, Rakhal and Lyondri, had been soundly rebuffed, and the old king was dying anyway, not worth the risk. His turn with Carolin would come again, of that he was sure.

There was work enough at Hali, particularly in the archives. He was not particularly interested in history, but access to the library offered the only hope of tracking down the daughter of Taniquel Hastur-Acosta.

At the approach of Dyannis, he set aside the scroll he had been indexing. She wore an ordinary gown, a pale soft green to set off her eyes and her tartan of Ridenow colors. Her perfume, subtly spicy, caressed him.

The years of study and mastery here at Hali had given her a poise beyond her years. Yet some core of her remained untamed. Once he had relished that rebellious, impertinent manner, but now he pulled away. She was unpredictable, answerable only to herself, and therefore dangerous.

"You've been cooped up here for the better part of a tenday," she said, but without any hint of a pout. "I've hardly seen you since your arrival."

He gestured to the pile of scrolls, some of them in such fragile condition that they would not survive more than another winter or two. "The work—"

"Has lain here for longer than anyone knows and is not about to sprout legs and go anywhere. But you must please yourself." She pulled up a stool so that, short of unspeakable rudeness, he had no choice but to sit with her. "What have you been excavating?"

"Genealogy records."

"Oh. Whose?"

"Obscure branches of the Hasturs. There are still traces of the breeding programs from the Ages of Chaos, including some lethal recessives. We need to know who carries them today, if only to prevent their reemergence."

"Bless Aldones, we don't do that any longer," she said. "I think we are living in a great age of progress. You should hear my brother talk, he's so full of new ideas. An end to *laran* warfare, new ways of treating disease, even training commoners who have talent—and, would you believe?—someday we may accept women as Keepers!"

"That's ridiculous!"

"No, it's true. Do you remember the rumor about Arilinn last autumn—Felicia, it was—she's a technician, but when Auster had his first stroke, she took over as Keeper. They say she saved the whole circle from a *clingfire* explosion."

Eduin shrugged, feeling only the icy chill in the pit of his stomach. He had done his best to forget the incident. Arilinn had refused to promote him to under-Keeper, when he clearly merited it. Instead, the head-blind fools had chosen that sandal-wearer, Varzil, and now perhaps a woman! The insult still rankled him. He had not felt sorrow at Auster's death.

By her expression, Dyannis expected a response, some show of interest. "Yes, I remember hearing something like that," he said. "I pay such gossip little heed. People who have nothing better to do are always spreading fantastical tales."

"Well!" She clapped her hands together like a child. "This is a whole lot more than idle talk. Felicia is actually going to be trained as an under-Keeper at Hestral Tower."

"Another rumor."

"No, it's true. Marelie was working the relays and had word directly from Hestral."

"That's fitting." He snorted, barely masking his contempt. "An insignificant Tower for a nobody pretender."

"Eduin! What's gotten into you? Don't you think this is exciting—for a woman to be even considered for such a post? And of course it would have to be a place like Hestral. You wouldn't expect Arilinn or Hali to take such a chance, would you? Barak's as hidebound as a Nest of Dry Towners. Besides, Felicia's not exactly a nobody. She may be *nedestra,* but she's of the royal Hastur line. She might even be in those records you're studying."

Something came alert inside Eduin. "What do you mean?"

"Promise you won't tell, but she's the daughter of the famous Queen Taniquel. I know it's supposed to be a secret, but it's so exciting that I just had to tell someone!"

Eduin felt the breath leave his body. *Queen Taniquel's daughter!*

"The very same," Dyannis chattered on. "She visited Hali some time back, along with my brother. I think he's a bit smitten with her, if you ask me—he could barely think about anything else. He wasn't indiscreet in his thoughts, and I'm sure he believed himself shielded, but after all, I *am* his sister. . ."

Queen Taniquel's daughter! Exultation flared within him. Quickly, he clamped down on his emotions, lest they arouse the insatiable curiosity of Dyannis.

"You're right," someone said with his voice, "this is an exciting development. That is, if it's true. It may all come to nothing. No matter how carefully we choose our under-Keepers, many cannot withstand the training. And then there are losses from marriage and family affairs and the normal course of life."

Death. Some of them die. How easy it would be to add another death. A woman foolhardy enough to try a Keeper's work? No one would suspect . . .

"I am sorry," Dyannis said, her voice shifting to gentleness. "That was tactless of me, to bring up your own disappointment. Yet take heart.

You may yet find your place, where your talents will be appreciated and cultivated."

He let her talk on for a little while, making comments when he was expected to. Then he excused himself and made arrangements to work on the relays that night.

Eduin finished the work assigned to him and waited for a pause in the incoming messages. It came early in the evening, because there was little news. He was alone in the circular room. The other worker had retired after a period of silence on the relays. In an offhanded way, he'd offered to stay on alone.

Bending over the glowing blue screen, he reached out his mind to his counterpart at Hestral Tower.

Eduin, came a mental voice, vaguely familiar. It was Serena, a sound enough *leronis* if a bit of a gossip on the relays. *We heard you had left Arilinn. Whatever are you doing at Hali?*

Not much. Biding my time. Combing musty old records. His mouth twisted into a dark smile at her responsive giggle. Then, with all the finesse he could muster, he pitched his mental voice for just the right degree of causalness and impact.

Might there be a place at Hestral for another matrix technician?

✦

The next spring, Varzil was formally presented as Keeper of Arilinn Tower to the *Comyn* Council. The assembly rose as he entered the very same chamber where, so many years ago, he had stood before them, awaiting their approval. He recognized many of the same faces, although they were more weather-worn and gray-haired. Some of the elderly were absent, replaced by younger men. His brother Harald now occupied the space for Ridenow of Sweetwater, among their more illustrious relatives. In an idle moment, he wished Carolin had been able to attend, but he was at Nevarsin and Rakhal had come instead.

Varzil concentrated on the assembly before him. In a sense, he no longer needed these men; he was a Keeper, above the censure of ordinary people. Yet, to do what he meant to do, to follow through with his dream of a pact of honor, he must have their support and cooperation. Some had already formed their opinions, both good and bad, while others were willing to wait and listen. A few despised him for what they saw as weakness, as a traitor to his caste with his talk of training women and commoners, his willingness to experiment. There was little he could do to persuade them otherwise. Instead, he owed his loyalty to those who saw him as a harbinger of positive change, a way through the darkness of chaos.

I bear their hopes, even as St. Christopher bore the Child of the World. Though Varzil was no *cristoforo,* he found the image appealing. As he acknowledged the Council's endorsement, he prayed for the strength to carry that burden.

At the conclusion of the presentation, Varzil took his seat as representative of Arilinn, knowing that he had earned his place here not by accident of birth but through his own merit.

That evening, Varzil joined the festivities. Wine flowed freely, not all of it well-watered. He drank little, for he'd long since realized he had no head for it, and there was too much important work to do at the Tower to take more than an evening's break. Rakhal drank a great deal, and Varzil was grateful he did not need to have anything more to do with him beyond a polite greeting, whether he was Carolin's cousin or not.

Later during the session, Varzil found time to speak privately with his brother. Harald had solidified into a powerful, broad-shouldered man, his yellow hair and beard now darkened into bronze. He would not hear Varzil's regrets for not being able to return home after the death of their father.

"It would have been suicide," Harald insisted. "We were fighting catmen on one hand and those *gre'zuin* from Asturias on the other. What could you have done except present an easy target? Father was already in his grave. You did much better to save your duty for the living."

"Yes, that's very much what Father would have said." Varzil thought that his brother was coming to resemble *Dom* Felix in more ways than one. Under the solid girth lay a core of unbending steel. He had grown into a man not lightly to be crossed.

Harald went on in a softer tone, "He would have been proud to be here, to see what you've made of yourself. He would not say so aloud, but he—" Harald stumbled, his voice roughening with emotion, "he regretted standing in your way when you wanted to study at Arilinn. He was wrong to oppose you."

No, *Dom* Felix would never have admitted such a mistake. His own fierce pride forbade it. Only Harald, who had persuaded him, whose life was saved by those very talents *Dom* Felix had belittled and despised, could do it for him.

Now the mental images, glimpsed from his brother's memories, shifted from anger and scorn to dawning pride.

"My son is a laranzu *at Arilinn."* The words echoed in Varzil's mind, and he knew his father had indeed said them.

"Look at you, Keeper of Arilinn," Harald said. "Yes, he would have been proud."

"I thank you," Varzil said in the awkward silence which followed. "For a man who never intended any of his children for the Tower, he ended up with two of us."

"Dyannis, well now, that's another matter." Harald looked uncomfortable. "She was to come home after a season or two, when a good marriage was arranged for her. You may remember, the first one came to nothing when the lad perished from a leg wound gone bad. It's time we made another. We're not so strong that we can afford to pass up any advantageous alliance."

Harald clearly expected Varzil to agree with him and perhaps even suggest some wealthy and influential *Comyn* lord of his acquaintance. Varzil, drawing upon his Keeper's reserve, replied calmly, "I would not take such a step without consulting Dyannis herself. If it is her wish, I will not stand in her way. She has always been strong-willed, and her training will have given her even greater independence."

"Insolence, you mean? The sooner we get her out of there, the sooner she will accept her duties and settle into becoming a properly biddable wife."

Varzil laughed. "Obviously, you have not spoken with our little sister in some years, or you would not dare to suggest such a thing! Harald, she has made a place for herself at Hali, even as I have at Arilinn. She is a skilled *leronis,* beholden to no man. I do not think she will lightly surrender the freedom she has worked so hard for."

"She is still a Ridenow. She has an obligation to her family."

"But we are no longer beset by enemies at every side," Varzil pointed out. "We sit in Council here by our own right. Carolin, who will be the next Hastur king, wishes only peace and friendship between our lands."

"That, too, can change." Harald looked angry now, his dark brows furrowing. Varzil caught the edge of his thought. *We have been enemies before, and even your Prince Carolin may prove false if it serves his own interest.*

Varzil saw no point in arguing over the abiding love and trust he shared with Carolin, or even citing the old proverb, *The word of a Hastur,* as an unbreakable oath. Instead, he said, "Then it is even more important that Dyannis remain at Hali Tower, for there she is a Ridenow among Hasturs, living and working together. No oath or marriage vow could create a deeper bond than that between *leronyn* of the same circle. Those allegiances should not be tossed aside lightly."

When Harald looked skeptical, Varzil dropped the argument. He had done what he could for Dyannis. If he had failed to dissuade her from an ill-considered affair with Eduin when she was but a girl and new-come to the Tower, then Harald stood no chance of convincing her to leave if that was not her own desire.

How few times in life, he thought, does fortune grant us a truly free choice? He touched the ring on his right hand, and felt an answering pulse of energy. In his mind, Felicia still lay within the circle of his arms, her face glowing, her lips warm with smiles and kisses. Her Gift had demanded that she leave, even as his forced him to stay.

Varzil suppressed a shiver. There was no reason to doubt the wisdom of her choice, only that moment of hesitation. Had it been a flash of prescient warning, or only the natural anxiety of embarking upon something so daring, so new? He wondered if he had done his sister a favor by allowing her to remain where she might some day face a similar fate.

BOOK III

31

Colder than Zandru's seventh hell, went the old saying. Carolin thought, not for the first time, that it ought to have gone, *Colder than Nevarsin in winter. Or spring. Or autumn. Or any other season.* The monastery of Saint Valentine of the Snows had been built among the arms of the glacier ice, carved of the solid rock of the mountain. There were many pleasures that came with being the heir to the Hastur throne, but the temperature of Nevarsin was not one of them.

He had brought his sons to live and study with the monks even as he had planned, and had stayed longer than was strictly necessary. As he had vowed on Alianora's deathbed, he had placed her rosary with the other tokens of devotion upon the sanctuary altar. Over the course of a month, he had met with his distant Aldaran kin, the Keeper of the Tower, and the Father Master of the monastery, drawing out each session to delay his returning alone to Hali.

Meanwhile, he would not disgrace his house or himself by grumbling. As he lay on his narrow cot under his blanket of thick sheepswool, he reflected that he had the privilege of a blanket and warm food to eat, and he could exercise as he wished and sit by the fire in the guest house. Young boys, novices in the Order of Saint Christopher, even his own sons, had none of these luxuries. He'd heard the whimpers of those newly

281

arrived. Soon, the monks said, they would accustom themselves, learning to regulate their bodies to generate heat and thrive on whatever food was provided.

The bell for arising had already rung and Carolin had delayed long enough. Although as a guest he not bound by the rigid hours of prayer and work, he preferred to observe the rhythms of the community. In this way, he gained a greater sense of the lives and cares of the *cristoforos*. That knowledge had already given him new insights into his own people.

Carolin set his teeth together to keep them from chattering and heaved himself out of bed. Once he'd broken the ice on his basin, the worst would be over. He forced himself to wash properly. If he could not control feeling cold, as the monks could, at least he could master his own actions and not race through his morning ablutions like a cat in a river.

He dressed with care, taking an extra moment to settle the wide leather belt. Like his wool tunic and pants, it was dyed a soft gray. Over it would go the tartan of Hastur blue and silver. He smiled, remembering the red belt he and Orain had fought over as boys.

Orain . . .

He had not thought of his foster-brother this last handful of tendays. Orain was back at Hali, in Lyondri's service.

Carolin went down to the guest house refectory, where one of the *cristoforo* brothers offered him steaming porridge. A cup of wildflower honey and a pitcher of cream, clearly from the same pottery, sat in the middle of the bare wooden table, along with a bowl of fresh apples. Carolin thought that no formal breakfast at Hali, served on gilded porcelain with utensils of precious silver, had ever been as satisfying.

He paused for a moment beside a courtyard to fasten his fur-lined cloak and listen to the choir practicing in the adjacent chapel. The sweet voices of the boys soared above the others, ethereal, almost other worldly. What an uncomplicated life they led, their lives confined, prescribed . . . predictable.

Some birds cannot be caged, he thought. *Without the freedom of the sky, with all its uncertainties and danger, they waste away.*

Carolin had not gone more than a few paces beyond the guest house into the gray-walled streets of the city itself when a boy rushed up to him.

"*Dom* Carolin Hastur." A statement, not a question.

Carolin recognized the boy as one of the novices from Nevarsin

Tower. He was the son of *Dom* Valdrin Castamir of Highgarth. The cold had whipped the blood to his cheeks.

"Young Derrek." Carolin inclined his head politely and watched the boy beam with pleasure. "What brings you abroad on such a frosty morning?"

"*Vai dom,* I am bid to bring you to the Tower. A message has come through the relays this very hour. From Hali."

So it has come.

The news could mean only one thing, Carolin thought as he followed Derrek Castamir through the tangle of narrow streets. Here, stone buildings clustered so close together, the sun never shone in many a shadowed corner.

Once past the Tower's outer gate and cloak hall, Carolin stepped into a chamber not unlike the common room at Arilinn. Warmth and light filled the space, from the generous fire and the *laran*-charged globes.

The Keeper of Nevarsin Tower came forward to greet him. He was an Alton by his features, running a little to fat but still in his vigorous prime. Carolin had called on him upon arriving at Nevarsin, but had not seen him since.

The Keeper drew Carolin aside. His face, which seemed formed for merriment, was grave. "Word has reached us along the relays from Hali."

"My uncle—King Felix—"

"Has joined his illustrious ancestors."

Bowing his head, Carolin allowed himself a moment of silence. *Chieri* blood had brought the Hasturs many Gifts, but in this case long life had not been one of them. The man, King and uncle, whom Carolin had loved as a child had ceased to exist for many years.

And now, after waiting for so long, I am King. Aldones grant that I be a worthy one!

The enormity of what lay before him rose up like a river in flood. The funeral—the coronation—establishing his own court—formalizing relations with neighboring kingdoms—calming dissident voices—reviving the Hastur Council to control abuses of *laran* weaponry—and most of all, the dream so long delayed.

The pact.

Carolin straightened his shoulders. "I thank you for bringing this news to me so swiftly. Now I must go and prepare my return to Hali. Please send word to my men that I will depart as soon as I may."

"Your people at Hali say that an aircar will be waiting for you at Caer Donn."

Carolin nodded. The treacherous mountain winds made flights to Nevarsin all but impossible, even in the mildest weather. The guards who accompanied him as a Prince must serve him as well as King.

The Keeper watched him with that steady, piercing gaze of the Towers. "Then I bid you, *Adelandeyo,* Carolin Hastur-King. Walk in the Light."

And may the gods smile upon you, the Keeper added silently, *for you of all men will need their blessing.*

◆

"We must make haste while we can," Carolin told his men. At his heels, they clattered through the city gates and down the well-traveled road. Longlegs, his black Armida-bred mare, pricked her ears, eager to run. Beyond the city, dark-bellied clouds hung like funeral draperies.

They had gone two days into the valley when the storm struck. Whiteness blanketed the mountainside behind them. Ice-edged wind slashed through their traveling cloaks, whipped the horses' manes, and stole the breath from their lungs. Pellets of hail battered them. The horses flattened their ears against their necks and plunged on.

At last, the winds subsided and the hard frozen nuggets gave way to softer flakes of white. The sky darkened, heralding an early dusk and plummeting overnight temperatures.

There was no returning to Nevarsin, not with the storm settling in. Nor could they camp along the road. They would have to make the best speed they could to reach a travel shelter before dark.

As the day wore on, snow began to fall steadily. Thick and wet, it soaked their woolen cloaks and packed the horses' hooves, giving them slippery footing. The little convoy slowed even more. The men drew their hoods close around their faces. The horses lowered their heads, tails clamped against their rumps, and trudged on.

Carolin wondered if he were a fool to have set off so soon, but he could not see any other choice. He could not sprout wings and fly to Hali, nor could the land wait until spring for its new King. At Arilinn, he had heard of ancient techniques for bringing people physically through the relays. He thought the knowledge lost in the Ages of Chaos, as so much else had been. At any rate, it would not serve him now.

In a way, this delay was a blessing, a time to fully prepare himself for what lay ahead. He had been anticipating the day when he became King for so long, now that it was upon him, he realized the enormity of the responsibility. He had seen in his uncle how easily a King might wield injustice, in Rakhal, the temptations of ease, rich food, endless wine, and willing women, and in Lyondri, how the power to seize a man's possessions or even his life could corrupt even an honest man.

I must never forget whose king I am. The thought came to him that to rule a land was to be bound to it, to keep faith with the loyalty given him, to set aside personal self-interest.

So will I swear, standing at Hali in the rhu fead *and the holy fire of my ancestors.*

So had he already sworn in his heart. At that moment, Carolin imagined that Aldones himself, Lord of Light and father to that very first Hastur whose name he himself bore, heard his oath. He saw himself kneeling before a figure so shimmering and brilliant, he could not look directly at it. Hands reached down and he placed his own between them, as vassal to lord.

No words were spoken, yet he felt his innermost secrets laid bare and measured in that pure radiance—his moments of petty temper, his disappointed hopes, his pride, but also his generosity, his courage, his love of honor. A silent promise arose from his depths, *As long as I breathe, I pledge to be a just lord and shield against all evil to my people.*

The ritual words usually concluded, "The gods witness it, and the holy things at Hali." Carolin needed no formal affirmation of his oath. As the vision faded, a warmth lingered on his brow like a token of benediction.

✦

Late in the afternoon, they came upon a village, little more than an inn and a couple of barns with pole corrals in back. Smoke rose from the chimneys and lights shone from the windows.

"I don't remember this place," Carolin's captain said.

"Nor I," Carolin replied, reining his horse toward the friendly-looking lights. "Do you think we've been caught in a Ghost Wind and it's really just a pile of rocks? Or even better, a banshee lair?"

Behind him, the men laughed, the tension of their journey broken.

"*Vai dom,* we came through here on a fair day, with the beds of

Nevarsin waiting for us. There could have been a dozen villages with dancing girls and roast rabbit-horns hanging from every branch, and we'd never have noticed."

Carolin swung down from his horse. They went into the inn, a single common room with a staircase at the rear. The trestle table that occupied most of the floor was uneven and much-repaired. A battered pot hung above the fire and a woman bent over it, stirring. She wore so many layers of skirt and shawl that it was impossible to determine her size or age. Without looking up, she said, "They've all gone back—"

She lifted her head and broke off, seeing Carolin in the doorway. "Oh! My lords!"

"Forgive the intrusion, my good woman, but could you provide us with a hot meal?"

They crowded into the room, damp cloaks already steaming in the warmth. The woman bustled about, taking out wooden trenchers and cups from a cupboard, dishing out helpings of soup thick with boiled grain and root vegetables, and filling pottery pitchers with ale from a barrel. The food was plain, but needed salt. She'd probably learned her cooking at the Nevarsin guest house. The ale, however, was superb, tasting of sun and malted grain.

As they were finishing the meal, two men entered, stomping off the clinging snow. By the welcome the woman gave them, they were clearly her husband and brother. The husband served up another round of ale for everyone. He hovered about the table, talking affably. His wife disappeared out back to begin another batch of loaves.

Despite the warmth of fire and ale, Carolin could not shake a feeling of growing urgency. "How far is the next village?"

"Oh, half a day, be it a fair one, m'lord. But you'll not be wanting to travel on so late in the day. Here's stout walls and a merry fire. Soon there will be my good wife's hearth cakes. We've but two guest rooms, but there's space to spread a cloak by the fire."

The man's arguments made sense, even if they were fueled by the thought of what all these services would cost. This late in the year, rich travelers must be few.

Carolin's captain leaned over, pitching his voice low. "*Vai dom,* you cannot be thinking of going on tonight."

"Be at ease, my friend. We will remain here and leave tomorrow with the first light."

The men made pallets of their cloaks in the common room, even as the innkeeper had suggested. Carolin went upstairs to one of the guest chambers, his captain and senior aide to the other. The room was narrow, with a single small window, set high in the rough stone wall, and of such thick glass that no details could be seen through it. As he had expected, the bed was too short for his height.

It was a good thing he had his own thick cloak to add to the patched blankets, yet everything was clean and very neat. With such ale and housekeeping, as well as its situation on the principal road to Nevarsin, the inn should have been prosperous. Was the poverty due to some personal difficulty on the part of the innkeeper, or taxes raised ever higher to support soldier and Tower?

I must see if I can ask discreetly, he thought as his body relaxed into sleep. *In the morning.*

♦

Carolin startled awake into a dim, hazy light. It was still night. Around him, the timbers of the house creaked and settled. He heard snoring from the other side of the thin interior wall. The fragments of his last dream dissolved around him, bits of sound and image. Someone had been calling to him—Varzil?

He focused his mind as he had been taught during that season at Arilinn so long ago. There was no answer, but he kept trying—listening. . . .

His thoughts drifted to the tasks which lay before him. Tales had come to him of actions both good and evil, of Lyondri's cadre of guards, of stones thrown in protest of taxes, of bribery and nepotism in the *cortes,* of harsh and trivial decisions by an increasingly senile King Felix. Over the last few years, he had been less and less able to influence his uncle, who had not wanted to listen to any hint of criticism or disagreement. Rakhal's flattery was far more pleasing. So, Carolin had bided his time, doing what he could. All that would change.

I am King now. These are my people. I will rule them with honor and justice.

Fine words, he knew, often crumbled in cold reality. At least, he would begin as best he could. He would gather advisers he could trust, men who would speak to him frankly and with no hidden purposes of their own.

A smile rose to his mouth. He would summon Varzil to Hali and together they would rebuild Neskaya, even as they had planned. It would be a symbol of a new age, a new hope for peace, a place where crown and Tower would lay down arms.

With that vision in his mind, he drifted back to sleep.

The next morning, the winds came up again, whipping the snow to a blinding flurry.

"We cannot travel in this," the captain reported. He'd gone to the stables to look after the horses and had been almost blown off his feet. "We'd be lost before we went ten paces."

Reluctantly, Carolin agreed. The night had left him with a sense of formless urgency. He told himself that Hali was safe in the hands of the Regents. The throne would wait for his return. He had no right to risk himself in a Hellers snowstorm. Meanwhile, the inn was snug and warm, and the landlord's excellent ale flowed freely.

32

A full tenday later, Carolin and his party at last set out again. The air was very cold and clear. Ice had crusted over the snow, but the horses were fresh and eager. Their breath rose in puffs of white vapor. Their hooves broke through the brittle surface with crunching noises to the jingle of bridle rings and creak of saddle leather.

When the sun had come full up, light filled the valley. Behind them lay the peaks of Nevarsin. The road curved before them, passing fields and farms silent under a blanket of sparkling white. The day warmed slightly, enough to melt the ice. One of the men began singing, a traveler's tune with a strong, driving rhythm. The others caught it up.

Carolin's spirits rose. What a day it was to be alive! The wind of their passing burned his face and ran thrilling fingers through his hair.

He sensed the hoofbeats on the road ahead before any of them heard the sound. With a signal, he slowed his men to a walk. The unmarked snow on the road ahead muffled the noise, but within a few moments, there could be no doubt.

A single rider appeared, a dark shape against the whiteness of road and field.

The captain nudged his mount to the front, placing himself between Carolin and the rapidly-approaching rider. He slid his sword free.

Carolin started to tell him not to risk the truce of the road by rash action. Unease brushed the edges of his mind. His pulse leaped in his throat. His black mare pranced and pulled at the bit.

The horseman raced toward them, bent low at full gallop. Neither his colors nor any identifying emblem could be discerned.

"Hail there!" the captain shouted.

Carolin recognized the horseman, not from the man's face but his seat in the saddle. Only one man he'd ever known rode like that. That tall, almost gaunt frame was unmistakable, even under the layers of flapping cloak.

"There's no need for steel," Carolin told his men. He released the reins and Longlegs surged forward. "Orain! By all the gods, what are you doing here?"

The rider pulled his horse to a halt and leapt to the ground. "*Vai dom!* I have not come too late!"

Carolin swung down from the saddle and caught Orain in a hard embrace. As his cheek touched the bare, unshaven skin of his friend, a jolt of emotion flashed thorugh him.

He drew back. Something was terribly wrong.

"I have heard the news of my uncle's passing, if that is what troubles you," Carolin said. "You need not have driven a good horse so hard to tell me. As you see, I am already on my way to Caer Donn, where an aircar awaits me. And," with a glance back at his guards, "I am well protected."

"All of Hali was making ready to welcome you," Orain stammered, his words tumbling together. "But Rakhal—he's seized the throne!"

"Rakhal? There must be some mistake."

"He claims that Felix named him heir on his deathbed, though Aldones only knows if that's true. The Regents, Zandru curse them, dared not stand against him."

Carolin scowled. The old king had grown weaker over the last few years. Many times, he held conversations with people long dead, mistook son for father, forgot where he was. He could easily have forgotten that the throne must by law and custom go to Carolin, the son of his eldest brother.

Orain shook his head. "You must not delay! Rakhal's already had himself crowned! He claims you are unfit and has declared you traitor and your lady wife a spy. Even now, the men are on their way to arrest you!"

Rakhal . . .

Rakhal with his soothing words, flattering and cozening the senile old man . . . Rakhal insinuating himself into positions of greater power and authority . . . Rakhal forming a cadre of guards loyal only to himself. . . .

How could I have missed the signs?

Somehow Rakhal had found out poor Alianora's secret and used it to convince the Regents to reject Carolin's rightful claim.

His life would not be worth a *reis,* once in Rakhal's hands. Rakhal dared not let him live.

"Rakhal's first act was to execute or imprison all those who opposed his claims, even old Lord Elhalyn, who had been King Felix's chief counselor for all those years," Orain rushed on. "Lyondri's thrown in with him and his men are already out in force, smashing anyone who says a word against Rakhal."

Carolin closed his eyes against the image of the streets of Hali, running with blood. Quickly, he gathered himself. There would be time enough for grief, for planning. Right now, he must act to save himself and his sons. He could become an outlaw, he knew, but there was no other choice.

He laid one hand on Orain's shoulder, and remembered that Orain had once been Lyondri's sworn man. "You must not return to Hali, my friend. If it were found out that you warned me—"

Orain bowed his head. *"Para servirte."*

A terrible thought crossed Carolin's mind, of his sons left behind, trusting and defenseless, at the monastery of Saint Valentine of the Snows. Rakhal could not afford to let them live, any more than he would spare Carolin's own life. The monastery kept no armed guards, not even for royal students, and the boys would have no reason to suspect a messenger from their kinsman.

Carolin's first impulse was to turn Longlegs around and gallop back to Nevarsin. The folly of such a move held him fast. He was no longer a private man, who could indulge such passions. He bore the fate of all Hastur. He had sworn it in his heart.

Delay or detour could be fatal. If Orain had reached here, so far along the road, then Rakhal's minions or, worse yet, Lyondri's butchers could not be far behind.

How could I have been so blind to what Rakhal was?

His only hope—the kingdom's only hope—lay in immediate flight. The sooner he placed himself beyond Lyondri's reach, the better his chances.

"I cannot command you, my friend, I can only ask this, for it will place you in even greater danger," Carolin said.

"My sword and I are yours to command." Orain had reined his horse closer, his face even more gaunt than usual. "Once I swore service to Lyondri, but he has proven himself both dishonorable and corrupt. I do not break faith with him, for he has already forsworn his faith with you, who should have been his King. Ask anything I can give, *vai dom,* and it is gladly yours."

"Then go on to Nevarsin as quickly as you can, and take my sons from there to safety."

Orain frowned. "Two such tender lads cannot travel far in this weather, even on good horses and with warm clothing."

"Make for Highgarth, the seat of *Dom* Valdrin Castamir. I trust his honor and integrity. He will not fail us. I will meet you there when Kyrrdis next greets fair Idriel in the morning sky, but if I do not come, you must take them yourself beyond the Kadarin River, into the wild lands. If I still breathe, I will find you there. Guard them well."

"My life upon it." Orain bowed his head, then turned his horse and galloped headlong along the road to Nevarsin.

Carolin watched the flurry of snow kicked up by Orain's retreating mount. The loyalty of such a man was a gift beyond price. He prayed he would be worthy of it.

But only, he reminded himself savagely, *if I stay alive!*

"Ride now!" Carolin mounted up and his horse gave a little rear, throwing her muzzle skyward as if in challenge. "Let us ride together.

◆

The black mare slipped and scrambled on the loose rock of a trail which was little more than a thread between massive outcroppings, like bleak and angry bones of the earth. The lesser mounts of the guards struggled behind, heads lowered in mute endurance. Sleet fell slantwise, driven by fierce mountain winds. At times, Carolin heard the ululating cries of wolves, calling to one another. He did not know if they were welcoming him as one of them, or joining in the chase.

Days melted into one another, and Carolin and his men grew more and more like the wolves, shaggy, watchful, cautious. They reached the broken lands which led to the Kadarin. Twice now, they had to beat back outlaws, desperate men who preyed on travelers. One of the horses had been lamed in an attack, and two men injured.

Along the trail, Carolin had woken from sleep more than once, sweating with urgency. He wished he had *laran* enough to identify the danger, for danger it was.

They are searching for me, he thought. *Lyondri's trackers, Rakhal's* leronyn.

Rakhal would have the Towers of Hali and Tramontana at his command, with the power of their circles, of *clingfire* and sentry birds and spells to bind a horse's feet or cloud a man's thoughts. Carolin thought of his friends and kin, of Lady Liriel at Tramontana, of Dyannis Ridenow at Hali, little Dyannis whom he had partnered at dance at Midwinter Festival so many years ago, and most of all, of Maura. Was she even now bending her thoughts against him? No, he could not believe that.

Not for the first time, he wished for Varzil with his courage and steady wisdom. He remembered the attack at the riverside on the way to Blue Lake, how Varzil had sensed the *clingfire* dart even before it burst from cover. He could use that kind of watchful protection now.

I am here with you, ghosted through his mind. It was not a direct contact, for that was impossible over so many leagues, and although Varzil was a powerful telepath, Carolin was not. He sensed that Varzil held him in thought, that even in these desperate times, he was not forgotten.

✦

Carolin stood before the roaring fire in the great hall of Highgarth, relishing the feeling of being warm and dry again. He had lost track of the days of hiding, traveling by night, jumping at shadows. Too many times, he had thought only of enduring the next hour of cold and hunger, the next stretch of trail.

If it goes on like this, we will forget who we are and why we seek this terrible refuge. The lands beyond the Kadarin had a fey, wild magic that sank its claws into a man's soul.

Orain had been waiting for him, along with his two boys. They ran to Carolin, as delighted to be set free from the Castamir nursery as to see him. So far, their journey had been more of a holiday than a desperate flight.

Valdrin Castamir had welcomed Carolin as lord and brother. "Many will stand with you against Rakhal the Usurper. He trades upon men's greed, for few would support him otherwise. Already we have heard stories of how he seizes the lands of any man who fails to please him and gives them to his flattering lackeys. Even smallholders who should have been apart from these troubles become his victims. He surrounds himself with those who tell him only what he wishes to hear, instead of restraint and mercy. And Lyondri Hastur, his executioner, has become a wild beast fattened on blood. *Vai dom,* the situation will only worsen as Rakhal tightens his grip."

Valdrin's words pierced Carolin's heart. He glanced from the old lord to Orain, watching him with shining eyes. These men would follow him, even at the cost of their own lives. They saw in him a symbol of hope, a just and honorable King.

I would be those things to my people, though I know they do not come from me, but only through me.

Over the next tenday, Carolin met not only with *Dom* Valdrin and Orain, who had quickly become his most trusted advisers, but with smallholders and minor lords within the area. A common thread of fear ran through them all. Sooner or later, on one pretext or another, they each risked prison or worse.

Dom Valdrin urged Carolin to use Highgarth as his headquarters, the center from which to launch his campaign to retake the throne. "These people lack only a King to follow."

Carolin shook his head. "I would not repay your loyalty by placing you at such risk. If Rakhal learned that you had aided me, he would stop at nothing to destroy you."

He must return to the wilds, he knew, to cold and hunger and always glancing behind. For the moment, his sons were safe, but how long would that last? Though the very thought sent a shiver of fear through his marrow, he must take them with him.

"Do not ask me to leave you again," Orain said in a private moment. "Every day, I feared the worst."

Carolin laid one hand on his foster-brother's shoulder. "I shall almost certainly need you as emissary, for I cannot be in more than one place at the same time. I cannot imagine anyone I would trust more to speak for me." Then, when he saw Orain would protest further, "I am no longer a private person, I am Hastur of Hastur. We both of us serve a greater cause."

Orain bowed his head in mute agreement and offered no more objections.

Over the time he spent at Highgarth, Carolin's small band of followers had grown. Sons of neighboring estates, afire with idealism, begged to join him, as did a number of Castamir's own men. Carolin divided his forces, for he must travel quickly and with as little notice as possible. To the guards who had accompanied him on that desperate flight from Nevarsin, he offered a choice.

"You served me as a Hastur Prince and heir to the throne," he told them. "I am grateful for your loyalty. But I cannot ask any of you to go further. Some of you have families, or oaths of loyalty which bind you elsewhere. Any man who wishes to return to Hali may do so with my thanks."

Some of the men fell to their knees and vowed they would follow Carolin to the Wall Around the World, but the captain, with tears in his eyes, begged leave, for his wife was sewing woman to Lyondri's own lady, and he feared for her life should he be named deserter and traitor.

Carolin embraced the man. "Go with the blessings of all the gods, for I greatly fear the war which sets kinsmen against each other, and men forced to choose between the lives of their loved ones and their own honor."

At Orain's urging, Carolin determined to disguise himself as one of his own men under the name of *Dom* Carlo of Blue Lake.

"That will help to spread the word that you are free, even if in exile," Orain said. "That knowledge alone will help to keep hope alive in men's hearts."

On a morning when the air held the first soft promise of spring to come, Carolin, his sons, and a small band of loyal men rode forth from Highgarth for the perilous journey back to the Kadarin wild lands.

33

It was a good thing, Eduin reflected, that he had learned patience, for it was the better part of a year before he arrived at Hestral Tower. He had been ready to leave as soon as word came from Loryn Ardais, Keeper of Hestral, that a *laranzu* of his skill and training was most warmly welcome. Before he could make arrangements, however, all Hali erupted with news of the old King's death. That in itself would have meant only a short delay for the funeral, but word that Rakhal and not Carolin had taken the throne rocked the city.

News came daily of this lord or that declaring for either of the cousins. Lyondri Hastur and his men stormed through the streets, struggling to restore order. Not a day passed without some other man, lordling or trader or disaffected soldier, being named outlaw. Carolin himself had fled beyond the Kadarin River, living among bandits, with a bounty set upon his head. For an entire season, the Keepers at Hali forbade any travel outside the Tower. The roads were not safe in these perilous times.

So Eduin remained, doing the work assigned to him. He'd lost all interest in the archives, but he had learned how to present a good appearance, and he wanted no cause for rumor or complaint on his account.

In moments of refuge behind the telepathic damper at his door, he both grieved and exulted in Carolin's exile. With Rakhal firmly upon the throne and growing more ruthless every day, Carolin's chances of survival diminished. Eventually, Lyondri's assassins, the cruel weather of the Kadarin badlands, or some fool desperate for the bounty would put an end to him.

Sometimes when Eduin thought of Carolin lying in a pool of his own blood or starved and frozen, battered by the elements, a shiver of almost physical pain would pass through him. Then his stomach would clench around a knot of ice. In its spreading chill, all anguished thoughts, all memories of friendship would fall away. Was this the price of the Deslucido Gift, or something deeper and more sinister?

In the name of Aldones and all the gods, what had been done to him?

◆

On Midwinter Festival Night, Eduin allowed Dyannis to lure him into her bed once more. At first, he had every intention of maintaining his distance from her. She knew entirely too many people, and never gave a thought to what she said. He could not afford to raise any suspicions. He told himself it was over between them, and at the time, he meant it. His life was not his own, nor had it ever been. He'd been a fool to hope otherwise.

He stood at the threshold of her chamber and felt the *kireseth* singing like poison in his veins. Dyannis stepped past him to throw back the curtains. It was a clear night, and the multihued radiance of three moons suffused the room. He felt as if he stood on the edge of some enchanted world, a place of pearly light and magic. Not even the faint orange glow from the banked fire dispelled the illusion.

Dyannis turned to face him, her eyes gleaming silver. With a slow, liquid movement, she reached up to free the clasp that held her hair coiled at the nape of her neck. It came loose in a cascade of red-gold silk. She looked so beautiful, he wondered if she had cast a glamour over him. His heart beat like a wild thing as she came toward him. Her lips parted in a smile and her fingers on his face were warm.

"My love," she whispered. Something in the night, the singing and the ritual, or perhaps it was only the effect of the drug, gave her words a curious echo. Each syllable rippled through his body. Spheres of color and heat sprang into life. An intoxicating fragrance arose from her skin.

She covered his face in kisses. "My first love. How I've missed you."

Hearing those words, something gave way inside him. It was as if she had opened up a secret door to his heart. She pressed herself against him, so that the boundaries of their separate bodies began to dissolve, even as their minds joined. The curves and sweet warm valleys of her body welcomed him like the home he'd never known.

Eduin woke near dawn with nausea trembling through him. He crawled to his own rooms, where he lay on top of his solitary bed, retching. He'd always had a sensitive stomach for *kireseth* and its distillations. This reaction went beyond the merely physical. He was disgusted with himself for having given in to the temptations of the moment. He should never have allowed himself—he should have made her go away forever. He had not been able to bring himself to do it. Now, no matter where he went, no matter what he did, she would be part of him. It was crazy, he knew, but he could feel the lingering warmth of her loving like a snake coiled around his heart.

She is the sister of Varzil Ridenow, he who is the bosom friend of Carolin Hastur and lover of Felicia Hastur-Acosta!

He sat up, raking his hair back from his forehead. Emotions roiled and clashed within him like storm clouds above the Hellers. Surely his very soul would tear apart under the strain. He could not go on.

Aldones, help me! Over and over, he prayed for a way through the tangle.

There was no hope for it. If the Lord of Light would not take this love from his heart, then Zandru, Lord of the frozen hells, must be his master.

Turn my heart to ice, so that I may never feel again!

As if in response, a chill rippled through his body, seeping into his core. His heartbeat steadied.

My heart to ice . . .

He repeated the words in his mind like a sacred chant. Already, the sensation of cold was fading. He thought of the monks at Nevarsin and how they took no heed of weather or temperature, looking only to their inner life.

And so, too, must he hold fast to his purpose.

◆

Winter dug its claws into Hali. There were fewer executions, as if no one had the heart to fight both cold and Lyondri's men. Daily living was difficult enough. For a tenday at a time, snow so blanketed the city that trade slowed to a bare minimum. The Tower drew into itself.

The bad weather was not without its blessings, for Eduin rarely saw Dyannis. They were both working long shifts in the circles, charging the great *laran* batteries that supplied heat as well as light to the castle. Rakhal had increased his demands and now frequently traveled by aircar over his new kingdom. When Eduin encountered Dyannis, whether passing in a corridor or across the dining area, they spoke only a few words. Intense matrix work depleted sexual energies for both men and women.

Spring crept into Hali like a thief, its presence barely noticed. Dyannis was called back home on some family business or other; Eduin didn't inquire. He was both dismayed and elated when she sought him out on the eve of her departure.

"When you first came to Hali, I wondered if we would be as we were," she said, with a shy lilt to her words that meant, *when we were first in love.* "I did not know if I hoped or feared it more. Not all the smiths in Zandru's forge can put that chick back into its egg, so they say. Not even for you," she spoke the word with a tenderness that sent a familiar fluttering through his breast, "could I return to the young girl I was then. But when I was with you, I wished it were possible."

And so you avoided me, when I thought I was avoiding you.

"Exactly," she said.

"But—Midwinter Festival Night—"

Dyannis tossed her head, and in his memory, Eduin heard the little tinkling bells she had worn at the Hastur court ball when he had first held her in his arms. "One last perfect evening. For remembrance, if you will. Before we each go on to the lives the gods have chosen for us." She drew so near that he inhaled the fragrance of her hair, washed with some herbs that left it smelling of sunlight. Rising on her tiptoes, she brushed her lips, butterfly-soft, against his.

"I believe you will do great things. When I hear men sing of them, I will remember that night."

She left him then without a backward glance. The moment he had waited for had come, she was gone, and instead of relief, he writhed inside with longing to call her back. If she had begged and pleaded for a pledge of everlasting love, then he would have had little difficulty pushing her from his mind. Against this dignity, this simple faith, he had no defense.

✦

Summer settled like a golden haze over the city of Hali. The cloud-lake glimmered in the sunshine, its waters in constant motion. On the long twilit evenings, Eduin walked in solitude along the sandy banks. He found a curious comfort in the restlessness of the mists.

I am like the lake, he thought. *Always changing on the outside to hide what lies beneath.*

On one such outing, when his thoughts were particularly somber, he returned to be summoned to the chambers of the Keeper, Dougal DiAsturian. A number of the circle's *leronyn* already sat, waiting.

"Ah, Eduin, thank you for coming," Dougal said, gesturing for Eduin to take his place.

Eduin sat, feeling the shift of emotional currents in the room. Had something happened beyond Rakhal's astonishing overthrow?

"Dark times are upon us all," Dougal said aloud. "Although it is our wish to remain at peace with all men, we may not have that choice. We here at Hali and our colleagues at Tramontana are bound to allegiance to the Hastur King."

"That is true," Marelie, the middle-aged woman who often worked the relays, pointed out. "But which one? Rakhal sits upon the throne, right enough, yet many loyal men believe it should be Carolin."

"That was what everyone thought, before this terrible business," one of the *leronyn* said, shaking his head. "Rakhal had the blessings of the Regents. They claimed to have evidence of Carolin's perfidy and unfitness for office, but it was never made public."

"The issue of succession is not ours to decide," Dougal brought the discussion to a halt in a voice ringing with authority. "If Rakhal or any other crowned King commands us, then we must obey. It goes without saying that one use he has for our talents is the pursuit and capture of the exiled King Carolin."

Several of the workers shifted uneasily in their seats.

"Exactly," Dougal said, responding to the flare of emotion. "Several of the *leronyn* at Tramontana, who are kin to both Rakhal and Carolin, have asked that they not be ordered to make war upon their families. King Rakhal has agreed to release them, provided they also swear that they will not participate in any attack against him. I am empowered to offer all at Hali the same agreement."

Eduin remembered that Maura Elhalyn, who had known both Rakhal and Carolin from childhood, now served at Tramontana Tower, as well as Liriel Hastur.

"Why should Rakhal agree to such a thing?" Marelie asked.

"Because he is not an utter fool," Eduin burst out heatedly. "He knows that to compel any of us to act against blood ties and conscience is to court rebellion. That he cannot risk, or he will find himself without a single Tower to call upon."

Several of the others looked at him with shocked expressions, but the Keeper nodded. They both knew that only within the confines of the Tower was such speech safe.

One of the women said, "I cannot claim any such allegiance to Prince Carolin, but I despise being drawn into a feud of brother against brother."

"Aye, for is it not said that when kinsmen quarrel, enemies will quickly step in?" another commented.

Eduin nodded, remembering the discussion he had had with Varzil about the rulership of the Towers. How long ago that seemed, when they were all at Hastur Castle for Midwinter Festival! He had been so young, so naive. All the passion he'd felt had drained from the memory. What did it matter who gave the orders, whether the Towers governed themselves or followed the commands of some ignorant lordling?

Ice shivered through his belly. Let king and Tower go their ways, let them all destroy one another. Only one thing mattered, and if remaining loyal to Rakhal would help him achieve that goal, he would do whatever was necessary.

"Is it sure that we will be asked to make *clingfire* and lungrot plague spores for Rakhal?" Marelie asked. "I would much rather use my skills for healing than killing."

"I will do what I can to assign you to those tasks," Dougal said, "though I fear we may have no choice. And you, Eduin, what is your position? I know that Carolin Hastur studied at Arilinn during your time there, and I believed you to be close friends."

The knot of ice tightened. "Yes, I was acquainted with Carolin," Eduin said, "and I spent a Midwinter Festival with him at Hali as his guest. It is not my place to judge who shall rule, any more than it is mine to tell a farmer when to plant his wheat or a shepherd when to cull the flock. My allegiance is to my Tower. I will do whatever work is given to me."

Dougal bent his head in acknowledgment. "Would that there were more with your clear loyalties, Eduin. It would make the world a much simpler place."

The world, Eduin thought as he returned to his own chambers, was not a simple place. It was complex, often puzzling, and always dangerous. And loyalty had nothing to do with it.

✦

Dyannis had not yet returned and summer was just turning into autumn when Eduin set off for Hestral Tower. To his surprise, a royal steward arranged for a horse and escort for him. The two swordsmen wore Hastur colors with an insignia that marked them as members of Lyondri's special cadre.

Several times along the road, the guards called a stop to visit a local manor house or question an innkeeper. Eduin quickly realized that they were searching for information about the whereabouts of Carolin and his sons, or word of any man who had helped them on their flight. As long as they treated him with reasonable civility and got him to Hestral Tower, it was no business of his what else they did.

They reached Hestral late in the afternoon, when the harvest sun poured down golden across the rolling hills. Here two traders' routes crossed the Hestral River, forming a natural crossroads. The town sprawled down to the river wharves, a collection of rambling, one- and two-story buildings, many of them in antiquated half-timbered style, half-buried under sword ivy, their roofs sagging with age.

On a rise sat a heavily walled fortress. In contrast to the liveliness of the town, with its bright pennants and throng of people and their animals, the fort presented an insular, brooding aspect. It must have been built originally as a guard post.

They made their way through the town market square where farmers sold hard gourds and turnips, rounds of *chervine* cheese and bushels of grain. This late in the day, only a few women with baskets over their arms remained to haggle with the vendors over the day's leftovers. Their voices rose like the shrill cries of birds. A pack of half-grown boys with sticks raced between the carts, chasing a ball and raising clouds of dust.

The bustle of the marketplace battered at Eduin's mental senses. He slammed his barriers into place.

A man hawking baked goods stepped backward into the path of Eduin's horse, which threw up its head. The man stumbled and the few mis-shapen buns left on his tray tumbled to the dust.

Though he wore the apron of his trade, the baker spoke boldly. "Now, there, yer lordship, you must buy my fine buns!" He held out a hand, palm up.

"Show proper respect to your betters!" one of the guards snarled. "In Thendara, you'd be whipped for such insolence."

The baker's man scowled. "But this is Hestral, not Thendara. And here a man must pay for what he's ruined, whether it's buns or pots."

The guard lashed out with one booted foot, but the baker's man twisted so the blow missed his face by a hair's breadth. He darted away. The second guard held up a cautionary hand. "If not him, then we'll find some other. There'll be a right time and place to teach such rabble their manners."

"Aye, and a healthy respect for His Majesty's colors."

Tentatively, Eduin lowered his mental barriers. The hum of so many people within a confined space swept over him, but it was not as bad as he'd expected. Most of the mental impressions were quiet, everyday pleasures. A cascade of images brushed his mind, like jewels strung one after another: the brightness of sunlight on running water; a child's laughter; water curling around bare toes; a fish quick and slippery darting through the shadows; the smell of rivergrass—

Eduin! There are you, come at last!

A woman strode toward him, a basket swinging from one hand and two adolescent boys in tow. Except for her crown of tangled flame-red curls, she could have been any of the townswomen, out to buy a few last vegetables for dinner.

For a moment, Eduin did not recognize her. When he'd last seen her at Arilinn, she had been thin and pale, only lately recovered from illness. Now she walked with a long, free stride, kicking the damp hems of her skirts. Sun and exercise in the fresh air brought color to her cheeks, and health had softened the angles of her body.

His stomach curdled. It was *her*.

"Eduin, don't you know me?" She'd reached him and stood at the head of his horse, shading her eyes with one hand.

He inclined his head. "*Domna* Felicia."

One of the boys giggled and the other hushed him up.

"You must forgive their manners," Felicia said in an easy way. "We've been down by the river, communing with frogs. They're not back to human level yet."

Her words and manner were disarmingly friendly, yet he sensed in her an *awareness* of the world around her. Any overt attack, physical or mental, would surely fail.

Quickly, he reined his thoughts under control. "Are you heading back to the tower? I must present myself to the Keeper."

"We have looked for you this last tenday," she replied. "I will return with you, for it's clear we'll get no more work from these two today."

Felicia refused Eduin's offer of his horse, walking beside him. The guards followed.

"The Keeper of Hestral must be an unusual man, to train novices in such a way," Eduin said, searching for some neutral topic. "We certainly did nothing like that at Arilinn."

"Arilinn is the very embodiment of tradition," Felicia said. "Loryn Ardais, who is Keeper here in Hestral, does not subscribe to the theory that nothing should be ever done for the first time. As he is so fond of saying, 'Innovation does not necessarily portend deterioration.' As for the frogs—well, perhaps there is more than a little playfulness in that exercise. How else can we expect boys to sit still for their indoor lessons, except by rewarding them with warty, slimy things?"

"You do not object?" You, who are *Comynara* and *leronis?*

Though Felicia's expression was perfectly serious, Eduin caught the undertone of merriment in her voice. "I have always thought that the best use of our Gifts is to create harmony with the world around us, not separation."

"So you would oppose using *laran* to move a storm from a place where it would create a flood to one where it would relieve a drought?"

"Hardly that. In fact, one of the projects in which I hope you will join us involves some new ways of detecting those weather conditions that can give rise to forest fires so that we *can* intervene. One of the workers in my circle has Rockraven ancestry that gives him a very strong weather sense, though it's erratic. But enough for now! You are not here an hour, and already I am giving you a dissertation on my work!"

They neared the gates. Eduin felt the shimmer of power. Felicia passed her free hand over the *laran*-keyed lock and the spell shifted but did not dissipate. One half of the gate swung open and she gestured for him to enter.

The two guards nudged their horses forward. Ears back, tails held at an angle eloquent with reluctance, the beasts shuffled a pace or two.

"Good masters, you must leave your weapons outside," Felicia told them.

"We go armed by the orders of His Majesty, King Rakhal," the senior of them said, glaring at her.

"It is by the orders of the Keeper of this Tower that no one shall enter bearing arms." She spoke the words as simple fact.

"You have fulfilled your mission in escorting me here," Eduin intervened. "Surely you are not required to go within."

Unless you suspect the Keeper of Hestral Tower of harboring fugitives. Were that the case, he added, there would be little which steel could accomplish.

Eduin dismounted, untied his saddlebags, and handed the reins of his horse to the nearer guard. He took out the small purse that he had been given for expenses on the trail. It still held a few silver coins. "Here's for your trouble."

The guard took the purse, weighing it for an instant before tucking it inside his jacket. "No trouble, my lord. We will leave you here, then, and wish you good fortune."

Felicia watched them ride back down the hill.

"What would have happened if they had tried to take their swords inside?" Eduin asked.

"Hmm?" She sounded a little distracted as she turned to close the gate. "Metal acts as a conductor of energy, somewhat like lightning, so it heats up. The last time anyone tried was ten years ago. A thief, the story goes. He'd only a dagger, which he carried in a sheath filled with spring water because someone had told him it would protect the weapon against magic. I'm told it made a spectacular explosion. The townsfolk still sing a drinking ballad about it."

Inside lay a little courtyard with a well and rows of dwarfed fruit trees, and a tiny kitchen garden. Beneath a trellis of yellow rosalys, a young woman sat playing a *rryl*. The sound had not carried beyond the gates.

The girl set down the *rryl* and darted toward them. She was barely in her teens, with a fresh innocence that reminded Eduin of Dyannis when they had first met. As Felicia introduced them, the girl lowered her eyes.

"You must forgive our Alys," Felicia said, "for she is new-come to Hestral and has not lost her shy ways. Ah!" she turned toward the portal of the Tower, where a man in the flowing crimson robe of a Keeper emerged. "Loryn, here is Eduin of Hali, come at last to join us!"

Loryn Ardais seemed to float above the ground, so smooth was his stride, his feet hidden beneath the rippling folds of his robes. His hair was a dark, intense red, almost black, and his gaze entirely too penetrating as he inclined his head in greeting. "Come inside and meet the others," he said gravely. "We are very happy to welcome you to our fellowship."

The introductions went smoothly, for Hestral was far smaller than Hali. Even the common and dining rooms had been framed on a more modest scale.

Left alone at last, Eduin surveyed his own chamber on the second floor facing the river. It looked comfortable enough. Beside the fireplace stood a washstand holding a basin, an ewer of water scented with petals from those very rosalys he had seen in the garden, and a bar of fine soap. Best of all, it possessed only a single wall in common with another inhabited room. He unpacked his few belongings, beginning with the telepathic damper he had brought from Hali. Setting it on a table beside the door, he tuned it to its highest setting. The familiar buzz and wash of deadness reassured him that it had survived the journey intact.

His cloak went on one of the hooks, his extra shirt and linens into the small, exquisitely carved chest at the foot of the bed. He listened for a moment before checking to make sure the corridor outside was empty. Then he closed the door once more. Though there was no lock, he did not think anyone could enter unawares.

From the pocket sewn into the lining of his winter cloak, he drew out a pouch of triple-layered silk. With a tug on the drawstrings, he turned it upside down, so that its contents, a single blue gem, fell into the opened palm of his hand.

Such a small thing it was, so harmless in appearance. It looked like nothing so much as an unkeyed matrix, and one of only mediocre quality. He had carried it from his father's cottage, hidden it at Hali, and now . . .

Holding it to the light from the river view window, he marveled again at his father's consummate skill. He himself, or any qualified matrix technician could have constructed such a device, but it would have been many times this size and used multiple stones. This one caught the light only dully, as if a twist of fog marred its center. He had carried it, undetected, through the warded gates of Hestral. With it, he would at last fulfill his oath and bring about the destruction of the last remaining heir of Taniquel Hastur!

34

The next months passed uneventfully as Eduin settled into life at Hestral Tower. Loryn Ardais ruled with a light hand, not only allowing but actually encouraging his people to develop new ideas. He was, he told Eduin, very much in sympathy with the ideas of Varzil of Arilinn. *Laran* was at its best and noblest when used for peaceful purposes. War not only demeaned but tarnished the Gifts.

Eduin had countered with the list of new developments in *laran* weaponry. He steered the conversation toward the topic of the use of a trap-matrix keyed to an individual's signature for selective assassination. Had the news of Gwynn's failed attempt—and the device he'd used—reached this far? He needed to know how suspicious the folk here at Hestral were before he set his own plans into motion.

Loryn brushed the topic aside. "Innovation in the service of a single goal—the destruction of fellow human beings—may result in a few new devices, but the very process of creativity is stifled. You see, once you define your goal so narrowly, once you say, I must have a weapon against an invading army, or I must target a single leader for assassination, then you close your mind to all else. Your creativity becomes so tightly funneled, you cannot follow your spontaneous impulses, your curiosity."

"If we have no goal in what we do, what is the point of all this?"

Eduin gestured to the matrix laboratories, the library, the living quarters of the workers, the Tower itself. The thought of unbridled *laran* experimentation, without direction or limitation, disturbed him. It would be like living without purpose. "Are we not to accomplish any useful work at all, then?"

If Loryn noticed Eduin's discomfort, he gave no response. "We have not even begun to discover all the ways our Gifts can be used. Do you think we were given talent and intelligence, not to mention the privilege of our caste, to spend our lives making weapons for one petty war after another? Or to light the palaces of kings while peasants live in darkness?" He drew himself up, with that sense of *separateness,* and Eduin remembered that as a Keeper he was ultimately answerable only to his own conscience.

Eduin had never expected to find such sympathy of ideas in a Keeper. Bile rose in his throat at what he must do, how he must betray the trust of these people.

"Forgive me if I spoke out of turn," Eduin said. "I meant no offense."

"You are but newly come among us," Loryn said. "If there is one thing which I wish for this Tower, it is the freedom of each person to discover his own vision. It is no easy task rendering those into a harmonious whole, but it is always worth the effort. We live in a complex world, where there are no simple answers. Every man, from loftiest *Comyn* to lowliest peasant, has his own view of the ills of the world and how to make them right. Do you think that a man's position grants him any special wisdom above all others? Even if we could all see into the future, as Allart Hastur was said to do, we would never agree on the single best course of action."

"Then how are men to decide anything?" Eduin burst out. "Why do we not run amok, each man following his own inclination?"

"Because we are men, and not beasts without the power to reason, with no thought past the moment's gratification," Loryn said gravely. "Because we can listen to one another, we can exercise our compassion as well as our critical faculties, we can consider the common good. More often than not, it is what we do before we take action which shapes our fortunes."

Eduin bowed, not trusting himself to say more, and excused himself.

Only when he was back in his quarters with the telepathic damper turned on, did he allow himself to relax.

He sank down on his bed, waiting for his racing pulse to slow. The breathing exercises he had been first taught as a novice would help, but he could not so easily tame his thoughts.

What Loryn hinted at was impossible, a world where men made decisions cooperatively. It would not work in a Tower and it would mean disaster for the world at large. How could a circle function without willing surrender to its Keeper? How could harvests be gathered, children be raised, justice be served, without the rule of liege lord?

If a man could shape his own life—

He dared not imagine what his own would look like. His father's mission had given his life its form and purpose. Without that guiding quest, who was he? What was he? How could he justify the things he had done—the things he would yet do?

Useless thoughts! He flung them away, lest they leach away his very manhood. That way lay madness as well as paralysis. Only women and cowards indulged in such notions. He must act quickly, before the poison of this place had time to work on him.

The next evening, between the dinner hour and the time when the work of the Tower was to begin, he sought out Felicia. He found her in the common room, sitting by the westward-facing window with a cup of herbal brew. It smelled of mint and honey, with something he could not name. He hoped it was not for some women's troubles, for that would temporarily prevent her from working in the circle.

In response to his inquiry, she smiled gently. "Thank you, Eduin, I am quite well. I am only a little—well, I am too old to be homesick, so perhaps I should say *nostalgic*. It must be the weather, reminding me of the place I lived as a child. My nurse used to make me a drink like this and I find it comforting, a fairly harmless pleasure. But you yourself have been home, I believe. A family illness, was it not, that took you from us at Arilinn?"

Damn her to have remembered!

"Yes, my father. But he is well now."

She smiled again and said she was glad of it. He rushed on to ask about her weather project, and she brightened even more.

"Ah! It is a good thing we are all as stubborn as Durraman's donkey, or we would have given that up!" she answered. "Poor Marius—one day he can sense the air currents as clearly as his own hand, and then next, they're gone, or worse yet, he cannot tell the difference between a storm front and a flock of geese. I have been wondering if a matrix lattice might help. If we can construct *laran* batteries to store energy and then deliver it at a controlled rate, then perhaps we could do the same here."

"That is an intriguing idea," Eduin said. *A matrix lattice!* He could not have wished for a better opportunity.

It took very little to convince Felicia to accept his offer of help. He was, after all, a highly skilled *laranzu*. At Arilinn and then at Hali, he'd learned to fabricate artificial matrices and assemble them into complex linkages.

"I think we must begin with the specific," he said, "although once we have discovered the underlying principles, we may be able to design a system which any circle can use."

"Yes, I think so, too." Felicia set down her half-drunk cup of tea. "We know little of talents like this, let alone why they are so often inconsistent. Perhaps in learning to modulate Marius' Gift, we will learn more of the basic processes."

Her brow furrowed in concentration. "Weather sense is not uncommon, even in ordinary folk. Varzil told me the shepherds at Sweetwater can sense an approaching storm. Perhaps there is some small kernel of *laran* there, or it may simply be unconscious attention to natural details— the pattern of birds in flight, the songs of frogs, I know not what. There are many tales of animals warning of bad weather or earthquakes."

Eduin nodded. He had wondered if the beasts possessed some special sense akin to *laran* or if people simply took particular notice of the time the dog howled before a forest fire, but not the hundred times it did so when there was no such catastrophe.

He said so aloud and Felicia responded, "That is one reason I am training the boys under my tutelage as I do. Of course, they have little objection to splashing in the river on a hot summer afternoon, and wet, slithery things have always held a special fascination for boys. It seems to me that we know a great deal about rapport with sentry birds, but very little with the far more numerous creatures of the wild."

"That is because sentry birds are useful in war," Eduin said, "and there will always be more need for them than for songbirds."

Felicia glanced out the window, looking pensive. Eduin caught a glimmer of her thoughts, going to Vazril, far away. "If the gods shine upon us," she said, "we may live to see a time when that is no longer true. A time when songbirds are valued above instruments of war."

Eduin dared not frame the thought that sprang to his mind, that whatever the future held for the rest of Darkover, she would have no part in it.

✦

Loryn Ardais received their proposal with a gratifying show of interest and support. Within a tenday, they had a laboratory all of their own, access to Hestral's store of unkeyed starstones, and the equipment for assembling lattice arrays. Felicia, acting as Keeper for the project, began assembling a circle, although most of the work would be shared between her, Eduin, and Marius. Marius, it turned out, was one of the boys Felicia had taken to the river on the day Eduin arrived.

Through the short, bright autumn and into the next winter, they continued the painstaking process of selecting, modifying, and arranging various stones in combination. Each time Eduin tried to link another stone to the one they had selected as anchor, the combination would not resonate with Marius' personal matrix. There was something in the linkage which created interference patterns. Eduin tried various other stones, both natural and artificial, in every combination he could think of. Felicia tried setting up a bond with Marius unaided by his starstone, and that was a dismal failure, nor could Marius key into a second stone. There was something unique about the way his own enhanced his erratic talent.

By the first warm afternoon of the new year, Eduin began to despair of the project, both for its own purpose and for its usefulness in advancing his own cause. He had hoped that once the lattice was complete and functional, once the circle would use it with Felicia as Keeper, he would be able to strike, and in such a way as to escape obvious suspicion. He must not sacrifice himself or there would be no one to continue the mission against the rest of the Hasturs.

Even isolated as Hestral Tower was, news reached them of armed resistance to Rakhal's rule, of increasingly punitive measures, and of men turning to Carolin's cause.

Reluctantly, Eduin began to think of other possibilities. Although still technically an under-Keeper, Felicia now possessed that intense awareness and sympathy of mind necessary for centripolar work in a circle. He could not catch her unawares with any direct attack, as he had long suspected.

The setting sun created a glow like a furnace outside the western window. Marius and Felicia were already in the laboratory. Eduin entered and went to his workbench. Felicia, usually so even-tempered, emitted frustration. Marius cringed as if expecting to be personally blamed for the failure of the project.

"Eduin, come and look. You're much better at technical details than I am. Marius tried reconnecting the tertiary layer here and here—" she pointed, rattling on, "and now the anchor stone's gone flat. It doesn't make sense. The two designs should be equivalent. What do you think? They *shouldn't* nullify each other, but that's exactly what seems to be happening."

Eduin took the slender metal probe and gently brushed the connection between the core stone and one of the tertiaries she'd indicated. On impulse, he decided to reroute the connection through one of the secondary nodes, a particularly large and brilliant natural stone. It had, he remembered, been one of the group from Aldaran territory. At Arilinn, it would have already been broken up into small stones, but Loryn had preserved it whole. It was the equivalent of a third-order matrix in a single stone.

The instant the connection was complete, Eduin felt the entire array quiver as if alive. Marius, standing behind him to look over his shoulder, gasped.

"That's it!" Felicia cried. "The fault was not in the connections, but in the primary stone. It's a solitary!"

Eduin nodded. He'd never encountered one before, but he had heard about some starstones that, no matter how powerful or sensitive when used alone, lost their connective qualities when linked to others. They sometimes make good talismans when keyed for specific, limited purposes. One this size might well be put to such use.

They spent most of the night working with the new matrix configuration, tuning it to Marius' *laran* signature. Marius, wrought up by their repeated failures, showed signs of fatigue. Despite his attempts to contain them, the boy's anxieties seeped out, doubts about himself, his talent, what would go wrong next. Before long, all three were snapping at one another.

Behind Felicia's unguarded thoughts, Eduin caught some deep, formless anxiety. Did she suspect him? No, even under the stress of frustration, her manner was as open and friendly as ever.

I must take care of Marius, she repeated silently to herself. *He is so young and vulnerable . . .*

So even if she sensed a threat, or had any foresight of disaster, it was on the boy's account. *So much the better.*

Better? Felicia responded.

For a terrible instant, Eduin froze. How could he have come this far and then been so careless in his thoughts? She was a *Keeper,* by Zandru's frozen hells! Telepathic rapport came as naturally to her as breathing. And he had given himself away—

Ice flared, digging claws deep into his gut. He slammed up his psychic barriers and reached for the *laran* trigger his father had implanted. Light washed through his mind, cool and blue as truthspell. All doubt fell away, all emotion quenched.

When he turned toward her, his thoughts were utterly calm. Certainty emanated from his mind.

"Better for Marius, I mean." How innocent his voice sounded, how untainted by any doubt. "For both of us to watch out for him. To make sure he comes to no harm."

"We need a break," Felicia said, getting to her feet and stretching.

"Please go, both of you," Eduin told the two others, "The next part is technical. I don't need the help and you'll only distract me. With luck, tomorrow we can try it out."

"Come on, Marius," Felicia said, moving toward the door. Marius followed in her wake like a younger brother.

After their footsteps fell into silence, Eduin let out his breath. He completed about half the remaining work, all the time listening for any sound of return. Then he headed back to his own chamber. If he encountered either of them, he could truthfully say that he had taken a break before finishing up.

He sweated all the way back to his room. It was near dawn by the light simmering outside the diamond-mullioned windows along the corridor to the sleeping chambers. The night's work was over, and most of the Tower workers would be in the kitchen or dining room, replenishing their energies. Below, the village stirred to life.

A servant, a girl from one of the outlying farms, passed him just outside of his room with an armful of linens. Eduin's nerves shrilled alarm, but he forced himself to walk slowly and confidently. She bobbed a curtsy as she hurried by. He told himself that he did not owe her an explanation, that it was not her business to question a *laranzu* in his own Tower.

His father's stone was hidden exactly where he had left it, a neat packet in its layers of insulation. He slipped it inside his shirt and hurried back to the laboratory. With a sense of relief and elation, he closed the door behind him. The room was exactly as he had left it, even the array of tools aligned precisely on their tray.

Eduin knew precisely where to position the stone, how it would re-flect the blue-white light of the other stones and fade to invisibility. He had only to finish keying it to Felicia's mental signature and place it within the matrix.

The lattice still hummed with her pattern. As Keeper, Felicia was the interface between the device and the human circle. In addition, he'd managed to come by a strand or two of her hair for the genetic material.

With the final adjustments, the stone brightened. It was now fully activated and ready for the triggering event—contact with the mind to which it had been attuned. With any luck, that would take place tomor-row night.

Tomorrow night! So soon, after so long a search!

Eduin grasped the stone carefully with wooden tongs and began low-ering it into the lattice. Just then, a noise outside the door—the scuff of footsteps—reached him. He froze.

Before he could move, the door swung open. He whipped his head around as Marius entered.

"Oh, you're still here," the boy said. Without waiting for an answer, he crossed the room. He picked up a scarf from underneath his bench, where it had fallen. "I forgot this," he said with a trace of nervousness. "I'm sorry I interrupted you."

"It's all right," Eduin heard himself say. Only after Marius left did he take a full breath. The boy had a perfectly legitimate reason to return to the laboratory, he hadn't been spying, and he had noticed nothing amiss.

The stone fitted into its setting with a satisfying *chink!* Eduin stepped back to inspect the lattice. Just as he had anticipated, there was no visible difference, nothing which could not be explained as his final adjustments.

His task complete, Eduin headed for the kitchen and a badly-needed meal. Now he had only to wait for the inevitable workings of justice to unfold.

35

Carolin and the band of loyal men who had sought him out camped in the rugged hills that looked down upon the valley of Highgarth. They had ridden many leagues, and his muscles ached with fatigue, yet sleep eluded him. He knew better than to wander from the safety of those sworn to protect him, for Rakhal had again raised the bounty for his death or capture, high enough to tempt even honest men.

The night was mild and the pastel multihued light of the moons softened the fractured rock of the crags. Highgarth Castle sat upon a promontory, a mass of solid rock which jutted over the widest bend of the river, protected on three sides by currents too wild to ford and by a single, easily defended trail on the other. Even at this distance, Carolin made out a pinprick of light here and there along the castle walls.

Yet . . .

For the past tendays, as they made their way from Carcosa, unease had gnawed at the back of his mind. His skin prickled at every crackle of twig and passing shadow. He was, Orain said, jumpier than a half-witted rabbit-horn.

He knew he was taking a terrible chance, and not only for himself, in returning to Highgarth. Valdrin Castamir had already put his life at risk by providing shelter during that hectic flight from Nevarsin. The old soldier had served Rafael Hastur, he who had been King and Hastur of Thendara before dying under mysterious circumstances and leaving Felix, even then doddering toward senility, to take the crown. Such loyalty ran deep.

If I am to rally forces strong enough to stand against Rakhal, then I will need such men.

They had set up camp just as the great Bloody Sun dipped behind the silhouetted crags, but Carolin could not bring himself to approach any closer. Wrapped in his tattered cloak, he crouched on the steep rock and watched the silver ribbon of river.

Watch. Wait and watch.

He felt Orain's approach, a shadow against the night.

"*Bredu,* do not trouble yourself," Carolin said. "I will not risk myself without good cause."

"You already risk yourself simply by being anywhere on this side of the Kadarin," Orain replied. "But I have long since accepted the futility of telling you so."

Restlessness trickled through Carolin's veins. He wondered if Orain were not right, that they should never have crossed back into Hastur lands. Seeing his sons safely into the care of his far-flung kin, the Hasturs of Carcosa, beyond Rakhal's reach, was his first purpose. The wild lands were cruel enough to a grown man, let alone two boys, even though they complained so little. A fall from a horse, an avalanche of mud or snow, a fever, an attack by cloud leopard, wolf or even banshee, any of these could so easily take a child's life. They were too precious to risk.

The time was coming when he could not continue to hide, when he must return to his own lands with the growing number of men who had gathered under his banners, and meet Rakhal in battle. Once his sons were settled out of harm's way, Carolin had taken the longer route back in order to seek *Dom* Valdrin's counsel.

If only Varzil were here . . .

He remembered their pledge, to rebuild the Tower at Neskaya as a symbol of hope and peace. In these times, it seemed impossible that such a thing would ever come to pass. Yet, with men like Orain and Valdrin at his side—

"You are right," Orain said. "Something *is* amiss. At this hour, there should be more light—torches and fires for cooking. We should see some

trace of them, as well as the smoke. And we have seen but little movement of men or horses."

"You must not go down," Orain said, and his voice had an edge like
obsidian. "Not until we know for sure. The place is not deserted and this
quietness may have some good cause; all may yet be well."

"We will wait, then," Carolin said, "and see what we can discover
from here. The morning may show us more. But in the end, we must find
out if anything has befallen *Dom* Valdrin and his folk."

"I will go, or one of the others."

Carolin shook his head. "If one of you were to fall into Lyondri's
hands, he would use any vile means to wring my whereabouts from you.
I cannot ask it—"

"And you cannot go, and risk everything!" In the dying light, Carolin
could not read the expression in the eyes of his foster-brother, but he
recognized the surge of obstinacy.

"Tomorrow we will discuss this further," Carolin said.

◆

Toward dawn, Carolin fell into a broken slumber. He startled awake at
the approach of young Mikhal, who had come with him from Nevarsin
and had taken the last watch of the night.

"*Vai dom,* and you, too, Lord Orain, come quickly. Something is
going on down there. There are soldiers. And, sir, they wear Hastur
colors."

Jittery energy surged through Carolin's veins. A glance showed him
that Orain had come instantly alert also. In silence, they followed the boy
to the outcropping which afforded the best view of the valley and the
castle below.

Dawn had spread across the arc of cloudless sky, although the shadows still held a knife-edged chill. Despite the clear day, a faint mist clung
to the valley, like a gauzy veil which softened edges and muted colors.
The blue-and-silver banners which hung from the castle turrets looked
tarnished.

Orain laid one hand on Carolin's shoulder and pointed, but there
was no need. In the castle courtyard, only partially visible from this angle,
a small crowd massed. Probably every man in the castle was out there.
The Hastur soldiers arrayed themselves in tight ranks in the center and
around the periphery.

A force of occupation—conquerors, not guests. With eyes wide and dry, Carolin watched the drama playing out below. His own men joined him.

Four men, each surrounded by a knot of Hastur guards, halted in the open space at the end of the yard.

"Gods, no," one of Carolin's men cried, "they cannot mean to—"

"No more!" Orain growled. "The only way we can help them now is to bear witness."

One of the soldiers, a giant of a man, struck the first prisoner with a massive two-handed sword. In a single blow, the prisoner crumpled to the ground. Carolin could not see clearly at this distance, but he was sure the poor man—*Dom* Valdrin, his friend and ally—had been beheaded.

Soon, one body joined the other in a ragged line. The castle people drew together visibly. A terrible emptiness filled the canyon, broken only by the keening of the wind.

It was not until the Hastur soldiers began a rapid yet orderly departure that Carolin was able to tear his eyes from the courtyard. He raised one hand to cover his sight. The movement seemed to crack his body into a hundred shards. Breath rasped in his throat. His thoughts had gone numb, empty. In a moment, he knew, he must come back to himself, say something to the men, give orders, be the king they needed. For now, he offered this silence within himself as tribute to the men who had just died in his service.

Crouched at his side, Orain muttered, "*Vai dom*—Carlo—you must not blame yourself."

"I do not." Carolin found his voice and it sounded like flint striking steel. "I blame Rakhal and his executioner, Lyondri. Gather the others, Orain. Let us go down and see what may be done for *Dom* Valdrin's people."

Carolin got to his feet, but Orain suddenly grabbed him and threw him to the ground, under the low, spreading branches of the nearest tree.

"Look there, aloft!" Orain cried.

Above them, hidden until now by the hills, an aircar glided soundlessly across the sky. Another quickly joined it, each lit within by pale blue. The men which guided them appeared only as ghostly figures. Carolin could not make out any identifying colors or device, but the shapes were sickeningly familiar.

He had flown in those very vessels, now in the service of his cousin Rakhal. One of them might have been the same which carried Varzil to his home at Sweetwater and then back to Arilinn. Why should Rakhal send them into such rugged territory, to the home of a man who had not been to court in years?

Carolin sensed rather than saw the side of each aircar slide open and a cluster of fragile glass teardrops tumble free. The contents of each vessel glowed, each a tiny liquid ember. Slowly they fell, then faster and faster, streaking downward toward their target.

Carolin scrambled to his hands and knees for a better view of the castle. Gouts of flame exploded like miniature suns, to fall in eye-searing brilliance and then burst upward. Rain after rain of orange fire pelted the castle. From every surface it touched, fire answered it, rising higher and brighter until it seemed the stones themselves were burning.

Clingfire! *Sweet gods, no!*

Something hot and acrid exploded at the back of Carolin's mind. The basic order of fire and earth and air twisted madly, elements set in unholy alliance or warped from their very nature. Ice and fire shivered over his skin. His muscles locked and for a long moment, he could not draw breath.

"Aldones save us!" Orain cried, his voice a sob. "Ah, Rakhal! Zandru curse him a thousand times! How could he do it?"

The crack of shattering stone came roaring up from the valley. Rock would not ignite, not even in *clingfire,* but it would splinter and collapse in the intense heat. Everything else—wood and cloth and human flesh—burned.

Pain lanced through Carolin's mind, not once but a dozen, a hundred times, each like a molten dagger. There were men down there, men now shrieking in agony as the unquenchable fire consumed them.

I swore I would protect my people against all harm, and for that loyalty they burn. . . .

Rakhal, as Aldones lives, I shall burn that hand from you with which you have sown disaster and death . . . and Lyondri I shall hang like a common criminal, for he has forfeited the right to a noble death!

At this distance, Carolin could not hear the screams of the men who had loved and aided him, but all through that night and the many nights of dreadful flight which followed, he felt them like the points of a hundred daggers turning slowly in his breast. Never before had he thought his *laran* a curse.

✦

Carolin and his men traveled quickly, hiding by day and riding hard by night. Once a small company of armed soldiers flying pennants with Lyondri's insignia galloped by as they sheltered in a tangled wood. Orain swore they'd been seen, but the soldiers took no notice and pressed on on their own business.

They made for the Hellers and Nevarsin. The monks cared nothing for the struggles of the lowlands, but they offered Carolin and his men shelter, saying that he had harmed no one, whereas his enemy, Rakhal, would kill him for his own ambition. They would not join in Carolin's cause, but neither would they surrender him.

During one brief daytime stop, when even fitful sleep would not come, Carolin lay wrapped in his cloak and tried to rest. At his side, Orain snored softly, and Carolin dared not move for fear of waking him. Since their flight from Highgarth, Orain had driven himself almost to exhaustion until Carolin had to command him to let other men stand watch in turn.

Rest, he told himself. *Sleep . . .*

He did not want to close his eyes, for in the darkness of his mind, the fires of Highgarth still burned. He shivered, his soul sickened by the memory.

He saw a Tower crumbling into ruin, blasted by a rain of fire, the bodies of men and women blazing like torches. *Varzil! Maura!* he cried out, but his friends were not among them, yet they were so many. A great black stallion lay in a pool of blood. A land once green with pastures became a barren desert broken only by the twisted skeletons of trees. A young woman with eyes like a hawk's wept helpless tears in the night. Orain twisted in agony under Lyondri's knife. Varzil stood bathed in white fire, his eyes blind with pain and loss and terrible purpose.

Blood everywhere, blood and fire and death.

Would this be the fate of everyone who followed him, everyone who trusted and believed in him?

High in the mountains, in the shadow of Aldaran, an army waited for its King. Would he lead them to victory or to ruin? This war between cousins would set brother against brother, father against son.

Had Rakhal ruled with a fair and just hand, had he treated his people as a king should, respecting and protecting them, then Carolin would have gladly yielded up the throne to him. If he had learned nothing else during his exile, it had been how little he wanted to be king.

Though he might fail, he had no choice but to try. He had sworn it, and of all the things left to him, his honor was the most precious.

✦

As the hills grew steeper and more rugged, the weather turned foul. Carolin and his men traveled now by day, for few other men used the mud-churned roads.

They passed under the shadow of a ragged grove of pitch-pine. Carolin drew a halt, signaling with hand instead of voice. No one spoke. Only the steady whisper of the rain and the breathing of the horses broke the silence. The sound came again, a faint rustle, the muted clink of unshod hoof on stone. His fingers tightened around the hilt of his sword, but he did not slide it free.

Chervine, not horse. A man on foot, maybe more.

Carolin's skin tightened. As one, he and his men turned to face the sound. The next moment, a heavyset man appeared, leading a laden stag pony. Behind him, silent and dour, came two others in animal-skin cloaks, armed with heavy staves. Their leader's clothing, once fine, was torn and stained, Carolin suspected, with more than trail mud.

For a long moment, the two parties stared at one another. Honest men did not roam these rugged hills, not in the rain. Carolin and his men looked like outlaws themselves in ragged clothing, having long since done away with any badge or emblem which might identify them.

Carolin's black mare snorted and pawed the ground, restless with the tension. He patted her neck. "We bid you good travel, strangers," he said, pointedly not asking their business.

The heavyset man did not reply at first, perhaps measuring the odds of battle or flight.

Carolin said, "I think you are neither thieves nor felons, but desperate men like ourselves. You need have no fear from us. We are no threat to any man who offers us none."

At his words, the other man's stance softened. He nodded. "Like better men than us, we seek exile here."

"Then be on your way," Orain said, nudging his horse to the fore, "for we are no hunters of men."

"That you are not," the man said. Clearly, he had made up his mind to speak, rather than pass by in silence. "I think there is one who hunts you, perhaps the same as seeks me."

"Who might that be?" Orain said.

"By the word of the usurper whose backside warms the throne at Hali, I am a landless man. The crime for which I lost my farm and was flung into Rakhal's prison under sentence of losing a hand and my tongue? My children shouted, 'Long live King Carolin!' as one of Rakhal's men passed by my village. So here I am, ready to serve any king who will bring down Rakhal and his henchman, Lyondri."

"We, too, serve the exiled king," Carolin said, "but if you would join our company, we can offer no sure hope of victory."

"I ask only to fight against my enemies," the man said in a voice resonant with bitterness. "I have heard that King Carolin is gathering an army somewhere in the Hellers. If it is your purpose also to join them, we might share the road."

Something of the wolf stirred behind Carolin's slow smile. "Then we ride together, friend. How are you called?"

"Alaric." The man gave no other name, for here in this lawless place, he had left the past behind.

Alaric. Like my little son.

✦

They rode together, even as Carolin said, for another tenday, until they came to a little valley overlooked by a castle. Built into the living rock of the crags, it was little more than a fortress, but the men who lived here were distant kin of Valdrin Castamir and gave Carolin and his men welcome, though the news they brought was bitter.

"I can spare only a few men," *Dom* Cerdric told Carolin, "for in these lawless times, we are beset by Ya-men from the heights on one side and bandits which haunt these passes on the other."

Instead, he presented Carolin with an even greater gift, three sentry birds. They were great powerful birds, resembling *kyorebni,* the savage scavengers of the heights, more than proper hawks. Long feathered crests arched over their eye sockets. Their heads were naked and wrinkled, and their beaks gleamed like obsidian. Though they were far from beautiful and an odor of carrion arose from them, they were a magnificent gift. A trained *laranzu,* his mind linked with one of them, could spy out the land, locate enemy forces, track the movement of armies.

You will be my eyes, and perhaps through you, I may bring about a speedy end to this war, Carolin thought. From Nevarsin, they might contact Tramontana, to see if any of the workers there might join them.

Dom Cerdric's saddlemaker attached blocks to three of the saddles for the sentry birds to perch upon. When offered fresh meat, however, the birds refused to eat. Before long, they became listless and irritable. Some of the men had trained hawks, but could not make out what ailed the sentry birds. Carolin began to think the gift was in vain, for the birds were failing and might not live until they reached Nevarsin.

Late one day, they climbed a little forested knoll. Away to the northwest, a high mountain loomed. Beyond it in the failing light, snowcapped peaks glimmered like pale shadows. Orain spotted a curl of smoke just off the road ahead.

Carolin's *laran* stirred. He sensed no threat, although an undercurrent of fear ran through the mind of the boy—no, a young woman—who crouched in the thickest part of the trees.

Another dozen paces took them around a curve and into sight of a small clear space with the remains of a fire. The coals had been carefully covered so that no chance spark might set the hills ablaze. Whoever she was, this girl was forest wise.

"Come out, boy," Orain called. "We mean you no harm."

The girl emerged from the thicket, leading a horse which by its coat and staring ribs had lately seen hard travel and poor fodder. Carolin recognized the girl from his waking vision outside Highgarth, the proud bearing, the eyes shadowed yet alive with fire, like those of a bird of prey. She herself looked like a runaway hawkmaster's apprentice, with her rough garb and improvised perch on her saddle.

As her gaze met his, Carolin felt an instant kinship with her. Like him, she traveled in disguise, shadowed by fear. Would that he might meet the future with the same courage he saw brimming in her eyes.

At the girl's signal, a magnificent *verrin* hawk swooped down from the sky and caught her lifted forearm. She looked tenderly at the bird. "She is mine, for I trained her with my own hand."

From her red hair and sure manner with beasts, Carolin wondered if she might have MacAran blood, as well as a touch of their empathic *laran.* "In this wild land," he said, "your hawk could fly away if she would, and in that sense at least, you own her as much as any human can own a wild thing."

She caught his meaning and gave him a smile of rare radiance. But when he asked her name, she looked away and muttered, "Rumal."

Keep your secrets, then, little hawkmistress. No harm will come to you or your hawk from any man of mine. From her bearing and speech, she was gently-raised, perhaps in the lands north of the Kadarin. Her horse, although thin, had good breeding. He could not imagine what had driven her to travel like this, alone, wearing a boy's boots and breeches, her true nature concealed. Yet he sensed that she, too, was an exile, homeless, driven from her kin through no fault of her own except her own honor.

On impulse, Carolin asked the girl if she knew anything about treating ailing sentry birds, and was surprised when she approached them without fear. When told the birds had been fed only the best and freshest meat, even when the men went short of food, she replied, "There is your problem, sir. Look you, these are scavenger birds, which feed on half-rotted meat. They must have fur and feathers, too. These birds are starving because they cannot digest what you've given them."

Each creature feeds according to its nature, Carolin thought as Rumal set about arranging for carrion for the sentry birds. The birds permitted her to handle them, and he saw how quick and light her hands were. Soon she and Orain were deep in discussion about what to name the birds. *If only men could learn to live in the same way.*

What if it were Rakhal's nature to pillage and abuse his people, or Lyondri's to destroy anyone who stood against him?

That is what a king is for, to restrain such men.

Rumal went about her self-appointed tasks, as much a member of the party as if she had always belonged. After some grumbling, for Alaric resented having to make do with his little stag pony while Rumal rode a proper horse, the men accepted her as the boy she pretended to be.

Orain in particular took a liking to her, and when they reached Nevarsin, bought her a warm vest and stockings. When she caught a fever, he dosed her with an herbal brew his mother had taught him to make.

So she finds a place with us, where there is no other, Carolin thought. He saw in her a kindred spirit, but could not foresee how well she would repay the kindness.

36

The fugitive King Carolin had so far eluded capture. Scattered rumors of his death proved false. The harsh treatment dealt anyone who aided or sympathized with him served only to strengthen support for him. Neighboring kingdoms snapped at Hastur's borders, searching for any sign of weakness.

Often, Varzil thought of his friend, wandering the lawless lands beyond the Kadarin. Sometimes at night, he caught fragmented dream images, Carolin shivering by a pocket fire or with his sword drawn and crouched in a fighting stance. Carolin still lived, of that he was sure. He clutched that knowledge to him like a talisman.

Arilinn Tower, though not directly involved in the unrest, still felt the shifting tensions. Once messages flowed freely along the relays between all the Towers. Now Hali and Tramontana would fall silent or send only guarded communications. Almost every Tower from Dalereuth to Hali had begun making *clingfire*. Only Hestral and Arilinn were so far exempt. Since the incident which cost Auster his life, Arilinn had made no more weapons.

Varzil had been instrumental in keeping Arilinn apart from the conflict, although here, as elsewhere, the demands increased with each tenday: medicine, *laran* batteries for aircars or lighting, the building of fortifications or repairs. Despite Barak's reservations, Varzil now had the status of *tenerézu,* a fully qualified Keeper. Arilinn could not function with a single Keeper in these times. Varzil had been adamant in working only on peaceful uses of *laran.*

Varzil sometimes spoke over the relays with Dyannis at Hali. She sounded worried and distant. Rakhal Hastur threatened Serrais, seat of the Ridenow chiefs, and she feared she might be forced to make weapons to be used against her own kinsmen.

Carolin promised us that we might elect to remain neutral at such times, doing only peaceful work, she said. *But the new king thinks otherwise.*

Surely Rakhal would not force Lady Liriel or Maura Elhalyn to fight against Carolin, Varzil said.

No, she answered. *To do him justice, Rakhal offered exemption to those who had blood-ties to Carolin, so long as they swore not to engage in any hostile action against him either. But he has since reneged on that bargain after Lady Maura and several others left Tramontana. Maura said she could not continue to serve Rakhal after what he had done—but Varzil, was she not to marry him? I thought so when we were together at Hali that first Midwinter Festival.*

So we all thought, Varzil answered. He did not want to imagine what turned her from a man she had defended so loyally.

As for me, Dyannis went on, *Rakhal has no care for any Ridenow sentiments. He has lost too many of his own* leronyn *to neutrality to be willing to release any more of us. I think he is growing desperate. What if he orders us to attack the Great House at Serrais, or even Sweetwater, for as you must have heard, Harald has declared his support for Carolin. I love my work here, Varzil, but I love my family also.*

Varzil caught the wistfulness in her mental voice, as if she were a child caught in an unpredictable and hostile landscape. Yet beneath it rang a core as tough and resilient as whipcord. Neither Dougal DiAsturian, the Keeper of Hali Tower, nor King Rakhal himself would find her pliant, were they to command her against her own conscience.

◆

The next time Varzil took his turn in the relays, he signaled Hestral Tower. Within moments, distance compressed and he touched the mind of Serena, one of the monitors.

What news from Arilinn? she asked.

He passed on the messages for that evening. Some were complex, answers to inquiries Loryn Ardais had made of the Archives of the *Comyn* Council, stored in the Hidden City. Some of these dated back to the height of the Ages of Chaos and documented some of the more bizarre types of *laran*. During this time, inbreeding and genetic manipulation resulted in strange and unpredictable Gifts. Loryn was particularly interested in the ability to sense the vast electric and magnetic fields of the planet itself.

The Arilinn Archives were huge and records of this age poorly indexed. It would help, Varzil said, if he knew precisely what bloodlines Loryn was investigating and to what purpose. Silently, he prayed it was not for the development of some fearsome new weapon. The Aldarans were rumored to be able to generate storms of devastating force. He shuddered silently as he remembered his visions, so many years ago, at the bottom of the cloud-lake at Hali.

One of the younger workers, a Rockraven boy, seemed to have some measure of this talent, but so little was known about it that trying to train it seemed like stumbling about in the dark.

Bumping into shadows and hay-ricks, Serena added. *Let me summon Felicia to speak with you. She of all of us knows most, for she is developing a matrix lattice that we hope will allow Marius to focus his talent. She thinks that if we can determine the right conditions far enough in advance, we can shift cloud patterns and moist air, or perhaps even discharge the electrical energy in some harmless way. Only last winter, we lost five families and as many fishing boats to a fire-storm.*

After a few moments, Felicia's clear mental voice reached him, embracing him in welcome.

I am so glad to hear you, my dearest! Serena said there was some problem about our researches, but I think she was only looking for an excuse for us to talk!

Varzil could almost see her smile, the quick bright light in her eyes. *Are you well, beloved?*

Exceedingly! Again, came a sparkle of delight. *I am working as a Keeper most of the time now, although not yet in name—Darkover is not quite ready for that! When I arrived, I was prepared to do battle with Loryn Ardais, to refuse to work on instruments of destruction, even if it meant doing nothing more challenging than distilling* kirian *and tending sick babies.*

Varzil chuckled silently at the image of Felicia, her hair tied back in a kerchief, a screaming, red-faced infant in her arms. In his mind, her expression softened into tenderness. She lifted the baby and he realized the child was theirs. His heart shuddered with longing, but he knew it was no true clairvoyance, only a desperate hope.

In my heart, I share your wish, Felicia responded. *I pray for a time when we may live it together.*

Loryn is a surprising man, she went on, returning to business, *a Keeper who encourages independence in others. I have his full support on my weather project. Eduin has been here this past season, and he has been helping me a great deal. Tomorrow night we'll be ready to test the lattice he's constructed.*

She described what they hoped to do. Varzil was impressed by the creativity and depth of her work. Barak would never have permitted her such scope or allowed her to use her remarkable talents so rapidly.

And your feelings of trepidation? he asked. *Have they been laid to rest?*

She fell silent for a moment. *In truth, I do not know. There has been so much work to do, so many exciting new things, I have not thought much about it. Before I came here, I had not realized my own ambition—I certainly was not encouraged to follow it at either Nevarsin or Arilinn! After all those years spent hiding my parentage, it was not easy to draw attention to myself and my abilities. I am anxious from time to time, but it is on account of the* leroni *in my care and the enormity of what we aim to accomplish. We stand upon the brink of a new age, beloved, and you and I will be part of its making.*

Varzil sent her a pulse of love and pride. *If you are not too tired, let me know the results of your experiment. I'll wait tomorrow night in the relay laboratory.*

Be assured I shall. Until tomorrow night—oh, one thing more. I heard a lovely old saying, "Your words brighten the sky." I've been waiting for the chance to say it to you . . .

"Your words brighten the sky," Varzil repeated after they had broken rapport. Her presence filled him with the sweetness of a summer dawn. He longed beyond words to hold her under that shining sky.

◆

The next night, Varzil had no work of his own. For the past tenday, he had been directing a circle repairing some of the houses within the Hidden City. As in the Tower itself, no nontelepath might pass within those precincts, so *laran* workers instead of masons placed the new stones. This labor also required daylight, but fortunately there were few ordinary bystanders. Any *Comyn* with business in the Hidden City knew better than to disturb a working circle.

This had been a particularly demanding day, using the combined mental power of the circle to lift, resurface, and replace several massive stones. It was not hazardous work in itself, but the power required drained vital energies. Afterward, he insisted that Fidelis monitor each member of his circle to make sure no one was dangerously depleted.

"No one but you yourself," Fidelis told him. "You of all people should know better than to stay up half the night on the relays and then put in a day's work as Keeper on a project like this. You are hereby ordered to eat and then sleep."

Varzil readily agreed to the food, but would not break his rendezvous with Felicia. Fidelis was a good enough telepath to pick up the flicker of his thought.

"You will make yourself ill if you abuse your body in this manner. How can you set an example as Keeper, or truly be responsible for those in your circle, when you yourself behave in such a reckless manner?"

"I am a Keeper, and know my own limits."

"You are an idiot if you do not listen to your monitor!"

Varzil refused to be drawn into an argument. He knew that Fidelis spoke out of love. "I promise I won't allow myself to get too tired."

"I have ordered you to rest. If you refuse, I cannot force you. I ask you to consider the consequences, not only to yourself, but to those in your circle, if you collapse because of stubborn pride."

Varzil told himself that his emotional well-being was as important as any other aspect of his life. He was tired, true, but not too tired to work effectively. He relented enough to eat a hot meal before resting on one of the cushioned divans in the common room.

He started awake at the sound of footsteps and voices. "Has word come from Hestral?"

Marella turned from Richardo at her side, with a startled expression. Both of them were robed for *laran* work, and she looked pale and drawn. "No, nothing from Hestral. But there's word from Hali that Rakhal Hastur has executed Lord Valdrin Castamir and all his sons and then sent aircars with *clingfire* to burn Highgarth Castle to the ground."

"Horrible," Richardo said.

"Valdrin Castamir?" Cerriana, coming downstairs a pace behind them, asked. "What has he done to so anger King Rakhal?"

"He gave shelter to Carolin as he fled to safety," Varzil said. "And Rakhal, who had been as a brother to him, could not abide that act of loyalty."

"Don't let Barak hear you say such things!" Marella said.

"Barak may hear whatever I say," Varzil said quietly. "Carolin is the rightful King of Hastur, no matter how many castles Rakhal destroys. If there were any remaining doubt of Rakhal's fitness to rule, his actions have proven him a scoundrel and a tyrant."

"No man dares say so aloud," Richardo said, "lest he suffer the same fate as Lord Castamir. Rakhal may be ruthless, but he's not stupid. The people he used as examples to others were chosen carefully. Keeper or not, you would be wise to keep your opinions to yourself, Varzil. Not even the walls of Arilinn will shield you, should King Rakhal decide to put an end to your accusations."

"What are you saying, Richardo?" Cerriana cried. Two spots of hectic color rose to her pale cheeks. "Neither Rakhal nor any other Hastur lord has power here!"

"I say simply that we live in a world in which it is better not to interfere in the doings of kings, lest we suffer the same fate as Tramontana and Neskaya!"

Varzil straightened. "Ah, but Tramontana has been rebuilt and Neskaya may yet be, if Carolin Hastur regains his throne."

"Richardo is right," Marella said, shaking her head so that her curls trembled. "It is none of our concern who rules at Hali, so long as we at Arilinn are left alone. Our continued safety lies in keeping to our own affairs."

"Silence will not bring about justice," Varzil said.

"You are a fool, Varzil Ridenow," came a voice from the far end of the room. "And it is only because of your Keeper's skill that you have a place among us." Face dusky, brows furrowed, Barak strode across the room. "Arilinn must remain apart from the affairs of kings! We take no position on any of these events, none! You have made your opinions clear. Every time we are asked to make *clingfire,* we go through another round of debates with you! Do you think your red robe will exempt you from the consequences of your rash words? We may not live in the greater world, but we are as subject to its laws as any other men!"

Varzil, who had risen to his feet at the entrance of the senior Keeper, bowed his head. He should have known better than to let himself be drawn into such a debate. Though he regretted nothing of what he had said, he now saw the folly of having spoken so frankly. Barak would not be swayed by argument, but would see any dissenting opinion as a challenge to his authority.

"Perhaps I spoke out of turn," Varzil said in a low voice. "I can only claim fatigue and concern for my friend Carolin Hastur as an excuse for my lapse in judgment. I hope that at Arilinn we have not come to the point of condemning a man for a few unguarded words rather than actual deeds."

"I pray that day may never come," Barak said. His tone was still gruff, but his countenance grew calmer. "No one can accuse you of shirking your full share of work, Varzil. If anything, you take too much upon yourself and this—this misunderstanding is the result."

"We live in times when much is demanded of us," Varzil said. Bowing, he excused himself and made his way back to his chambers.

Although Varzil lay upon his bed, breathing deeply into the core of his body, sleep came slowly and with it, dreams of fire in the night.

✦

Felicia listened gravely as Eduin explained he would not be available to work in the circle for the next two or three tendays.

Earlier, Eduin had sought out Loryn Ardais. He'd prepared what he was to say, for he needed a believable reason to absent himself from the laboratory. When the trap sprang shut, he must be elsewhere and beyond suspicion. He composed a series of reasons for transferring to Loryn's circle. It wasn't difficult to convince Loryn of Eduin's eagerness to work with him.

"But surely you must want to be part of the trial of the device, after you spent so much time on its design and construction." Felicia's eyes were puzzled. For a single heartbeat, her skin paled.

She recovered smoothly, moving into a gracious statement of thanks for his contributions. "I hope you will be able to rejoin my circle before long," she said.

Let her take some small measure of comfort from the pretense that she was a Keeper, Eduin thought as he watched her retreating back. She had not yet earned the right to wear the crimson robe. And now she never would.

✦

On the third night with yet no word from Hestral about Felicia's experiment, Varzil's composure wavered. He could not think of any happy reason for her silence. The relays operated on their regular schedule with other news. Carolin Hastur had not yet been captured, and every day brought some new rumor of an army that had gathered around him. There had been food riots in the poorer areas of Thendara, put down after considerable bloodshed by Lyondri's enforcers.

Vague fears nibbled at his mind, thoughts of what might have happened at Hestral. Was some illness preventing the circle from meeting? Felicia seemed to have made a complete recovery from her lung fever, but he'd heard that sometimes there was residual scarring, leaving a predisposition to future infections.

Had some disaster befallen Hestral, that the Tower had fallen silent? There had been no news of such, but Hestral did not send messages every night, and it might be some time before its absence took on any significance.

Or had Felicia attempted the experiment, and had it gone badly? Was Hestral even now mourning the loss of an entire circle? Varzil felt sure he would know if something had happened to her. When he reached out, he felt the subtle pulse of her presence. She was alive and well.

Varzil attempted to quiet his mind, to practice the detachment and patience that he had worked so hard to master. He knew that the longer he allowed such thoughts to prey upon him, the more frantic and unbalanced he became. He told himself he was a grown man, a trained *laranzu,* and not some lovesick boy.

Meditation eased his anxiety, but only for a time. Instead of resting, he paced the hallways until Lunilla ordered him out of doors. He put on ordinary clothing and went down into the city as he used to do in his first years. Arilinn was yet untouched by the turmoil racking Hastur lands, although fear ran like a barely-felt rumble beneath every conversation.

Varzil bought some fruit at the market and wandered by the shops. Fine cloth, knives with jewel-set handles, bridles of tooled leather, even carpets from the legendary Ardcarran looms passed before his eyes like dust. After a short time, the memory of Carolin rose like a ghostly form just beyond his vision.

Though he had never been gifted with prescience, Varzil shivered. There was more to his feeling of unease than frustrated longing. The brightness of the day, for it was midafternoon now, only accentuated the feeling that behind the facade of glare and normality, shadows gathered.

"Vai dom?" a voice asked. "Did you wish the head scarf?"

Abruptly Varzil came to himself. He stood at an open-air stall at the far end of the market square, holding a square of tartan suitable for a girl-child. He had no memory of having walked here or any thought as to why this particular garment should have attracted him.

The merchant, an aging man with the slack skin of one who has lost too much weight, too rapidly, watched him with an expectant expression.

"No," Varzil said, replacing the scarf on the table and walking away before the merchant could offer it to him as a gift. He didn't want to bargain for favors, which was what would surely happen should he accept.

I cannot go on like this, he thought as he headed back to the Tower. *Torn between two people I love, one in danger and beyond my help, the other in no trouble that I know. I will only make myself ill and endanger those who rely upon me in the circle.*

For the first time he could remember, Varzil did not know what to do or even whom to turn to for help.

37

Days passed, and still there was no word from Felicia. At the insistence of Fidelis, Varzil called a halt to the construction work and forced himself to rest. He was having increasing difficulty sleeping, even with a telepathic damper to reduce the psychic distractions. If Hastur had been at peace, he might have taken a journey to Hali to see Carolin and the lake, and to visit with Dyannis. The exercise of travel and the change in scene would do him good. But Carolin was in exile, fighting for his life as well as his throne. The roads were increasingly unsafe and Arilinn itself was an embattled island.

He sat outside in the garden and here found unexpected solace in the company of the *kyrri,* the small furred servants who were the only living things other than *Comyn* to pass the Veil. Ever since the first morning he had woken outside the Arilinn gates, he had had a special fondness and respect for their kind. Now, two or three of them seemed drawn to him, offering their wordless comfort. He knew better than to try to touch them, for their bodies generated electrical currents that could create a nasty shock. Their nearness and the soft chirping noises they made among themselves soothed his frayed nerves.

Nearly a tenday after his last contact with Felicia, Varzil fell into a restless sleep. He dreamed in patches, moments in which he knew that he was searching for someone, or someone was searching for him. He woke, heart pounding, confused and grateful to be in his familiar bed.

Later in the night, he wandered through the Overworld, that strange and formless place where neither time nor distance had any meaning. He saw a Tower racked by lightnings and at first thought it was Hali from the far past, during the Cataclysm. Fire burst from the upper spires, drenching all the land around in twisted orange light. Then he seemed to be standing upon a rise or promontory, looking down upon a castle in flames. His vision took on an eerie doubling, if he were seeing through the eyes of a sentry bird or another man. The images flickered by too quickly for him to be sure.

Varzil . . .

It was only a whisper, a breath across his mind.

Carolin? The ephemeral mental touch bore none of his friend's masculine resonance.

Varzil . . . help me . . .

The words were faint and distant, sifted across leagues and through the psychic shields of two Towers. He struggled to maintain that state of receptivity, half-dream, half Overworld. Fear trembled at the borders of his mind. The presence faded.

FELICIA!

Silence answered him.

In desperation, he summoned a mental picture of her as they had last touched across the relays, the tone and texture of her thoughts, the pride and playfulness, the unexpected turn of thought that was as much a part of her as breathing.

She was there and not-there, and with the fleeting contact came a jumble of other images, as if a panel of stained glass had been fractured into a hundred colored shards.

He glimpsed a room, recognizable as a matrix laboratory, though only a portion of it was visible. Another sliver showed two robed *laran* workers, hands joined, heads bent in concentration—*Felicia's circle?*—and yet another revealed an intricately patterned matrix. Power pulsed through the crystalline lattice in blue-white flashes. He saw Felicia's face bathed in that eerie radiance, as if in truthspell. Her eyes were closed, her countenance one of unearthly calm. Another glimpse showed a young woman, swathed in white, turning toward the giant artificial matrix with an expression of alarm.

Felicia!

He sat bolt upright. The air rang with her name.

"Felicia!"

The ring which she had given him, which never left his finger, erupted into brilliance. For a terrifying moment, Varzil could see nothing, not with his *laran* senses, not with his physical eyes. Then the light subsided, leaving the room in shadow. Only a dim glow persisted, pulsing gently like the living heart of the gem. It felt warm.

Varzil scrambled to his feet and snatched up the nearest garment, a robe in summerweight gold and green. Barefoot, he raced through corridor and down stairway, taking the steps two at a time.

Gavin! Lerrys! I need you! Varzil sent a mental call to the two strongest technicians in the Tower, with a single mental image of what he wanted to do.

He had never been athletic, and by the time he reached the level of the relay chamber, his breath was rasping through his lungs and he'd broken into a hard sweat.

When he shoved the door open, hands trembling, Cerriana was already rising from her place before the relay screens.

"Varzil! What's wrong?" *Are you ill? Injured?*

"It's Felicia! Something terrible has happened. Cerriana, you must send me through the relays to Hestral Tower."

"Varzil, I cannot! That hasn't been done since the Ages of Chaos! We are not nearly strong enough—"

"We *have* to be strong enough!"

Ah! Gavin is on the way, and Lerrys—And I. Valentina Aillard stepped through the door. She wore the white robe of a monitor, yet some trick of light, perhaps catching the intense flame color of her hair, tinted the garment red. She looked as fragile as always, slender and pale as a *chieri* of legend, yet the very air around her vibrated with power, steel and silk rather than oak.

Gavin burst into the room an instant later, with Darriel Alton and Richardo on his heels. "Lerrys caught a backlash earlier tonight. Fidelis dosed him with *kirian* and he's sleeping it off. Are we enough?"

Varzil, his eyes still on Valentina, nodded. Darriel and Richardo were both highly competent, schooled in Arilinn's demanding standards.

"I will tell the folk at Hestral to make ready," Cerriana said.

Using the relay screens as a focus, they placed themselves at equidistant points surrounding Varzil. In an instant, he gathered them into that seamless whole which was a circle. He had worked with all of them before, although less often with Valentina. With the proper training, he realized, she herself could have acted as Keeper of this circle. He wondered if Felicia's experiment would put an end to the effort to train women as Keepers.

Varzil's skin tingled with the electrical fields of the workers. Each shimmered like a focal point of swirling power. The screen crackled with energy.

He drew upon the forces surging through the circle and shaped them into a cone of power with himself at the apex. At the same time, he felt an answering resonance in the relay screens hundreds of leagues away, in Hestral Tower. Vision faded as senses overloaded and the reek of ozone filled his nostrils. His awareness of his body drained away, replaced by a flare of energy so bright and potent that for that instant, he seemed to be composed of lightning.

Ice shuddered through him. He gasped, but his lungs drew in no air. A piercing crack and jolt of sound tossed him like a broken doll. It faded to a vast singing silence.

Nausea swept through him and suddenly he had a body again and was kneeling on a stone floor.

"Varzil? Varzil of Arilinn?"

A woman bent over him, the monitor he had glimpsed from Felicia's shattered telepathic communication. He opened his mouth to reply, sucked in air. The room turned gray and cold around the edges. He tried to rise, but found he had barely the strength to hold up his head.

"It's all right," she said, and introduced herself as Oranna MacLean. "The energy drain of traveling through the relays is extreme, but there is nothing wrong with you that food and rest cannot cure. I have studied the procedure in the records."

As he followed her gaze, he saw more of the room. He recognized it as a relay chamber very much like the one he had left, yet with the differences of architecture, the placement of the screens, the minor ornamental touches, which assured him that he was no longer at Arilinn. The workers who had gathered around him, masking their curiosity under a discreet distance, were strangers.

Varzil accepted a plate of the familiar, heavily-sweetened food suitable for strenuous *laran* work, nut candies and honey-laced dried fruit. His body responded with a rush of mental clarity.

"What need prompted you to travel at such risk?" Oranna asked. "Not that we are unhappy to see you, but our own Keeper, Loryn Ardais, cannot welcome you properly or, I am afraid, give you any immediate aid. We have a crisis of our own—"

Varzil found his voice. "Where is Felicia? What has happened to her?"

"Oh, Varzil, it was such a terrible accident!" Oranna replied. "Come, if you are able to walk now, and you will see for yourself."

Varzil was still weak enough to appreciate a shoulder to lean upon, especially when negotiating the stairs. The matrix laboratory had clearly been constructed for some other purpose and later remodeled. Panels of oiled wood partly covered the red stone walls. A worktable dominated the center of the room, and on it sat the shattered ruin of a matrix lattice. Parts of it remained intact, the crystals catching the light like tiny bits of stars. Blackened powder covered one side. A few robed workers stood just inside the door and in one corner a youth scarcely out of boyhood huddled on the floor, weeping. Beyond him—

Felicia!

She lay on the floor beside the worktable, covered by a blanket. A man in the crimson robes of a Keeper crouched at her head, his back to Varzil.

For a heart-stopping moment, Varzil feared he had come too late, that she was already dead. He could not sense her mind and her body appeared as inert as clay.

The Keeper looked up. In the light of the glows, his hair looked black, his eyes pools of shadow. The lineaments of his features conveyed a quick mind, a deep and abiding curiosity.

"Varzil of Arilinn?"

"Vai tenerézu," Varzil replied, bowing. To his surprise, his voice did not tremble. "What happened here?"

"I have stablized her as best I can. We will bring her down to the infirmary for a more thorough examination."

You must prepare yourself for the worst.

Varzil flinched. *But she still lives!*

There is life and then there is life.

Varzil, despite his fatigue, insisted upon helping to carry Felicia. Her flesh felt warm and resilient. She was lighter than he'd expected, as if the greater part of her substance had been burned away. Her face was very pale except for the faintest brush of rose across her cheeks, yet her lips curled softly. There was no terror in her expression. The few faint lines that marked her skin only added to her character.

From the placement of its windows, the infirmary had once been a solarium, which now looked out upon darkness. Oranna arrived before them, arranging a cot in the center of the room with ample space for a circle to gather. Around her stood a group of workers, some robed for *laran* work. One of them was Eduin.

Varzil lowered Felicia to the table. "I will take care of her."

"You will do nothing of the sort," Loryn said. "You are not yet recovered from your own transit through the screens."

Loryn had the least invasive psychic presence Varzil had ever experienced, an extraordinary self-sufficiency and flexibility without any apparent need to impose his will on any other. Varzil liked him immediately. He lowered his *laran* barriers, just as if Loryn were his own Keeper.

Ah! Loryn replied telepathically. *Such is the bond you and Felicia shared. We, too, hold her dear. You did well to come to us. No one who loves her so deeply should be deprived of the chance to bid her farewell.*

"She still lives," Varzil repeated aloud, conscious of how stubborn he sounded. "There must yet be hope."

"There is always hope," Loryn agreed. "Come now, let our monitor do her work. I will assist her, but you must not interfere. You are much too close emotionally to Felicia to be objective."

Reluctantly, Varzil agreed. He himself had said very much the same thing upon occasion. Powerful emotions, love or hate, jealousy or anger, garbled perceptions and warped judgment. Married couples were not allowed to work in the same circle at Arilinn. The demands of celibacy from the intense psychic work were too great for most relationships. He and Felicia had both been Tower-trained before they met; they understood the physical limitations as the natural price of the use of their talents.

As he looked down at Felicia's tranquil face, Varzil realized that the core of their relationship was neither romantic nor sexual, although these aspects, when they could be enjoyed, were certainly pleasurable. They shared a sympathy of spirit that transcended the flesh.

I will never know anyone like her again, he found himself thinking, and then recoiled. Surely, she would recover with such competent care. She must.

He stepped back even as Eduin moved to his side. "Varzil, I am sorry to see you again under these circumstances. You are most welcome, though you have come to Hestral at a dark hour."

Varzil had not expected such kindness. "I did not know you were here at Hestral. We heard only that you had gone to Hali after your visit home. How does your father?"

"He has recovered, thank you. During my time at Hali, I had the chance to consider my own future. Arilinn trained me well, but left me with little room to develop myself. Here at Hestral, there are no such limitations."

Eduin smiled at Varzil, his eyes steady, his psychic aura unblemished. Perhaps, Varzil thought, he had at last found the place where he no longer needed to hold himself apart, to conceal who he truly was.

◆

Varzil was weaving with exhaustion when, a short time later, an elderly man entered, introduced himself as *coridom* of the Tower, and said that a guest room had been prepared. Hestral Tower had no wards such as Arilinn with its Veil that forbade the entry of non-*Comyn*. Men and women from the village came in daily to clean and cook.

The *coridom* shuffled along the hallways, leading Varzil past the rest of the living quarters to a narrow, poorly lit chamber. Mustiness tinged the air, as if it had been little used, although the bedding was quite clean and the meal laid out on a tray set on the chest of drawers steamed with appetizing aromas. Varzil gulped down the food, scarcely tasting it, and tumbled into bed.

He woke some hours later, ravenously hungry. From the light sifting through the single window, he guessed the time to be an hour or two past sunrise, not more. After several wrong turns, he made his way to the infirmary, where he found Loryn and Oranna beside Felicia's bed.

"Varzil, I am so sorry." Oranna's voice was as thin and gray as her cheeks. "We tried everything we could."

A shimmering field of *laran* energy surrounded Felicia's still form. Up close, it was fully transparent, with only a hint of scintillation to betray its presence. All color had drained from her cheeks, leaving only a waxen mask. Varzil watched the shallow, hesitant rise and fall of her chest.

"Yes," Loryn said, "her heart beats, her lungs breathe. This much we have been able to do, but for how long, we cannot say. She took an immensely powerful stream of energy through her body. Not even her spinal reflexes survived intact. Worst of all, her *laran* centers have been badly damaged."

So even if she recovered— Varzil reined in his thoughts. "Surely with time and skilled *laran* healing—" he began.

Oranna shook her head. "I have seen several such cases, and have never found any documentation in the medical records of a true recovery. Certainly not from this severe an injury." She went on, a little defensively, for she looked much too young to have any depth of experience, "I was fostered near Temora, where there have been a number of outlaw circles over the years. They work without the safeguards of a Tower and take all manner of risks. And too often pay the price. There was one woman—I cringe to name her *leronis*—who was able to keep working. I don't know how she did it, but I was never part of her Nest and so not privy to the details. I suspect—and Loryn agrees—that her injuries were not as severe as she put about, that she used the circumstance of the accident to her own advantage."

"That is no justification," Varzil said tightly, "to abandon Felicia without trying."

"I have already done my best for her," the healer responded in a pale, taut voice. She pressed her lips together, holding back tears, wavering on the edge of exhaustion.

"We will have no dissension among ourselves," Loryn said. The gentleness of his voice masked his sorrow.

To him, she is gone already.

She is indeed gone, my friend, came Loryn's telepathic voice. *Believe me, we have done all that could be done. Do you think you were the only one who loved her, who would do whatever was necessary to have her back in our midst? We must face reality. Her brain is damaged past repair. All we have been able to do is to keep her body alive.*

Varzil closed his eyes as grief washed over him. It came as a wave, built to a peak that left him shivering, and then subsided. Loryn asked his permission to release the energy fields that maintained Felicia's life.

How can I let her go?

She is gone. Now is the time for acceptance, and for mourning.

Passing one hand across his eyes, Varzil turned away. Loryn withdrew the telepathic contact in respect for his privacy. On Varzil's finger, the white stone pulsed gently. She had given it to him on a night of passion and hope. Would it be all he had left of her? He cupped it in both hands.

As his lips touched the gem, warmth surged through him. For an instant he felt Felicia's presence. Not her thoughts, nothing so clear as that, but the unmistakable stamp of her personality. His first thought was that, against all evidence and everything Loryn and Oranna had said, she herself still lived in her body.

But no, that was not possible. He knew the truth of their words.

Memory came in a flash—Felicia calling to him, driven by such desperation she was able to cross leagues and formidable Tower barriers. The darkness of his room at Arilinn—the flash of the crystal—

Somehow, she had transferred her mind, or some part of it, to the ring.

If that were so—his thoughts careened on like beasts driven mad by a storm—and some way might be found to restore her body—if enough of her mind survived—if the crystal were complex enough to sustain her—

If—if—if!

With a cry, Varzil covered his face with both hands. He needed time to think, to calm himself. Hope and despair clashed within him, jumbling all reason.

Time—

Time also to discover exactly what had happened, so that he might find the key to her recovery. If he understood *what* and *how,* he might also discover the way to reverse it.

Varzil gentled his voice as he turned back to Loryn. They were all distraught by the suddenness of the events, he said. No one wanted to take premature action that they would later regret. Surely, there was no harm in maintaining Felicia's body in its present state. For a time, at least, until more could be learned about what had happened.

Loryn listened, nodding compassionately. In the normal course of events, without the extraordinary resources of a Tower, Felicia would already be dead.

"You are right," he said. "We all need time to accept this terrible tragedy."

"I would like to investigate," Varzil said. "There are many things I do not understand."

Loryn regarded him calmly. "If it will ease your mind, you have my leave."

Oranna came over and laid her fingertips on the back of Varzil's wrist, a telepath's light contact, a world of sympathy in a single gesture. "We can create a stasis field which will isolate and protect her. Her life forces are already very low, but within such a field, time would lose all meaning. An hour, a day, or even a century might pass without any decay."

"I thank you," Varzil said. "I—I have heard of such a technique at Hali, at the *rhu fead*. In ages past, things too dangerous to be handled or destroyed have been safely kept in this manner. I did not think the knowledge still remained." He smiled, half-bitter. "Perhaps we at Arilinn, with our pride in our traditions, have much to learn from other Towers."

"Perhaps," Loryn agreed. "And perhaps you also have much to teach. We have become strangers to one another, each hoarding our own knowledge and skills, each terrified that the other will make some discovery leading to a tactical military advantage."

"This much is true," Varzil replied with feeling, "and it must stop. Perhaps we cannot bring an end to all disputes, armed or verbal. But we can at least attempt to contain them within the sphere of physical conflict."

"Ah!" Loryn said. "Even here at Hestral, we have heard of Varzil's Compact of Honor. I had hoped for the opportunity to sit and discuss it with you."

"Compact of Honor? Carolin Hastur and I just called it our Pact, but I like the sound of that."

Loryn was about to say more, but paused. Someone had approached the infirmary door and sent a telepathic query instead of the usual knock. The Keeper excused himself and went to the door. Varzil caught a glimpse of a young woman, her face troubled. Either she had not yet learned to mask her feelings or else something had disturbed her deeply.

"I will be with them presently," Loryn said. "They can wait outside the gates. We do not permit armed men to enter Hestral Tower, and certainly not before breakfast."

Varzil caught the slight lift of the other man's shoulders, the ring of authority in his voice.

"What was I saying? Ah, yes. Your Compact. Throughout Darkover, there is a longing for peace, for justice. We of the Towers cannot sit by, complacent in our seclusion, while kings and lordlings set the very land ablaze. Once we made *clingfire* at the command of the Hastur Lords, and to this day still hold a stock of it, hopefully forgotten. Perhaps one day, not only will the stuff be forgotten, but the very word will have lost all meaning. Can you imagine that? A time when no one knows what *clingfire* is?"

"I, too, hope for a day when such words are but empty sounds." Varzil followed Loryn into the corridor. "It is not *my* Compact, as you call it, but rather a dream I share with Carolin Hastur, who has been my friend since we were boys together at Arilinn. I fear that it will be many years before there is hope of persuading men to follow it."

"Do not lose heart," Loryn said, "for here is one man—and one Tower—ready to listen. We will speak more of this later. For now, the hospitality of Hestral is yours, and I hope you will stay with us for a time, at least long enough for resolution of this incident. Go with Oranna. Rest and eat."

Varzil bowed and, thanking Loryn for his graciousness, headed back toward the laboratory. He had arrived in the middle of the night, uninvited, in the middle of a crisis, and had found an unexpected welcome. These armed men Loryn spoke of, whoever they were, would get a far cooler reception.

38

Oranna led Varzil down a wide staircase and into Hestral's common room, part dining area, part meeting place, and part sanctuary. Like the rest of the Tower, this room had once served another purpose. The walls were rich red-brown brick flecked with bits of mica that winked softly in the morning light. The windows had been thrown open, so that the breeze carried the faint scent of rosalys. Instead of a central divan, wooden chairs sat arranged in small groups. They were of unfamiliar design, with curved backs and armrests, covered with cushions in bright orange and yellow.

Eduin looked up from where he was sitting alone by the empty fireplace. After a moment of hesitation, he came toward them. "What news?"

"It is as we feared," Oranna said in a voice strained with fatigue.

She went to the table that ran the length of one wall underneath the opened windows, took up a plate, and filled it with the food arrayed there. Most was familiar to Varzil, but a few dishes, such as the stewed mushrooms dotted with pea-sized balls of fresh cheese, surprised him.

Eduin sat with them as they ate. After he and Oranna had exchanged a few pleasantries, he said, "Did you hear the ruckus at the gates earlier?"

"I fear it bodes nothing but trouble," Oranna said, in between mouthfuls of crumbled cheese and honey-glazed apple. "Until now, we have had an overly easy time of it here at Hestral. But we cannot remain apart from the world's sorrows forever."

Excusing himself, Varzil walked over to the window nearest the corner. From this vantage, the gates themselves were obscured, but he had a fair view of the men and horses arranged outside. The sun reflected off their shields and lances. Even knowing little of military matters, Varzil recognized the groupings, the banners of blue and silver bearing the badge of Lyondri Hastur. This was no simple escort but a show of rank by numbers. This was a party armed for war.

✦

Hestral's layout was simple and central, the commons having once been the great hall of its original design. The working areas comprised one wing, with living quarters diametrically opposite. The matrix laboratory was very much as Varzil remembered it from his arrival, only now the full morning sun streamed through the eastward facing windows. It had been a pleasant space, well proportioned and comfortable.

No one had yet come to set right the overturned benches or clear away the pulverized crystal which made a halo around the central work-table, broken by a swathe where Felicia had fallen.

A young man, still robed for circle work, huddled on a bench beside the table, gazing down at the ruined lattice. Shadows hid his face. By his posture, he looked to have not moved for some hours. He had probably been there all night.

"I still can't believe it," he stammered, flinching at Varzil's approach. "It worked so well the last time we tested it. It was *designed* to prevent this kind of power surge."

"Felicia told me a little about the project," Varzil said, "but I'd like to know more."

"It's all my fault!" The lad turned and Varzil saw him clearly for the first time, a rawboned, gangly youth not yet at peace with his growth. Fading acne reddened his face. Varzil recognized him as Marius, the Rockraven boy whose talent was the focus of Felicia's research.

"How is it your fault? Did you attack Felicia? Did you deliberately channel destructive energy in her direction?"

"No!" The boy's voice cracked. "No, I would *never*—"

"Then you have nothing to reproach yourself with, certainly not something you neither caused nor could possibly control. Exactly what *did* happen?"

"I don't know! I've been racking my memory, trying to find a reason! There's nothing—"

"Just start at the beginning. How did this—" Varzil indicated the matrix apparatus, "come about?"

The boy took a deep breath to steady himself. "Our goal was to modulate *my* weather talent. If only I'd been able to manage it properly, none of this would have been necessary. I have something of the old Rockraven weather sense, did you know?"

Varzil nodded and sent a pulse of calm to the boy's mind.

"It seemed to be more than just a talent for sensing patterns in wind and cloud. Lots of people can do that, even if they don't know it. They think it's the birds nesting a certain way or the growth of a sheep's wool that tells them a bad storm is coming. I—I have moments when I see these flows of energy, at least that's what Loryn and Felicia say they are. To me, they're like rivers and streams, so big and deep and strong I don't have words for it. Ordinary storms—those waft about in the air. These rivers lie deep underground, and everything—" he gestured to include not only the room, the Tower, the valley, but all the lands beyond, "—everything resonates to them."

Aldones! He sees the lines of magnetism of the planet!

"I can't see them all the time," the boy rattled on, "not even when I concentrate, and I've never been able to *do* anything with them. Felicia thought that some day I might."

If you could, every tyrant on Darkover would be after you. Varzil did not want to imagine what uses Rakhal Hastur might put the boy's talent to.

The youth went on to describe how Felicia planned to use a specially constructed matrix to focus and balance his natural ability, enhancing or buffering it as needed.

"It should have worked! All the preliminary tests we did were wonderful—as if I'd suddenly taken off blinders I'd worn all my life. But we hadn't used it as a circle—that was the first test. We started off in the ordinary way and then, when we were settled in our circle, I felt Felicia make the bridge to the lattice. Something—I don't know—something hot and white exploded right where she was. She tried to hold the circle.

I felt her struggling. There was this jolt like being hit with bucket of live coals. I've still got a headache from it."

Varzil paced the room, his mind ranging through the psychic space. The atmosphere still quivered with the residue of destructive energy. He couldn't identify it. There was no trace of outside intrusion or any invading personality. His circuit took him to the door, where a telepathic damper sat on a table beside the platters of food, beakers of sweetened wine, a folded shawl. He touched the damper and felt the faint, fading pulse of its interference fields.

"This was turned on?"

The boy looked startled. "Of course. Don't you use them at Arilinn?"

"Indeed. And no one entered the room physically?"

"No, nothing like that. Why are you asking? It was an accident!"

Either that, or Felicia's own carelessness. Varzil could not bring himself to believe that she had somehow brought this on herself. She was too competent, too well-trained by Arilinn's exacting standards, to attempt work beyond her ability, especially when the minds and lives of others depended upon her. In their last conversation over the relays, her words had rung with assurance and competence. She'd known what she was doing.

Varzil gestured toward the ruined matrix. "I must study this. Perhaps I can discover some flaw, some reason for what happened."

The boy moved back to the table. "I hardly see how. Eduin worked on the design with Felicia and then constructed it. He—"

"*Eduin* constructed this? And was he—" *O, Dark Lady Avarra!*—"was he part of the circle?"

"No. He was working in Loryn's circle."

Varzil forced himself to breathe slowly, to think. His heart pounded in his chest and his hands threatened to shake. "Isn't that unusual? For a technician to build something this complicated and then leave its operation to others?"

"Why, yes, I thought so, too." The boy blinked rapidly and the red haloes around his acne lesions darkened. He wavered on his feet.

Varzil recognized the danger signs of exhaustion. Clearly, the boy was too overwrought, too tormented with guilt to see reason. Varzil wanted to examine the ruined lattice undisturbed, to ponder Eduin's part in the disaster.

"Varzil?" a girl's voice, light and pleasant, interrupted him. She stood in the doorway and Varzil recognized her at once as Serena, whose mind he had touched many times over the relays. She smiled back at him. "Loryn asks if you would join him in his chambers."

Varzil put his arm around the boy's shoulders. "Marius," he said gently, "you must get some food, then go to bed. You aren't going to do anyone any good if you become ill."

Some of the brittleness seeped from the boy's muscles. He nodded and led the way from the laboratory.

◆

Loryn Ardais was one of those men who by their constitution showed little outward trace of fatigue, yet Varzil noticed the slight sag of his shoulders. The man had worked through the rest of the night and then met with an envoy and his armed escort.

Do not admire me for a trait that is none of my choosing, Loryn said telepathically. *I owe my constitution to the gods; it is no credit of mine.*

He went on aloud, "I asked you here to consult with you as a fellow Keeper. Most of the time, I rule Hestral with an easy hand. My people are skilled professionals and perfectly capable of their own reasoned decisions. But in the world at large, only one voice may speak for the Tower, and that is mine."

Varzil thought a moment. "So you sent Hastur's men on their way without whatever they came for. Do you need my blessing for that? I give it freely."

"Do you remember my mention of a stockpile of *clingfire,* made by one of my predecessors and all but forgotten?"

"I remember that we spoke of a future when not only the stuff itself, but the secrets of its making and its very name would vanish with time," Varzil said.

Did Rakhal Hastur find out about it? he added mentally.

Yes, undoubtedly from the records of that same king who commanded its manufacture. These would be kept at Hali.

Varzil shuddered inwardly at the notion of handing over a supply of *clingfire* to Rakhal Hastur.

"Did Rakhal say why he wanted it? Or shall I guess it was to pursue his war against Carolin and his allies?"

Loryn raised one hand in a dismissive gesture. "I do not care why he wanted it. I wish I had destroyed the stuff the very hour I learned of its existence. I told the Hastur captain that is what I had done."

"You lied?"

"I *anticipated,*" Loryn replied with such an expression that Varzil almost smiled. "Now I need—I *ask* your help in bringing truth to my words. I would have this thing done in secret, so that if any of my people are questioned under truthspell—an eventuality I pray will never happen—they can all swear they knew nothing of it. It is much to put upon you, Varzil. This is not your problem. I thought you might feel some kinship of spirit with us, if only for Felicia's sake."

"I am not protesting," Varzil said quickly. "I heartily agree with what you have done. I am honored you would look to me for this."

Loryn looked at him with a curious expression, half in wonder, half in appraisal. "Your reputation has preceded you, Varzil of Arilinn, as a man of honor and vision."

"Please, do not flatter me," Varzil said, cutting Loryn off before he could utter more praise. "I have already said I will do it. You need not cozen me with sweet and improbable words to enlist my help."

I have done nothing so praiseworthy, Varzil thought. *Not yet, at any rate. I have done my work as best I can, and on occasion shared the dreams of others.*

Your modesty does not become you, Loryn answered silently. *Nor does reticence further the wisdom behind your words. Yet, I will leave the subject. We will have more than enough troubles in the days ahead.*

"I fear we have not seen the last of Rakhal's soldiers," Loryn said aloud.

Varzil realized with a pang that his investigation into Felicia's accident would have to wait. The *clingfire* must be dealt with as soon as possible. A time of rest and grieving would give him a plausible public reason to remain at Hestral without arousing anyone's curiosity.

"The welfare of the Tower and all who dwell herein must take precedence over any individual desires," Varzil said, though each word turned in his heart like a dagger.

Kings know this; Keepers know this. And I—Aldones save me—I have a greater duty.

"Do not regret that you are a man with a man's heart," Loryn said gently. "All things happen in their proper season."

◆

Loryn had fitted out a small stone cellar for their work in dismantling the *clingfire*. The windowless space was set below ground level and had been cleared of all combustible material. Even the makeshift benches and worktable were of brick, the vessels of glass.

The cellar, hidden from the sun and shielded by the earth itself, struck Varzil as the worst possible place for their mission. Destroying *clingfire* ought to be an act of public conscience, not a secret. Perhaps one day, it would be.

Varzil lowered himself to his seat. The cold edge bit into his flesh. There were only a handful of vessels, begrimed with dust and cobwebs. Even so, their contents glowed slightly like banked embers.

Loryn, wearing padded gloves, set aside all the vessels but one, which he placed in the center of the table.

It was not enough to simply isolate the *clingfire,* setting it apart from anything combustible. So far as Varzil knew, *clingfire* did not degenerate with age, but would stay potent for years, perhaps even centuries. It must be rendered into its component parts. These would then be teleported to widely separated locations deep within the earth. Fortunately, none of the processes involved the most dangerous step of its original manufacture, the distillation under high heat. Working together, two Keepers should be able to handle the material safely.

"I have not done this before," Varzil said, "although I am familiar with the theory. I look to you for instruction in the practice."

Loryn's mouth twisted in a rueful half-smile. "Sadly, I *have* done this before. My earliest training was at Dalereuth, where making *clingfire* was an everyday event. So much so, in fact, that from time to time a contamination would not be discovered until afterward and then the product could not be used or even safely stored. Once—" Loryn rolled up his sleeve to display a pitted scar running the length of his forearm, "a batch corroded through its container. We had used glass, as we do here and everywhere else, I suppose, because it is chemically inert, but this stuff—"

He jerked the sleeve down. "This stuff not only ate through the glass, it seemed have an intelligence of its own, the way it sought out human flesh."

"That would be horrendous indeed," Varzil said. "Ordinary *clingfire* is deadly enough."

Loryn projected the image of the steps they must follow and the two set to work. It was simple, but not easy. Each slow, meticulous step required unwavering concentration. Without a circle, they must generate their own psychic power.

By the time Loryn called a halt, Varzil was near the limits of his own endurance, so soon after his transit through the relay screens. Sweat filmed his face and trickled down his sides. His mouth felt dry and pasty.

He rose, noting the faint unsteadiness of his knees, and looked down at the first vessel. They had been working for two or three hours, and had finished only a quarter of it.

"True," Loryn said, catching his unvoiced thought. "But that small portion is gone forever."

Varzil nodded. "To move slowly and thoroughly is perhaps the wisest course of all. When faced with an evil, it is tempting to want to obliterate it instantly. I fear this is what leads good men to adopt rash solutions which only create worse problems."

"Even good men can be driven past patience and reason," Loryn agreed.

✦

Gray with fatigue, Varzil headed for the infirmary. He did not consider the wisdom of sitting there, rather than attending to his own physical care. All he knew was that he *needed* to be near Felicia, as a drowning man needed air or a Dry Towner needed rain.

Stiff joints protested as he climbed the stairs from the stone cellar. He paused several times to gather the strength to take the next step. At the portal to the commons, the mingled aromas of hot apple and meat pastry assaulted him. His mouth watered and his leg muscles quivered.

You must eat, he told himself, listening to the rumble of his stomach. *Or you will make yourself ill. You are responsible for more than your own welfare. Would you let your willfulness expose Loryn to the dangers of* cling-fire?

The voices in his mind were a mingling of many—old Lunilla, back at Arilinn, Fidelis, Oranna, even Felicia herself. It had ever been a failing of his, to push himself, deny himself, as if his passions could eliminate all more mundane concerns.

Serena, who had been working the relays, came rushing into the room just as Varzil began his second pastry.

"Everyone! There is such news!" she exclaimed.

"What has happened?" Eduin asked from across the room.

"I have had word from our fellow *leronyn* at Tramontana!" she rushed on, her features flushed with excitement. "They will make no more *laran* weapons for King Rakhal, nor will they be a party to his wars against Carolin Hastur, who they now hail as the rightful king. In short, the entire Tower has declared its independence. Several of its workers have already gone to offer their aid to Carolin—I should say King Carolin."

"At last," Eduin said, "a Tower has the courage to stand for itself instead of toadying to some arrogant Lowland *Hali'imyn!*"

"Carolin has sworn he will use neither *clingfire* or any other *laran*-made weapon," Varzil said.

"The more fool he," one of the men said, shaking his head, "for Rakhal will not hesitate to use whatever is in his grasp."

Loryn appeared in the doorway. He and Varzil exchanged glances. "Then it is just as well," the Hestral Keeper said, "that we have none to give him. He must be desperate indeed to send to us for it."

"I think he must be," Varzil said thoughtfully, "for did he not use *clingfire* against *Dom* Valdrin Castamir? The stuff is so difficult to make, he cannot have much remaining to him."

"Aye, perhaps he now regrets squandering it so early in his reign, when now he has greatest need of it," someone else said.

"All the better for Carolin's poor men," Serena said.

"One day, men will go to war without such weapons, if they go to war at all," Varzil said.

"You are such a dreamer," Eduin said, "for what man would throw away his sharpest sword and fight only with his bare hands—especially when his enemy still goes armed with steel? I say, let Carolin and Rakhal fight it out on the battlefield, one king is as bad as another. Our only real hope is that we of the Towers make our own decisions about how to use our talents. *We* choose to make *clingfire*. *We* choose the ones we give it to."

Varzil, pondering Eduin's words as he continued to the infirmary, thought that despite their differences, Eduin was right. In the end, in order for the Compact of Honor to succeed, the Towers themselves must choose.

39

When the last particle of *clingfire* had been separated into its component parts and sent into the bowels of the earth, when the stone cellar had been cleansed of every remaining trace of their task, Varzil ventured back to the matrix laboratory. He did so with some trepidation, for the destruction of the *clingfire* had required all his concentration. Now, the powerful emotions he had held at bay returned.

His thoughts kept returning to the last conversation he had with Felicia over the relays. He'd asked if her earlier fears had been laid to rest. From the first, she'd sensed something dark, ominous. He'd persuaded her to go against her own best instincts.

The blame is mine. If only I had listened . . . She trusted me and I betrayed her. I saw only what I wanted to see . . . a woman Keeper . . . someone to change the face of Darkover . . .

Do not trouble yourself, came a thought, framed by the mental voice he knew so well. *The choice was mine alone, and mine alone the risk.*

The piercing guilt subsided, but only for a time. He sat beside her, hands clasped around her ring, searching her face for any impossible sign of life.

If only I had listened . . .

✦

Loryn had ordered the laboratory chamber sealed, and no one had disturbed it. Varzil stood for a long moment, studying the matrix lattice. It sat like a misshapen lump in the center of the table, half charred, half fallen in upon itself. Enough of the structure remained intact to make out its original shape.

It had been a thing of beauty, crystals mounted on struts of glass, held with wires of copper and other metals, some of them braided. Even mangled, it caught the light of the glows and fractured it into tiny rainbows. The colored light reminded Varzil of the Veil at Arilinn, mysterious in its beauty, yet disturbing.

Stepping closer, Varzil bent to inspect the damaged section. Here, metal and glass had fused and blackened. He closed his eyes and shaped his thoughts into a probe.

To his surprise, the lattice hummed in response to his *laran,* as it had been designed to do. He followed the resonance from stone to stone, studying how the device amplified certain mental vibrations and damped others. Many pathways no longer functioned, but he seized upon what remained.

The design was brilliant, the execution subtle and elegant. Yet even as he admired Eduin's work, Varzil searched for some imperfection, some flaw.

There must be a reason!

But he could find none. The intact portion of the lattice was perfect.

The fault, then, must be Felicia's.

No! Varzil stormed. *I will not believe it!*

At his sides, his hands curled unconsciously into fists. The muscles of his back and shoulders tensed as if for combat. His thoughts twisted as if straining at invisible chains.

Zandru curse it all!

His fists slammed down on the table and sent the lattice trembling. Powder sifted through the openwork structure and over his feet. A shard of crystal bit into the heel of one hand. The pain drew him back to himself, to the mental cry that still echoed in the room.

With a series of ragged breaths, Varzil struggled to rein his emotions under control. His mind cleared—

—just in time to sense the faint spark of energy from *within the blackened area.*

Realization shocked through him. He'd assumed that section of the device utterly destroyed, and to appearances, it was. Something in his agonized outburst woke a lingering resonance there . . .

Heart pounding, he circled the table for a closer look. Heat and *laran* overload had twisted and melted the delicate framework. Blackened bits that had once been glittering crystals stared sullenly back at him. He knew better than to physically touch them. Once again, he sent out a mental probe, this time aimed at the heart of the ruin.

Silence answered him, a muffling of psychic energy so dense and complete, he might as well have tried to communicate with an operating telepathic damper.

Again, Zandru curse you!

Even charcoal would have been more sensitive to his thoughts, Varzil fumed. The very absence of any answering vibration only aroused his suspicions further.

There had been *something* in that section of the matrix, something whose remains, even warped and broken, still operated to keep it hidden. Only one type of device Varzil knew could produce such an effect. He had seen one before in the bird-thing which had almost claimed Carolin's life at Blue Lake.

A trap-matrix. But such a device required a single, specific target . . .

Could Felicia herself have been the intended victim? Felicia, who had not an enemy in the world?

Who? Why?

Mouth dry, Varzil lowered himself to the nearest bench. He slipped the ring off his finger, clasped it between both hands, and closed his eyes. Clear light pulsed gently from it. Something faint and far-off stirred across the surface of his mind, like birdsong on a frosty spring dawn.

Felicia . . .

Varzil, my love . . .

He wanted nothing more than to rush toward that voice, no matter where it might lead him.

Are you really there? he asked. *Or is it my own heart that answers me?*

I cannot tell. Her voice sounded small and forlorn, lost in some unimaginably vast space. *I can barely sense you, and the Overworld pulls me more strongly with every passing moment . . .*

"My love, what happened in the circle? How came you to this state, half in one world and half in the other?" Varzil spoke aloud to help focus his thoughts.

I remember . . . gathering up the circle . . . I was so excited . . . to be able to focus Marius' Gift . . . She trailed off and for a long moment, Varzil feared he had lost her.

And then? Something went wrong? What?

The next instant, he sat in this room, only in a different position. Around him, he felt the warmth and movement of other people. His own mind linked to those of the circle, weaving their psychic energies into a single flow, like a braided river. Oranna's mind moved from one person to the next, easing tight muscles, keeping heartbeats regular. Though his eyes were still closed, he knew the matrix glowed with light. It seemed to have a life of its own, amplifying and redirecting the energies which he fed into it.

With this, we can dissipate killing storms or bring rain to the worst forest fires . . .

Gladly, he poured the united energies of the circle into the lattice. It sang with power.

More . . . and faster . . .

At the very border between mind energy and crystal, something flared, only a minute spark. Suddenly, the lattice did not resonate with the energy he fed it.

It pulled. It took.

It *demanded*.

He tried to resist, to slow the flow of *laran* power that now threatened to cascade beyond his control. The device should not be beyond the ability of a circle of six to control. Should he call for help? No, he could—he *would* master it!

The *laran* streams bucked and fought, swelling to torrential dimensions. Rivulets broke off like frayed threads, snapping and crackling. He held on, held on . . .

Pain shrieked through him, not along his physical nerves, but the channels carrying his psychic power. Needles of fire like grappling hooks pierced him, held him. He twisted this way and that, trying to break free.

Horrified, he realized that his struggles only tightened the hold of the thing upon his mind. He threw all his power into a single leap, a single name hurled into the night—

VARZIL!

And then, silence.

Slowly, Varzil got to his feet. He felt sickened by what he had seen and felt, but even more by what he must do now. The trap-matrix had been carefully planned, placed in secret and with great skill. No outsider could have done it. Only someone intimately acquainted with Hestral Tower and Felicia's own psychic signature could have constructed and triggered such a device. That meant the assailant must be a member of the Tower . . . in all probability one of Felicia's own circle.

◆

"Truthspell?" Loryn repeated, one eyebrow lifting in surprise. "Surely that is an extreme action, when we have no proof there actually was a trap-matrix."

Loryn had been unable to elicit the same reaction from the fused lattice array, and Felicia's ring seemed to be attuned to Varzil's mind alone. It was only Varzil's word that the lattice had been sabotaged in a way that targeted its Keeper.

My word is not the word of an ordinary man. I, too, am a Keeper.

"Absent that hard proof, we must use what tools we have to discover the truth," Varzil countered. "If I am wrong, I will most humbly apologize—"

"No, that won't be necessary—"

"If I am right and we do not do this thing, then you harbor a scorpion in your midst. Once a man has plotted a death, executed it, and survived unpunished, *he will kill again.* He will find reasons to eliminate those who stand in his way."

Whether they be kings or commoners . . . or fellow leronyn.

Loryn ran one hand over the side of his face, drawing the skin taut. Clearly, he did not want to think ill of his own people. The intimacy between a Keeper and his circle was of mind and spirit.

"I am sorry to have brought this crisis to Hestral, which has offered me the hospitality of a second home," Varzil said gently. "In the short time I have been here, I have come to love you as my own kin. Yet to remain silent, to keep what I know to myself, would be a far greater betrayal of your trust."

After a long pause, Loryn said, "You have done right. If I hesitate, it is not from any anger at you. If your suspicions prove right, you will have done us a great service. I will convene the entire Tower and question every one of us as you have asked. Truthspell will resolve the matter in a way which will leave no doubt."

✦

True to his word, Loryn assembled the workers and students of Hestral Tower that very night. He chose an hour when most would normally be awake. All work was suspended, even attending to the relays.

Varzil sat to the side of the room, watching and listening. The murmurs of curiosity and surprise, both spoken aloud and in thought, reminded him of the beating of wings or the fall of rain on a lake surface.

Frightened birds. Disturbed water.

An unspoken signal rippled through the company, leaving silence in its wake. Loryn moved to the front of the room and began to speak. The softness of his voice had the effect of intensifying the attention of every single person in the room.

"We stand here in grief today because of the loss of Felicia Leynier. Everyone here knows that two months ago, she was severely injured in her work as Keeper, in what seemed to be an accidental backlash. Recently, however, some evidence has come to light which suggests that this terrible accident might not have been mischance."

He paused, letting the others absorb his words. Varzil, his senses attuned to the gathering, caught their stray thoughts.

A design fault? A flawed crystal? Did she make some error in judgment?

No one as yet suspected it might have been sabotage. Loryn went on in his calm, reasonable tone, explaining that in order to find a meaningful correlation between isolated details, the community must act in unity. Varzil admired how he brought them together, subtly eliciting their cooperation, without ever implying that the purpose of this investigation was to uncover a traitor in their midst. The innocent among them would think the questioning aimed at uncovering particulars which had no significance in and of themselves but might produce a pattern.

The guilty one . . . the guilty would go along, for it was too late to object without the appearance of having something to hide.

"I have asked Varzil, who is *tenerézu* in his own right and the only one of us not present on that dreadful night, to cast the truthspell. In its light, we may put a rest to this dreadful business."

Once again, Varzil sensed a ripple of emotion encompass the room, this time a fervent prayer. He unwrapped his starstone and held it aloft, speaking the ritual words which would trigger the spell. "In the light of this jewel, let the truth illuminate this room in which we stand."

His starstone flared to life and so did the white gem on Felicia's ring. Moment by moment, the eerie glow of truthspell seeped through the commons until the combined radiance bathed the faces of everyone in the room. Varzil could tell from the characteristic cool warmth on his skin that his own features also reflected that blue-white glow. If anyone knowingly spoke a falsehood, the light would vanish from his face.

One by one, Loryn called forth the members of Felicia's circle. "Tell me what happened on that night," he said, leaving it to each person to offer what he remembered.

Varzil listened with half a mind, reserving his concentration for the truthspell and scrutinizing the face of each speaker for the slightest change in the blue glow. There was none, not even when Marius Rockraven, sobbing, hid his face in his hands. Loryn, with the first trace of sharpness, ordered him to drop his hands so that everyone could see his face. Tears blotched the boy's cheeks, and his stammered words sometimes verged on incoherence, but the light never wavered.

Neither Marius nor any of the circle added anything substantial to what Varzil already knew. The device had been tested in all its parts and had never shown any erratic response. No one had been overtired or unfit. Oranna's testimony in particular reinforced the care and thoroughness of the preparations. Felicia had gathered the circle with skill. There had been no forewarning of disaster.

The members of the circle described what happened next in different ways, using their own personal imagery. Just as each individual in a working circle presented a psychic presence according to the distinct pattern of his *laran,* so each experienced mental events differently. One person described a clashing and tearing of metal, another a bolt of searing light. All agreed that Felicia had tried to hold the circle together as long as she could, and that was perhaps why she herself had been injured. The consensus was that without her quick-minded and selfless action, they all might have suffered the same fate. She had died to save them.

When the circle had finished their testimony, Loryn glanced at Varzil, as if to say, *There is no villain here, only a heroine and the people who loved her.*

Varzil indicated with his glance that the questioning should continue. He dared not, by look or thought, indicate where his own suspicions lay. *Hold the truthspell . . . Listen and watch . . .*

A heartbeat and a breath restored his detachment. The next person to speak had little immediate knowledge of the project, only chance comments overheard at social occasions. One by one, the questioning proceeded, until it was Eduin's turn.

Eduin stepped forward, positioning himself to face Varzil directly. In the blue-white radiance, his face looked set and grim, far older than his years. He held his shoulders proudly, almost defiantly.

"You all know that I designed and constructed the matrix lattice Felicia used for this project," he said. "And it is not true that the device was without flaw. At first, in the early stages, it failed to integrate properly." He went on to describe technical details relating to materials and connections. "Felicia herself discovered that the primary stone was a solitary, and hence incapable of resonating in a coordinated manner with the other components."

"And the night of the accident?" Loryn asked. "What do you know about that?"

"I know no more than any of you, for I was not present. I had another commitment. I had already discussed this with Felicia, so my absence was not unexpected. I was not needed. She and I had completed all the testing. The lattice seemed to be in every way ready for execution."

Eduin turned so that the entire company could see his face. "I know of no reason why my device should have failed. If there was some fault which I overlooked, then the responsibility must be mine alone. I stand ready to accept whatever consequences may come. My only regret is that there is nothing in my power to undo what has happened."

Eduin spoke with such dignity and understated passion, that Varzil himself wondered if he had misjudged the man. Surely, if Eduin were guilty, if he had placed the trap-matrix within the lattice, he would not offer himself for judgment in such a forthright, public manner.

When the final questioning was over, Varzil dissolved the truthspell. The room emptied quickly. He slumped in the nearest chair, his mind too numb to think.

I must surely have been mistaken—I was confused by grief, exhausted by destroying the clingfire. *I had not rested properly. How could I perceive things correctly under those circumstances?*

Eduin, who had lingered to exchange a few words with Loryn, walked over. "I know this is a difficult time for you. Please believe me when I say that I harbor no ill will against you. We were boyhood companions together at Arilinn. We may not have always been friends, but we are now men and *laranzu'in,* capable of setting aside childish disputes. I hope that when the grief has lifted from your heart, we may be again on good terms."

Varzil thanked Eduin for his good will. "I do not know how much longer I will be at Hestral, but for the sake of my sister, Dyannis, whom we both hold dear, and for the years at Arilinn, I will do my best."

40

The Midwinter which Varzil spent at Hestral Tower was the most dismal he could remember. Storm followed storm, so that there was little difference between night and day. As the holiday approached, a pall settled over the entire population. Little hints of joy hovered in the shadowed corners, like thieves in the night or children who had crept downstairs after being sent to bed. No one could summon the energy for merrymaking. Outside the walls, the village sparkled with holiday bonfires, song, and the spiced aromas of cakes and mulled ale.

On Festival Night, the people from the village made a little caravan, bringing baked goods and garlands bedecked with red-and-blue ribbons. They sang as they climbed the hill to the Tower, their voices ringing in the still cold air. The night was very clear, the stars a milky sweep across the blackness of the sky.

The company of the Tower had gathered, as usual, in the commons. Loryn bade the villagers enter and welcomed them courteously. They sang a few songs and some of the younger people joined in. Then several got out flutes and drums. Each of the villagers took a partner from the Tower for a simple reel or two. A grandmother with cheeks like ripe apples drew Varzil into the dance and then winked at him with such spirit that he laughed aloud.

After the dancing, Loryn raised his hands and blessed the villagers, wishing them a year of prosperity, their fields and animals fertile, their children healthy, their borders safe.

"A man can't ask for more than that, *vai dom,*" one of the village men said, tugging on his forelock as he followed the others from the hall.

After they had gone, a hush fell across the room.

"It is usual at this time to invoke Aldones and Cassilda, Lord of Light and His Lady," Loryn said. "They, too, suffered loss. Grievous loss. Yet in their story, all men find hope."

"Aye, that's so," one of the older men said to a murmur of agreement.

"Yet I think, in this season, it is not to Light that we must look, but to Darkness. To Avarra, Dark Lady of the Night. To Zandru, master of the hells. Even as our world spins into the deep of winter, when it seems that the warmth and light of the sun will never come again, when life itself is held in abeyance, so are we here, in the winter of the soul. The wolves of chaos roam the countryside. Hope dwindles.

"Hope dwindles, yes, and men pay homage in blood and fear to the powers of the darkness. But hope does not die. All things have their season, and from each season we draw a different kind of strength. Trees send out their deepest roots in the snow, and the sweetest cherries ripen after a hard winter. So, too, with men, for it is these times which harden us, and in these darkest of nights, we face what we most fear and conquer it.

"So at this time, I do not offer you Cassilda's gift, the fruit of the *kireseth.* Instead, I bid you look to the winter of your own soul and the spring which will surely follow."

Stunned past reply, Varzil waited as the other Tower workers filed out, singly and in groups of two or three, to find solace where they could.

"Loryn, whatever possessed you to speak like that? We are all grieving, it is true, but—" he struggled with his own sadness, "—but surely this is a time for fellowship and revelry. Even in the midst of sorrow, we need the rhythm of the celebrations."

Loryn passed one hand in front of his eyes, as if to clear his vision of some invisible veil. "I—I do not know. I spoke as the words came to me. Perhaps it was Zandru himself who put them in my mouth for the purpose of generating despair."

"Despair? No, for you also spoke of hope," Varzil said. "But it seemed to be a hope of endurance, rather than renewal."

"Ah, my friend, that may well be, for in my dreams, some shadow yet hovers over us. I fear we have not seen the worst."

Varzil laid his fingertips gently upon the other man's arm. For a moment, he felt ashamed that he had been so lost in his own private grief for Felicia that he had been blind to the suffering of those around him. "Well, it is said that nothing is certain but death and next winter's snows. Whatever new hardships lie ahead, we shall meet them together."

Loryn shook his shoulders and his eyes cleared. He took Varzil's hand in his, an uncharacteristically direct touch between telepaths. "I am glad you are here."

Together, the two men left the commons hall, even as the fire was flickering out in its grate. Silence settled over Hestral Tower, a deep numbing quiet, and its inhabitants slept dreamlessly through the longest night of the year.

◆

There had been no question of Varzil returning immediately to Arilinn, for that winter was the worst within memory. The overcast days stretched on as one bank of swollen gray clouds followed another. Swirling gales made aircar flight impossible even in the lowlands. Roads and fields froze solid and animals shivered in their barns. Wolves came ravening down from their forests to harry the very young or the very old. Many babies sickened and died.

At Hestral, as at every other Tower within the relay network, there was more than enough work to do. Varzil was grateful to be occupied and useful. There were many sick people from the village and surrounding areas, cases of everything from frostbite to lung fever to the illnesses of the mind from too much close living and not enough sunlight. Some patients could not be sent home immediately, but required a period of convalescence. Loryn finally turned the common room hall into an infirmary. The kitchen was often given over to the preparation of medicines, so that the mingled smells of herbs and tinctures lingered in the air.

On too many nights, after he'd finished a long shift and was too exhausted to sleep, Varzil made his way down to the stone cellar. Felicia had been moved here at Oranna's suggestion not long after Midwinter, when space in the infirmary was needed by others. Oranna had, at Loryn's behest, constructed a small lattice that would maintain the stasis field without continuous input of thought-energy. She'd incorporated it into Felicia's pallet.

Felicia lay with a white blanket pulled almost to her chin. The cover was for the comfort of those who loved her, for although the cellar was almost as cold as the ground in which it was embedded, Felicia herself could suffer no hurt from it. No decay could touch her within the faintly shimmering field. Time itself slowed to a bare crawl. Centuries might pass without the slightest hint of change, except the slow accumulation of dust that managed, particle by particle, to sift through the energonic net of the field.

On such nights, Varzil lacked the strength to weep. His heart ached within him like an ancient wound. He thought of soldiers who had taken hurts in battle, wounds which throbbed with remembered agony decades after the flesh had healed, and of old men whose swollen, arthritic joints warned of storms approaching.

He would cup the ring between his hands, pressing its faint glow over his heart. Sometimes, the stone seemed to answer him; a whisper of presence, sweet as the first buds of spring, would brush against his mind.

Beloved, I am here . . .

And then the dark would cover him. He could no longer hold the bone-deep chill at bay. He would drag himself back to the realm of the living, to sit beside the small fire in his own rooms, rocking himself, gathering himself for the next day's work.

✦

Like all things, that terrible winter eventually passed. Spring came hesitantly, as if unsure of its welcome. The men who ventured forth into the muddy fields or stared up at the pale sky had not enough strength left to believe in it. Slowly, day by day, one blade of grass at a time, winter faded. One day, the fields were bare, lined by skeletal trees. By twilight, the rich damp smell of the earth was matched by the bright perfume of new leaves, of first blossoms. Everywhere, birds perched, wings fluttered. Nests sprang up like some new tree growth.

All through Hestral Tower, Varzil felt a quickening. Here and in the village below, people laughed as they stretched their arms and threw their heads back in the sun. Farmers sang in their fields. Herds bent their heads to the new grass and lost their winter gauntness.

As soon as the afternoons were warm enough to risk opening the windows, even a fraction, the *coridom* began a systematic cleaning and airing of each Tower wing in succession. The number of sick in the infirmary dwindled and the commons was restored to its usual service. Although Varzil still went down into the stone cellar regularly, he spent less and less time there. The ring, with its spark of living light, held far more of Felicia than the cask of her body.

Once winter's iron grip had broken, even the spring rains fell more gently than in other years. Travelers dared to venture forth. At first, only the hardiest of traders braved the muddy roads, but as one tenday melted into the next, more and more appeared.

And with them, soldiers.

The roads had barely dried, though the fields and hedgerows still glittered with moisture, when a company of armed men clattered up to the gates of Hestral Tower. They carried pennants with the Hastur fir tree, silver against blue.

Loryn went down to meet them at the gates of Hestral, along with his senior workers. He'd taken the time to put on his Keeper's robes and insignias of rank. "Come with me, Varzil, for I may have need of your counsel."

At his touch, the matrix lock released and the gates swung open. The Hastur captain sat on a tall dun horse with his men arrayed behind and to either side. His face and posture were vaguely familiar to Varzil; they must have met during the Midwinter Festival Varzil had passed at Hali, he and Carolin and his cousins, Lyondri and Rakhal, he who now sat upon Carlo's throne. And Maura and Jandria and her brother Orain. And Eduin.

The captain stared overly long at Varzil, clearly recognizing him in return.

My presence here may put Hestral at risk, Varzil sent the telepathic thought to Loryn. *Men have been executed and their homes burned to the ground for their sympathies. Rakhal knows of my friendship with Carolin Hastur.*

I do not think Rakhal Hastur would foment trouble with Arilinn, Loryn answered, *for he is too canny to risk the enmity of a Tower not under his control.*

Varzil followed Loryn through the open gate, acutely aware that beyond the protection of the matrix which kept out all weapons, he entered a world where another set of laws held. He lifted his chin. As *laranzu* and Keeper, he was hardly helpless. He knew how to defend himself. Only a madman would attack a Tower-trained worker, and then only once.

Still, the company of soldiers looked larger here, standing before them, than seen from above. The faces of the men were ruddy from long riding in the brisk spring air. A pair sat a little apart from the others, the hoods of their gray traveling cloaks drawn up around their faces. Varzil recognized them instantly as *laranzu'in* from Hali Tower, but although their minds might have touched many times on the relays, or one of them might have tended him after his adventure in the cloud-lake at Hali, the situation forbade them from greeting each other.

This is what war does, rends kin apart and sets men to kill those they once saved.

A young man, scarcely more than a boy, nudged his horse to the front, took out a trumpet and blew a fanfare, cried out, "By command of Rakhal Felix-Alar Gavriel, King at Hali and Hastur of Hastur!" then rattled off a string of additional titles and finished, "I bear a message for the Keeper of Hestral Tower."

The insult of omitting Loryn's name and rank was blatant. The Hastur force had not come with any conciliatory intention.

"On behalf of Hestral Tower, I greet you," Loryn said. "Our customs do not permit any men bearing arms within our precincts. If you will leave yours outside, you are welcome within. There we can discuss our business in comfort and privacy."

Nicely done, Varzil thought. With impeccable politeness, Loryn had made it impossible for the Hastur captain to do anything but answer directly.

The captain shifted in his saddle. "I'll stay as I am, although I thank you for your hospitality. My mission requires no secrecy. All here know that I have come on behalf of my liege and King, Rakhal Hastur, for the *clingfire* which is his due."

"I fear you have come in vain," Loryn responded in the same easy tone as before. "I have already sent word last year that what your master seeks no longer exists. It was destroyed some time ago."

"*Clingfire,* destroyed?" The captain made a gesture of derision, as if Loryn had made a casual reference to destroying rock or iron. "Even if it were possible, what fool would so disarm himself?"

Loryn paused for a moment before replying, "A fool, perhaps, who would seek some other solution to men's differences than raining liquid fire upon them. Ravaged lands nourish neither victor nor vanquished. I pray that thought will be of value to His Majesty, for it is the only answer I can give. I am sorry to send you back empty-handed. If he insists upon having *clingfire,* he will have to look elsewhere for its making."

"We thought you might have some such excuse." The Hastur captain squared his shoulders. His horse pulled at the bit and danced sideways. He hauled on the reins to hold it still. "So I am bid to say to you that one way or another, we will have *clingfire* from this Tower, as is our right. If your predecessors have been so unwise as to do away with it, then you shall make more. And speedily, too, for we have wars to fight, and they cannot wait."

Loryn, there is danger here. These men care nothing for honor or justice, only power. Go carefully.

I know, Varzil. I feared such a time might come even before the first messages from King Rakhal last year.

Varzil realized what Loryn meant to do and why he had asked for his support. Varzil might not speak formally for Arilinn Tower, but in a very real sense, Arilinn stood with Hestral.

"Hestral Tower makes no more *clingfire,* nor any other *laran* weapon," Loryn said.

"What madness is this? It must be *his* doing," the Hastur man pointed at Varzil. "Even in Hali, we have heard of Varzil of Arilinn and his seditious notions. He would persuade Towers to go renegade, to flaunt the lawful commands of their king!"

"It is true I have spoken my mind on the subject of *laran* weaponry, at Hali as well as Arilinn," Varzil said quietly. "I oppose those which kill from afar, so that the men who wield them need never look upon the faces of those who suffer, or put themselves at equal risk. But I have made no attempt to persuade *Dom* Loryn. He is Keeper here, the master of his own conscience."

"Perhaps not for long. Loryn Ardais, will you deliver up a stock of *clingfire,* as you have been rightfully commanded to do?"

"That I cannot," Loryn replied.

"Then at the order of Rakhal, Hastur of Hastur and King at Hali, I name you traitor! From this moment forth, your life and that of any who follow you is forfeit, and any man may slay you without penalty. Your bones will be buried in salted ground and your soul consigned to Zandru's coldest hell. You—"

Loryn tilted his head back and laughed. "You will have to catch me first! And if you'll pardon my saying so, you haven't had a good deal of luck catching Carolin Hastur either."

Don't taunt him, Loryn.

It is too late for soothing words. I would know the worst he has come to do.

"I give you until dawn tomorrow to consider your rash words, Loryn of Hestral. Then I will have either your obedience or your head—"

Loryn raised one eyebrow in skepticism.

"—if I have to tear down Hestral Tower, stone by stone, to get it!"

41

The Hastur captain departed within the quarter-hour. Later that day, the senior workers of Hestral Tower gathered in the Keeper's quarters to make plans. It was characteristic of Loryn that instead of issuing orders, he encouraged discussion and listened with grave concentration.

"Rakhal's affairs must be going badly indeed to render him so desperate," Varzil remarked. "Surely he must know how unlikely he is to get *clingfire* or anything else of military value from us. The tighter his grip, the more men are drawn to Carolin's cause."

"I have never heard that higher taxes and harsher punishments inspired men's loyalties," Oranna remarked. Her family had come from one of the little border kingdoms that Rakhal had swallowed up soon after taking the throne.

Loryn brought the debate back to what kind of attack Lyondri would most likely use and the best defensive strategy.

"You say there were two *leronyn* with him, Varzil," one of the older men said. "Did you recognize them?"

"I do not know them well," Varzil said. The Hali workers had kept their *laran* barriers raised, against the custom of friendly greeting between colleagues. "I suppose if we had handed over the *clingfire*," he went on,

371

"they were to have taken it into their care, but I do not think they expected it."

"I agree," Loryn said, nodding. "This captain wasn't chosen for his meekness or tact. His presence is a gesture of intimidation to anyone else who might defy Rakhal's orders. Hestral is a small Tower, and we do not supply anything of strategic importance to Hastur."

"Only healing and knowledge!" Oranna said. "We may be small in size, but what we do is hardly inconsequential."

"I agree with her, Loryn," Varzil said. "We could disappear overnight, and Thendara be no worse for it. Our importance is more symbolic—" *for what other Tower has dared to train a woman Keeper?* "—and now Loryn has made us a symbol indeed."

"A symbol of defiance, you mean," Eduin said, deliberately misunderstanding. "We could not have done anything else. They came here thinking to bully us ito submission, but they will come away with another lesson. *We* will teach *them* not to make idle threats against Hestral, or any Tower."

"What, are you suggesting we make our own *clingfire* to use against them?" Oranna said.

"I am merely pointing out that we are not powerless," Eduin said. "Too long have we of the Towers been servants to these Hundred Kings, many of whom have no more *laran* than my lady's lapdog! But it was not always so. At my last post, at Hali, I spent many long hours in the archives, cataloging and copying the old records. Once the *Comyn* made their own laws. Men were judged not by some accident of birth and rank, but by the strength of their *laran* and the uses they put it to. There were no limits save those of our own will! Any venture we could conceive, any problem which caught our imagination, any quest of mind or flesh—all this lay before us, ripe for the taking!"

"You speak of the Ages of Chaos," Varzil said gravely, "and of the abuses of power which ended them. The genetic breeding programs, designed to produce even stranger and more potent forms of *laran,* left us a legacy of horrors. Today we must still contend with the sicknesses that sprang from inbreeding. I fear it will be many generations before we can recover."

"I spoke of an Age of Opportunity, of freedom from the narrow vision of the head-blind," Eduin rushed on, but Loryn silenced him with a gesture.

"Some day we may have the pleasure of debating the morality of our ancestors and whether their world was indeed superior to ours. For now, we—like every generation before us—must face our own test. I cannot in all conscience accede to Rakhal Hastur's demands, and as Keeper, I am responsible for every person within these walls. If there are any who cannot abide my decisions," and here his gaze lingered first on Eduin, then Oranna, and finally Varzil, "I will attempt to arrange a truce under which you may leave Hestral for your own homes."

"Leave Hestral!" Oranna cried. "Abandon my home to that—that debauched *oudrakhi!*"

"You mistake me, Loryn," Eduin broke in, tight-lipped. "My intent was that we must resist not only this order, but *all* orders from usurpers! I will stay and fight with you. I beg you, give me command of Felicia's circle, so that I may smash Rakhal's army into bits!"

One of Loryn's eyebrows twitched upward, but his features remained otherwise composed.

Oranna said, "Are you mad, Eduin! You may be an excellent technician, but you cannot simply step into such a role, especially at a time like this. Besides, we already have two Keepers."

"Varzil?" Eduin cast him a sidelong glance. "He is only here because of Felicia's accident. He is not one of us."

"Let us hear from you, Varzil," Loryn said. "Eduin is right in this much, for our quarrel with Rakhal Hastur is none of yours. Arilinn is neutral in this affair."

"But I am not," Varzil said. "Carolin Hastur is my dearest friend and Rakhal, his enemy. Moreover, I have sworn to oppose all abuses of *laran*. In that sense, this quarrel is very much mine, not because I have sought it out but because I cannot turn away, not when it is within my power to resist."

Loryn nodded, his features lightening with relief. "Then together we will defend ourselves and our principles. Go and get something to eat, all of you. We must be ready when the Hastur forces make their first move."

The next moment, however, there came the faint, unmistakable clangor of bells from the village below. From his vantage point in the Tower, Varzil saw the soldiers swarming up the hill, the ranks on horseback and on foot. Blue-and-silver pennants rippled in the wind of their passing. The afternoon sun set their swords and spear points ablaze.

"Sweet gods!" one of the workers exclaimed. "He's sent an army!"

"He means to make a quick victory here," someone else said.

"The gates are spelled against any who bear arms," Loryn said, "but they are not the only way into the Tower. These men may bring grappling hooks and ladders. The walls must be reinforced. For this, I will need all your strength."

Varzil hurried after Loryn and a hastily assembled circle. He had not worked with these people before, excepting Eduin, and that had been many years ago at Arilinn.

They used the laboratory which had been Felicia's, for it overlooked the road leading from the village. The chamber had been cleaned and the worktable replaced so that no trace of the ruined matrix remained. Sweet herbs freshened the air and the residue of a cleansing spell still hung about the corners.

Loryn did not so much gather up the separate minds of his circle as open a space between them. Varzil found himself gazing into a well of clear light. It reflected the faces of the men and women of the circle, not as they appeared in the flesh, but with a timeless sense of presence.

Look, Loryn's mental voice resonated like the slow sweet tolling of an immense bell. *Look there.*

Varzil gazed into the chasm of light, and for an instant saw only a swirling of clouds. This quickly dissipated and in the clear space, he seemed to be everywhere at once. He saw the Hastur soldiers rushing the gates and felt the energon flows of the matrix locks rise and tighten at the approach of steel weapons. Drawn swords flashed into shafts of brilliance, as if catching the glare of the sun. Light and heat, as intense as any smithy's fire, burst from blade and spear point. A dozen or more blazed as if ignited from within.

The foremost soldiers hurled their weapons to the ground. A few fell to their knees, clutching their hands, while behind them, others hesitated, glancing from their wounded comrades to the Tower before them.

Sorcery . . . The whispers spread through the ranks.

"Forward! Attack!" screamed the captain.

Horns blared. A few of the men who had dropped their weapons turned and ran, but most of them held their ground. The bravest formed a wedge and hurled themselves bodily against the gates. At the first touch, the gates turned as hard as rock. Matrix-spelled, the wood could not be split by any ax or bent beneath any weight. With that preternatural clarity of vision, Varzil saw the forces binding each fiber glowing blue.

The harder they press the gates, the more unyielding the resistance. The vigor of their attack supplies the energy for the defense.

At the same time, Varzil realized the walls were of ordinary stone. They had been masterfully placed, but the passing centuries had weathered the rock and cracked the mortar. No spells bound them together. They could not withstand a determined *laran* assault.

The walls! he cried.

Watch, Loryn answered.

Smoothly, Loryn directed the linked minds of the circle into a river of power that flowed over the old fortress. In the clear light of their united minds, the walls now glowed faintly blue.

The Hastur men retreated from the gates. Many of the foremost had thrown down their swords and knives during the first onslaught. Some reached down with visible hesitancy, and then gathered up the weapons.

Loryn made no attempt to launch a counterattack, although the enemy was clearly demoralized and vulnerable. He allowed the soldiers to retreat back to the village.

Eduin scrambled to his feet, hands curling into fists. "Are we going to sit up here, doing nothing but deflecting one attack after another? Those filthy *ombredin* will not stop there. You know what will come next—fields and crops set ablaze, starvation next winter, hostages taken and executed, Zandru knows what other outrages."

"They will do these things whether we retaliate or not," Loryn said. "We cannot stop them by giving in."

"We *must*. Loryn, surely you see that! We can do far more than simply stand against them. We have the *laran* power to smash that army and send the Hastur captain running back to Thendara with his tail between his legs like a craven dog!"

Loryn shook his head. "Eduin, have you learned nothing in your time among us? I know very well what you mean to do, and it is not to shower those men with flower petals. If we use our *laran* against them, we may indeed prevail for a few days or even weeks. Sooner or later, they will come against us with a force we cannot match, whether *laran* or some terrible machine of war. We may not rain down *clingfire* or bonewater dust upon them, but that will not prevent them from doing the same, or worse, to us. Instead, let us keep this battle small and insignificant. Our best hope lies in persuading them that we have nothing they want."

Varzil did not think Rakhal Hastur would be swayed by this reasoning. A mouse might escape the notice of a hunting banshee by making itself very small, but only for a time. Sooner or later, the carnivorous bird would scent its prey and strike. So, too, would the men outside.

Eduin's posture clearly expressed his opinion that Loryn was a fool, but he had the sense not to say it. Tight-jawed, he excused himself and stalked from the room.

Varzil watched him go. Eduin's words filled him with apprehension. "He was ambitious when we trained together at Arilinn," he commented to Loryn, once they were alone in the chamber, "and I fear his disappointments and my own advancement have festered in his mind. He so clearly expected to be selected as Keeper, for he certainly has the innate strength."

"Eduin, like each of us, must find his own way. As for the other, you are right. He has powerful Gifts. I think eventually he might make a Keeper, but I have never seen in him that sympathy of mind to bring together the disparate personalities in a circle and make of them a single, harmonious whole. In another man, one less talented, I might say the fault lies in his own nature, but Eduin . . . there is something, some part of himself which he keeps apart and hidden. Yet," he continued, "Eduin has served Hestral well. His loyalty is above question."

"You have created a Tower of individuals who follow the dictates of their own conscience," Varzil said, "and now it is too late to instill blind obedience."

"I believe you are right," Loryn replied. "Even if I had known what would happen, I would not have chosen otherwise." A smile, like summer sun on water, flickered across his weary features. He took Varzil's proffered arm and leaned upon it, though such close physical touch was not the custom of telepaths. "Do you think our brothers down below have chosen this day's work as freely as we have?"

"I suspect few of them are here of their own accord," Varzil agreed, "but only by the command of their masters. And that is both their strength and their weakness."

"Yes, exactly so. Should we do as Eduin suggests and rain down destruction upon them because they are too loyal or too frightened to rebel against their lawful masters?"

"You already know my answer," Varzil replied.

"Ah yes, Varzil the idealist."

Loryn moved toward the door. "Now I must finish this day's business. You should rest as well, for we will need all our strength against whatever they throw at us tomorrow.

42

Mounted men rushed the gates of Hestral Tower in volleys, only to be repulsed. They had learned from their earlier failures, for this time few of them carried metal weapons. Instead, they brought up a battering ram, a solid old tree from along the river, many of its branches still intact.

Crash! Crash!

Varzil joined the circle to reinforce the gates. Hour after hour passed as the thumping and pounding reverberated throughout the Tower. The men below worked in relays, so that as each group tired, another came to take their place. They broke off only as the light faded from the sky.

No sooner had Varzil eaten the food laid out for him in the commons hall and returned to his chamber, aching with weariness in every joint, than a cry went out from the watchers posted high in the Tower. The attack had resumed.

The three *leronyn* in Lyondri's army came forward, barely discernible in the gathering dusk. They gathered together near the base of the hill, well out of reach of any physical counterassault, and spun their own circle. To Varzil, on watch, it had the semblance of a spider's web.

And they will have as little power over us as the silk they spin, came Serena's mental voice.

Varzil was not so sure. What did any of them truly know of *laran* warfare, which pitted one Tower against another, save for ballad and whispered tale? The Peace of Allart Hastur brought a time in which those horrors were all but forgotten.

The spells came snaking up the hill like threads of darkness. Moment by moment, they gathered substance. They darted at the walls, as if seeking to insinuate their slender tips between the particles of mortar and enter through the very pores of the stone.

With every contact, Varzil felt the glitter of clashing energies as the *laran* shields held. The blue glow intensified. He bent all his trained power to the pattern that Loryn had set into the walls below.

Hold . . . hold . . . hold . . . pulsed through the circle, each syllable a separate heartbeat. Varzil had no other thought than the energon flows binding each mote of stone and mortar. In his mind, he saw the walls as a patterning of elemental forces.

Hours slipped away in a numbing trance. From time to time, he became aware of the touch of Oranna's mind as she monitored the condition of his body. It was a flicker only, for he had long ago learned the proper posture and breathing for strenuous *laran* work. All she could do was ease and support, for there was no question of dissolving the bonds that unified them. The Hestral circle dared not falter. Any break in their concentration might give the *leronyn* below the opening they needed. They could only endure and hold fast until the psychic battering ceased.

Eventually, in the darkest hours, Varzil felt an emptiness in place of the relentless pressure of the Hastur circle.

Loryn dissolved the circle. One of the workers gasped for air before collapsing forward on the table. Oranna rushed to his side. Her face, too, was so pale as to appear bloodless. Numb and drained, Varzil made his way to his chamber, where he fell across his bed, still in his working robes.

✦

That afternoon, Varzil was heading down to the kitchen when he heard voices, hushed and tense, below him. The speakers were hidden by the curve of the stairs, their voices echoing in the tall open space.

"With every word, you disprove your own argument," Loryn whispered.

Varzil turned to go back upstairs. There could be only one person Loryn would speak to in that way.

"Never mind about me! When are you going to do something, instead of sitting here like a pile of laundry, passively deflecting whatever devilry they think of?" Eduin demanded, his words now rising with each phrase. "Can't you see that only encourages them to escalate the attack?"

"I have said there will be no more discussion of this. Dissension only aids our enemies by setting us against one another. If you cannot accept this, then I will arrange for you to leave Hestral under truce or else confine you to solitary meditation."

"No!" Eduin's breath came audibly, bordering on a sob. "I want to fight the Hasturs!"

Some sense in Varzil came alert. Eduin meant more than merely defending the Tower against Rakhal's arrogant demands. In a moment of unguarded passion, Eduin had phrased it rightly. He passionately wanted to fight Hasturs, but for what reason, Varzil could not guess.

◆

The next morning, a messenger rode up the hill under truce colors and demanded Hestral's surrender. He returned without an answer. Then the soldiers arrived in their formation and began the day's attack. That night, the three workers from Hali tried different spells upon the gates, all with as little success as before. Both sides seemed to be settling into a pattern.

The *coridom* had asked Loryn's permission to return to his family and Loryn agreed, sending the man out under a banner of neutrality. One of the Hastur guards met with him and, after a few words, attacked the old man with the flat of his sword. The *coridom* scrambled back up the hill, panting with terror.

Varzil watched from the tower balcony. He felt the binding upon gate and wall strengthen, even as the *coridom* slipped through. There would be no second time, if the Hastur captain knew his business.

During a brief respite, Loryn organized the Hestral workers into two circles, the second one under Varzil, and a group of watchers. This way, everyone might rest while the Tower maintained a continuous guard. The whispered wisdom was that as long as Hestral stayed on the alert, there was nothing the besiegers could do.

Varzil stretched his aching body on his bed and folded his hands across his chest. The posture, one he had used hundreds of times for deep meditation, triggered relaxation. He tensed every part of his body and then, using his breath and energon control, released it. His heartbeat slowed and each inhalation brought a flood of oxygen to his cells. A tide of cleansing energy rose and fell, from the center of his diaphragm to the tips of his fingers and toes. His thoughts quieted.

With deliberate intent, he extended his consciousness deeper. Originally, he had practiced the technique to drop into rapport with another worker. Now he shaped his focus, keeping his mind receptive. He felt the wood and leather of his bed, still humming with life, and below them the carpet . . . the stone floor . . . the swirling air beyond the outer walls . . . the singing joy of the river . . . the fields like cradles of life, teeming with roots and stalks and many-legged creatures . . . and finally to the far mountains, reaching like monks in prayer to the arching heavens. With each breath, he gathered them into himself, he felt their strength and stillness fill his energon channels and then recede.

Something pulsed nearby, bright and warm. A strangely familiar perfume suffused him. He thought of an arpeggio played on a *rryl,* of sun dappling spring leaves. Sweetness rose in him, answering, as if his own heart were a bell lightly tapped.

Felicia.

Though his body did not move, his mind shifted toward the ring on his hand. Her wordless presence answered him. One way or another, the siege would be resolved, the realm would pass from one liege to the next, and yet the mountains would endure, spring would come again in its proper time, lovers would find joy in each other's arms, babies would cry aloud in delight.

And this, he thought as he rose from the depth of his healing trance, *this we will have forever.*

✦

Dusk blotted light from the sky. In the preternatural vision of the circle, Varzil, working as its Keeper, saw the fires that sprouted from the main buildings of the village. A group of villagers stood in the marketplace. Their cries rose toward the smoking heavens. Women clutched their young children tightly against their skirts, while their men muttered curses and clenched fists or hidden knives, but made no overt move against the armed and mounted men. One villager, a stout, bearded man with massive shoulders, shouted for a fire brigade. The Hastur captain struck him with a sword and he lay unmoving on the shadowed field.

"So much for your precious Tower!" the captain growled. *"Did you think*

they'd protect you? They shut themselves up like cowards while your homes are burning! Where are they? Why do they not come to your aid?"

The next instant, fractured lightning shot through the Hestral circle. Rage surged up in Eduin; the chamber reeled with it. Someone cried out—Marius Rockraven. Varzil, in centripolar position, took the brunt of the energon flare. Oranna smoothed over the shock, her mental touch like balm over his nerves. He felt the circle grow clear and steady once more.

The village burned like a torch against the night. The terror of the villagers rippled through the darkness like invisible smoke.

Varzil stretched out his mind. Up the river, he sensed a buildup of moisture, a tension between earth and sky.

Marius? Can you feel the rain clouds?

The boy's awareness unfolded like a fisher's net. *Yes . . . It is not a storm yet, but if the winds shift like this*—a series of images which Varzil felt as layers of color and heat—*it will be.*

Marius, you must bring the rain here.

The boy's reflexive shudder rippled through the circle, but the unity held.

—not without the matrix—I can't—I'll ruin everything—

Varzil caught bits of frantic thought, and with the same deliberate care he had used to break down the *clingfire,* he separated out each particle of fear.

You can do this, Marius. You were born with the strength and talent for it. See how naturally your mind reaches out to the weather currents. Trust your instincts instead of trying to control them. Let your senses guide you.

But I don't know how!

This is not a thing you need to know, only to feel.

Under Varzil's words, Marius grew calmer. The patterns of his mind changed from a gossamer net, barely solid enough to hold the gentlest breeze, to a silken tapestry, supple and light but impenetrable. Varzil anchored him as he spread wider and higher. The clouds had not yet formed completely, moisture-laden air with only the potential to condense. Marius wove his mind through the layers, tapping into the temperature and electrical potentials.

Don't think about what you're doing . . . Varzil said. *Just feel it . . . You don't have to control the clouds, only give them direction.*

Thunder rumbled beyond any human ears, a shivering in the air, a tinge of ozone. Clouds piled one on the other, growing rapidly in size and speed as they responded to the *laran* forces. Varzil, and the circle with him, rode the currents, felt the gathering power.

Now the burning village came into view. Already, the roofs and upper stories of the headman's house and the larger craft halls were gone and their beams burned with a deep steady blaze. Adjacent buildings made a smear of brilliance against the night. Brightness answered from deep within the clouds, jagged explosions of lightning. Faces turned upward, ovals of paleness reflecting orange flame.

Anger pulsed once more from Eduin and his thoughts rang out, *Hit them with the lightning! Kill them all!*

No . . . Smoothly, firmly, Varzil directed the interwoven *laran* forces with his own will. He sent Marius an image of water running free.

Just let go. Let the clouds do their work.

The next instant, rain began to fall. Smoke billowed from the burning buildings. Men cried out, in joy and in alarm. In the Hastur camp, the *leronyn* desperately tried to summon a wind to dissipate the storm.

Still the rain came, no longer sweet and gentle, but harder with every passing moment. The storm took on a life of its own, and it seemed that every effort of the Hastur circle to divert the clouds only aroused them to greater fury. The artificially summoned winds lashed the rain, driving it against the smoldering buildings. The soldiers rushed for cover, leaving the villagers to fend for themselves. The swollen river lapped its banks.

Smoke still rose from scattered pinpoint sources as the last remaining fire succumbed to the rain. The square was transformed into a field of beaten mud. The winds subsided, leaving the rain to fall like a misty veil.

Marius freed the storm to go where it would, where the natural forces of air and temperature took it. Eventually, it would run its course, but for the moment, it seemed caught between hill and river.

Only then did Varzil release the circle. His hands trembled as he ran them through his hair, an old gesture he used to gather his composure. Across the table, one of the women drew a sobbing breath.

The rain fell, lightening steadily, for three more days, during which the Hasturs made no attempt to attack again. Hestral Tower used the respite to rest. Villagers began moving to outlying farms, their belongings piled on carts or packs. Even the youngest child trudged along under a heavy burden. Serena, following them on the matrix screens, reported the theft of food, horses, and cattle. The Hastur army wasn't going to give up easily; they were clearly settling in for a long siege.

43

A tenday later, Varzil was sitting in the common room, lingering over a mug of *jaco* laced with powdered roasted blackroot. Serena, who had taken the last relay shift of the night, crossed to the sideboard and poured herself a mug. Settling herself in a chair beside Varzil, she sniffed and wrinkled her nose.

"Ugh. Blackroot. I hate blackroot."

Varzil grinned and indicated his own half-full mug. "So do I. In a few more days, it'll be just blackroot if we want anything hot to drink. Either that, or some herbal concoction which is even worse." He paused. "Any word from Hali Tower?"

Serena shook her head. She looked younger than her years, with bruise-colored circles beneath her eyes. "They haven't formally broken off contact, they just say they have no messages, nor will they receive any. I suppose it's to be expected. How could they remain apart from this—" She gestured toward the window overlooking the fields where the Hastur forces were encamped. *Unless they mean to defy the Hastur King, as Tramontana did.*

"Any word on my inquiry?" he asked. "The records?"

"No, but I do not think they would keep that sort of information from you. It may well be that it does not exist, or has been lost over the years."

Varzil ran the fingers of one hand over Felicia's ring in what had now become an unconscious habit.

If there is any way to restore her . . .

Varzil, there's movement down below, came the mental voice of Marius, on watch that morning.

Varzil went to the window. The Hastur soldiers had indeed begun to gather at the base of the hill. As yet, there was no sign of impending attack. The men were not even in formation. The rain had barely ceased, and the ground was still muddy. If they charged, it would be uphill and on uncertain footing, highly vulnerable. No wonder the captain was cautious.

It was time to form the circle that would keep Hestral safe for another day. Varzil took one last bite of nutbread and headed for the chamber that by now had become like a second home to him. He sent a telepathic signal to the other members of his circle to meet there.

Something was subtly wrong, for the *leronyn* he summoned were already enmeshed in some kind of circle, along with others who normally worked with Loryn.

Halfway up the stairs, Varzil felt the screams from the fields below, even though he could not hear them. The sensation of gut-clawing cold struck him, so sudden and intense it was almost a physical blow. It was as if a thousand fevered nightmares had been condensed into one horrific vision and then hurled like a projectile. He staggered and caught his balance against the wall. His fingers scraped against the stone hard enough to draw blood. The pain brought him back to his own body.

He had caught only the edge of a powerful fear spell, and then only because his thoughts had been open, his barriers lowered. It had not been aimed at him.

Who, then?

Varzil spread his *laran* senses outside the Tower walls and down the hill to where he had last seen the Hastur men. With his inner eye he saw them now, staggering or lying curled on the ground, racing here and there, struggling with one another. Though he could not hear them, their mouths stretched in howls of agony. One man had clawed out his own eyes, leaving bloody sockets. Another had drawn his sword and was hacking away at his leg. Blood spurted from the arm of another where he had already severed his wrist with a battle ax.

Confusion rose like a dreadful miasma from the field. The very air, through his psychic senses, seethed with panic, with the stench of terror too great to bear. These men were not cowards, but seasoned veterans. Yet the bravest of them could barely keep his feet.

Blood drenched the soft wet earth, mixed with other things. Two men, officers by their helmets, had taken their swords to their own bellies and lay writhing in the blue-gray ropes of their intestines.

The Hastur soldiers struggled as if blinded or bewitched by things that were not there. In flashes, as if his own vision were illuminated by mental lightning, Varzil saw what they did. Demons straight from Zandru's hells, blue with cold, clung to the bodies of the men. The demons were as varied as nightmares, horned and many-legged, some with forked tongues as thick as a man's wrist, others with seven eyes or scorpions' tails, the claws of a cloud leopard or the hideous hooked beak of a banshee. Many held whips or hammers with which they beat at the men or bound them, sinking fangs deep into flesh.

Illusion, all of it. *Something—someone—*had roused the deepest childhood terror of each man's mind and brought it into searing form.

Pity swept through Varzil. He had had his own share of frightening dreams as a boy. But he had always known they were dreams and that soon he would awaken.

Blessed Cassilda, who has done this?

His own guts turned cold as Varzil realized he would find the answer aloft in the Tower. He climbed a stair and then another. It seemed to him that everything which had gone before in his life had been easy, whether it had been running away that first night he came to Arilinn or facing the catmen in their caves or even what he had witnessed at the bottom of Hali Lake. Those times had been frightening and difficult, but he had had no choice. Fate had brought him to them and it had never occurred to him to run away.

All he had to do was close his mind and retreat back down the stairs. Eduin's circle would do its work. One by one, the Hastur men would fall prey to their own madness until nothing remained of the army. Word would speed back to Rakhal that Hestral Tower was not to be trifled with.

And men would die, those who still fought for life, helpless against the spells that bound their minds. Pain and death would be the price of Hestral's freedom.

He had stayed at Hestral, rather than retreat to Arilinn under the safety of his neutrality, because of his oath to oppose any abuse of *laran*. Whether that came from Dalereuth's illegal *clingfire* laboratories or from the *leronyn* below or from within Hestral itself made no difference.

He climbed.

They were very much as he expected to find them, a rough circle with Eduin seated in the Keeper's position and four others, all strong men. No white-robed monitor sat to the side, ensuring their health. Eduin's face was a mask of concentration and black triumph.

Varzil paused on the threshold to steel himself for what he must do. From his very first days at Arilinn, he had been taught the sanctity of the circle. Once joined, their very sanity was given over to the hands of their Keeper. He was the sole director of their combined mental and physical concentration. There could not be two Keepers in one circle, which is why he had subordinated himself so completely to Loryn's command when they first mounted the defense of Hestral.

Nor could a circle be lightly broken. Even with a monitor, it was dangerous to disturb the convergence of *laran* energies. Too abrupt a dissolution, and nerves could misfire, causing seizures and worse, hearts could stop completely or beat in such an uncoordinated manner that death would surely follow. Energon channels, which carried both sexual and psychic energy, could overload. The backlash could sweep the circle, affecting every member. Varzil had heard of one such case where all that was left of the unfortunate *leronis* was a charred husk. When he had first heard the tale back at Arilinn, he had thought it an exaggeration, a teaching story, but he did not think so now.

Eduin was a strong telepath, skilled enough to focus and direct the *laran* of a circle, even an improvised one like this. Only a Keeper, or someone with that potential, could create the nightmare illusions in so many men below.

Pity rose up in Varzil, mixed with loathing of the waste of such talent. He did not know why Eduin had never been selected for Keeper training, first at Arilinn and now here at Hestral, this most experimental of Towers. Whatever chance Eduin might have had, he had now thrown it away. No Tower would train a man who had proven himself so reckless, so willful, so defiant of every principle of circle discipline.

If Eduin were the only one involved, Varzil would have jarred him out of his trance, even if it meant seizing Eduin's starstone with his bare hands. He knew the risk of serious, even fatal consequences. Carolin had almost died that way, that winter at Hali.

Eduin had been there. . . .

Fury surged through Varzil. He had suspected Eduin then, but had no proof. Carolin, in his firm belief in the goodness of other men, had defended Eduin. But Carolin had been wrong about his cousin Rakhal, too.

The others in Eduin's circle, men who believed they were protecting Hestral Tower, *they* did not deserve such a fate.

Instead of intruding upon the circle, Varzil took a moment to calm himself and focus his own thoughts. He knew Eduin's psychic signature all too well, from the long hours they had worked together at Arilinn. Eduin had developed over the years, grown stronger and brasher, but he could not change the basic pattern of his mind. Varzil attuned his own *laran* energies and slipped into rapport with the circle.

No one had noticed his approach, but that was not unusual for the degree of concentration involved. He felt not a ripple of response, only a slight intensification of Eduin's exhilaration. With the addition of Varzil's mental power, Eduin's emotions veered toward euphoria.

It is ill done to take joy in another man's destruction.

Eduin's attention turned then from the bloody field below to Varzil's presence within his own circle. Before he could react, Varzil struck, jamming the energy connections that bound Eduin to the others. As neatly as a boning knife slipped beneath the skin of a felled deer, he inserted himself into the circle as Keeper and shoved Eduin out.

Eduin's cry echoed in the chamber like the ring of iron on stone. As quickly as he could, taking care for the safety of the other *leronyn,* Varzil dissolved the circle. One by one, they opened their eyes, stretched taut shoulders, looked around.

"Varzil! What—"

Varzil moved swiftly to the table, where Eduin slumped over, graceless and unmoving as a corpse. He knew from the light rapport that remained between them that Eduin was not dead, only deeply unconscious.

"By Aldones' Holy Light! What happened?"

Varzil straightened up, drawing all the authority of a Keeper about him. "What you have done here violates our most sacred oaths. You have used your powers to enter the minds of other men with deliberate malice. Why not burn down the gates and issue a formal invitation to Rakhal's men while you are at it? Today you have done far more to destroy this Tower and everything it stands for than to defend it."

"We thought—Eduin said—" one of the men stammered. At Varzil's words, his face went ashen with shock.

"We have no time for excuses now," Varzil cut him off. "There is no telling what may come of this, but we must be prepared. You—and you—carry Eduin to his chambers. You—fetch a telepathic damper."

"He already has one," the man said, visibly miserable. "He needed it—he *claimed* he needed it for his privacy."

"Did he, now? How very convenient." Varzil heard the venom in his own voice. If he gave into anger and vengefulness, then what would become of justice?

An invisible shadow passed over him, a shadow of light instead of darkness, and it seemed to lift him out of himself. For a moment, his human frailties receded and he saw himself as the origin of that light, casting it from one end of Darkover to the other, a beacon in the darkness, a name on men's lips stretching into the unimaginable future.

The pulse of radiance faded, leaving a sense of wordless compassion. Varzil moved to Eduin's side and laid one hand on his forehead. The gesture was part comfort, part diagnosis, part blessing.

The poor benighted fool. We may never know what drove him to throw away all that potential, all that brilliant talent. May Aldones grant him peace, for the human world is not likely to.

"Carry him gently, and stand guard over him that he may not do himself any harm," Varzil told the others. "I will confer with Loryn about what is to be done next."

One of the men picked up Eduin's arm and draped it across his shoulders. "And us, *vai dom?* What about us?"

Varzil suspected they would devise their own punishments, far more severe than anything he or Loryn would impose.

✦

Below the Tower, the muddied road and fields lay quiet except for the soldiers carrying away their dead or maimed comrades. The Hastur *lero-*

nyn moved about them, using their powers to ease the worst. Some of the remaining villagers came out to help, but under no discernible coercion.

The sky clouded over later that day and then it began to rain. There was almost no wind and the rain, falling straight as the Arilinn Veil, was surprisingly warm. Varzil thought the heavens themselves wept for what had been done, and then as quickly dismissed the idea as self-indulgent fancy. Or perhaps guilt, because he had suspected Eduin, he had seen every indication that Eduin might try something desperate and foolish, and yet had done nothing to prevent it. He had left the matter to Loryn, which was correct according to Tower etiquette, but did not absolve him of the responsibility.

He would see justice done by Eduin, though he did not know what form it might take.

In the Keeper's private chambers, Varzil listened to the testimony of the other workers in Eduin's circle. They entered one by one, shamed and chastened, with varying degrees of defiance. The watery gray light made the room seem colder than it really was. Loryn himself sat immobile, leaving Varzil to ask the questions.

"I thought—this siege will go on and they will sit there, slowly draining our strength while we starve," one man said. "All the while our friends in the village lose their homes, their crops, who knows what else. I thought Eduin had the right of it."

Loryn did not answer, either aloud or in his thoughts. He looked gray, on the edge of shock, an exhaustion of spirit as well as flesh. His shoulders sagged.

"We had the power to destroy them," the man went on, his words tumbling one over the other but with an odd cadence which told Varzil these were not his own, but Eduin's. "Why not use that power? Why not make the price of aggression too high for even a madman like Rakhal?"

"Those men down there did not choose that fate," Varzil pointed out. "They are ordinary soldiers who fight with sword and spear and they were following the commands of those they had sworn to obey. What defenses had they against an attack on their very minds? You, on the other hand, decided they should die in terror. Do you take upon yourself the prerogatives of a god? Have those men somehow turned into beasts you may slaughter as you will?"

Although Varzil spoke mildly, the man's certainty crumbled. "I—I am no such monster. I thought it was the right thing to do. Eduin was so persuasive, so sure. He said that since we have the power to stand against tyranny, we must use it."

"Is Eduin the keeper of your conscience?" Varzil demanded.

For a stunned moment, the man stared at him. "Who, then, am I supposed to believe?"

Who, indeed? Varzil asked himself. *A Keeper too weak to instill proper discipline? A usurper king bent on only his own lust for power?*

The Compact, if it ever came into reality, would be only a beginning, a single underlying point of honor between all men. The Towers themselves needed more, because they wielded so much greater potential for discord and destruction. Varzil did not know what form that might take—a league of Keepers, a codification of ethics and tradition. Something must be worked out, or Darkover would descend from instability into chaos.

Nothing in this world is certain but death and next winter's snows, went the old saying. Add to that, Varzil thought, the propensity of men to abuse however much power they had.

When they had finished, all but one truly regretted what he had done. Varzil suggested to Loryn that he be removed from work and, when the fighting was over, be sent to Arilinn or Hali for better training. The man accepted the judgment with surprising good grace, as if he realized that this was his only chance to continue in a legitimate Tower.

Serena tapped on the door. "Eduin's waiting if you're ready for him."

"Let him come," Loryn said.

Eduin walked in and, with a nod to Loryn, sat in the chair in the center of the chamber. Though his *laran* barriers were tightly raised, Varzil sensed the waves of fury resonating through his mind.

I had them! I would have won the day, but for that interfering, sanctimonious Varzil! And now he is to sit in judgment of me. Insufferable!

"Eduin," Loryn began in a heavy, slow voice, "you have committed a grave offense against both this Tower and the principles of human decency."

Eduin's chin jerked up. "I am not the offender, as well you know. It is Rakhal Hastur and his wolves—although that is an insult to the wolves—who generated the present crisis. I—*we*—were not the ones to initiate this violence, but we will be the ones to end it. That is, if we are not crippled by those with their own private grievances to pursue." He glared at Varzil.

Varzil blinked, startled by Eduin's vehemence. "We have never had an easy comradeship, you and I, if that is what you mean. That is not the issue here. I am neither your prosecutor nor your judge. Your actions alone indict you."

"Eduin, you brought together a circle although you have not been trained as a Keeper, and against my direct wishes," Loryn said. "Matrix work is difficult and dangerous enough, even with the best training. You risked not only your own life and mind, but those of the men who trusted you. This—" he sighed deeply, as if the very act of speech pained him, "—cannot be allowed. Not only that, you escalated the conflict with Rakhal Hastur's men. You—"

"I *ended* the conflict! I did what no one else in this Tower had the *cojones* to do." Eduin gestured toward the gates and the fields beyond them. "Who is left to attack us now?"

"That is not the point," Loryn said. "If you will not listen to reason, I have no choice but to confine you under guard until your fate can be decided."

Eduin scrambled to his feet and pointed at Varzil. "This is all *his* doing!"

Varzil, stung, rose also. It seemed only right that he should face Eduin's accusations on his feet.

"Can't you see?" Eduin screamed. "He's using the incident to promote a personal vendetta against me! Ever since we were students at Arilinn, he's disliked me. He's used every opportunity to besmirch my character, to turn others against me. Carolin Hastur was my friend until Varzil poisoned his mind. Even his own sister was taken in by his self-serving manipulations! You have a scorpion-ant in your midst, Loryn! Take care you do not nurse him at your bosom, or you will discover to your sorrow how treacherous he can be!"

The door flung open and two of the senior workers rushed in. One carried a telepathic damper, the other an open vial. Varzil caught a whiff and recognized one of the many distillations of *kireseth*. Some worked by lowering *laran* barriers, but others, like this one, temporarily blocked all psychic abilities. Its use was rare but not unknown, for *laran* was no guarantee of self-control. Sometimes, an adolescent in the throes of threshold sickness became so disoriented as to pose a danger to himself and all around him.

Eduin recognized the drug, too, for he drew back. "You will have no need for such with me. *I* am not your enemy."

"Will you give your solemn word that you will make no effort to escape or harm anyone in this Tower?" Loryn said.

Eduin's shoulders lifted minutely. "As long as Hestral stands and the Hastur menaces us, I will abide by your rule. Will that satisfy you?"

"I think it must," Loryn replied. He signaled to the others to escort Eduin back to his own quarters.

Varzil thought that Eduin had chosen his words too carefully, but could discover no fault in what he had said.

"I do not know what has distressed me most," Loryn said, "these days of attack and siege, or Eduin's misguided heroism, or his excuses. I am tired, Varzil, tired of this interminable tension between hope for the future and despair that no matter what we do, things only get worse."

Varzil sought for words, but none came. Loryn had aged visibly since he had arrived at Hestral, and he did not think the present warfare was entirely responsible.

A Keeper carries a heavy burden, he thought. *Not only for the work we do, but for what we* are. He wondered if it were too great for any one person to bear. *But what choice has Loryn? What choice have I? We neither of us can undo what we have become.*

The thought came to him, with a little shiver of premonition, that the same was true for Eduin.

44

One long day stretched into another without any further attack from the Hastur camp. The rain stopped and the mud dried. After a single sunny day, however, the sky turned gray and sullen, brooding. All of Hestral Tower rested, at first gratefully, then with increasing anxiety. Any attempt to leave the Tower walls was promptly turned back by the remaining soldiers. Food supplies dipped even lower, although there was water enough from their own deep wells.

"I don't understand why they don't just go home," Oranna said fretfully. Varzil had joined her at the commons hall window watching the sunset with mugs of steaming plain water. She disliked plain water even more than brewed roasted blackroot. "We won't give in to them, and if they weren't strong enough to overpower us before, they certainly aren't now. Sooner or later, we'll break out. I don't understand what Loryn is waiting for."

Varzil held his peace. He had been on watch all afternoon and was too tired to argue. He and Loryn had been in contact with the other Towers, searching for a way out of the impasse.

"It is not yet over," he said. "The Hasturs are waiting for something, or they would have left already."

"Reinforcements from Thendara? Would they be so foolish?"

Varzil was certain of it. "Next time, they will take no chances, but will send an overwhelming force. There are many who would see a successful resistance as a sign, a call to action. At the same time, Rakhal dares not put himself into a public position of incompetence, which will surely happen if he makes a show of force here and then fails."

She looked thoughtful. "Then why press the issue at all? Why not accept our first answer, that we had no *clingfire* to surrender? Whatever was the King thinking of?"

"Ah, who can tell? It was many years ago when I met him, and even then he was so involved in court politics, it was difficult to tell what sort of person he was. Once, Carolin loved and trusted him, and showered him with favors. Yet people change, or perhaps life itself changes them, and sometimes they hide their true nature."

"Perhaps somewhere there is still the man who was worthy of Carolin's goodwill," Oranna said with a brief, bright smile.

Varzil found himself smiling back at her. "You have such faith in people, *carya*. It is part of what makes you a good monitor. I fear that in this case, it is misplaced. Let us hope that even men such as Rakhal may come to see reason."

He broke off. That had indeed been Loryn's hope, that by refusing to retaliate or further provoke their besiegers, Hestral might calm the situation until a peaceful settlement might be found, some kind of compromise.

Varzil went to sit in one of the big comfortable chairs beside the now-bare fireplace. His body, tense and aching with fatigue, sank into the cushions. He let his head rest against the chair's high back. As he closed his eyes, his thoughts wandered to that time, so many years ago, when he had entered the cave of the catmen with no idea of how he might succeed, only the determination to do whatever was necessary to free his brother.

If I, a mere boy, could reach the catmen, who were not even human, then surely it must be possible to find some way out of this deadlock . . . some way besides Eduin's.

Varzil drifted toward sleep. Once more, he wandered through caves dim in the light of hand-held torches. Passages opened before him. He pushed on, searching for something. The tunnels grew darker as he outstripped the fragile orange glow. Ahead, he saw light like a pale shadow. It grew stronger, colorless and cool, as he rushed toward it. He recognized it as the Overworld, and he knew that something—or someone—drew him there.

The darkness of the cavern dropped away. Between one hurried step and the next, he burst into the gray landscape of the Overworld that lay above and beyond any physical dimension.

A woman stood before him, arms outstretched, gauzy gown blown in an unfelt wind. A clear white radiance, like the light in the heart of the ring stone, shone from her body. Her hair framed her face in an aureole of red curls. His heart leaped as he recognized her—

Felicia!

A smile brightened her features and she moved toward him. He saw that her mouth moved, shaping his name, although no sound reached him.

Varzil . . . Varzil . . .

The voice was not Felicia's, but another's, and it did not come from ahead of him, where Felicia beckoned, but from behind, from the twisted cavern passages. He hesitated, knowing he must answer that summons, yet unwilling to turn away. To see her, whole and beautiful, before him, to take her into his arms, even insubstantial Overworld arms—

VARZIL!

The next instant, he was back in his chair in Hestral's commons, and someone was shaking his shoulders, shouting his name. He started awake. His eyes focused on the face bent over him—Marius Rockraven. The boy's cheeks were pale and his eyes looked bruised. Behind him, Varzil spotted Oranna and Serena.

"Varzil!" Marius cried again. "Please wake up! We need you!"

Varzil swept the dregs of fatigue and sleep from his mind. He sat up. "What has happened?"

"I was at the relays—and word came from Hali—for Loryn. They said—it couldn't wait. But Loryn—I knocked, called him—he didn't answer—I didn't want to wake him if he was that tired." Marius gulped. "Should I try again? What do I tell Hali?"

"It's all right," Varzil said, getting to his feet. The brief sleep had been unexpectedly deep and the worst of the ache had faded from his muscles. "Oranna, go check on Loryn."

"On my way," she said, and whirled to go.

"I'll talk to Hali." Varzil started toward the stairs leading to the relay chamber. Marius hurried after him.

Varzil settled himself on the bench and found it still warm. The relay lattice hummed with light. Marius had adjusted it to his own comfort and Varzil found the tuning hard-edged. He unfocused his eyes, letting his thoughts sink into the pattern, and shifted it. Even as he did so, he felt the mind on the other end of the invisible linkage.

Loryn of Hestral? The mental voice held no warmth, yet sounded vaguely familiar. Varzil wondered if it might not be one of the *leronyn* he had met during one of his visits to Hali Tower, perhaps even one who had helped him after his adventure in the cloud-filled lake.

No, he cannot come at the moment, Varzil answered. *I am Varzil Ridenow, Keeper. I will accept whatever messages you have for us. How fares our sister Tower at Hali?*

Varzil? Varzil of Arilinn?

Suddenly, the contact flickered. Varzil frowned, puzzled. The relay linkage remained intact, yet he had lost all sense of another presence.

Varzil! He recognized his sister, Dyannis. Her mental voice was stronger than the last time they'd spoken when he was still at Arilinn. Her present agitation rang through the contact.

Varzil! By all the gods, what are you doing at Hestral Tower?

He smiled, although she could not see it. *Little sister, it is good to touch your mind as well. I have been here the better part of a year. It's a long story, and not altogether a happy one.* How could he tell her of his suspicions of Eduin—or of her lover's rash actions? Chill whispered along his nerves, for Hali Tower was bound to Hastur.

Never mind! She was almost shouting now. *Varzil, get out of there! Get out now!*

Dyannis, we are under siege by Rakhal Hastur's army.

I don't care! Find some way—don't wait—

Dyannis broke off and the first mental voice returned. *Varzil of Arilinn, you have no part in this quarrel. Sadly, we cannot count you or anyone else within your walls as neutral. As a result of the unprovoked and unlawful attack upon his soldiers, King Rakhal Hastur has declared Hestral Tower renegade. If you do not surrender immediately, you will be destroyed.*

The words had the ring of a speech memorized and reluctantly delivered, yet Varzil could detect no hesitation. However the *laranzu* who had spoken them might feel about those commands, he would indeed carry them out.

I will deliver your message, Varzil said. *But I cannot tell how soon you*

*may have your answer. Our monitor is attending to Loryn of Hestral even as
we speak.*

*We have no discretion to wait. Our orders are direct and specific. Varzil,
if it is within your power to make him see reason, I urge you to do so for—for
the sake of all those within your walls. Or if he cannot answer, then you must
do it for him. If there is any chance—I will do what I may to buy you a small
measure of time.*

It was both warning and concession, and Varzil knew it. *I thank you
for whatever you can do.*

Varzil let the contact drain away. Slowly he got to his feet. Marius, at
his side, looked to him, eyes brimming with emotion. Clearly, the boy
had been able to follow enough scattered thoughts to catch the essence
of the message.

"Loryn will never surrender," Marius said.

"No, I think not," Varzil replied, striding toward the stairs. "I very
much doubt if he would be able to enforce it if he did. But we must
accord him the courtesy of his own decision."

Even as he reached the archway to the topmost stair, Varzil felt a
massive shuddering of psychic energy through the Tower. The earth
heaved and bucked like a rebellious mount. He grabbed the archway to
keep his balance. Someone below screamed.

Another impact jarred the Tower, or perhaps it was an aftershock
from the first one. Varzil knew of a certainty that Hestral was now under
attack, and not by a minor aggregation of *leronyn,* such as traveled with
the army. The energy could only be generated by a full circle within the
protection of a Tower, their powers focused and amplified through a
matrix screen.

Varzil had not gone more than a few steps down, with Marius at his
heels, when another wave hit, followed an instant later with a deafening
crack!

Loryn! Varzil reached out mentally.

HESTRAL IS UNDER ATTACK! The Keeper's silent command
filled his mind. *EVERYONE WHO CAN, JOIN WITH ME! WE MUST
FORM A CIRCLE!*

Who is behind the attack? Serena cried silently.

Hali Tower! Varzil answered, pitching his mental voice to carry
thoughout the Tower. *At Rakhal's command. They tried to warn us—*

A horrendous rumble issued from the northern corner of the Tower,
the dormitory wing. Varzil, his *laran* senses stretched wide, felt stones

shift and slide, walls buckle, wooden beams splinter. The entire section shuddered like a hamstrung beast.

Varzil rushed sown the last few steps to meet Loryn and a handful of senior workers, responding to Loryn's silent summons.

"There's no time to reach a laboratory!" Varzil cried.

He jerked open the door of the nearest room. It was the old infirmary, where Felicia had first been taken. It took only a few minutes to pull benches and pillows into a rough circle.

As each one quieted his mind and breathing, settling into rapport, Varzil assessed their condition. They were all worn thin by unrelenting vigilance. Loryn himself was near exhaustion, his focus patchy. He'd been deep in healing trance when Marius tried to wake him, and its residue clung to him like a clouded film.

Loryn, let me serve as Keeper, Varzil said. *I am stronger for this task.*

Loryn's refusal was swift. *The fault and hence the responsibility for our situation are mine alone. If I had not been weak, Eduin would have not acted rashly. I must deal with the consequences.*

Yet all of us will suffer if we cannot defend ourselves. Should we not then each contribute as we are best able?

I am Keeper of Hestral Tower. This burden is mine!

Rather than provoke further dissension, Varzil settled into the circle. He allowed Loryn to integrate his psychic energy into the flowing whole. As he fed power into the circle, his concentration deepened. There were only five of them, a small circle working with only their personal starstones. At the back of his awareness, he sensed another presence, a warmth, an invisible radiance.

I am with you . . . sang a precious, familiar voice.

Once more, Varzil found himself looking into a clear lens through which he could see energy as well as physical objects. Hestral had been built centuries ago as a military fortress, strong enough to withstand the most determined physical assault. It stood upon solid rock, which would not yield easily. Only a tenday or so earlier, they had used their *laran* powers to reinforce the physical bonds between the particles of stone and mortar. What the Hastur army *leronyn* had sought to rend apart, they had preserved, not by any direct opposition of power, but simply by willing stone to remain itself.

As before, Varzil's vision penetrated into the substance of wall, roof and floor, wood, stone and mortar. He saw the energy form of Hestral like a second Tower overlapping the real one, shadowy and yet more real.

Without these interlaced bonds, the physical Tower would crumble into nothingness.

The attack from Hali came in bursts of invisible fire. Each one touched the outer edges of Hestral's energy form like a wave crashing against a boulder, seeking a crevice or gap.

Hold . . . hold . . . hold . . . pulsed through the Hestral circle like an echo of that earlier defense.

Rock—solid . . . mortar—sealed tight . . .

As before, the bonds between the particles of stone strengthened. Each succeeding blast of power spattered and flowed harmlessly over the surfaces. It fell away, leaving both the physical and the energy form of Hestral Tower untouched.

Let rock be rock . . . each thing according to its nature . . .

Elation swept the circle. With each passing moment, the walls maintained their solidity, the stone smooth and dense, heavy with the weight of the earth. This attack was more intense than the previous attempts, but the circle was well able to counter it. Loryn's strategy was working.

Beneath them, Hestral Tower shuddered again. Varzil followed the course of the energy blasts from the outer walls deep into the earth beneath. In horror, he realized that the first attack from Hali had been a feint, a maneuver to lure their attention away from the real object—not the walls of stone and mortar, but the bedrock upon which Hestral Tower stood. The underlying layers of rock and soil crumbled and gave way.

Varzil saw within his mind what his fleshly eyes could not. In the dormitory wing, the massive beams that supported the upper structures tilted as the foundations fell away at strategic, targeted points. The weight of stone and wood, tipping and sliding, came crashing down on what was left of the substructure. Like slivers of silvery pain, he felt the screams of those who were trapped, ripples of panic in others rushing to their rescue along the shifting, uncertain corridors.

Dismay shook the circle. There was no use in trying to shore up the Tower. The disintegration had already progressed too far. Even if the bedrock could have been welded solid in an instant, the entire dormitory wing was unstable. It was rapidly collapsing under its own weight.

Hali Tower paused in their onslaught, but only for a moment. Varzil, attuned now to their method of their attack, sensed the next target almost at the same moment. Hali was systematically demolishing the key supporting structures.

Varzil did not know how long they might hold out, or how long Loryn's will to resist would last. The Keeper held the circle in an iron grip. Iron, he reminded himself, could be brittle if stressed too far.

The floor beneath them staggered, slipped. Although the blast from Hali had not been aimed directly beneath the infirmary, the devastation from the dormitory wing had destabilized connecting structures, setting off a chain of collapse.

Loryn, we cannot stay here, he said silently.

At that very moment came a crash so loud and percussive, it stunned him. The air burst from his lungs; his psychic vision darkened. He reeled with the sudden, jolting return to his physical body. Heart hammering in his chest, muscles quivering, he scrambled to his feet. The floor at the far end sagged. A cot slipped toward the depression, colliding with an upended stool.

VARZIL!

The cry came not from one of the other *leronyn,* now stumbling toward the doorway, but silently.

Felicia?

White light surged around him, filled him, blinded him. His body tripped and caught itself against the wall beside the door. From what seemed an immense distance, someone cried, "Loryn! Help him!" and "Varzil, are you hurt?"

The light drew him up like a vortex. He had no strength to fight it. For a terrible moment, he found himself stretched and scraped thinner than the finest parchment, then twisted and wrenched—

Around him, stone walls toppled. He saw them as shadows of white against white, bathed in stark brilliance. Dust and powdery shards rose like a stormcloud. Something sharp and hard shattered, throwing out slivers that shot right through him.

Ahhhh!

The shriek of pain shifted his vision once more. With the eerie doubled sight that came from being partly in one world and part in another, Varzil looked down/around at the little stone cellar where he and Loryn had so painstakingly disassembled the stockpile of *clingfire.* Here, on the very table they had used, Felicia's body had lain, held in stasis.

Instead of the table, and the shrouded form of his beloved, Varzil stared at a pile of rubble. One wall had fallen and the adjacent ones were about to give way.

NO!

He threw himself where the table had stood, thinking only to pull the stones away, quickly while there still might be hope. He thought nothing of their weight, of his own danger—

His hands passed, ghostlike, right through the stone. The ceiling crashed down through him, completely filling the remaining open space.

The white light seized him once more. He was no longer in the little stone cellar, or the infirmary either, and he was not alone. Though he was again blinded, he was filled with that familiar presence, light and sure.

Quickly! Felicia's mental voice sang in his mind. *We must force Hali to end this madness before anyone else dies!*

Sweet gods—

Her face floated before him, very much like the last time he had seen her, a vision spun of dreams and the memory of the heart. A smile, inexpressively sweet for all its briefness, flickered across her lips. She reached out one pale hand to him—

—and he stood at her side in the Overworld. Her fingers slipped through his, insubstantial as mist. He saw that, like the strange gray plain, she had turned colorless. Already her eyes, once so full of intelligence and emotion, were fading. She gathered herself with visible effort. An instant of clarity kindled. Her lips moved—

Go—

Though she stood as still as before, she began to recede. A great maw of distance opened up between them. Varzil thought he had only to reach out and touch her, to take her in his arms once again, to taste her lips—

Felicia took a step away and shook her head. He understood; he was no raw novice, but *laranzu* and Keeper. He had been trained in the dangers of the Overworld, and most especially the certain failure of trying to maintain contact with the dead. Once he gave way to this temptation, he knew, there would be no turning back. No matter how far or how fast he ran after her, she would elude him. Time, which was difficult enough to keep track of in the Overworld, would lose all meaning. He would go on and on in fruitless chase, bound by desperation and hope, until his physical body withered and died.

And so would those who depended upon him.

*Go—*she had urged him. Begged him.

Though it felt like tearing his heart from his breast, he turned his back on her and summoned the Overworld landmark of Hali Tower.

45

Varzil pictured Hali as he had first seen it, a slender white Tower with the cloud-waters of the Lake at its base. The image wavered, mingling with the vision of the same Tower at the far distant time of the Cataclysm and his all-too-brief warning. He bent his will and concentration on the flashes of present-day personalities—Dougal DiAsturian . . . the *laranzu* from the relays . . . Dyannis . . .

Varzil, no! wailed through his mind, distorted, barely recognizable.

He had never worked in a circle at Hali. From his visits, he knew only a little of the layout. He remembered the room in which he had woken, the kindness of the healers who tended him. Details evaded him; he had been a boy then and had just suffered a tremendous shock.

It was years ago, he told himself. *They will not remember me.*

Yet he recalled the translucent blue stone of Hali Tower, used not as accents but in huge opulent blocks, tokens of a time when the will and pleasure of the *Comyn* lords was the only consideration. Once more, he looked down upon a circular room, generous in proportion, and the enormous artificial matrix at its center. A circle had gathered here, eyes closed in concentration, heads of flame and copper hair bowed, hands linked. Energy, visible as a coruscation of blue-white, bathed their faces. In mem-

403

ory or perhaps in sympathetic resonance, he felt an answering surge along his own *laran* channels.

His mental vision leaped into focus and he stood, not as a passive observer looking down upon the room, but at its very center. The faceted white light of the matrix surrounded him.

Somehow, Felicia had linked him with the device, and it had drawn him here.

Heads remained bowed, for the discipline of the circle held.

I am Varzil of Arilinn, guest and comrade to the leronyn *of Hestral Tower. I speak for them, for all of us. I ask you, mind to mind, where there can be no secrets, no betrayal, to stop your attack. Towers must not wage war upon each other. We must put an end to this madness before it destroys us and everything we have built!*

The Keeper, Dougal DiAsturian, a heavyset man whose hair and beard were more silver than red, answered. His expression did not alter in the least. *Have you come to surrender? It is too late. King Rakhal has given the order that we must continue our attack until Hestral is razed to the ground.*

I have not come to surrender, Varzil replied, *for that would not solve anything. Only a generation ago, Towers fought each other at the whims of kings. Have you forgotten Neskaya and Tramontana? Yes, you at Hali can prevail against Hestral, a small and insignificant Tower. But what will you have gained? A show of brute strength? Is this why the gods bestowed our Gifts? So that we can carry out the orders of bullies like Rakhal the Usurper?*

Watch your words, least you indict yourself. I think you, too, are a partisan here.

Varzil wanted to strike back, but he restrained himself. His goal was not to solve the problem of who was rightful Hastur King, but something far more important. Anger and righteous indignation fell away from him. It seemed he stood once more in a cone of light, which illuminated and purified all thought.

It does not matter who rules this Kingdom or any other, he said, *for it seems to be human nature to squabble over land and power. I say, until such time as men have learned to resolve their differences with words instead of swords, let them have their swords. Let us not turn our own powers, which can create marvels and which bind us in an intimacy of mind which ordinary men can never know—let us not abuse these Gifts so they become instead curses.*

A nice sentiment, Varzil of Arilinn, and spoken by one whose only weapon is eloquence!

So the Keeper of Hali thought Varzil spoke from weakness, with everything to lose and only the desperate resource of persuasion. There was no point in arguing further, for anything he said now would only reinforce that belief.

This is no child's game of bluff-and-blunder, Varzil replied calmly. *Even if you blast us into nothingness, you cannot win. You will be forever a pawn in the hands of Rakhal and his like, a dangerous and powerful toy.*

In his mind, he formed the image of two boys, barely past adolescence, thwacking away at each other with wooden practice swords. Varzil, like every other *Comyn* youth, had spent hours on a field like this one. His lack of aptitude had earned him more than his share of bruises. Now he drew upon those memories to fill in the sensory details—the smell of the dust, the sweat trickling down the side of his neck, the weight and awkward balance of the wooden sword as he tightened his two-handed grip. Just as he had projected his thoughts at the catmen and had honed his *laran* in his years at Arilinn, so now he sent the mental picture into the very heart of the Hali circle.

One sword caught a boy across the shoulder and sent him staggering. The sound of a bone breaking reverberated through the circle. Somehow, the boy managed to hold on to his own sword with his free hand. He screamed and charged, swinging.

The other boy, visibly surprised by the intensity of the counterattack, fell back. He lifted his sword to ward off the blows. Wood struck wood with bone-jarring impact. The mingled smells of adrenaline and dust hung in the air.

For a time, the first boy prevailed, carried by the impetus of his own fury. It quickly burned itself out. He retreated, stumbling, but not before he had smacked the other across one cheek. The blow raised a bloody welt.

Back and forth they went, each one pressing the advantage in his turn, each one defending himself with increasing desperation until the roles changed once more. Before long, they were coated in sweat and bruises, their shirts torn, their wooden swords splintered. The pauses between attack and counterattack grew longer. Each time one or the other was knocked down, he rose more slowly. Their breath came fast and harsh.

Finally one boy, the one whose collarbone was first broken, fell to his knees and stayed there. His adversary bent over, bracing himself on bent knees. There was no disguising the light of malicious triumph in his eyes.

What is the meaning of this? roared Dougal. *Do you think to frighten us with a tale of childish squabbles, or so impress us with your own* laran *talents that we will give in to your demands?*

Varzil drew himself up, and it seemed that the light cloaked him, sustained him. He felt Felicia's presence, her trust in him and in what he must do.

Have you never heard the old saying, It is ill done to chain a dragon to roast your meat? he asked.

The fallen boy lifted his head and yelled a command, *Dragon, come!*

The sky darkened and a shadow swooped down, its form immense and distorted. No living man had ever seen a dragon, and it was far from sure they had ever existed on Darkover, save in folklore and proverb. What Varzil intended to evoke was the awesomeness of the legend, its raw inhuman power.

The creature blotted out the blood-red sun. Wings, leathery and pinioned, but blurred with motion, churned the dust.

Still standing, the other boy shrieked in terror, and then issued his own command. Before the claws could rend his flesh, a second shape, equally hideous, appeared.

The battle cries of the dragons shivered the air, brassy as thunder. Gouts of flame, hotter than any Hellers wildfire, swept the practice field. One blast caught a boy full in the chest and left him a charred husk. The shout of glee from the other was cut off as a spiked-barbed tail as thick as a man's waist slashed across him. Two scaled bodies, steaming as they grappled with each other, slammed into the earth where the boy had fallen.

The field became a smear of blood-soaked mud, of ash and splintered bone. Claws slid over armored scales and dug deep. Ichorous fluids spattered the earth, which cracked open. Fumes burst from the fissures.

Tattered wings beat the air. The dragons lifted into the sky. Thick black smoke billowed from the intertwined bodies. Yellow blood, reeking of sulfurous smoke, sprayed in all directions. The dragons bellowed, blaring mindless fury. The din escalated and then cut off suddenly. In the metallic silence, a single form of smoke and scales plummeted downward.

The shock of its impact splintered the bedrock beneath. A miasma of dust and brimstone-yellow vapors spread for leagues across the scorched and cracked earth.

Who is the boy and who is the dragon? Varzil demanded.

This— the Keeper's mental voice faltered for the first time. *This is a tale to frighten disobedient children, an attempt at intimidation, nothing more. Nothing real.*

A TALE? NOTHING REAL? Then I will show you what is real and what is nightmare!

With a power he had not known he possessed, Varzil reached for that other Hali, the one from the distant past. He pictured it in his mind, dredging memories he had tried to bury forever.

Two circles now occupied that same room, yet only the present circle was aware of the other. The circle from the past was totally absorbed in their own desperate struggle.

Outside the phantom walls, the sky crackled and thunder rolled, even as they had in Varzil's vision. The heavens turned white. A torrent of blackness swept down from the north—from the Tower at Aldaran. In the city of Hali, pale ghosts of people thronged the streets. Their terror rose up like curls of smoke, mingling with the vapors from the lake and the blazing wooden buildings. Unnatural thunder built, shivering through earth and stone.

What—what is happening? came from the circle in the present. *What trick of illusion is this? Who would dare to attack Hali Tower?*

I show you what I have seen with my own eyes, Varzil answered. *What has already come to pass. What may come again.*

As before, the storm from the north reached down to the land. Light exploded over the Tower like Zandru's own lightning and then slowly faded.

From the circle in the past, power swelled. Steam arose from the surface of the lake. The very substance of the water shifted as more and more power poured into it, both from above and below, where the Hali circle-that-was summoned its counterattack. Molecules tore apart as jolt after jolt of energy shot through the Lake.

The Cataclysm! Dougal cried silently.

They each thought they had a weapon so terrible that nothing could stand against it, Varzil said. *They began as you have, in loyalty and obedience . . . and pride.*

He paused, for no words he could summon, no eloquent turn of phrase, could match the power of this vision which now filled the mind of every person in the Hali circle. No one with a shred of *laran* could escape the impact of the images, the terror of the burning city, the rending of elemental physical forces.

In the space between one heartbeat and the next, Varzil caught a glimpse of what must come next. Forces this enormous, once unleashed, could not be easily contained. Storm and wave were nothing compared to the energies behind them.

The fallen columns at the bottom of the lake . . . even now . . . pulse with power.

He turned all his concentration back to the present. Thunder receded, leaving dull silence. The ghostly forms of the second Tower and its inhabitants faded like mist at dawn. The present circle, along with the contours of their work chamber and the matrix lattice, which had seemed solid to him, wavered, thin.

Yet to these people, Varzil himself was the phantasm, the apparition. The contact with their joined minds diminished. He saw himself through their eyes, a figure limned with brilliance.

The circle was broken. Dougal DiAsturian lifted his head, his eyes clear.

Go in peace, Varzil Ridenow, for never again shall we of Hali meet any other Tower in battle. You have my oath as a Keeper upon it.

Walk with the gods, Varzil thought, and then a vortex of darkness took him.

◆

Varzil woke to the sound of a woman humming. His body ached in every joint and muscle, and his eyes had gummed closed. He reached up with one hand to wipe them clear and found that his head was wrapped in bandages. The effort of struggling to sit upright left him gasping, his heart fluttering in his chest. Gentle hands pushed him back against his pillow.

"Varzil, it's too soon for you to be up," said Oranna's voice. "Leave those bandages alone if you want the use of your eyes again."

"What has happened? Have I been ill—the attack from Hali—tell me!" he cried.

Felicia—

But there was no answering pulse of sweetness in his mind.

"Loryn will tell you all the details himself. He's given specific orders to be informed the moment you were awake." Oranna clucked her tongue very much like Lunilla.

Varzil felt a brush of warmth against his skin and Oranna's voice very close to his ear. "We feared we'd lost you, that you sacrificed yourself to save us. Loryn told us you went into the Overworld to stop the attack from Hali. Aldones only knows how you managed that, but we—*I*—am grateful."

Then she was gone, and a few minutes later, Varzil heard footsteps, quick but irregular and marked by the tapping of a cane. Wood scraped over stone floor as a stool was drawn up by his bedside.

Varzil, my friend, it brings me such joy to see you awake, even if you are more bruise and bandage than intact skin.

"Loryn! Tell me what happened!"

"Rather *you* should tell *me*. Things happened rather quickly once the ground under the infirmary started to collapse." Loryn sounded weary, his voice on the edge of hoarseness.

It did not take long for each of them to tell their separate stories, although Varzil left out the moments with Felicia in the Overworld. If Loryn sensed the omission, he refrained from any mention of it. Some things were too private to be shared, even in the intimacy of a Tower.

The spells of unbinding that Hali had used on Hestral's foundations had stopped immediately and some of the damage had reversed itself. Even so, much could not be undone. The entire dormitory wing had become dangerously unstable and would have to be torn down and re-built in a different location. Other structures could be reinforced, given time and the use of matrix technology.

The human loss could not be so easily replaced. Five people were dead or missing. Eduin's body had not been found. He'd been confined to his own chambers in the dormitory wing, but his rooms had suffered only minor damage. In the confusion of the attack, it was not impossible that he could have slipped away, rather than face the charges against him.

"If Eduin still lives, I doubt any of us will hear of him again," Loryn said. "He may have deceived us in other ways, but there was never any doubt of his instinct for survival. I fear you were right about him. His treachery was my responsibility as Keeper. I was too tolerant, too trusting."

"Do not judge yourself harshly," Varzil replied. "It is hardly a moral imperfection to see the good in other men. If Eduin deceived you, he deceived us all. Whatever he did, it was from his own will and choice, and not because any of us failed to stop him."

Loryn's voice faltered as he told of their efforts to excavate the little cellar.

"We tried. Varzil, we tried." Fingertips, dry and trembling, brushed the back of Varzil's wrist.

Varzil opened his mouth to answer and found that he could not breathe. He drew his hand away, clasping it in the other, and touched the faceted edge of the ring gem. It felt warm. Long after Loryn had left and the stillness of night enclosed him, he lay on his cot, one hand cupping the ring.

As he drifted off to sleep, a delicate white haze misted over his inner vision, like the rays of a flawless star against the velvet sky.

His heard ached past any words. It was natural to grieve, he told himself, to honor loved ones in their passing. He remembered her words,

"It is not lily days which shape our souls, but the frozen winter nights, when we find ourselves in the pit of Zandru's Forge and discover who we truly are."

Like a clay pot placed in a fire, like a tree that has weathered a killing ice-storm, he had not come unscathed through this time. It had shaped him, for good or for ill, and defined who he was. What he did with it, what he made of his life, that was now up to him.

BOOK IV

46

Lifting his eyes, Carolin searched the dawn sky, misty with the promise of rain. High summer had come to the Kilghard Hills, although frost still lay on the ground in the morning. Carolin, walking the camps and meeting with his captains, felt a subtle lightening of heart, as if, with the change of seasons, some deep and fundamental shift had begun.

With his *laran,* he sensed the building excitement in the men who marched under his banner, their passion and loyalty, the pattern of their myriad individual stories. Intelligence came from Hali that Rakhal was massing forces under Lyondri Hastur. If he moved as expected, Carolin would at last meet him, near Neskaya here in these hills.

This morning, Orain accompanied him to meet with representatives from the Sisterhood of the Sword, many of whom had pledged themselves to his cause. He had hoped to see Jandria, who had left Rakhal's court to pierce her ear and don the red vest of a Swordswoman, and he was not disappointed. She waited for him beside one of her Sisters.

Carolin's heart rose as he recognized the young woman who had traveled with him to Nevarsin under the name of Rumal. They had parted company shortly thereafter; he had not expected to see her here. She had clearly prospered, for her features no longer bore an expression of haunted desperation. Her tunic and breeches were well-made and even her boots looked the right size, not some boy's outworn castoffs. She kept her eyes downcast; either she had not recognized her old friend, *Dom* Carlo of Blue Lake, or was too shy to say anything.

She held the reins of the most magnificent horse Carolin had ever seen. The stallion was clearly of the same breeding as his old Longlegs, and she had been a fine mount. This fellow was taller and more power-fully built, with intelligent eyes and a mirror-glossy coat. He nuzzled the girl's shoulder as if they were old friends.

"You lend us grace." Jandria bowed politely to Carolin, and went on to present the horse as a gift from the Sisterhood, trained by their finest horsewoman. "Romilly?"

Romilly? Ah, so that is her real name.

Romilly blushed, keeping her eyes fixed upon the horse's sleek nose. "His name is Sunstar, Your Majesty, and he will carry you for love, for he has never felt whip or spur."

Yes, that is just how Rumal—how Romilly would train a horse.

When he spoke those same words aloud, her head jerked up. Her eyes widened in recognition and he smiled as tently as he could. "I am sorry to have the advantage of you. I thank you and the Sisterhood for this magnificent gift and for your loyalty."

He swung up on the stallion's back and the horse moved off willingly, with no more than a nudge from his knees. Romilly must have trained him with her *laran* as well as bridle and saddle, for the animal seemed to sense what he wanted without any need for direction.

On such a tall, fine horse, Carolin towered above the men on foot. Their eyes followed him through the camp. He wanted them to see him and know that he was here with them, not closeted away behind stone walls.

It was not until late in the day that Carolin had a chance to meet with the *leronyn* who had left their Towers to join him. At his request, they presented themselves to the central tent, adorned with the silver-and-blue fir tree banner of the Hasturs. Ranald Ridenow had already been acting as one of his officers. Two more had just arrived from Tramontana Tower—Ruyven MacAran, Romilly's own brother . . . and Maura.

Ruyven was clearly a MacAran; he and Romilly bore the same unmis-takable features. In his dark, unadorned robe, he looked as somber and ascetic as a monk.

Maura bowed to Carolin with the exact degree of reverence for a lord and king from a *leronis* whose skill is beyond question. She wore a gown of pearly gray-green, and her hair, as bright as any flame, was braided and coiled low on her neck.

Recovering his speech, Carolin thanked them both. They sat together, refusing his offer of wine, and discussed the flying of the sentry birds. Knowledge of the exact location and strength of Rakhal's forces could make a crucial difference when they actually clashed. Forewarned, Carolin might chose his own battlefield, using the land itself as his ally. Perhaps, if the gods willed it, there would be fewer lives lost.

Ruyven must have caught Carolin's thought, for he said, "If we can come upon them unawares, or force them to charge at us uphill, then our smaller numbers may prevail."

"May Evanda grant they have no sentry birds to spy on us in return," Maura said.

Carolin said, "We have received no reports of any others from here to the far Hellers."

"That is good," Ruyven replied. "By your leave, *vai dom,* Ranald and I will link with you, so that you may see for yourself how the land lies."

Carolin nodded. The troops were his to lead, their victory or death upon his head. His training at Arilinn made such a linkage possible.

"Romilly will fly that bird," Maura added, "and I the other."

Carolin smiled. "Then my bird will fly true, for I never saw anyone, man or maid, with a surer touch."

Ruyven rose and, bowing more deeply this time, took his leave. "If we are to fly the birds tomorrow, we must be well rested."

Maura sat quietly as the door flap fell closed. Outside, guards shifted, watchful. Dark had fallen, but the lantern filled the tent chamber with honey-soft light.

Carolin could not think of what to say. In an instant, he had gone from king and general, leader of armies, protector of his realm, to a man bereft of even the simplest speech.

As if catching his confusion, she lowered her eyes. "I do not know what you must think of me, to have turned my back on Rakhal in this way."

"Why are you here, Maura?" The words tumbled from his mouth. "If you felt you could not take sides in the war, surely you could have been excused from your duties and returned home to your family. You need not have come all this way—and placed yourself at such risk."

"I have sworn not to fight against Rakhal." Gray fire flashed behind her eyes. "It was a condition of my release from his service, and I must honor that promise. I could not have done otherwise, for he would have forced me to go against you. Now that I have seen what he truly is, or what he has made of himself, I cannot remain apart. Whatever happens now, Rakhal has brought it upon himself, he and Lyondri both!"

She paused, her chest heaving, then quieted herself. "I came because my conscience would give me no rest if I did not. You must regain the throne, not simply for your own sake, but for that of all these lands."

It is not to me alone that she offers such devotion, but to all our people, he reminded himself, even as his heart swelled with joy.

"*Vai leronis,* I thank you for your loyalty, but I would not have you expose yourself to the dangers of the battlefield—"

"And I would not have you at any greater risk than need be, not while I have the power to aid you!" she replied. "Are you ordering me away to safety, at the possible cost of victory, simply because I am a woman? Would you give such a command to Jandria, who wields a sword with as much skill as any of your men? Or to Romilly, whose link with the sentry birds may be the decisive factor in your victory?"

"Jandria chose the way of the sword," he protested. "She knows the risks—"

"And I do not? Carlo, the choice is not between security and death. It is whether we stand against the evil of our times or else do nothing while it swallows up everything we hold dear. There is no certain safety for any of us—not even in the Towers."

◆

Mounted on the black stallion Sunstar, Carolin rode near the head of the army, along with Maura and Orain. All about him, he saw great open tracts of deserted land. Now and again, a farmstead lay empty, its wells broken, its house and outlying buildings either burned or fallen away with time. His heart ached to see the decay. When Maura remarked on his somber mood, Carolin said, "I remember how green and fertile this country was. Now it's little better than a wasteland."

"The war?" she asked, frowning.

"Yes, but not this one. Back in my father's time, I think. People have not lived in these parts for some years. In the aftermath of conflict, there are always bandits, men bereft of their homes by war and their consciences by the horrors they have endured. They ravaged all through these parts, taking or destroying whatever was left. Decent folk moved closer to the protection of Neskaya."

"Do not lose heart," Maura said. "See how the land renews itself. With a little care, it will once again be green and rich. Like the men in exile, it waits for your return."

He looked away. "We have known each other too well and too long for such flattery. I am only a man, not a god."

"How do you think the gods do their work, if not through good and decent men?" she demanded.

Carolin remembered the moment on the journey from Nevarsin, when he had just received word that he was in truth king, and it seemed a luminous figure placed hands around his and accepted the oath of his heart. Whether it was some vision born of his childhood dreams, the *rhu fead* and holy things at Hali, or perhaps even a whisper of Aldones himself, did not matter. As King, he had sworn. As King, he would live or die by that promise.

They rode along a watercourse, a narrow brook which tumbled down a cascade of piled, weathered rocks, then flowed smooth and broad across a fertile meadow starred with little blue and golden flowers. The light of the day faded in the east, casting a pearly glow from one horizon to the other, a muted kiss of sky to fragrant earth. Before the night was past, three of the four moons would dance together in the sky, two of them near full.

"I can imagine *chieri* coming down from the forests to dance here on a night like this." Maura arched her back in the saddle and sighed. "What a pity we cannot have Midsummer Festival."

No, not here, not while this gruesome business still lies before us. Carolin straightened in his saddle. "If it be the will of the gods, we shall celebrate it together at Hali."

"Evanda grant it so," Maura said seriously. "I long to return home."

"To Hali, then, and not to Tramontana?" Carolin asked, keeping his voice light with an effort.

"Hali has ever been my home, and the people there most dear to me."

"Did none of the young men beyond the mountains," he joked, making a pun on the name of Tramontana, "shake your resolve to remain maiden for the Sight?"

She laughed, a strained sound that tore at his heart. "On the day when you ask me, Carolin, I shall not send *you* away disappointed."

For a long moment, he could hardly believe what he had heard. Beneath him, Sunstar jigged and danced with the surge of emotion. Somehow, he found his voice. "If the Council will permit us to marry, I—it will be so."

He nudged the stallion with knee and rein, guiding the horse close to Maura's so that he could lean over and brush her cheek with his lips. Her skin was soft and smelled of sunshine and the sweet herbs she used in her hair.

In a low voice that none but she could hear, he said, "If I have said nothing of my desires, it is because I feared you still grieved for Rakhal, that your heart was not free."

"He thought he could come to me over the bodies of my kinfolk—of *you,* Carlo—and that I would fall at his feet in gratitude when he offered to make me his queen," she replied with quiet spirit. "I felt ashamed that once I had believed in him, even defended his actions, denying his true nature. I knew then that I—I felt—"

She stumbled, then gathered herself. "I will not have it said that I turned away from Rakhal when I saw the war went badly for him and chose you instead, because I desired the crown so much I would take whichever man could give it to me."

Maura's voice faltered on the last few words. She sat upright in the saddle, and in that moment, she looked both courageous and forlorn. Carolin reminded himself that she was no frail, simpering lady, but a trained *leronis* and *Comynara* in her own right. She had maintained her commitment to the virgin Sight against all of Rakhal's blandishments, and then had outraged her Keeper and the very formidable Lady Liriel Hastur by training her own *verrin* hawk. In the camp, she had fed and tended the sentry birds with her own hands, had ridden and lived with the men without a hint of scandal.

Why should she care what people thought?

I would not have you *believe it of me, that I wanted you only for the crown you offered.*

Moved by wordless impulse, Carolin reined Sunstar close to Maura's horse and reached for her. She came into his arms as if she had always belonged there. He lifted her into his own saddle. Joy swept through him.

He had set aside all hope of this dream of love, had never looked for it, had thought it impossible since the night he realized he could not feel anything beyond respect for his own lawful wife. He had always loved Maura, but the love had grown from the affection of childhood to this shining transcendent moment.

"I am sorry I teased you about Tramontana," he murmured into the silken braids of her hair. "I should have known—I was not sure you felt—as I do—"

She shifted deeper into his embrace and her mind brushed his. All doubt fell away. His heart seemed to fill his entire body. He closed his eyes, unable to speak.

Sunstar pranced, shaking his head to send the bridle rings jingling. Carolin calmed him with a touch of the reins.

"In these uncertain times, we must seize what happiness we can," Maura said, "and treasure each moment together. "You were right, though, about the Sight. We are still at war with Rakhal, and we cannot afford to discard any resource. No matter what our hearts may yearn for, we must act rationally."

At that moment, there was no greater gift she could have offered him. She understood the demands of his rank, of the oath he had sworn, just as she, too, was bound by what she knew to be right.

"I will not have you as anything less than my queen," he whispered.

"Do not say that, beloved. We neither of us know what the future holds. What we have today," she smiled up into his eyes, "must be enough."

◆

A tenday later on the road, the weather turned gray and drizzly, with little spats of gusty rain slashing across the plains. Even when the clouds broke, the wind remained high. Cloaks and tents became soggy. Tempers frayed. The horses plodded on through the churned mud, and now and again, a wagon became mired.

Every passing hour brought the battle closer. The day felt closed in, as if, Carolin thought, they were marching blind.

He sent word to fly a sentry bird. It must stay low enough to spy through the mists, even though it was not their nature, for he needed to know where Rakhal's armies moved.

Romilly, riding apart with Ranald and Maura, guided the sentry bird, the one she called Diligence, eastward to where they had last seen the enemy forces. In rapport, Carolin flew high over the ranges, soaring on strong pinions.

Rain slanted from the northeast. Flight became a slow, sullen effort, each wing stroke forced against the bird's stubborn wish to fly home and huddle in damp misery upon her perch.

Through a break in the clouds, Carolin scanned the deserted land blow. Low on the horizon, smoke rose, as from an encampment of men.

Through the bird's eyes, he saw the outskirts of the enemy camp . . . men and horses, tents and supply wagons. One wagon in particular drew his interest, although the bird instinctively shied away. Sensed through his *laran,* something black and acrid hovered about it like a miasma. With a sickening wrench, Carolin recognized the foul taint.

Clingfire! *May Zandru curse him a thousand times, Rakhal has brought* clingfire *to the battlefield!*

Closer . . . he heard Romilly urge the sentry bird, *closer . . .*

Too late, the bird's attention veered to the arrow speeding toward her. As if a red-hot wire suddenly seared her breast, Diligence swerved, wings beating, screeching in pain, fighting to stay aloft, to stay in rapport . . .

falling like a stone . . .

the gray rain and the green hills fading . . .

Carolin slumped in the saddle, his breath catching in his chest. He struggled to orient himself again, to separate himself from the dizziness and the pain. Linked through Romilly to the bird, he had felt the creature's death as if it were his own.

Romilly's anger, swift as a plummeting hawk, swept through him. He heard a voice, Ranald's, saying, "I am so sorry . . . you loved her," and Romilly's heated retort, "I hate you all! You and your accursed wars, none of you are worth a single feather from the tip of her wing."

Ah, Romilly! Carolin thought, sick at heart. *What have I asked of you? And what more must I ask?*

When next he met with Romilly, he struggled to put his own feelings into words. "I am sorry about Diligence. But can you not look at this from my point of view, too? We risk birds, and beasts, too, to save the lives of men. I know the birds mean more to you than they ever can to me, or to any of us, but I must ask you this: would you see me or Ruyven or Orain die instead of the sentry birds? Would you not risk the lives of the birds to save your own Swordswomen?"

At first, he saw the conflict within her, the burning wish to throw his words back at him, to demand what harm the birds had ever done to Rakhal that they should pay with their lives.

A wave of sadness passed through him. "This is what every commander of men must face, weighing the lives of some against the lives of all. I wish I need never see anyone who follows me die . . . but I have no choice. I owe my very life to those I am sworn to rule."

She dipped her head and agreed to fly the one remaining sentry bird as Carolin required. So it was that, several days later, he had advance notice of the impending attack.

◆

Rakhal's army swept down over the brow of the hill and Carolin's own forces charged to meet them. After the first tremendous shock of encounter, the field exploded in frenzied action. Men on foot and horseback hurled themselves forward, captains shouted commands, trumpets blared.

From the ground, all was confusion. Linked with the sentry bird, seeing partly through avian eyes, partly through Romilly's, and partly his own, Carolin directed his forces to where they were most needed.

"There!" he shouted, pointing out the black wagon. "We must seize the *clingfire* before it can be used against us!"

Through the bird's eyes, Carolin saw the picked group of men leave the main body of Lyondri's army and sweep toward his own blue fir-tree banner.

Sunstar! Carry my king to safety! Romilly's mental cry reached both man and horse.

The great black stallion reared, lashing out with his front hooves, and thundered away. Carolin's men followed, maintaining a compact group around him.

The party Carolin had sent after the *clingfire* wagon drew nearer their target, through the thickest part of the fighting. A flight of arrows arched upward, toward the main body of Carolin's forces. Their tips glowed like molten orange fire. *Laran,* twisted and tainted, shocked through the air. Carolin flinched under its touch, even before the first arrow found a living target. Sunstar threw his head up, pulling at the bit.

The din of battle drowned out the screams, but Carolin felt each one as a fiery arrow through his own flesh. Beneath him, the black stallion recoiled, then gathered himself.

Leave the wounded to us! He heard Maura's voice as clearly as if she stood beside him.

He started to cry out, to warn her back from the killing frenzy. She was *leronis,* a trained monitor, and could help those men as he could not.

Above it all, Romilly's sentry bird wheeled, sending Carolin images of his own men moving ever closer to the black-shrouded wagon. From this height, he could not make out Maura in the cluster of fallen men, but he sensed her presence, the clear blue flame of her power, the sure movement of her hands.

"Carlo!" Orain shouted out a warning. Lyondri had sent out another charge. There were more of them this time, slashing through the foot soldiers. Orain's mount went down. He scrambled up, fighting on his feet.

Carolin wrenched free of rapport with the sentry bird. The next moment, he was fighting beside his men. Sunstar bellowed out his own battle cry. Men and beasts screamed, swords clashed. The reek of blood and sweat mingled with the stench of burning flesh.

A horseman slammed through Carolin's guard, laying about him with an enormous battle-ax. Blood smeared his helmet and the armor that gleamed through the rents in his tunic. Lyondri's badge flashed on one shoulder. His huge yellow horse plunged forward, ears pinned back, jaw dripping bloody foam. The horse reared, neighing. The ax swept up.

Carolin raised his sword as he reined Sunstar into place so that he could strike. The black stallion lost his footing in the churned mud and almost went down. Carolin glanced up at the falling ax. Sun glinted red along the curved edge.

Orain hurled himself between Carolin and the axman. The ax came down on his sword, deflected, steel skittering over steel. Orain staggered under the impact, but did not give way.

The next instant, Sunstar scrambled to his feet. His powerful hindquarters flexed and he sprang forward. Reflex aimed Carolin's sword, for there was no time to think, only to act.

Between one heartbeat and the next, the warhorses collided. Carolin's sword tip curved upward, under the assailant's breastplate. He felt it slide in. Sunstar swerved, pulling the sword free.

Two of Carolin's guards grabbed the axman even before he toppled.

One held the yellow horse as Orain scrambled onto its back. Orain's lean face was a mask of blood and dust and smoke, but fire lit his eyes. He lifted his own sword in salute, then wheeled the yellow horse to face the next onslaught.

Carolin could no longer fight a defensive position. The battle hung upon a thread and the key was the *clingfire.* The dreadful arrows were far fewer now, but still they came. Whatever they touched, flesh or bone or leather, grass or wood, ignited. Each man that fell was either dead or, worse yet, spread the unquenchable fire to any who sought to aid him. In the end, no matter how great the courage of the men or the healing of Maura and the others, the *clingfire* would defeat them.

The force Carolin sent to take the wagon battled on bravely, but met fierce resistance and heavy losses.

I must put an end to this thing.

"With me!" He shifted his weight. The stallion reared, pawing the air, drawing the eyes of all his surrounding guard. "Ride with me now!"

"King Carolin! King Carolin!"

Sunstar bounded forward, a torrent of sleek black power. Orain spurred his yellow horse ahead, clearing the way. A stride or two later, more men streamed to join them.

Through the eyes of the sentry bird, Carolin spotted his target. The wagon had come to rest, defended by a circle of soldiers. At Carolin's approach, his own men redoubled their efforts.

The wagon shimmered in Carolin's sight and then vanished. He bit off a curse. It had been an illusion to hold their attention while the real wagon was removed with Rakhal's army.

Trumpets rang out across the field. Once more, Carolin drew upon the linkage with Romilly and the sentry bird, still hovering above the battle. He saw Rakhal's troops wheel and flee, saw his own men pursue them for a space. The rapport with the sentry bird dissolved, and Carolin caught a last image of Romilly slumping, sickened and exhausted, in her saddle.

A *laranzu* stood on the place of the false wagon, his gray cloak blown about him. His hood had fallen back, his features unreadable. He held something in one hand, clasped against his breast.

"Hold!" Carolin cried. His voice penetrated the clamor. Men disengaged, remaining in fighting stance and yielding no advantage.

He lifted his voice, so that all might hear. "Lay down your arms, and I will grant you the king's amnesty!"

One of Lyondri's men shouted, "It's Carolin himself!" and surged forward. Orain swiveled his yellow horse across the man's path and cut him down.

The *laranzu* held his ground. Fear and despair emanated from him.

What has Rakhal told him about me, that he so fears surrender?

"Come no closer!" the *laranzu* called. "You know what this is and what it can do!" He lifted his hand, and Carolin saw a glass vial. Shadow and ember coiled within it.

Zandru's frozen hells! Was the man willing then to immolate himself, rather than surrender?

"I ask you again to lay down what you hold," Carolin replied. "That infernal fire knows neither friend nor foe, but consumes all life. Have you not seen the lands to the east, still barren from a war fought before either of us was born? Have you not tended the children of those who dared to venture into the wastelands? First *clingfire,* then bonewater dust and root blight and what more? *These* are the true enemy, not I, not your master, nor any other mortal man. Look about you, and tell me what defense these soldiers have against *clingfire.* I say, let them fight as men, with honor and steel. I say, use the Gifts the gods have given you for healing, not for death. If you will yield, I offer you safe conduct back to your own Tower."

A hush fell over that corner of the battlefield, and even the men still struggling paused. Carolin's sight blurred, as if a veil of glowing silver had fallen over him. Sunstar pawed the ground, then stood like a rock.

Chest heaving, the *laranzu* shook his head. "You will only use it against my people."

"I swear I will not use it at all, except to see it destroyed," Carolin said. "By the light of Aldones and the holy things at Hali, I swear it."

The next moment, the men guarding the *laranzu* broke, some of them throwing down their swords and standing with empty hands outstretched, others running away. The *laranzu* carefully lowered the vial of *clingfire* and approached Carolin.

"*Vai dom,* I did not believe the stories which came to us through the relays," the *laranzu* said, "but now I have seen and heard. I have read the truth of your thoughts. Though I be exiled for it, I will make no more war upon you."

"You need suffer no exile for such a choice," Carolin said, "for there will always be a place for you among us. If you will go into the field and help those men who burn with this accursed stuff, I welcome you into my own company."

One of the surrendered soldiers gasped, for this was not how Lyondri or his captains treated their prisoners. The *laranzu* bowed deeply, and then went to do what he could for the wounded. Carolin gave direction for the safeguarding of the *clingfire*.

All about Carolin lay men and horses, dead and dying. Blood darkened the churned earth. Unexpectedly, the thought came to him that Roald McInery had said nothing about the stench in his *Military Tactics*.

As the battle fever drained from his veins, a terrible weariness set in. All the hurts he had scarcely felt now burned as if he'd been lashed by *clingfire*. Orain swayed in the saddle, rubbing the back of his free hand across a gash in one cheek.

Carolin roused himself. The dead were beyond his help, but the living still needed him. He steeled his voice, sending renewed strength into his officers. He ordered tents set up for nursing the wounded and repairing equipment, picket lines for horses, latrine pits, and such burial as could be arranged for so many.

Ruyven and Rakhal's *laranzu* had joined Maura, seeking out those who could be helped, while others went to give the last few dying horses the mercy stroke. The Sisters of the Sword gathered up their own.

By the time everything immediately necessary had been done, Carolin was weaving with exhaustion. Inside, he reeled with death upon death, men and horses and even Romilly's ugly, faithful sentry birds.

Orain, who must have been even more weary, finally insisted that Carolin rest.

"How can I?" Carolin protested. "The men—and the Swordswomen, too—who fought at my command—"

"There is nothing more you can do tonight. Look, the last of the daylight is almost gone. The men will look to you tomorrow; you must be ready to lead them again."

Carolin allowed himself to be led to his own tent, his armor and clothing stripped off. An aide brought a bowl of steaming water, soap, and towels. Carolin could not imagine how the man managed to find these things, but he accepted the ministrations gratefully. Every joint and muscle in his body throbbed. He fell across the sleeping pallet and sank into its softness. Darkness took him.

Distantly, as if floating up from a formless abyss, he sensed the presence of another person. The pallet shifted. The edge of the blanket touched his cheek. He smelled the faint fragrance of rosalys and sunlight.

Beloved, I am here. Maura's mental touch, as sweet as dew upon parched land, swept across him. Her arms went around him, slim cool fingers brushing his lips, his eyelids. *Rest now.*

47

The morning after the battle, the sky opened and drenched the field with rain. Great carrion birds fed on the bloating carcasses of the horses. The healers continued their work, now aided by Orain's grown son, Alderic, who had just arrived. Alderic had Tower training and had come to lend his skill to tending those suffering from *clingfire* burns.

Carolin met with his advisers, and it became clear that they must move camp. The rotting carcasses would soon bring disease, and, more importantly, would hamper any attempts to maneuver, should Rakhal's forces return to strike at them again.

Though he hated to ask it of her, he sent Romilly to fly the remaining sentry bird to spy out Rakhal's path. Romilly would not look at him, though she agreed without argument. There was something wrong with her eyes. He remembered that she had trained many of the horses slain yesterday. With her MacAran gift, she must have felt the death of each of them. Many of her Sisters of the Sword had perished also.

She is a girl, not brought up to hardship. She must have proper care, as soon as may be. Perhaps Maura, being a woman, would know what to do.

Romilly sent the bird up and with the help of Ruyven Carolin followed it in rapport, flying in slow circles, gradually widening. The rain lightened, so that a strange watery sunlight penetrated the clouds. Before long, the bird spotted movement in the distance. Carolin recognized the pattern of Rakhal's army, riding swiftly toward the hills.

To Carolin's eyes, the fleeing army seemed shrunken in size. Off to the north, he spotted another body of men and horses, riding hard away from the main force. Rakhal's men were deserting him, but not, Carolin thought, from cowardice. They had fought as bravely as any.

They knew what Rakhal was capable of, and seeing that Carolin was not easily defeated, they made their choice. Despite his weariness, and lingering sickness of heart at the carnage, Carolin's spirits rose.

The main body of Rakhal's army halted at the brow of a little hill, seizing the most advantageous terrain. From there, Carolin's army would be forced to charge uphill at them. Rakhal's horsemen quickly formed a perimeter, surrounding the foot soldiers and bowmen. They ringed the hill, so that as long as they held firm, it would be impossible to breach their defenses.

This, then, would be the decisive battle. But upon whose terms? Carolin was unwilling to waste the lives of his men in a useless charge against formidable odds. Roald McInery had described how a fortified hill could be taken, but had advised against it. Somehow, Carolin must lure Rakhal down or at the very least, break the line of defense. It would be difficult enough, charging uphill against a disordered enemy.

Orain, who had been riding a little apart, talking earnestly with his son Alderic, kneed his horse closer to Carolin's, so that they might speak in private.

"By your leave, my lord, I have in mind a plan, an old mountain trick. Give me a dozen or two of your men, as well as *leronyn* to cast an illusion that we are four times as many. We can deceive Rakhal into an attack, leaving the main part of his forces open. Then you can come and take him on the flank."

"It just might work." Carolin considered, though he did not like sending Maura and Ruyven directly into battle. Most *leronyn* did not even carry swords to defend themselves.

What had he himself said to Varzil after the assassination attempt on the way to Blue Lake?

Would you have me cripple myself trying to prevent every conceivable catastrophe? Life must be lived on its own terms, and part of being a Hastur, let alone a king, is the ongoing risk.

Varzil had answered, mind to mind, *I would not live my life walled in by imagined terrors. I cannot ask my friend to do the same.* Aloud, he had added, "Once you said there were two kinds of power—that of the world and that of the Tower. We must have both, if we are to succeed."

Then Carolin remembered Maura's words, *There is no certain safety for any of us.* She was no plaything, to be protected from danger or given as a prize to whoever prevailed on the field. Every day, in the Tower, she took unimaginable risks, even as Varzil did. Were her choices any less honorable because she was a woman? Had she not gone out into the battle, using her *laran* against the *clingfire,* doing what no ordinary man could do?

To protect her is to diminish her. He remembered how Alianora, who would have quailed to come within five leagues of a battlefield, had died. He had not been able to protect her, either.

"Once Rakhal's line breaks, we must take the heights as quickly as we can," Carolin said. "Rakhal is already desperate. He sees his own men deserting him, and we have him penned on that hill. He will not hesitate to use *clingfire* or anything else he has, if he believes all is lost."

Orain nodded grimly, and Carolin saw this was also in his thoughts. Of all of them, Orain best knew Rakhal's mind.

Carolin gave orders for riders to accompany Orain and positioned his forces to strike quickly at the first breach in the perimeter.

A short time later, two dozen of Carolin's men, headed by the small band of *leronyn,* rode toward the hill. They slowed as they neared its base, circling away from the gentlest slope to the steeper, rockier ascent. Carolin, watching from the safety of his own guard, saw a cloud, dense as smoke, rise quickly to engulf them. It could not be natural dust, however, for the earth was still damp.

The cloud billowed to many times the size of the attacking party. Figures emerged, the blurred shapes of riders, not two dozen now but a hundred or more in tight formation, racing out ahead of the real men. Pennants of Hastur blue and silver streamed out behind them. Carolin had seen these very horsemen before, for they were Rakhal's own men in flight. Orain had used the image as a mirror, this time rushing toward the defended hill.

For a time, Rakhal's men held firm under the approaching assault. Bowmen moved to the fore and sent down a hail of arrows, using the height of the hill as an advantage. Their aim fell short, however, for they shot at the false image of the soldiers speeding toward them. They missed the real riders toward the rear.

Carolin could not see his riders, but he sensed they had drawn together, sending the illusion out in front of them. As he watched, the shapes within the cloud altered, so that they no longer resembled a company of living, breathing creatures. The horses' heads elongated into pale bony skulls, tapering and reptilian. Their riders became skeletons lit from within with devil fire. Whips and chains, shimmering with unnatural light, lashed the air above their heads. Moving between them, the lean shapes of gigantic hounds wove in and out, their eyes glowing like red coals.

In the name of Aldones, where had Maura and the others gotten these horrific images?

Around him, Carolin's guards muttered prayers to the Lord of Light, to Holy St. Christopher, Bearer of the World's Burdens, even to Zandru, Lord of the frozen hells. He could not suppress a shiver of terror, for this was no ordinary foe, but a nightmare from men's darkest primal fears. Echoing his guard, he gave silent thanks that the unholy host was racing away from him, not toward.

Loathing stirred in Carolin, as if he had touched something unclean, a pollution of the soul. He had kept his resolve not to use *laran* weaponry, yet how easily he had agreed to this use of psychic power, this warping of the minds of men who had no defense against it. Was this not as despicable, as horribly obscene as *clingfire?*

I have no choice. It is the only way to save the lives of my own men.

So kings and generals thought, from the Ages of Chaos to the end of time. There would always be good reasons. Men would say, *Just this one battle, just this one time.*

What kind of king will I be, with such a beginning?

A better king than one who never questions his own actions, a thought whispered through his mind, and Carolin felt Varzil looking over his shoulder, nodding.

It will take more than the resolution of any one man to make such things unthinkable, Carolin thought.

That is why we must do it together, you and I, castle and Tower. But first you must win back your throne from Rakhal, who has no such compunctions.

You are right, my friend. Carolin narrowed his attention to the impending battle. Sunstar snorted and arched his neck.

Closer and closer, the ghost army approached the hill. It flowed up the steepest part without slowing. The defensive line faltered in a dozen places.

"Stand firm! Stand firm!" Rakhal's own voice rang out.

Orain's company slowed, letting the bespelled forces continue on. As the ghostly riders climbed, their speed increased. Sparks flew from the curling whips and the hooves of the foul steeds. Carolin imagined slaver, glowing an unnatural yellow, dripping from the jaws of the gigantic hounds.

Rakhal's captains tried vainly to hold their forces. These were seasoned fighters, surely aware of the uses of *laran* in battle, yet there was a limit to what men could withstand. Pushed to the breaking point, the bravest would flee in terror, or plunge into the oncoming foe, each according to his nature.

The foremost of the ghoulish forces had almost reached the top of the hill. Carolin's men held their position on the flat ground.

In an instant, the defensive line broke. Rakhal's horsemen charged down the hill, straight into the cloud of magical images. The portion of the perimeter facing the attackers gave way, and riders from other areas rushed after them. Even as Orain had predicted, the flank was now vulnerable. Carolin signaled for his own riders to begin their assault.

The horrific shapes, dragon horses, spectral riders, and demon wolves, vanished. The cloud of dust fell away. Fire burst upward through the ground, a conflagration in vivid green and blue. The flames disappeared as quickly, replaced by a river of blood that flowed uphill.

The horses of Rakhal's men slid to a halt, snorting in terror. A few threw themselves over backward, thrashing as they crushed their riders. Other men fell from their plunging, maddened mounts, or jumped free and sprinted away.

A few, braver than the others, still held their ground, "It's a trick! A trick!"

The warning came too late. The line of Rakhal's defense had broken. Horses stampeded, trampling the fallen riders. Officers struggled to reassemble their men. Trumpets sounded, a confusion of signals. Foot soldiers gathered with their backs together, unsure whether to stand and give battle or retreat.

"Now!" Carolin cried.

Carolin's forces charged, flowing like a living river through the scattered defense. Momentum and rising exhilaration carried them forward.

Sunstar plunged on like a beast possessed, shouldering aside lesser mounts. All about him, Carolin's men shouted and whooped in triumph.

The charge slowed at the pit of resistance, no longer slicing through the enemy lines, but fighting at close quarters. Now Carolin sensed the black miasma of the *clingfire* wagon. Through the fray, he saw Rakhal's bowmen gather around it, dipping their arrows into the caustic stuff.

"The wagon!" he shouted, pointing with his sword. "We must take the wagon!"

He urged Sunstar forward, but Rakhal's men rushed up, and not even the great stallion could push through their ranks.

Orain, by some chance, was not so heavily pressed. Shouting, he wheeled his horse toward the wagon. Alderic and Ranald galloped on his heels. Carolin felt the *leronyn* link minds; he threw his own *laran* power into the bond, even as he had learned to do at Arilinn. Orain, too, was there, and somewhere behind them, adding their strength, Maura and Ruyven and Romilly.

Blue fire erupted from the earth, raging outward in a solid band. Suddenly, it shot upward to form a wall. It rolled out toward the wagon, engulfing any who stood in its path. The bowmen who had been dipping their arrows into the *clingfire* spun around. Their weapons tumbled to the ground. Faces paled in the oncoming cerulean brilliance. The roar of the blaze swallowed their screams.

The blue fire struck the wagon, blazing upward. Thunder crackled overhead. An inferno of coruscating blue and white burst skyward.

Rakhal's men, those beyond the sphere of fire, scattered and ran for their lives. Where the *clingfire*-dipped arrows had fallen, grass burst into hot orange flame. It sped up the wooden wheels, surging over the sides and protective canvas. With a sound like heaven itself shattering, the wagon exploded. Fiery fragments and white-hot dust spurted skyward.

Carolin shuddered as the acrid stench of *clingfire* swept over him. Every instinct recoiled against it, but he steeled himself to hold firm. He must not think of the terrible danger, only upon what he had come to do.

Burning droplets fell on the bowmen and fleeing soldiers. They ignited like living torches. Their bodies twisted and shriveled, blackening, as the fire consumed them. The rest of Rakhal's forces, hearing the shrieks of agony of their own fellows, panicked and scattered. Many ran right on to the swords of Carolin's own men.

Hold the circle! Ruyven cried silently. *We must put out the* clingfire *before it rages out of control!*

Join with us! rang through the psychic firmament. *In the name of everything holy, everyone who has* laran, *help us to hold the* clingfire.

The smell of charred flesh saturated the air. Rain began to drizzle again, but the *clingfire* burned on.

Hold . . . hold . . .

Carolin felt the *clingfire* as a living thing, drawn from the pulsing heart of the planet, yet imbued with malevolence toward all living things, ravenous and implacable. It raged outward, consuming everything it touched, wagon, men, and grass. A halo of blue light, flickering like the gentlest of flames, sprang up to surround it.

Hold . . . hold . . .

The fires burned inward now, the blue of the *laran* spell mingling with the glowing red-orange of the *clingfire.* It left a ring of blackened earth, where there was nothing left to consume.

"Look there!" Orain cried, pointing beyond the burning *clingfire.* "See where Rakhal flees with his sorcerers!"

"After them, men!" Carolin shouted. "Take them now!"

Carolin nudged Sunstar with his heels. For an instant, the horse froze, back arching, terrified of the fire.

What had Romilly said as she offered the horse as a gift? *He will carry you for love.* Neither spur nor whip could compel courage. Shuddering yet steadfast, the stallion moved forward.

Now I will put an end to this barbarity, Carolin thought.

Rakhal's standard came into view, with his men fighting furiously, covering their retreat. Step by desperate step, they fell back before the onslaught of Carolin's men.

One of Rakhal's soldiers lunged at Carolin, sword in hand. On Carolin's signal, Sunstar reared high, pawing the air. The man fell beneath the blows. One massive hoof struck the man's head. Carolin lost his balance in the saddle for an instant, but as quickly recovered.

Another soldier rushed up with a lightning flash of steel. The stallion swerved. Too late, Carolin saw that he himself was not the target, but the horse beneath him.

His mind was so open, so attuned to the warhorse, that for a terrible moment, it seemed that the sword sliced through his own neck, his own throat, and that it was his own life's blood which spurted away into the dust.

Reflexively, he kicked his feet loose from the stirrups and rolled free. Sunstar dropped to his knees, shaking his massive head, struggling for the strength to rise . . .

. . . *fading, like the sky at twilight, lingering for a blessed moment. Pain fell away, and terror, and memory* . . .

The horse never felt his body strike the ground. A terrible emptiness filled Carolin's mind, the utter absence of the stallion's vigor and courage. The man Sunstar had killed lay beneath the horse's body. Sunstar's head had been nearly severed.

There will be a time to mourn, Carolin promised himself, *for this death and for so many others.*

All around him, his men were fighting hard, pressing back the enemy. Steel clashed against steel. Rakhal's men no longer shouted his name as a battle cry, but struggled on in silence.

Carolin's guard clustered close around him. In a break in the fighting, a man in a blood-stained Castamir tartan led up a small, mud-smeared chestnut mare. She rolled her eyes as Carolin gathered the reins, but stood for him to mount. After Sunstar's powerful rounded back, she felt slight, hardly able to bear his weight. When he touched her with his heels, she moved off skittishly.

Even mounted, Carolin could not make out much of the battle beyond a small circle. He longed for a vision of a sentry bird, but he could not simultaneously fly and fight.

Just then, the remnants of Rakhal's army made a last, frenzied assault. They charged into the main body of Carolin's force. Carolin and his guard were swept away by the attack. Rakhal's men fought recklessly, heedless of risk.

For a time, Carolin's guards were pressed hard. They drew together, fighting at close quarters. Carolin kept a tight hold of the chestnus mare. Infected with battle fever and terror, she whinnied and pranced, pulling hard at the bit.

The battle shifted as the momentum of that last charge faded. Carolin's men began making headway as Rakhal's fell back, step by bloody step to the very edge of the hilltop.

Before long, the worst of the fighting ended. Men still fought on here and there, but most of Rakhal's forces had either fled or thrown down their weapons and fallen to their knees.

Carolin wheeled the little mare around the summit, scanning the fields below. There were so many dead—men and beasts. The circle where *clingfire* and blue *laran* flames had mingled still gave off throat-searing, greasy smoke. They dared not leave it until every mote of the infernal stuff was gone.

He called to the nearest officer. "What of Rakhal? Captured or killed? Where is Orain?"

"*Vai dom,* there is no sign of either of them, or of Lord Lyondri."

Dead? Escaped? That could not be, for Orain would never let Rakhal slip through his grasp, not while he had breath and strength to hinder him.

Carolin stood in the stirrups, searching through the smoke for the yellow horse. His eyes stung and he wiped them, smearing his face with sweat and grease.

"*Find them!*" The command came roaring out of Carolin. "*Find them now!*"

The officer, looking very pale and young, bowed his head. He spurred his horse toward the main body of the army.

"My lord," the chief of Carolin's guard said, "we have taken the field, and await your orders."

Carolin nodded. There was nothing he could do about Orain or Rakhal for the moment. He must establish a headquarters so that the necessary work might proceed, everything from tallying and burying the dead to arranging latrine facilities to tending the wounded and sending word to Hali.

48

Dusk came early, as thickening, black-bellied clouds blotted out the late afternoon sun. In between receiving reports and meeting with his officers, Carolin paced the length of his field tent, too overwrought to sit still. The losses, although fearsome, were less than he'd first thought. Rakhal's men had taken the brunt of the *clingfire,* or the damage to his own forces would have been much worse. Even so, he had gone numb, hearing the roll of those identified as slain.

Mikhail Castamir . . . Ranald Ridenow, whose quick thinking and *laran* skill had saved the lives of so many others . . . Alaric, the landless man who had ridden with him from the Kadarin . . .

With each report, he braced himself for the names he most dreaded hearing.

Orain . . . where was Orain?

Neither he nor the yellow horse had been found. By now, it was clear Rakhal and Lyondri had escaped, together with their *leronyn.* Carolin tried to convince himself that Orain, along with the party of men he commanded, was still on their trail.

Faithful, tenacious Orain who was once sworn to Lyondri's service and now had every reason to hate his former master unto death.

Lyondri's death? Or Orain's?

No, he must not think that way. He was king. His men looked to him for command, for steadfast courage. He was their heart, their sword. Doubt was a luxury only ordinary men could afford.

He sensed Maura's nearness even before the guard outside spoke. Other voices joined hers, another woman and two men. The tent flap lifted. Alderic and Ruyven followed Maura inside, with Jandria a pace behind.

Maura's face was very white. Her hair hung in sweat-damp tendrils. A jagged scorch mark covered her sleeve from shoulder to elbow. She moved stiffly, but did not seem to be hurt. When she saw Carolin, her smile lightened her whole body. He ached to gather her into his arms.

Ruyven inclined his head. Like the others, his face was ashen. "I regret we could not come sooner."

Carolin made a dismissive gesture. "What is the situation?"

Ruyven raked his hair back with one hand, a gesture that reminded Carolin of Varzil. "We have ascertained that the *clingfire* is completely extinguished, and have done what we could for those still within our power to help."

Carolin steeled himself to ask, "What of Orain? Has he been found?"

"There is no trace of my father," Alderic said. In his voice, in the weariness of his spirit, Carolin saw that he had searched the battlefield from one end to the other, with his mind as well as his eyes, and had encompassed more death than most soldiers saw in a lifetime.

"We have looked everywhere for him," Jandria said. "He is gone . . . and so is Romilly."

"Romilly, missing?" Carolin echoed. His heart clenched.

"Neither of them is among the slain," Ruyven said, and Carolin remembered that he was Romilly's own brother. If he and Alderic, who had Tower training, could not find her, then she must have run far away.

"At first, we thought she might have sought comfort in the Sisterhood, as she had before," Jandria said. "None have seen her since the battle. We feared the worst, but have not found her body."

"I would know if she were dead," Ruyven said, shaking his head.

Not dead, then, but fled into the madness born of too much pain, too much death.

Romilly was like a wild creature in her innocent trust, the generosity of her love. She had felt the loss of the sentry birds as if they were her own children. How much keener and more devastating must the death of Sunstar, trained with her own hands and heart, have been for her?

It was too much for her to bear. He himself had asked ever more of her in the name of saving human lives. Had he been selfish to demand so much for his own cause?

We must find her!

Maura met his eyes with that direct, unflinching gaze. "We will not abandon her. She may be too wounded in spirit, too sick at heart to hear us, but we will not stop until we have found her."

Carolin nodded. As for Orain, there was nothing more to be done, except wait for news.

"My father is not on the battlefield," Alderic said again. "We think he and his men must still be on the road to Hali, following Rakhal and Lyondri."

Carolin pressed his lips together. Yes, Rakhal would go running back to Hali, even in defeat. He was not the sort to forsake the luxury of Hastur Castle for the wilds beyond the Kadarin. Let him think himself safe in the city he had once ruled with a brutal hand. If he managed to reach it before Orain caught him, it would buy him only a short reprieve.

"Go now to the rest you so richly deserve," he said to his *leronyn.* "We will do what is needful here and as soon as may be, we will ride for Hali also. If Aldones smiles upon us, we will find Orain there with Rakhal in his custody, or else encamped at the gates, waiting for us."

Jandria and the men withdrew, but Maura remained behind. He held out his hands and she came to him. Her hair did not smell of the usual intermingled sunshine and sweet herbs, but of smoke and the faint, acrid tang of *clingfire.*

Carolin seated her in one of the folding camp chairs and lowered himself in the other. He offered her a goblet of the wine he had not been able to touch earlier. "Now tell me, *preciosa—*"

Just then, he heard a commotion outside the tent, men's voices, a horse's hoofbeats and labored breathing, a sharp cry of command. The tent flap lifted and the guard stuck his head in.

"*Vai dom,* it is one of the men who rode with Lord Orain."

Carolin leaped to attention. "Send him in."

He recognized the man, a boy barely the age he'd been when he went to Arilinn, but one of the fastest riders in his company. From the way he handled horses, Carolin had wondered if he might not have a touch of the MacAran gift.

The boy wavered on his feet, gasping for breath. What was left of cloak and tunic were black with sweat and mud, blood as well. He took a step into the tent, raised one hand, and fell forward on to his knees.

"We—we had almost caught them—they set an ambush—Lyondri's men—came at us—" His voice cracked, on the edge of a sob. "We fought—Aldones knows how we fought—"

Carolin felt Maura stir beside him, but she said nothing.

"Lord Orain?" he said, dreading the answer.

The boy fell back, so that he sat upon his heels, body curved forward, hands braced on either side of his knees. His shoulders heaved with the effort to draw breath. "He lives—at least, when I left him—but—" He looked up, tears streaking the grime on his cheeks. "But, *vai dom,* the last I saw of him, he was the prisoner of Lord Lyondri. Those of us who could, continued the chase. I took the fastest horse and came back. Would that I had died with the others, rather than carry this news!"

"Be at ease, lad," Carolin said, and saw the responsive lightening of the boy's spirit. He felt a wave of compassion for anyone who bore such a burden, let alone one so young. In a moment, his own fury and grief would set in, but he had time enough to send the boy away with a morsel of comfort and to direct a guard to see him given food and a dry bed.

He turned to Maura as the dam burst.

Orain! In Lyondri's clutches! he stormed. *May Zandru curse both him and Rakhal with scorpion whips to the last level of his frozen hells! If they have harmed so much as one hair of Orain's head, I will tear them to bleeding pieces with my own hands—*

"Hush, love," she whispered, laying a finger across his lips. "You cannot know what you will find at Hali. The only thing certain is that you will cripple your ability to think and act if you go on in this manner. For now, there is nothing you can do for Orain, nothing except rest and prepare yourself for the journey tomorrow."

No soldier could have said it more clearly. He sighed, wishing he could so easily put aside the anguish raging in his heart.

"I will try to rest, since it is wise," he said, hearing weariness roughen his voice, "though I do not think I have ever felt less able to sleep."

"Leave that to me."

✦

Maura awoke in the middle of the night, sitting bolt upright. Carolin, rousing at her side, could not tell if she had cried out aloud or only in her mind. He reached for her, felt her trembling.

"What is it? What has happened?"

She was breathing fast and hard, as if she had been running. "I Saw—a terrible battle." From her tone, this was no ordinary dream, but a result of the Sight.

Sitting, he took her into his arms. "You are safe here. My armies guard us. Nothing can harm you."

She shook her head, creating ripples of movement in her unbound hair. "Not here—far away. Hali—the circle there—ordered to attack Hestral Tower."

Hestral Tower! Where Varzil had gone . . .

"They cast a spell of unmaking upon Hestral's very foundations, enough to bring the Tower down in ruin. Oh, Carlo, it is a terrible thing when one Tower makes war upon another. Many of us have kin in other Towers, or have trained together. Almost every night, we speak mind-to-mind across the relays."

"In the name of all the gods, why would Hali do such a thing?"

"They would not make *clingfire* for Rakhal." She shuddered, wrapping her arms around her body. "This was his doing. His, alone! But all is not lost. Hali broke off the attack before the destruction was complete. Varzil stood against them, bathed in silver light like Aldones himself. He—he showed them the horror of what they were doing and convinced them they must not fight one another." She drew a deep breath. "Now Hali swears they will never do so again, nor will they make any *laran* weaponry for Rakhal or any other king."

Carolin shook his head in amazement. Hali, of all Towers beholden to Rakhal, had in essence agreed to their pact. If any man could bring such a conflict to a halt, and in such a way that the Towers vowed neutrality, it was Varzil.

Varzil the Stubborn, Varzil the Resourceful, he thought. Varzil who faced down a pride of catmen to save his brother, who had foiled more than one assassination attempt, who shared his dream of a peace with honor for all Darkover. *Varzil the Good.*

49

Maura and Ruyven continued their *laran* search for Romilly as Carolin moved his forces through the outlying Venza Hills to the gates of Hali. He took with him all those men yet able to fight, leaving behind only sufficient numbers to care for the wounded. Fortunately, the lords and smallholders in that area were sympathetic, having suffered much under Rakhal's rule, so that food for men and beasts would not be a pressing problem.

As Maura had said, Carolin did not know what conditions he might find at Hali, although it was unlikely that Rakhal would be able to amass another army. Yet Carolin must move swiftly, before Rakhal could set another trap or dig in his position so deep, they would have to fight from one room of the castle to the next.

Every passing hour tore at Carolin's heart. Sometimes, as he gazed into the fires of his encampment along the road, it seemed that every one who had loved or trusted him met some terrible fate. All the men and horses slain in his cause, even poor Alianora dead in bearing his child, Romilly driven to madness, Orain . . . he dared not think of what Orain might be suffering.

A whisper brushed his mind, *I am here,* bredu, and he sensed in Varzil's presence an inexpressible comfort. *Do not lose heart, for the men who followed you, and the women, too, did so freely. Already our dream is taking hold. Towers are turning away from the folly of destruction, and everywhere men look to you in hope.*

Then, Carolin promised silently, he must not give way to despair. He roused himself to walk the camp, so that all would see him, hear his voice, feel his care for them, both his own men and the Swordswomen who had chosen to go with him. Along the road, the ranks had swelled with the shattered fragments of Rakhal's army. Some of the men, having made their submission to Carolin, asked to be released on parole and return to their farms, but others offered their swords to the true Hastur King.

At last, they came to Hali itself, the long dimness of the lake, the Tower like a pale slender finger of light rising on the far shore, and the city hunched and gray under a lowering sky. A length of wall, much of it still bearing the *laran* imprint of its hasty construction, encircled the city.

Before long, Rakhal sent out a messenger. Orain was his hostage, and if Carolin or any of his men entered the city in an attempt at rescue, he would kill Orain at once. Clearly, Rakhal intended to use Orain to parley.

Carolin sent back an offer of safe conduct for both Rakhal and Lyondri to beyond the Kadarin or wherever they wished to go, provided Orain was released unharmed. Lyondri's son might return safely to Nevarsin, or be reared according to his rank at Hali along with Carolin's own sons. It was perhaps too generous an offer, but he wanted to give Rakhal a solid reason to compromise. As long as his cousin saw no hope, his rising desperation would prompt him to more and more reckless actions.

Silence answered him. Hours passed, and then a day. The search for Romilly continued. Alderic pleaded with Carolin to offer himself in exchange for his father, along with a small treasure of copper and gold.

"I do not think Rakhal will listen," Carolin said, "but you may try." He hoped that Orain lived through this ordeal, if only to know what a fine and loyal son he had fathered.

Rakhal flatly rejected Alderic's proposal. Maura made the same offer, that she would give herself up to Rakhal, even going into exile with him, if that was what he wished. Rakhal did not even answer her.

Just before sunset, a horn sounded from the city and another messenger rode out. Carolin recognized him as a minor lord whose fortunes had fared badly after some reversals in the *cortes,* and who clearly had prospered under Rakhal's favor, by the rich cloth of his cloak and the silver ornaments on his horse's saddle. After an elaborate bow, he handed Carolin's officer a small wooden box, saying he had been bidden to deliver it into Carolin's own hands before speaking his message. Carolin took it into his tent where, surrounded by Maura, Ruyven, and Alderic, he opened it. The slender package of yellow silk was sticky with blood. His hands shook as he lifted it out and unfolded the wrapping.

Inside lay a severed finger, callused and caked with blood. It still bore a little copper ring set with a blue stone called a sky-tear. Carolin had last seen it on Orain's hand.

This very finger had clasped a sword hilt in Carolin's defense, wrapped rags around Carolin's half-frozen feet that first terrible winter beyond the Kadarin, nursed a handful of twigs into a fire. It had also raised a goblet of wine in celebration, stitched broken harness with precise skill, caressed a lover. Now it was no more than a rotting piece of flesh and the hand which bore it—

Carolin's vision went gray and then red. He felt Maura's touch as she took the hideous packet from him. She said nothing, offering only her silent presence. Alderic's anger rippled through the tent, and then he wept.

It was many long minutes before Carolin was ready to hear the rest of the message. Ruyven signaled to the guards that the messenger might enter.

The messenger bowed and assumed an oratory posture. "In the name of Rakhal Felix-Alar—"

"Yes, we know who sent you," Carolin snarled. "Just say what you have come to say."

The messenger swallowed, his cheeks blanching. "I am bid to say that unless you, Carolin, unlawful pretender to the throne of Hastur, surrender yourself and your armies to King Rakhal, he will return your paxman to you, one piece at a time. You have until dawn to give your answer."

His final words faded away into shocked silence. With another bow, this one considerably less assured than the first, the messenger withdrew.

Ruyven, looking even paler than usual, turned to Carolin. "You aren't seriously—you cannot consider—"

It took all Carolin's strength to walk calmly to the camp chair and lower himself into it. In truth, for a single heartbeat, he *had* believed the only way to save Orain's life was to do as Rakhal insisted. His own death would be quick enough, for Rakhal could not risk another claimant to the throne.

Then the enormity of Rakhal's demand, the monstrous truth of what and who he was, swept over Carolin. If Rakhal would do this to Orain— or, more likely, order Lyondri to do it—Orain who had been as a brother to them both from the time they were children, Orain who had served Lyondri faithfully for so long— *Then in the name of all the gods,* Carolin thought, *what will he do to my people?*

They all turned to stare at him. Carolin found his voice. "No," he said. "No matter what happens, I will not betray everything we have fought so hard for."

Maura said gently, "Orain would not have it otherwise. He would let himself be cut into little pieces to save you, to save the kingdom."

Rakhal knows that, Carolin thought. *He knows that I would give my own life for Orain. But it is not mine to give.*

"We all love Orain," Maura went on. "If there were a way to save him, any one of us would offer ourselves. That is not what Rakhal wants. I know how he thinks, although to my shame, I once tried to justify his actions. He wants above all to win, and he does not care how. He knows you love Orain, and he thinks that he can use that love to bend you to his will. But he does not know *you.* He sees you only as a fool who trusted too much. He cannot imagine that you are bound by something higher than your own personal feelings."

Carolin straightened his shoulders. Grief lapped at him, the pain of the loss to come and the knowledge that he was powerless to prevent the torture which Lyondri's butchers would surely inflict upon Orain, piece by piece, day by day.

"We will continue attempts at negotiation," he said. "Perhaps Rakhal may hold off while he believes we are giving in. Something we cannot foresee may yet turn up. Meanwhile, we will begin preparations to take the city by force."

Late in the day, Jandria came to Carolin's tent. He welcomed her and bade her sit beside him. In the lamplight, she looked haggard, with little remaining of her old prettiness, but she held herself with quiet competence. Whatever she had been, she was now a pledged Swordswoman, and sister to every other woman who wore the gold earing and red vest.

"We have made *laran* contact with Romilly," she said, brightening. "Maura and the others have been trying to reach her ever since she disappeared after the last battle. We thought she must be hiding, not wanting to be found, for Ruyven would surely have known if she were dead."

"She is alive, then." The knot of pain in Carolin's heart eased ever so slightly.

"Yes, although she has been living in the wilds like an animal. You were right, the battle was too much for her. Her mind was linked to the stallion's when he died. You know the bond she had with all the animals she trained."

Carolin nodded. *Too much pain, too much loss, felt so deeply, without any defense . . .*

He wondered if any of them were ever truly prepared for the horrors of war, the brutalities of men like Rakhal and Lyondri, the betrayal of kinsmen.

Jandria had paused and was gazing at him with a mixture of compassion and reserve. "Romilly will come as quickly as she can, although the Dark Lady alone knows when that might be. She, too, loves Orain and will not leave him in Lyondri's clutches if there is any way she can help."

✦

Romilly galloped into the army encampment two days later, riding a rangy, ill-bred roan gelding without any saddle or bridle. Carolin felt her presence even as she passed the outlying guards. Jandria rushed out to meet her, along with Alderic and Ruyven.

She looked weary, wearing a filthy, torn tunic and breeches, her hair matted and wild. Claw marks, still bloody, crossed her cheek and one earlobe was torn through. But her eyes were steady as she put off their questions.

"Later," she insisted. "What is this about Orain being held hostage by Lyondri? Tell me!"

Carolin held out his hands to her. His heart rose in his throat and spoke with its own voice.

"Child—" he began, and she came into his arms as if she were indeed his dear child. He hugged her hard, feeling the wiry strength of her body. Into the tangle of her hair, he murmured, "I thought I had lost you, too. You and Orain, who both followed me, not as a king, but as a fugitive."

He drew her into the tent, where they all gathered around, the people who had searched for her, Maura and Alderic, Ruyven and Jandria. Jandria insisted that Romilly take some cold meat and bread. Romilly ate as if she had not tasted food since the great battle. She would not speak of her flight or how she had survived in the wilderness, not even when Jandria, washing the cuts on her cheek, questioned her. Her thoughts were only for Orain, as Carolin knew they would be.

When he drew out the package with Orain's finger, she struggled visibly to keep from retching; her horror and outrage washed over him, echoing his own.

"Yesterday, it was an ear." Carolin's voice wavered, and he feared that if he went on, he would weep aloud.

Jandria said grimly, "I swear, I shall not sleep until Lyondri has been flayed alive!"

"Do not swear so," Maura said, "for we have all suffered enough at his hands."

"You come when we have almost lost hope," Carolin said. "We are on the brink of storming the city, knowing that our action will bring Orain a swift, clean death."

For the last two days, his men and *leronyn* had struggled to find a way into the city, but Rakhal had set sentry birds and savage dogs around the gates, which raised the alarm when a scout tried to sneak in. With their *laran,* they tried to follow the common soldier who brought the next bloody token, but Rakhal's own sorcerers had set a psychic shield around the city. In the end, they had no choice but to proceed with a direct assault. In preparation, Carolin sent a promise of amnesty for every man in the city who did not raise a hand against him. The Tower had already declared itself neutral as a result of Varzil's intervention; it would make no weapons and supply no *leronyn* for either side. Rakhal was cut off from any hope of reinforcement.

"We will take the city at dawn," Carolin finished.

Romilly listened thoughtfully, especially to his description of the animal sentries. "My *laran* is of little use against men," she reminded him, "and I have no power against Rakhal's psychic defenses. But I have no fear of any dog or bird, or any natural creature. Let me go into the city before dawn and search for Orain in my own way. If I can find him, and bring him out safely, then you can attack freely."

No, I cannot risk her, not when she is newly found! Then Carolin remembered that she was a Swordswoman, even as Jandria was. She had proven her courage and resourcefulness, in the wild lands, on the trail, in battle. She had no empty pride; if she said she could do a thing, whether it was nursing an ailing sentry bird or training a warhorse, it was done.

"You may try," he agreed. "At the least, we will have an idea where to strike first, so that they will put him to a swift death. Rest now, and wait until full dark."

She went off with Jandria to the tent of the Swordswomen. Carolin paced for a while, until it felt he must collapse under the weight of so many deaths, so many decisions.

He went out into the camp, as he had so many times before, under the wan light of a single moon. Men, gathered around their cook fires, lifted their faces as he passed. He paused here and there to speak to them. Gradually, the awful burden lightened, or perhaps it was the sense, gathered one moment at a time, that he did not carry it alone.

Romilly had left the camp by now, gliding like a shadow into the city, and by her own choice. Maura, too, had chosen, as had all who rode with him.

He himself had also chosen. He could as easily have stayed in the wild lands beyond the Kadarin, eking out a fugitive living. He might have sought asylum with his Aldaran kin in the far Hellers.

Memory swept him, the figure of light which had taken his hands and heard the vow spoken only in the silence of his heart.

He thought of Varzil, at Hestral Tower many leagues away, and how he had brought the siege to an end, not by force of arms or *laran* weaponry, but by the simple power of *right*.

There are two kinds of power in the world, he had said, *that of the Tower and that of the crown.* But each of them rested upon the free choice of those who served.

He would honor that pledge, keeping faith with his people and his dearest friends, his sworn brothers and his beloved, but most importantly, with himself.

50

Carolin slept fitfully, weaving in and out of broken dreams. He seemed to be moving through a preternaturally quiet city. Shadows, dense and quiet, clung to its streets like funeral draperies. From the edges of his vision, he caught furtive shapes and lights quickly covered. The scent and taste of fear hung like a black mist in the air.

Peace, peace . . . silence . . . Romilly's thoughts spread across the walls where the sentry birds sat like great misshapen statues. He felt their vigilance soften under her mental touch.

Peace . . . silence . . .

Somewhere beyond the wall, a dog snarled at a rat, then subsided. Horses drowsed in their stables, mice within their nests. Cats curled up on their hearths. Fretful babies quieted.

Silence, silence . . . peace . . .

The contact vanished and he jerked awake. Romilly must have passed beyond the *laran* barrier. He wondered if Rakhal had thought to watch the rest of the city as well, or if his *leronyn* were already stretched too thin, guarding the gates.

Evanda and Avarra keep her safe.

Before Romilly left, he had offered her any reward in his power to give, even marriage to one of his own sons, if she could free Orain or,

448

failing that, put a swift end to his suffering. She had looked at him strangely.

"I do this for Orain's sake and not for any reward," she had said, "because he was kind to me beyond all duty when he knew me only as a runaway hawkmaster's apprentice."

Now he had lost all trace of her. She was in the hands of the gods. He must try to find what rest he could before dawn, for he would soon need all his strength.

At last, he could remain still no longer. He summoned water to wash his hands and face, ate a cold breakfast, and prepared himself. Outside the tent, a faint milky tinge lightened the eastern sky.

Where was Romilly? Why had she not returned? Had something gone amiss and was she, too, now in Lyondri's hands? What if she needed more time to find Orain? What if the attack raised the alarm and resulted in her death as well as Orain's? Should he not wait a little longer?

His officers were already moving about, giving orders in hushed, tense voices; foot soldiers and horsemen alike finished a hasty meal, doused their fires, and took up their weapons. Along the picket lines, men saddled horses. Expectancy roiled through the camp.

Carolin met briefly with his advisers and officers, giving last minute encouragement. One of his aides went to bring the horse he would ride. It was not as fine and brave as Sunstar, but he doubted he would ever see the equal of the black stallion.

Maura, who had spent this night apart with the other *leronyn*, preparing for their role in the morning's battle, came to him. "All may yet be well. There is still no stirring in the city, not even the sentry birds, which should be waking at this hour. I suspect that is Romilly's doing. Will you not hold off for a little time and wait for her return?"

She had spoken the thought which was in his own mind, the temptation to cling to hope, to delay irrevocable action. If he did as his heart urged him, however, he might never recover the momentum of this morning.

He kissed her brow. "All is in readiness. If we are to take the city and end Orain's suffering, it must be now. Romilly understood this. We will attack as planned."

She walked with him through the camp. The first rays of sunrise cast a gentle glow over the ancient city and glittered on the battle standards.

Men led horses into position to the jingling of harness rings. They stood at attention as he passed.

Suddenly, a clamor erupted from beyond the gates, dogs yammering, birds screeching, and alarm bells ringing wildly.

"Look!" Alderic hurried up. "Look there, by the gate!"

Carolin strained to make out three figures racing away from one of the side entrances to the city. He recognized Romilly, her hair tied back under a dark scarf, her face smeared with soot, holding the hand of a fair-haired boy in a white nightshirt . . . and on her heels, Orain. Rough bandages covered one side of his head and one hand, and he limped badly.

With an inarticulate sob, Carolin ran forward and caught Orain in his arms. Orain reeked of blood and filth, but he was alive. He hugged Carolin back with fervor.

Carolin heard Romilly crying, "We're safe—we're safe! Oh, Caryl, we could never have done it without you!" He turned his head to see Lyondri's little son, his own namesake. The boy's tear-streaked face glimmered in the faint dawnlight. Carolin, in a single motion, enclosed Caryl and Romilly along with Orain in his embrace.

"Listen," Orain said, pulling away. His body shook with uncontrollable tremors. A second, even more frantic alarm burst from the city. "They know I am gone—"

"Our army is here to guard you," Carolin said. "They shall not touch you again, my brother. Now, I think, they will have no choice but to surrender, as they will have few supporters left in the city and nothing left to bargain with."

Orain flinched as Carolin, embracing him once more, brushed against his bandaged ear. In short order, Carolin took Orain back to his tent, where Jandria took charge of him.

Romilly again refused any reward, saying that she hoped Orain knew that even though she was a girl, she had no less courage. Something of her proud independence softened and she allowed Orain to rock her like a child, both of them weeping.

Orain reached out his free hand to Alderic. "I heard you had offered to exchange yourself for me. I know not what I have done to deserve it, for I have never been a good father to you."

Alderic was silent for a moment. "You gave me life, sir, and you left me free to follow my own path. I owe you for that, at least."

"You are all here and safe," Carolin said. "That is enough." To Lyondri's little son, he said, "Whatever your father has done, you are safe with me. I will raise you as one of my own sons, and I will not kill Lyondri if I can help it. He may leave me no choice, for I dare not trust him; but if I can, I will offer him a life in exile."

The boy replied, his voice shaking, "I know you will do what is honorable, Uncle."

Romilly got to her feet and took Caryl's hand. "My lord, may I take your little kinsman to the tent of the Swordswomen and find him some decent breeches?"

"Please, Uncle," the boy said, "for I cannot show myself to the army in a nightgown."

Carolin laughed, and it seemed a great weight had lifted from his heart. "Do as you wish, my hawkmistress. You have been faithful to me, and to those I love."

He caught Maura's smile. "I pledged to you that we would celebrate our Midsummer Festival at Hali, and indeed we shall. But first, I must take back my city."

✦

Carolin rode with his army to the main gate. Maura and his other *leronyn* came with him, and Jandria at the head of her Swordswomen, but not Romilly or Orain. They remained in the safety of the camp, having suffered too much already.

It would not be difficult to breach the walls or batter down the wooden gates. Rakhal's fortifications had been hasty, more for show than determined defense. Carolin preferred not to ruin the city he would rule, or shed the blood of his people if it could be helped. His herald cried out that the lawful king had returned, and bid the inhabitants cease resistance and welcome him. Again, Carolin promised that he would not harm any man who did not offer violence against him.

For a time, there was no response. The gates remained shut and silent. The first sign of surrender was the sudden falling away of the *laran* spells. Then came the sounds of fighting behind the gates.

"Rakhal's *leronyn* have deserted him," Maura said, "and his remaining men are at odds with one another." Her eyes had a slightly glassy look of inward concentration, and Carolin knew she had been searching outward with the Sight. "Look now to the side gate, the one Romilly came through. Those who wish surrender and reconciliation will try to open it."

Even as she spoke, the smaller gate swung open. Carolin's vanguard pressed through. At first, they encountered resistance, but the defenders were also fighting against their own divided forces. Soon, Carolin's men were able to win free and open the main gate, allowing his army to enter.

As Carolin's forces penetrated deeper into the city, ordinary people emerged from their houses. They stood on balconies and ventured into the streets. From their balconies, a few ladies waved brightly colored scarves.

"It's Carolin!" some cried, cheering. "King Carolin!"

Others responded. "Our rightful king! The king has returned!"

The most determined opposition came from small groups of men wering Lyondri's badge. They fought desperately, without hope of mercy, for they had given none. With the defeat of their master, they would surely be called to account for their brutalities. Ordinary men joined Carolin's soldiers and newly-loyal City Guards in the attack. One by one, faced with overwhelming force in a city just awakening to its liberation, Lyondri's men succumbed or threw down their weapons.

Maura pointed to a massive gray hulk of a house, more fortress than dwelling. "Yonder is Lyondri's stronghold, where he kept Orain captive."

"Will he surrender? Will he fight?" Carolin asked her.

She shook her head, swaying in her saddle. "The Sight shows many things, but not the hearts of men."

"And Rakhal?"

"In the palace. I think he is fled to the upper chambers—the room where we used to play at seeking—on rainy days—"

"Enough," he said gently. "You have given me what I need. No man could ask more. Return now to the safety of the camp."

Maura asked to remain instead with the other *leronyn,* though she agreed not to use the Sight further unless there was dire need. She argued that she was safer in the midst of Carolin's army than anywhere else.

"Let me come with you," Jandria said to Carolin. "For the sake of little Caryl, who aided Orain's escape, and for the love we once shared, I would not see Lyondri die needlessly."

The last of Lyondri's men waited just inside the barricaded doors. As Carolin's force broke through, the fiercest fighting erupted. Some wore soldiers' gear, but not all, and Carolin wondered if Orain's torturer were among them. These men were not cowards; they fought with grim determination. Jandria and her Swordswomen engaged them at close quarters, pressing them back.

They took the central hall and entrances to the corridors and stairways leading upward. With each passing minute, fewer defenders remained. Their blood spattered the threshold of a chamber which reeked of pain and despair. This must have been where Orain had been held, where—

Carolin wrenched his attention back to the moment, to the clash of steel, the weight of the sword in his hand, the shouting of the men around him. The last of Lyondri's men, four of them still on their feet and a fifth down with a spurting gash on one thigh, took up positions before the door of an inner room.

"Hold!" Carolin shouted. "You cannot win. Surrender now and I will spare your lives."

"Never!" one of the men cried. He held his stance, sword raised, eyes lit with desperation. "We'll go down in glory!"

"It is over." The door swung open and Lyondri stood there, his shoulder sagging as if under an unendurable weight. He stepped forward and the light etched deep lines into his face. His eyes, gray under pale lashes, widened as he saw Jandria in her red vest, standing behind Carolin.

"It is over," he repeated, as if to convince himself. Then he raised his voice. "Surrender to King Carolin, even as I do. It is my final order to you." Though he spoke quietly, the men lowered their weapons.

Lyondri came forward and made as if to kneel before Carolin. Carolin bid him remain standing, but ordered his men to search Lyondri and bind his hands.

Even in victory, I dare not trust him as I once did.

"You will not leave me even a little dagger, with which to take my own life?" Lyondri said with a bitter smile. "It must be, then, that you reserve that pleasure for yourself."

"You do not know King Carolin, or you would not say such a thing," Jandria said.

"Have you, too, come to gloat over me in defeat?" Lyondri snarled.

"No," she replied with a touch of sadness, "only to see if there was anything left of the friend I once loved."

"You speak as you think, expecting the same treatment you have meted out to so many others," Carolin said. "For Orain's sake, I should flay you alive and pour salt into each bleeding strip. But then I would become like you, Lyondri, and your evil would have triumphed. For my own sake, and that of your innocent son, I offer you your life, to do with what you will, so long as you never step foot across my borders again."

Lyondri hesitated. "Caryl is with you, then? I thought as much when he was not in his bed. I have no choice but to agree to your terms. You hold my only son as hostage against me."

He thinks me a monster because that is what he has become.

"I will keep Caryl with me, yes," Carolin said, "but not as a prisoner, nor will I punish him for your crimes. Your own conscience, if you still have one, must do that."

Disgusted, Carolin turned his back on one cousin he had once loved, and went to deal with the other.

✦

Carolin left a small force surrounding Lyondri's headquarters and pressed on to the castle. Some of the guards moved to block his progress through the outer courtyard, but when they saw how little chance they had, and heard his offer of clemency, most lost heart and surrendered to him, so there was little real fighting in the castle itself.

Just as Maura had Seen, Rakhal had barricaded himself in one of the upper towers. Carolin climbed the last range of steps at the head of a dozen of his best men. Every stone evoked memories of who he once was, living here in innocence and trust. Yet every breath now also carried the tang of freshly-shed blood. The muscles of his shoulders ached from the weight of his sword. His lips shaped the names of those who were gone forever, men he had loved, men who had died in his service, even the stallion Sunstar, all because of the greed and ambition of the man in the room above.

How can I show him mercy, after what he has done?

How can I be a just and faithful king to my people, as I swore to do, if I do not?

The latch moved freely under his hand. When they had played here as children, it had never been locked.

Watery daylight filled the little circular chamber, so that a gray film seemed to lie upon each stone, each curve of wood, and cushion. The windows had been opened fully. Rakhal stood beside one of them, his features backlit in silhouette, holding his fur-trimmed robes close against his body.

For a moment, Carolin thought he was looking into the past, seeing a ghost. Gone was the bloated, wine-soaked figure, the lecherous sneer, the habitually narrowed gaze. When Rakhal moved and the light shifted, he seemed not youthful but shriveled, as if consumed from within.

Two of Rakhal's men remained, placed defensively in front of their lord, swords drawn. Carolin sensed a third, lying in ambush behind the opened door.

"So it has come to this," Rakhal said. "The fool presents himself to claim his throne." He swung his arms wide, sending the full sleeves of his robe flapping like the wings of a misshapen bird. "You are doomed! The day of fire is coming, and you cannot hold it back!"

Carolin signaled to his men to be ready to take on Rakhal's defenders. His fingers curled around the hilt of his sword.

"Oh, yes," Rakhal went on, "I know your secrets, that *cristoforo* witch you kept as a wife, whispering the poison of weakness into your ears. I should have throttled the brats in their cradles, but you would have found out too soon. The castle was full of spies. Spies everywhere, mumbling in the corners, whispering in my dreams. You turned them all against me, even sweet Maura, but she would not let me—leave me— A plague on her, Zandru's pestilence take them all!"

His face convulsed, a rictus of anguish. "Attack!"

"Hold!" Carolin cried with such force that Rakhal's men hesitated. "You cannot win. You are trapped here, and greatly outnumbered. The city has surrendered. There is nowhere to run. Your deaths will serve no purpose. Will you not lay down your swords and save your lives?"

As for Rakhal—dare I let him live? He will never stop scheming, never stop hating.

Lyondri craved power, but never pretended to the throne. Having once been king, Rakhal would never lack discontented or corrupt men ready to follow him. The price of mercy might well be to set the entire kingdom ablaze.

With a hideous cry, Rakhal pointed at Carolin. "Kill him! Kill them all!"

Carolin shoved the door fully open, pinning the third man against the wall. He turned his body flat against the door so that his own men could enter first. The next moment, the room exploded into frenzied action. The chamber had been small when they were children; half a dozen grown men, slashing at each other with swords, filled it entirely. Even if Carolin wanted to jump into the fray, he could not find an opening.

The door jostled Carolin's shoulder. The trapped man was trying to get free. Carolin shoved back, as hard as he could, and was answered by a muffled yelp. Two more of his own men sidled past. He leaned against the door and shouted again for Rakhal's men to surrender.

Within a few minutes, the fight was all but over. One of Rakhal's defenders was down, disarmed and hamstrung. The other, faced with overwhelming odds, lowered his sword. Carolin, motioning to his men, released the door and the man pinned behind it tumbled free, only to face three sword points at his throat.

Carolin waited until Rakhal's men had given over their weapons and been bound before he stepped into the room.

"It is over, Rakhal." Carolin echoed Lyondri's phrase.

Rakhal gathered his robes around him like tattered dignity. "So you would like to believe. You could not hold the throne before; what makes you think you can hold it now? No matter how deep the dungeon or how long the exile, I will not rest until I have set your severed head upon a pike outside the city gates!"

"Let us not bandy idle threats before the men, cousin. Do you yield, and give yourself into my justice?"

For a moment, it seemed that Rakhal would concede. Then his eyes shifted. "If I cannot be king, then neither will you!" In a lightning swirl, a sword appeared in his hand, hidden in the folds of his robes. He leaped forward, too fast for Carolin's soldiers to react.

Carolin, forewarned by the slight movement of Rakhal's eyes, was already raising his own blade. He deflected Rakhal's thrust. Rakhal disengaged and swept in with a flurry, so fast and hard, it took all Carolin's skill to fend him off.

Rakhal does not care if he lives, so long as I do not.

Conscious thought vanished in the silver heat of the attack. Rakhal was pressing him hard now, fighting with reckless ferocity. The impact of clashing steel shivered up Carolin's arm. Nerve and muscle, drilled over countless hours in the practice yard, reacted—*acted.*

Breath and fire surged through Carolin, every sense sharpening. Adrenaline sizzled along his nerves. He caught the rhythm of Rakhal's blows, the pattern of advance and recovery, of slash and lunge. It was like dancing, one partner stepping forward in the same instant the other stepped back.

Rakhal slowed a fraction, the merest delay between blows. Without conscious thought, Carolin flowed into the opening. His sword shot forward, an extension of his will and hand. He slipped past Rakhal's guard.

The tip of his sword rested at the hollowed base of Rakhal's throat.

I have you now—

Never!

Rakhal twisted sideways, his eyes white and wild. The movement left a scratch, welling blood but not fatal. Carolin moved to close with him again.

Rakhal, instead of evading the attack, advanced, an oddly oblique charge. Carolin reacted, pivoting to meet him. His sword lashed out as if it, too, sought a speedy end to this deadly game. With a jerk, Rakhal's sword clashed to the floor.

Carlo! His other hand! Maura's silent warning shrieked through Carolin's mind.

Rakhal broke the distance, sidling to the outside and slipping past the outer reach of Carolin's sword. Barely in time, Carolin swerved. Rakhal's dagger stabbed cloth instead of flesh. Momentum carried Rakhal's arm in an arc and he twisted for another attack.

In these close quarters, the sword's length made it unusable on tip or edge. By some instinct, Carolin brought it up, vertical, like a narrow shield. He caught his cousin along the upper arm near the hilt and stepped into the blow.

Rakhal stumbled from the impact, but did not drop the dagger. He swung wildly, recovering to dart this way and that, as if in desperate hope to slip past Carolin's guard again. Blood spattered from the wounds on arm and neck.

The dagger—it's poisoned! Maura cried.

Dark Lady, now I must kill him.

A terrible stillness gripped Carolin's heart. He gave himself utterly to it. His weight shifted, his step lightened. It was as if the spirit of some predatory animal—a wolf or snow leopard—moved through him. He no longer saw a man before him, cousin—betrayer, playfellow, assassin—but only a pattern through which death might enter.

Rakhal scrambled back a step and then another until his back was to the open windows. His face convulsed, as if he realized his chance had passed. Carolin moved forward. He saw, under the spiral of Rakhal's robes, the curve of ribs, the exact path and angle to the heart. In the space between heartbeats, his sword pierced the air. He threw all his force behind it.

As he twisted away, Rakhal screamed, a roar of fury and despair. Carolin felt the moment of contact, an instant of resistance, and then nothing. Momentum carried him forward.

Rakhal toppled backward over the window ledge, jerking free from Carolin's sword. An instant later, his scream cut off.

Carolin rushed forward. Leaning over, he saw that Rakhal had fallen across a low wall surrounding the ornamental garden below. From the unnatural angle of the body, his spine had been broken. He did not move.

Dizziness, like a sickness of the soul, swept through Carolin. He would never, until the end of his days, be sure if he had slain his cousin or if Rakhal had chosen his own ending.

It did not matter. He had *meant* to kill him, and so bring to an end the degenerate monster who had seized his throne, but also the bright-eyed boy playing in this very room, the youth laughing as he danced with Maura and Jandria, the solicitous nephew tending upon elderly King Felix, the hunting companion and friend giving Carolin advice about court politics. The man who, for good or ill, had worn the crown of Hastur.

To be a king was to accept the full weight of what he had done. No excuses, no apologies. He alone.

Maura stood in the doorway. Her face was very white and tears glimmered in her eyes. "He chose to be what he was, even as I have. Even as you have."

What am I? What have I made of myself, that I could exile one kinsman and slaughter another?

She took a step toward him, so that the gray light fell like a radiance upon her. "You are Carolin, King, Hastur of Carcosa and Hali, *bredu* to Varzil of Arilinn, savior of Orain, father and friend, a good man who has faced extraordinary challenges and has kept faith with us all. And by Evanda's grace, you are also my beloved."

His heart was so full, he could not speak. In those few words, she had given him back the man within the crown.

She took his hand and led him back down the stairs and into the city, where his people waited for him.

The thought came to him that there was a third power in the world. That of the Tower, that of the crown . . . and that of the heart, and perhaps this last was the strongest of them all.

EPILOGUE

Carolin Hastur stood at the window of his private presence chamber and allowed his shoulders to sag. He'd been holding himself upright, masking his fatigue, for a chain of tendays now. The official coronation had taken place in Hali, among the holy things and the invisible presence of his august ancestors. He would not rule there, but in Thendara: a new capital city for a new era. Despite the grumblings of the self-appointed keepers of tradition, he had moved his entire court to Thendara Castle. The last Hastur King to live here had been Rafael II, who had also reigned in times of upheaval.

The move complicated all those things that were needful for a king returning from exile. Trials, executions, pardons, replacements of staff, inventories, the list had seemed endless, even with the indefatigable Orain as his paxman. Now, most of these were well begun. There would always be more—pockets of resentment, Rakhal's partisans, border skirmishes, and difficult legal cases—in addition to the ordinary business of running a kingdom this size. For the moment, though, he might take a rest and indulge his own pleasure. His promises to the people he would rule had been largely fulfilled.

There was one more promise to keep.

A rapping on the door that led from the outer chamber brought him

459

to attention. Carolin signaled to the guard on post there, one of the young officers who had served him so well on the last bloody campaign. The door swung open and a man stepped in, slender in his robes of green and gold, his face calm and intelligent.

For a long moment, Carolin stared at the transformation of his friend. It had been years since they had last beheld one another, years of separate struggle. Somehow, in his mind, he had not realized Varzil would have changed so much—the frosting of white around the temples, the lines of suffering incised on his face. Varzil had never been robust and the years had pared his frame, yet there was an air about him of such power that Carolin thought not even a mountain could bend him.

Varzil inclined his head, more in salute than homage, the measured acknowledgment of the master of one type of power to another. Carolin thought of how true that was—Tower and castle, each a world to itself, yet interdependent. Now Varzil waited for Carolin to speak first, as befitted a host and king.

"My old friend, how good it is to see you again," Carolin said. He started to lift his arms in a kinsman's embrace and then thought better of it. Although Varzil's expression was warm, he carried about him an ineffable air of detachment, as if he moved through the world, met it on its own terms, and yet remained essentially apart. He was, after all, a Keeper. And then Varzil broke into a grin and he clasped Carolin in a tight embrace.

"And you, Carlo. It has been too many years since we last greeted one another."

"Too many years," Carolin said, smiling a little more widely because of the familiar nickname. "Don't remind me. Come, make yourself comfortable. Will you drink?"

Carolin led the way to a couple of padded chairs arranged around a serving table with pitchers of wine, both chilled and heated with spices, and a platter of artfully shaped sweets. The guard at the door stepped outside, leaving the chamber in silence. Varzil sat very still, hands folded in his lap. Carolin had not remembered how small they were, and the ring which his friend wore was unfamiliar.

Within a few minutes, they passed the awkwardness of long absence and settled into conversation. Carolin told only a small fraction of his adventures, skimming over much of the dark times and entirely omitting many episodes. He judged that Varzil was doing the same. It did not matter. Neither was the chronicler of the other's life story. Far more important was the easy comradeship they slipped into, the flow of words and silence.

After a particularly long pause, Carolin said, "We have each suffered much and grown much, and yet it seems that only a little time has passed since we were boys together, sharing our dreams for the future."

Do you remember those dreams, Varzil? Do you still hold fast to them? I have never ceased to work for them.

"Even when you were in exile," Varzil said aloud, "and there seemed no hope of us ever meeting again in this world. Even then. I fear I have made somewhat of a reputation for myself in speaking out for your pact. Loryn of Hestral Tower started calling it the Compact of Honor, and so it has become for me."

Carolin chuckled. The reports had not exaggerated, then. "From what I hear, half of Thendara thinks you're a saint and the other half is equally convinced of your lunacy."

Varzil's hands moved, so that one lay gently over the other, covering the ring with an oddly tender gesture. "I do not care what they think of me as long as they listen to my words. The ideas are far more important than my own poor self."

"Your own poor self? Ah, but you were always too modest, Varzil, putting yourself forth as less than you are. Fate and the world have caught you up. You cannot escape. The people call you Varzil the Good and the Lord of Hali. They still tell of how you appeared to the Tower there garbed in living light, like Aldones himself. Some of my own people took it as an omen of victory, a sign that Rakhal's power was at last on the wane."

At this, Varzil looked away and made a deprecating gesture. "It is too much. I never intended such a legend."

"Do any of us? Doubtless, in some corner of this world, people recount very much the same sort of story about me, or will in a generation or two. Varzil—" Carolin watched as his friend reacted to the shift in his voice. Their eyes met, and the difference of years fell away. "Varzil, let's give them something to *really* talk about."

"You mean to carry through with our Compact? There will be much resistance. Kings are not overly enthusiastic about placing restrictions on their own military resources unless their neighbors do it first and no one wishes to take the risk of beginning." Varzil's expression lightened. "I do not know if it can be accomplished in our lifetime, or at all, but this I do believe, that if it is possible, we two must do it together."

Carolin spread his hands. "On this account, we can only do our part. Who will listen and who will join us, that is in the hands of the gods. I have something more definitive in mind, something we can most surely realize together. Men need more than promises to give them hope. I saw that all too clearly during my years of exile. I could not issue orders to my men and hide safely in my tent. To give them heart, I had to walk the camp, to let them see me and hear my voice. Ordinary men are neither beasts without imagination nor gods unto themselves. What they need now is a symbol, a concrete promise that the future need not be a repetition of the past."

Varzil's eyes widened with understanding. "The Tower at Neskaya. We spoke of rebuilding it, you and I together."

"That we did, and that it would be a place of study and of service, set beyond any petty involvements in the world's strife. Now that dream can be fulfilled. Will you work with me to build not only the physical Tower, but the real one? Will you be Keeper of this new Neskaya, this beacon of hope?"

Unthinking, Carolin had reached out his hands as he had so many times in the months just past, as one lord after another hand placed his hands between Carolin's own and pledged his fealty. After a moment's hesitation, Varzil reached out. He set one hand between Carolin's and the other to the outside, so that each held the other's in the time-honored gesture of loyalty.

"With all my heart, and with all the power that is at my command, I will."

"Then let us begin."